Ascension

To Kristine:
Thank you for reading.
I hope you enjoy it.

Nadine Lalonde
Oct 25, 2014

Ascension

Nadine Lalonde

Copyright © 2013 by Nadine Lalonde.

Library of Congress Control Number:	2013910639
ISBN: Hardcover	978-1-4836-5388-4
Softcover	978-1-4836-5387-7
Ebook	978-1-4836-5389-1

All rights reserved. No part of this book may be reproduced or transmitted in any form or by any means, electronic or mechanical, including photocopying, recording, or by any information storage and retrieval system, without permission in writing from the copyright owner.

This is a work of fiction. Names, characters, places and incidents either are the product of the author's imagination or are used fictitiously, and any resemblance to any actual persons, living or dead, events, or locales is entirely coincidental.

This book was printed in the United States of America.

Rev. date: 08/19/2013

To order additional copies of this book, contact:
Xlibris LLC
1-888-795-4274
www.Xlibris.com
Orders@Xlibris.com
122028

Contents

Prologue		9
Chapter One	The Killing Fields	11
Chapter Two	The Fog	33
Chapter Three	Life or Death	55
Chapter Four	Creatures of the Night	69
Chapter Five	The Making of Justus and Magnus	85
Chapter Six	Love at First Sight	105
Chapter Seven	Partners in Crime	140
Chapter Eight	"Who's on First?"	174
Chapter Nine	Obsession	199
Chapter Ten	Point of No Return	227
Chapter Eleven	Oh, Sweet Revenge!	245
Epilogue	The War Over Transport Routes Escalates	281

This book was made possible due to everyone I know; by each experience that has made me who I am today. I want to especially thank my children, Alexandra and Adrian, the reasons for my existence, and the best teachers that life can offer. I want to thank my mother, Laurie, my primary editor and test audience, for her generously donated time; Lauren Touchant and Caleb MacGillivray, my secondary editors, for their many suggestions; my brother Andrew and his friend Charlie Logan for providing a dose of male perspective. Finally, thanks to Oana Babeti for the amazing cover art.

PROLOGUE

"Mayor McKay . . . Mayor McKay," hollered a stunning, young, blonde reporter, stretching out her microphone, following the horde of journalists. Again, she prompted, "Mayor McKay, what's the city, what are the police doing about this 'College Rapist'?"

The robust, frayed-looking man that she addressed turned to look at her, and their eyes made contact across the crowd.

"Ms. Flaherty," he said sternly, "I thought I made it clear in my press conference that we're working with very minimal information and even less evidence. We've increased patrol in the target area. We're giving information sessions at the colleges and universities. We're convening a task force . . . I don't know what else you expect us to do."

Turning abruptly away from the crowd, he paused for a moment then turned back. He looked for the eyes that he had last made contact with and said, deflecting the responsibility, "You know . . . we can't be responsible for everyone. There comes a time when the citizens of our city must be responsible for themselves. If a woman goes to a bar and gets so drunk that she doesn't know what's going on around her, maybe the accountability falls there!"

A trembling voice rang out from the crowd, "I was raped by him, and I wasn't drunk . . . I resent your statement. A woman never deserves to be raped no matter what the circumstances."

The mayor's gaze shifted from the reporter toward the voice. The crowd went silent and parted as a young woman wearing a university sweatshirt stepped forward, gripping the mayor in her sights, tears streaming down her face.

"I don't mean to say a woman deserves to be raped," he retorted hesitantly. "What I mean is that the police can't be everywhere. People need to be vigilant so they can keep themselves safe." He paused briefly and took a deep breath, thinking carefully about the next words he would say. "Students drink. Alcohol inhibits the ability to be aware of your surroundings. It inhibits reaction time. It makes you more vulnerable. There's more than one rapist in this city, and people, especially women, need to be careful . . . always."

His appearance changed from annoyance to concern as he looked at the young woman. The awkward, brief silence was broken by another irate voice, this time a man.

"My daughter was assaulted in the subway, and even though she tracked down a cop almost immediately, nothing was done," said an average-sized man with a thick head of salt-and-pepper hair, standing behind his beautiful young daughter.

The crowd, as though at a tennis match, looked in unison to the man and his daughter, back to the mayor, then back to the man as he continued with his outburst.

He stepped out from behind his daughter, walking toward the mayor with fists clenched, and continued, "Are you going to blame her too?"

The mayor's entourage stepped in front of him, but he insisted on responding. "I have a daughter too. She rides the subway, and I share your concern for the safety of our public transportation system, but this is not the forum to discuss it."

The crowd formed a front with the man, supporting him as he demanded, "What is the forum to discuss a young woman being violated? What forum deals with the police not doing their job?"

One of the entourage members took the mayor by the arm, trying to direct him away from the crowd. Mayor McKay stood his ground and answered with a compassionate voice, "I can appreciate your frustration. The system isn't perfect and never will be. Who is the bad guy here? Not the police. Let's try to remember that. We're on the same team! If anyone has information regarding the College Rapist or any other perpetrator, I encourage you to come forward . . ."

Abruptly, the news report on the TV screen was replaced by a *Law and Order: SVU* rerun as a devious grin lit his face. He put down the TV remote and fondled the cross pendant on his chain. Relaxing in his armchair, satisfied, sipping his beer, he watched *Benson and Stabler* catch someone . . . someone like him.

CHAPTER ONE
The Killing Fields

"What's new about this attack, O'Shea?" Justus questioned as we all sat at the dining room table with Captain O'Shea on speakerphone. There was definitely a sense of tension in the air as everyone was getting frustrated that the College Rapist was leaving no evidence, no trail.

Embellished with a smattering of choice words, O'Shea managed to say that the incident occurred in Gramercy, in the stairwell of an apartment building. A twenty-one-year-old student on her way home from a club was attacked with the same MO as the other recent sexual assaults, or attempted assaults, in Manhattan East. Once again, the perpetrator escaped without leaving any evidence and couldn't be identified by the victim. Listening to the details of the case made my stomach turn. He apparently stalked his victims in bars and clubs frequented by college students then followed them and forced himself upon them. The victims who were left battered and violated could never identify him because he would hold them facedown with their hands bound. How could someone do such a thing to another human being? I had to leave partway through the briefing to clear my mind. I needed to be alone.

Up in my room, I looked at myself in my bathroom mirror wondering how I could do this. The eyes that looked back at me were tortured, my skin translucent. How could I live like this? How could I ever kill? I didn't ask for this! I didn't ask to be thrust into this world of violence! This wasn't me!

So distraught, I took a pair of scissors from the medical supplies that were still in my room and cut deeply into my wrists. It hurt, but not much more than getting scratched by a cat. I watched the blood flow from the wounds, a slow trickle, although I cut deeply. There was no spurting blood, and in no time at all, the blood flow stopped. Frustrated, I took the scissors and plunged it deep into my abdomen, and this too wasn't any more painful than cramps. I stood by my bed, hopeless, with a body so strong, so vital, and a will to live so weak. I dropped the scissors to the floor as I heard a knock at my door. I already knew it was Tavia by her scent.

"Come in," I said dully, although I really wanted to be alone.

She looked at me mildly shocked and voiced, "Oh, sweetie, what have you done?" as she saw the blood. She came to me and offered a hug which I accepted reluctantly but needed very badly. I had tried hard to be tough, to take it all in, but I couldn't anymore. I began to sob as a multitude of thoughts swirled in my head.

Tavia didn't say anything. She just knew that questions like "Are you all right" were useless because it was obvious that I was not all right. After a long while standing together in an embrace, I asked, "What will happen if I don't take blood?" Tavia was the right person for this question because she wouldn't wrap the answer up in judgment or drama; she would tell me the truth.

"Being such a young immortal, you would die," she began earnestly. I could see that she had to work at keeping her emotions at bay. "The process would take a few weeks and would be excruciating," she continued as she swallowed hard. I sensed she had witnessed this before. "You would have to endure the gradual death of all your body tissues bit by bit . . . you would suffer a lot."

"Is there a faster way?" I asked, thinking I already knew the answer.

"Fire is faster," she noted, giving me the response I had figured, and neither choice sounded ideal for suicide.

"You don't have to stay with us and live the life we lead," Tavia suggested. "You don't have to be involved with our vigilante pursuits. If that's what's making you hurt yourself and want to die. I would rather you leave than stay here so unhappy. I could find you somewhere to go with other immortals that live much more simply."

She held me in silence for a long while and then helped me get out of my bloody clothes. While cleaning up the mess, she told me that I seemed more tortured than most, and she didn't know how to help me. She said she thought of me as a daughter and was distressed because she didn't want to push me into the decision to stay with her, if I didn't really want to. I felt she regretted putting me through this pain. Of course she wanted me to choose her life, a life with this newfound family, but she didn't want to pressure me.

I lay on my bed, and Tavia sat beside me, running her fingers through my hair as she began to tell me her story.

"I was born in Edessa, part of the Near East, in the year 1127," Tavia began. "I had three sisters and two brothers. Most of my family was killed in the aftermath of the Edessa siege by the Zengid dynasty."

I looked at Tavia blankly and admitted, "I never paid attention in history class."

"Do you know a little about the Crusades?" she inquired.

"A little," I stated.

"Well," she began, "in the first Crusade, Edessa was taken by the Christians and was turned into the first Crusader state. My parents were born just after that. They married young and had seven kids. I had four sisters and two brothers. We had a decent life, nothing extravagant . . . lots of hard work just to survive day to day. When I was seventeen, during the Siege of Edessa, my family was slaughtered except for me, my younger sister, and my younger brother."

I listened intently as she continued to tell me her story.

"My sister and I were forced into marriage with the invaders," Tavia recalled, "and my brother was forced into slavery, where he died shortly after. I had three children that I loved, and I grew to like my husband. I needed him for survival, and he was a good man who had to follow military orders to survive."

We were silent for a moment, and I pondered how she could live with and have children with the person who killed her family and forced her into marriage.

"Back then," Tavia explained, "it wasn't unusual to lose family to war and disease. There was no social support. To survive, you did what you needed to do. Love wasn't really that important when you were starving!"

"You must really think that people now are such wimps!" I stated. "What's our biggest problem? Can we get cell service? Is the fast-food place open? Where's the closest bank machine?"

Tavia chuckled and pointed out, "As the world evolves, needs change. You can't compare times. As an immortal, I've lived through and seen times with worse challenges than I went through as a mortal."

I could see her point but still felt the need to express that I had lived a pretty good life in comparison to hers.

Tavia continued her story, "My husband was killed in battle, leaving me and my children destitute. Not long after, my children died of starvation, and I was resolved to die as well. Then I met an immortal named François de Poitier, a Templar knight, who gave me immortal life.

"Both of us, angered by the loss of family and by the loss of our mortal lives, became fervent killers. François, still devoted to the Christian cause, slaughtered Muslims by hundreds. We traveled throughout the Holy Land on a killing spree, and we eventually settled in Cairo, Egypt. We spent several years together, but I grew tired of the life we led. I didn't have the deep hatred that he possessed, and I couldn't go on killing for his cause, so I set out on my own."

I couldn't ever picture Tavia as a ruthless killer. It just didn't seem to be part of her nature. She made clear that when an immortal's killer switch is turned on, it's easy to give in to it.

"In Egypt," Tavia continued, "I met a young immortal that had been left behind by her maker, and needed guidance. I took Rebekah, still a teenager, under my wing, awakening my maternal instincts. For decades, we were together enjoying life in Cairo, the largest city in the East at the time. We learned to control our hunger, and we were experimenting with how long we could survive and thrive without feeding.

"During the early Mamluk dynasty, the Mongols and the Crusaders were kept from invading Egypt. The many battles allowed us easy, inconspicuous access to food, but still, we only fed enough to survive.

"The age of the Mamluks brought vast commercial expansion. Egypt's spice traders, the Karimi, were rich, influential men, and they dominated the trade routes across the Mediterranean, the Red Sea, and the Indian Ocean. Rebekah and I married Karimi traders and lived in luxury for several years.

"During one of the Mongol raids upon Egypt, I lost Rebekah. She was captured by a clan of Mongolian immortals." Tavia, who usually maintained her composure, looked distressed as she continued. "This clan was known as the barbarians of immortals and was feared by all throughout the East. Many of them who were older than me knew life before and after immortality as 'kill or be killed.' They controlled much of Russia and Asia and would go on crusades of their own to recruit for their clan. They would desecrate the food source in an area and then move on.

"I left Egypt and traveled to Russia, hoping against slim odds to find my immortal daughter. I never found her, but I did find Anton."

She looked at me, took my hand, and explained, "I told you my story not to make you feel sorry for me, but to show you that you never know what lies ahead. From the worst can come the best! I met Anton while on an almost impossible quest to find Rebekah, a quest that probably would have cost me my life had I succeeded in finding her with the Mongols. You are my daughter now. You are my first true immortal child."

"Your first true immortal child?" I questioned.

"Yes, in all my time, I have not changed anyone. You were special. I didn't take time to think about it. I sensed a connection that I couldn't ignore, like the missing piece of a puzzle," she answered while gently touching my face.

I didn't know what to say.

As she looked into my eyes through her tears, Tavia expressed with deep emotion, "I don't want you to live tortured and unhappy."

I had to look away. I didn't want to be causing her or anyone else pain.

She silently left my room. I needed to hear my own daughter's voice, although it was late in London, I called her.

Ana could tell that there was something wrong. She was always good at reading me. I minimized my situation and wanted her to tell me all about her life since we last talked. She had met someone and told me about him. Like most girls of her age, she could go on for hours—there were always so many details to include. I lay in bed, listening to the happiness in her voice, and I remembered how precious she was as a child. An easy smile lit my face for the first time in what seemed like weeks.

"Mom, even if I can't see you, just hearing your voice brings me comfort," Ana told me. "I can tell there is something wrong with you . . . if you're worried about me, don't be. Everything is fine with me. I'm enjoying my life in Britain, and I love school." We talked for another short while, and then Ana said, "Mom, I have to go now, OK. I love you!"

"I love you too, baby," I answered.

Ana could always read me like a book, and as usual, she seemed to know just what to say.

I lay in bed for another short while, picturing Ana's face, her smile, thinking of my father and his smile. I would have done anything to have my father alive when I was Ana's age.

It was dusk, and I needed some air. I needed to clear my head. I made myself presentable and slipped out of the house. I had always done my best thinking, alone, while out walking. I walked for hours throughout Manhattan and learned my way around the streets, thinking about my predicament and what I was going to do about it.

I was in Chelsea on west Twenty-sixth near Ninth when I heard a sound that immediately brought me back to my past and set off my fight-or-flight instincts. I followed the sound with immortal swiftness to an apartment building. The sound was coming from a fifth-floor apartment. I couldn't get into the locked entrance so I managed to scale the building using the balconies. Arriving at the source of the sound, my fury was intense. I easily broke the lock to the balcony door and emerged upon the little terrified voice saying, *"No, Daddy. No, stop!"* There, I laid my eyes upon a woman shielding her two young children from the blows of their drunken, incensed father. The woman, already bruised and broken, was crying and cowering doing all she could to protect her children. A young boy, with wide frightened eyes, was screaming, wanting badly to protect his mother.

The man turned to look at me, and I saw in his eyes that look, the one I had seen many times before the fist came down. A look that said, *You're the reason for my pain. You're the reason I can't escape this life . . . you're to blame for my unhappiness.*

He began to say, "What the . . ." and before he could finish his words, I had him by the throat, squeezing. I could feel his body fight to breathe against the death grip I had on him. His face turned red, and all the while, I looked in his eyes, watching them change from rage to fear for his life. I felt powerful. A power that I wished I would have had many years before, when I was the cowering woman trying to protect my child. He passed out in my grasp, and I snapped out of my own rage to see the woman, mouth agape, watching me with a look that I couldn't read. She was clearly horrified by the spectacle in front of her, but was she grateful that I intervened? She tried to hide her children's eyes from seeing their father in that state.

I dropped the man to the floor and uttered, "I'm sorry," as the children broke free from their mother and ran to their unconscious father. The woman, still stunned, looked at me with a combination of thankfulness and fear and I walked over to her, reaching out my hand to help her up off the floor.

Hesitantly, she took my hand and got up, straightened out her hair, and questioned feebly, "Now what do I do?"

"I'll call someone," I replied as I dialed Justus.

A short while later, an officer named Mel Dunn arrived at the scene. She was stoic and efficient in her process with the abused woman. She told me to leave but just before I did, the young girl, no more than six, came to me and said, "Thank you for stopping Daddy from being bad. He doesn't mean to be bad. He just gets real angry sometimes."

My heart just broke hearing these words that had come out of my own mouth before, trying to justify to my daughter why her father would hurt us. I smiled at the girl, hiding the sadness that I felt and quietly left.

As I reached the sidewalk, I broke down in tears, sobbing, releasing years of pent-up anger and hatred for my ex-husband Mike and for myself, for having endured it for so long. It was a cathartic moment, and I realized that I didn't hate myself for using violence to resolve this situation. I hoped that the man, the abuser, would remember the feeling of fearing for his life the next time that he raised a hand. I was definitely going to walk by that apartment building frequently and make sure that it didn't happen again.

Just as I was thinking this I stopped and wondered, *What would I do, if I found him hurting his family again? How far would I go?*

Justus and Magnus joined Captain O'Shea at the precinct as invited guests to the first meeting of a task force created to catch the College Rapist. There were officers from various precincts, and the task force leaders were Officers Dunn and Johnson. After introductions were made, Captain O'Shea outlined the project mandate, and an open discussion took place to brainstorm ideas. A plan was hashed out whereby the police would start posting undercover officers in the college area bars. There would be additional patrols of uniformed officers in the college bar district, and they would have information sessions on campus to promote safety measures.

Justus and Magnus, who were introduced as technical analysts, were to provide leads about which clubs and bars to watch more closely based on information gathered and analyzed by their team of specialists . . . basically Ethan.

As Justus and Magnus walked down the hall from the meeting room, they passed a blond man who caught their attention as he looked at them smugly, and peered just a little too long. His cold eyes and seemingly confident demeanor, arrogant even, gave both of them an uncomfortable feeling. Justus and Magnus glanced at one another, and simultaneously looked back at the passing man as he looked back at them, smiling slyly.

"That guy gets my hackles up," Magnus said to Justus.

"Yah, I know what you mean," agreed Justus, as the blond man entered the elevator.

They walked to Johnson's desk, and Justus asked, "Who was that blond guy that just walked by?"

Johnson answered, "He's one of the blond parade. They're coming in here by droves. We have a tip line reporting blond guys who look like the College Rapist composite, and we follow up each tip. They are invited to come in voluntarily for questioning and to give a DNA sample. My report says that the guy you saw is considered low risk. He's a financial guy, had plausible alibis for the nights in question. He gave a DNA sample without hesitation. We'll check on his alibis eventually, but we have over two hundred of these guys to review. He didn't set off any red flags with my team, so he is low on the priority list."

Still feeling unsettled, Justus and Magnus continued their work at the precinct, reviewing files for the College Rapist case, discussing technical aspects with their information technology liaison and finalizing timelines with Dunn and Johnson.

They arrived back home to find me waiting for them.

"Justus, I know you're busy, but I'm wondering if you can take me out and show me how to hunt animals?" I requested.

Magnus snickered as Justus paused momentarily and then said, "Uh, OK. This is kind of surprising."

"I know," I replied, "But I want to do it while I still have my nerve!"

Eyeing Magnus briefly, Justus confirmed that Magnus had their workload under control, so we left together on a hunting adventure.

"Are you sure you can't hunt a human?" Justus verified with a hopeful look as we left the house.

"Yes, I'm sure, but I've made some progress!" I said happily.

I told Justus about my encounter the night before and he was impressed and proud. What he thought of me was very important. I needed to know that I had his support, no matter how small my progress was. Justus was the second most important person in my new life, after Tavia.

We walked together idly toward Central Park, people watching, and talking. Justus told me about the task force and how O'Shea wanted us to help as much as we could to catch the College Rapist before he attacked again. We arrived at the park late enough to find it almost empty, at least in some places, allowing us to hunt freely.

I watched him as his demeanor turned from human to animal. His movement changed; his concentration focused. Suddenly, he leaped quietly, pouncing several feet away, and turned to look at me with a rat in his hand. I screamed at the sight of the rat squirming in his hand.

"Shhh!" he said. "You'll attract attention." Regaining my composure, I walked over to him and looked at the rat up close; it was trying without success to fight and flee. Luckily, my daughter had guinea pigs and gerbils, so I had handled rodents before. He showed me how to hold it to prevent it from biting me. Then the hunting lessons came. I had to learn to use my immortal hearing and eyesight, as well as my heightened sense of smell, all of which were superior to the rat's senses. It didn't take me long to learn to catch them, but I didn't want to kill them, not that night at least, as vile as they were. I could hear their little hearts beating.

Justus wounded one, and trying not to look too disgusted by it, he told me to come and drink. "It's going to die anyway. You'll just make it faster." The poor thing was making a noise I couldn't take.

"It's suffering," I screamed. "Kill it . . . please!" The scent of the blood was starting to overwhelm my senses. Justus just stood there with the writhing rat in his hands and finally, my brain couldn't think of anything else but the blood. Swiftly and without conscious thought, I found myself tasting the blood, feeling the warmth of it. I was holding the little dead carcass in my hand before I came to the realization that I drank it all, that it was dead. Sickened, I threw it away and for a moment I was angry with Justus for forcing this experience on me.

After a while, I forgave him because I knew it was for my own good, and I rationalized that the city had rats to spare!

For the next several nights, Justus came with me to hunt rats, and eventually, I went alone. Feeding on rats was repulsive, but it was a means to an end. I did feel stronger with fresh blood, but from what everyone told me, I could be feeling much better if it was human blood. After all, my DNA was still most similar to humans. My body still functioned with the base necessities of a human, but I could only get those necessities from one source . . . *blood*.

When I wasn't hunting, I joined some discussions about the College Rapist case, learning to tolerate more of the morbid talk a bit at a time. I also started to watch the surveillance cameras with Justus and Magnus, observing the activity in the city at night. I watched my family members kill people, and like watching a movie, I started to condone the killing because the "bad guys" deserved it.

The time came for me to witness firsthand what it was like to hunt humans. I hunted with each of my new family members at least once to see what they did, to understand their motivations, and to get to know them a little better. My thirst for human blood was becoming very intense, but I still couldn't bring myself to kill one. Even when I saw with my own eyes the vile things that rapists and killers did to innocent people, I still couldn't picture myself killing them.

Anton, Ethan, and Justus hunted indiscriminately; the blood of any rapist or murderer would do. Whatever came up on the menu any particular evening was fine. Tavia and Helene usually hunted together, and they preferred higher profile criminals. The type of criminals that needed to be watched for a while; the ones that often had others do their dirty work.

Yasmine usually hunted with Magnus, and they were on the borderline of cruelty with their victims much of the time. They enjoyed making them suffer and plead for their lives. Yasmine was particularly brutal with rapists. Both of them were like cats playing with mice before going in for the kill. Needless to say, I didn't want to hunt with them ever again!

The College Rapist was our biggest concern, but there was also another serial rapist who had been striking in Central Park. Tavia and Helene were in charge of watching over the park for the evening, and I decided to join them. It was just past sunset as we strolled down the Mall like three mortal women having a girls' night out. Our plan was to split up once we reached Bethesda Fountain.

Helene and I were not particularly close, but she wasn't really close with anyone, except Ethan. She wasn't friendly either and was always serious. I got the feeling that she hadn't led a happy mortal life, and that she was not exactly thrilled with being immortal either.

"Helene . . . Justus and Magnus told me a little bit about Ethan. How did you meet him?" I asked.

"We met in Britain during the Second World War," she replied.

Tavia added, "Helene was a nurse and worked in the hospitals during the war, tending especially to the air raid victims."

"Were you an immortal then?" I probed.

"Yes, I had been for almost a century," she disclosed.

"When were you changed?" I continued.

"Helene was changed in 1821 in Tripolitsa, Greece," Tavia responded, trying to elicit the story from her.

"During the War of Independence," Helene began. "I was thirty at the time, working as a nurse. I was alone because my parents had been killed when I was young. I had never married and had no siblings, no kids. The town was attacked by Greek revolutionaries fighting the Ottoman rule. People were being beaten, raped, and killed in the streets. It was unimaginable. I tried to help a few people but soon came to realize that it was useless. A few others and I hid in a tomb and managed to survive the attack but we were taken prisoner a few days later when we came out of hiding."

"That sounds horrible," I said.

"It was. I watched others get killed daily and wondered why I was spared. Day after day, wondering if this would be the day that I would die. One night, one of the revolutionaries came to me and told me that the next day, everyone held captive would die. He told me he could save me and asked me how much I wanted to live. I thought this was a strange question and answered that I wanted to live more than anything. He took me to a cavern and there, he drank from me. He told me he would be back every day, and he told me that I was going to get sick for a while, but then I would get better and stronger, and nobody could hurt me then."

"His name was Phineas," she said with a slight smile. "He did come back every day and drank from me a little bit. I was sick, and the transformation was almost unbearable. Soon, I started to be thirsty, like I had never been before. He came back one day with someone. My thirst was excruciating. He slit his prisoner's wrist and the smell of the blood took over my body. It was like all reason left me. I remember the feeling and sound of my own heart pumping exceedingly hard when the blood entered me—the exhilaration and energy that entered my body. It was amazing."

This was the most that Helene has ever shared with me. She went on, "Every day he brought me a new victim. I didn't care who the person was. I just wanted the blood. I asked him what I was and what he was. He told me as much as he knew about immortality."

She stopped talking, so I waited to see if she was going to go on. "OK, then what happened?" I probed, trying to elicit more conversation.

"One day, he just stopped coming," she remarked with no feeling.

Again I waited, but that was it, she said no more. We walked in silence for a while then I started a new conversation.

"I noticed that nobody gets involved with mortals much except for liaising with the police."

"Usually, the only ones who get involved with mortals are the newly changed immortals," Helene pointed out. "They still have attachments to mortals, but after several decades, they realize that it doesn't work out. It's complicated. Ultimately, someone gets hurt in the process."

"Justus told me his story about Elizabeth," I commented. "I could tell that he was deeply hurt by having to leave her. Magnus seems OK with brief mortal trysts," I added casually.

"Yes, he has no problem with breaking hearts," Helene snapped.

I knew that she and Magnus didn't see eye to eye, and her tone when speaking of him seemed very contemptuous. There was more to it than clashing personalities, and I doubted that I would get any more information about the friction between them, based on her body language.

We walked for another while in silence as I pondered life for Justus and Helene, both of them abandoned by their makers very early. I would be completely lost without them, my new family.

"If I didn't have you guys, I would be lonely," I admitted. "I can see how a newborn would be drawn to mortals, especially if they didn't have an immortal family."

"That's why we generally don't make new immortals, of course, you being the exception," Tavia disclosed. "There are so many things to consider, so much angst early in a newborn's life . . . so much to teach. It is like having a teenager for at least a century!"

Again, there was silence as I pictured myself and Yasmine as the bratty teenagers of the family, and I smiled. It seemed to me that they should have experience since Magnus seemed to be a perpetual teenager!

The park was now under a cover of darkness. Most of the people in the park had left. It was time for us to split up, but I could still think of many other questions that I wanted to ask. We continued down a path, and I asked, "What about love and sex? Is it different for an immortal? I'm feeling like I'm lacking something in my life. I was a single mother for several years, and I didn't date. I pretty much wrote off relationships and sex and was OK with it. Now, with this new body, new sensations, I'm finding that I am craving sex, but I think it is more than sexuality. I think I need some kind of connection with someone who can understand me."

"That eliminates mortals," Helene asserted. "Because they'll never be able to understand you!"

With a nod of agreement, Tavia added, "That's so true!"

"You both sound like you speak from experience," I said.

"Yes, we both do," Tavia answered with a look on her face that held both pleasure and pain.

"Some immortals are happy to have transient mortal relationships, like Magnus and Yasmine," Helene explained. "They are entertained with the superficial and are not at risk of falling for a mortal. You, on the other hand, strike me as someone who would."

"Really, you get that from me?" I questioned.

This time, Tavia was the one to answer. "It's strong in you, your ability to connect. I think it is your gift, your special ability."

Helene explained, "It usually doesn't take newborns this long to kill. Your connection to mortals, to others in general, is and will continue to be a hurdle for you in immortal life."

"I'm just a little slow to take up new activities," I expressed, lightheartedly trying to ease the mood that the conversation was taking. Both Tavia and Helene laughed, and we stopped walking, ready to break up and go our separate ways in the park.

I hadn't been paying much attention to my surroundings while we were walking. I was just following along obliviously, but I suddenly became aware that I was in a part of the park that I recognized. I stopped walking and stood for a minute, looking around in all directions.

"Are you all right?" Tavia asked.

I heard her talking but didn't hear the words. In my mind, I had flashes of memories. I saw the moon on a clear night. I had a rush of emotion flow through me—happy . . . happy to be alive. I could even smell the late summer flowers in bloom, but it wasn't late summer anymore. Then I heard a voice behind me. I turned to see the voice, and suddenly there was a flash of light and pain, then darkness.

Through my hyperventilation, I managed to get out, "It was here, wasn't it?" I was still spinning around and looking in all directions. I fixated on one spot and was drawn over to it. It was like the earth pulled me. I didn't feel my feet moving at all. I crouched down, and when I touched the ground, I put my hand in blood. I lifted my hand to look at it, and I saw blood for a moment.

I felt my head. The pain was blinding. My eyes were now shut. I could feel them on top of me, tearing at my clothes. I could smell the liquor and cigarettes. I tried to scream, but my mouth didn't work. When he saw me trying to talk, he punched me in the face, and then there was nothing.

I became aware that Tavia was beside me, touching me. I couldn't comprehend. I could see her mouth moving . . . what was she saying? I heard someone else, Anton, and through one eye, I saw him. I saw what he did. I could feel myself gasping, and I was cold, so cold. Everything around me was moving away in a wave, voices, images; even my body seemed to be moving away from me. Suddenly, there was a pain in my neck.

When I snapped out of it, I was holding my hand to my neck where Tavia had drank from me, to save me. She was in front of me, and I could hear her now.

She took hold of my shoulders and said, "This is where we found you. What's happening to you?"

"I saw it all in flashes," I shrieked. "I saw them. I saw you and Anton. I could smell them and hear them, my attackers. It was as though it was happening to me right now."

Tavia looked into my eyes, which always calmed me down. It was like looking into my father's eyes when I was a kid. Her gaze brought me back to the here and now. I was OK for a moment, looking at her, and then my ears picked up a sound from a distance.

I felt myself jolt, and I began to run amazingly fast. I could sense nothing except the noise that I heard, a scream, a scream like mine that night. My body was guided by what I heard. I was on autopilot, and before I knew it, I was there. I saw him on top of her, holding her by the throat, and suddenly the flash of light and the pain in my head . . . again, I felt ill.

I'm not sure that he heard me, or that she saw me. I was moving so fast. Time seemed suspended. I was holding him by the throat up in the air, just looking at his face, his surprised, shocked face. The sound of him gasping for air as I crushed his windpipe excited me. His feet were jerking and kicking as he tried to get out of my grasp. He was at my mercy and deserved none. I punctured his skin with my nails and let his blood flow over me, and that is when it happened.

Like a bloodthirsty, starved, wild animal, I ripped open his throat and let the stream of warmth enter me; it was the most heavenly taste imaginable.

Although I'm sure it lasted only for a couple of seconds, in that moment, time stood still. I could taste each drop. I could feel the warmth surging through me, around me, like sitting by a fireplace in a warm, soft blanket sipping hot cocoa. The more he drained, the more ravenous I seemed. I wasn't sure, but I might even have been making a sound, a primal grunt or groan like when bearing down to give birth or when having an incredible orgasm.

I could hear his heart, its strong pounding at first, and as it slowed, I began to see flashes, images in my brain. It wasn't my life I was seeing; it was his. I saw an abused and abandoned child. I saw a teenage drug addict. I saw rape, lots of rape. I felt anger, despair, loneliness, aggression, and finally, as his heart beat its final time, I felt remorse and gratitude and saw a smiling woman's face.

I threw him down to break my connection with him. I was freaked out by what I saw in my mind. How could I see images of him? I don't know him!

I heard Tavia and Helene tending to the assault victim. I approached my victim, the rapist, slowly and touched him cautiously, like he was a live wire that could electrocute me. Would I see more images? *Maybe the blood gave me hallucinations,* I thought. It certainly pumped me up and made me feel incredible. *Maybe blood intoxicates temporarily?*

I sat for a moment and turned my focus inward to my body, the sensations. What was happening to it? I could feel the warmth surging in me. I could feel a tingle in my limbs. I looked at my hands. I had color, and my skin looked alive. My eyesight was incredible. I had a huge amount of energy that felt like it was brimming over, wanting to spill out. That's when I noticed the blood on me, all over me, and I became aware that Tavia was standing over me, looking at me in disbelief, mouth hanging open. I was like a child caught with the cookie jar, covered in melted chocolate and cookie crumbs. She shook her head and stated, "What a mess! We can't have you walking around the park looking like that."

"I'm not sure what happened," I stammered. "It was all so fast and so slow at the same time. I was like a rabid wild animal. I'm not sure if I should be ashamed or proud of myself. I lost control. That can't be good."

"You did what comes naturally, especially at your age," Tavia replied. "You're still very young. You have shown a lot of restraint so far, and I don't imagine it will be difficult for you to manage your hunger. Don't read too much into this. It's your first kill, and it was obviously intensified by memories of your own assault. You'll definitely need to be a little less messy next time!" she finished with a grin.

Helene had already called Justus to come pick me up. Our contacts with the police department were arriving to take care of the mess. Helene looked at me and said nothing but winked.

The assault victim was physically OK but emotionally damaged. Helene told her what happened, that we hit the rapist over the head with a rock and he was dead. It was a plausible story and with her emotional state; that was the reality she believed. That was also the story that was officially noted with the police, and they took care of the entire situation.

Dr. Drake, the medical examiner of choice for these cases, arrived. "Another 10-33," he declared as he looked me over and then looked at Tavia inquisitively.

"She's new," Tavia remarked.

"Looks like it," he replied sarcastically. "Everything's taken care of here. You can go."

The responding Officer Johnson walked over to us and motioned to shake my hand but then took a look at me and put his hand down. "Thanks," he said and touched my shoulder. He gave me his jacket to cover up my mess and a cloth to clean the blood off my face. "My number is in the pocket. Call me if you need anything." They took no statements from us and sent us on our way as soon as possible, before a crowd could form at the scene.

"How does all of this work?" I asked Tavia.

"They have a procedure to follow when it's one of ours," she explained. "There are a few officers and Drake that we always call, and they know what to do. They're fast and efficient, and they get us away from the scene before any media arrive. It's a well-oiled machine."

The adrenaline of the situation was just starting to wear off as we met Justus at East Drive and Terrace.

"She's had enough excitement for one evening," Helene told Justus.

He stopped dead in his tracks, looking me over. "Your approach needs a little refinement," he observed through bursts of laughter.

"I killed someone," I said in a voice that was partially questioning.

"Yes, you definitely did," he said soberly.

I started to cry. Justus took me in his arms and held me while I sobbed. I'm not sure why I was crying. Was I overwhelmed by the entire situation? Was I disgusted with myself for being such an animal? Did I feel sorry for the victim . . . both victims? Was I just realizing who or what I really was? Was I happy that I helped someone? Was I happy that there was one less vile rapist on the street? Was I happy to be alive . . . or a version of alive? Was I happy to be immortal or did I hate it; hate what it turned me into?

Justus kissed my forehead and led me to the car in silence. Tavia and Helene had left us alone. We drove for a bit, and then Justus pulled over.

Looking at me with the sweetest eyes, he asked, "How are you . . . really?

"I'm . . . I'm not sure," I choked out through the heaves of my quieted sobbing.

A few minutes of silence passed as I ran my first kill over in my head. I closed my eyes, and I could hear my victim's heart beating, first strong and powerful, and then gradually slowing and becoming weaker and weaker. I searched for words to describe what I felt, but at the moment that I was killing him, there were no discernible feelings for him, for anyone. It was like eating a steak. A rare, juicy steak with baked potato and sour cream, topped off with my favorite Château Pétrus. I felt the same feelings I would have for that meal: satisfaction, satiation, and an endorphin rush. Consuming for the pleasure, not for the need! Was that wrong?

"I was like a starved animal, giving in to my primal urges," I said.

"Technically speaking, you were a starved animal," Justus asserted. "You hadn't had real blood."

He touched my face and stated, "You're warm and your skin looks healthy. Not that you weren't exceptionally beautiful before, but now . . . you're radiant. I can hear your heartbeat. Your body will change even more now that you have real blood. I'm sure you can tell that you're different?"

"Yes, I can tell. My body feels amazing," I remarked. "But is that worth killing someone, even someone that vile? Does this keep the balance on earth? Was he the yin to my yang? Who am I to judge and sentence him to death?"

Just then, a cyclist drove past us, and his bike hit a pothole on the street. He went flying off the bike and cut his hands and elbows, landing on the rough concrete. I could see with my enhanced vision the trickle of blood from his wounds, even in the dark. I could smell it, and my focus became drawn to it and only it.

Like an addict, the only thing that I could concentrate on was the smell . . . the smell of blood, warm, fresh, mortal blood. I wanted to be out of the car; I wanted to taste it, so I reached for the door handle. Justus hit the lock switch then grabbed me by the shoulders and looked at me straight in the eyes.

"Fight the urge," he encouraged. "You don't need any more tonight and not even tomorrow. Hold your breath, close your eyes, pinch yourself, or find some other way to take your focus off what you smell."

Time again seemed to go both in slow motion and as fast as light. I kept looking at Justus and decided to focus on his eyes. They were beautiful to look at, easy to get lost in and I did just that.

I was now in full control of my urge and could hear the cyclist cursing like a sailor as he picked up his bike, got back on, and drove away, taking with him the sweet aroma that almost drove me to kill again.

"Wow, I thought chocolate was hard to resist. I've never thought of killing for chocolate before," I joked, trying to lighten the mood.

"You've also never experienced the animalistic instinct to kill for your survival either," Justus commented not as lightheartedly. "You are not the same animal that you were before. Your base primal urges are much stronger. To understand yourself, watch a shark kill. Blood triggers a process in you that bypasses reasoning."

"How come you don't react in the same way?" I asked.

"Because it takes training to engage your brain in the process so that you can overcome the urge," he explained. "That process is just beginning for you now and is the second most difficult part of immortal life."

"What's the first?" I asked.

"Physical transformation," he answered.

"I would have thought giving up mortal life would be first," I pondered.

"Maybe for some," he noted vacantly.

"For the next several weeks and maybe even months, you can't be left alone, because now your switch has been flipped on. You're like a meth addict, and we have to keep you on the program to control your urges."

"That sounds grrreat!" I said sarcastically.

He started the car, and we drove off again. I still couldn't think of anything else but my kill. Nobody had mentioned anything before about having hallucinations during the process. *Maybe my head was damaged permanently when it was bashed in during my assault*, I wondered.

"Justus, is it normal to have visions?" I questioned.

"Visions? When and of what?" he probed.

"When I was . . . you know . . . killing, I had these visions that I can't explain," I replied, unsure of myself, wondering if I was abnormal . . . more abnormal than the average immortal.

"OK," he said, "I need to know a little more to be able to comment."

Clenching my fingers together, I answered, "Well, I saw flashes, like pictures or short video clips of him . . . my victim. I think it was things that happened in his life. I saw an abused and abandoned kid, a teenage drug addict, and too many rapes. It was like I could see and feel what was going through his mind in his last moments. Does that make any sense?"

Justus looked at me inquisitively in silence for a moment and then let out, "Hmmm."

"What?" I asked.

"Well, I've heard of it, but it has never happened to me," he stated. "I'm not sure if it has happened to anyone else we know, but we can ask."

"Does it mean I'm messed up? Is it because my brain is damaged?" I speculated while touching the spot on my head that had been bashed in. "It's kind of unnerving, but still, right at the end, I sensed gratitude that it was all over, like he was thanking me for putting him out of his misery."

"Well then, maybe you did a double good deed tonight," he added.

"Maybe," I whispered more to myself than to him.

We entered the house and found Magnus and Yasmine sitting on the couch in front of the television. They looked at me, then at

Justus, said hello, and went back to their movie. I went up to my room to change my clothes. I looked at myself in the mirror and could only imagine how much worse I looked before I cleaned the blood from my face. I tuned my hearing to the conversation downstairs among Justus, Magnus, and Yasmine. I wasn't sure just what Justus would say, and I wasn't sure what I wanted him to say.

It was clear by my appearance that something happened, so I'm sure that Yasmine and Magnus were curious. The way they behaved when we came in gave me the impression they had a heads-up on the situation. What I heard Justus say was that the story was mine to tell when I was ready to tell it. This made me smile because I felt that I could trust him. Real trust is when someone helps you through something and keeps it between the two of you.

I showered, put on some comfortable clothes, and ventured back to my friends, my family. I thought that maybe if I acted normal, like nothing happened, I could just sit and watch a movie and that would be that for the night. That's what I did. I walked into the room, found a comfortable spot to sit in, and watched the movie.

"What is this?" I asked.

"*Burnt Offerings*," Magnus answered.

"Never heard of it," I commented.

"It's a seventies classic," he stated in disbelief, "the inspiration to *The Amityville Horror* and *The Shining*."

Yasmine added, "Magnus is very serious about his seventies horror."

"I can see that," I said.

"He'll eventually make you watch all of them, believe me," she continued.

"Horror flicks from the sixties and seventies rule the genre," Magnus exclaimed with great enthusiasm. "There's nothing like *Psycho*, *The Exorcist*, *Halloween*, and *Rosemary's Baby*. You just don't get movies like that anymore."

"What about *Hellraiser*?" I remarked.

That got his attention. "You know *Hellraiser*?" he perked up, diverting his eyes from the television for the first time in our conversation. "There's hope for you yet! It's not a seventies flick but not a failure like many of the other eighties horror films. You must be a bit twisted if you like *Hellraiser*."

I sat back in my chair and pondered the word *twisted*, especially in reference to my activities of the evening.

My thoughts were interrupted by Yasmine bursting out with "Enough small talk already . . . What the hell happened tonight?"

Magnus made a sound like choking. Yasmine was peering at me with her large dark, piercing eyes, and Justus got up and walked out of the room shaking his head.

I sat silent, briefly reviewing the night in my mind, and tentatively stated, "I had my first kill tonight." I looked down, away from them because I felt guilty and shameful. Of anyone in the group, these two were the ones who enjoyed killing the most, so I didn't expect them to understand how I felt.

"That's like saying you had sex for the first time. Spill it, girl!" Yasmine ordered with fervor.

I couldn't quite muster her level of enthusiasm, but I decided to tell them the story as I remembered it.

"First I had flashbacks from the night I was attacked. That kind of put me in a hypersensitive state. I heard a scream and followed it. I was on autopilot, driven by instincts or something. Then it all happened so fast. I tackled the guy off her and held him by the throat. I either did it accidentally or on purpose, I can't remember, but I pierced his throat, and blood poured out all over me. Then I lost my mind and slaughtered the guy like a wild animal."

Magnus looked at me with no expression and said, "I forgot to mention the movie *Carrie* in my list of classics, which is weird because that's exactly what you reminded me of when you walked in here tonight."

Momentarily, I felt angry, then his face softened, and I picked up a sofa pillow and threw it at him.

"You know the seventies spawned a huge load of vampire movies," Magnus noted. "I'm going to go get my collection, and we'll pick one to watch . . . seems like a good night for a vampire flick!"

"Thanks, but I think I need to process what happened. I'm going to rest," I told them.

I lay down on my bed thinking about my kill, and as I drifted, my first days as an immortal came flooding into my thoughts.

CHAPTER TWO

The Fog

My life began the day it ended.

As I lay still with my eyes shut, my eyelids like weights, a vague sensation of heat in my right arm pulled me out of my stupor. My head felt heavy and fuzzy, like my brain was made of steel wool instead of gray matter. My right hand was pleasantly warm compared with the rest of my body, cold and listless. I slowly opened my eyes against the strong force that held them shut and through the haze, I could see I was in a small dim room that I didn't recognize. My heart pounding from fear, I searched through my mind for a hint of memory related to this place.

My eyes darted around the room; my vision was blurry. Everything was coming in and out of focus. The room was faintly lit by a small bit of light escaping from the edges of the thick, dark shade pulled over a window to my left. To my right, there were some medical supplies on a shelf and a closed door visible in front of where I lay. My breathing was fast and shallow. I felt dizzy and weak. I wondered, *Was I in a hospice somewhere? But where? Where could I possibly be?*

My thoughts, very easily distracted, turned to how cold I felt. I had a blanket covering me, yet I felt like I was made of ice. I was drawn to the one different sensation: to my right hand. It was oddly warm despite the fact that the rest of me was terribly cold.

With the little strength that I had, I lifted my hand toward my face, trying to focus my eyes on it. *My hand was unusually pale, or was it an effect of the dimly lit room?* I thought. I could see a tube going into my hand, a dark intravenous tube. I followed it with my eyes to see it ending at a large bag of dark liquid hanging on a pole beside the bed. On the bag, I just barely made out the "A+."

It took a few seconds for my brain to react, to register that it was blood going into me, and then suddenly, my heart found the strength to race again. My breathing worked up to a gasp as I realized I was having a reaction to the blood. I was a type *B* negative. I couldn't have *A* positive blood. It would kill me! Where the hell am I? Why wouldn't they know this?

I tried to scream, but my voice was so powerless that all I could get out was a faint whisper. I kept trying to make my mouth work, gasping and flailing, struggling hard to get out of bed. A loud clang rang out in the room as something metallic fell off the bed. I heard the sound of footsteps coming toward the door. I tried with all my might to make my mouth say, "Help me, I'm dying in here," but all I could get out was a dry-sounding croak from my pasty throat. Finally, the door shot open, and in a split second, someone was beside me. It was a woman, and she touched my head as she looked down at me lovingly.

With my eyes wide with panic, I begged, "Help me," in the meekest of voices.

"Sleep," she said. "Everything's OK."

My head was swimming. I was sure death was near. I was resolved that if I shut my eyes, I would die! Through my hysteria, I could see that she was accompanied by a man.

He whispered, "It's too soon!"

I could hear myself muttering, "I'm type *B*. I'm type *B* negative . . . I can't have this blood!" I tried to rip the tube out of my hand, but I had so little strength that it was futile.

"Take it out! Take it out!" I screamed, but the words came out as a mumble. The man held me down as the woman spoke.

"Everything is OK, Ivy. You're not ready yet."

Through tears of frustration, I heard myself pleading, "You're killing me. Stop. Please, stop!"

She put something in my IV, and despite the fight to keep my eyes open, they became so heavy that they closed slowly against my will.

Suddenly, I was really light, floating . . . floating in a warm white space. I was weightless. My feet touched the ground, and the white space transformed into my favorite park, the park where I always took Sam, my golden Lab, where he could run wild with the other dogs.

I felt warm and content, and I heard a voice that I recognized from behind me. It was the sweet voice of Ana, my daughter. I turned to look at her. She was very young . . . and Sam was with her. She ruffled his ears and kissed his head and said, "Go, boy, run with your friends." Sam took off to join a pack of dogs. I walked over to Ana and took her hand. She was smiling at me, a true happy smile, and I couldn't help but return the smile, all the while wondering how could I be here? Ana wasn't ten anymore. Sam died two years ago.

The warmth of the sun felt amazing on my skin. It was early summer. I could smell the blooms in the fields around us. I took a deep breath, one that seemed to go right down to my toes and suddenly came to the realization that this must be heaven. I didn't believe in heaven, or hell, or any particular religion, yet it was my first thought. I must be dead. Heaven must be a place where you can go back to your happiest time and just stay there. This was a comforting thought. If I could, I would stay here forever.

This time was indeed the happiest point in my life. I was finally divorced and safe. He was in jail; Ana and I could live freely without worry. I was always a little embarrassed about this when I thought of it. How could Ivy Lewis, the daughter of the great Meryl Howard—a superior court judge and former prosecutor of violent criminals—end up in a violent marriage, a battered woman? I shook my head as I always did to try and rattle the thought out of my brain. I looked back to Sam and Ana, and the warmth came back to me.

What a beautiful day, and if I was going to believe in heaven, I should also thank God for giving me this wonderful daughter and this freedom . . . freedom that I never had before. I sat on the same carved bench that I always did, drinking my warm coffee and watching the two beings that I love the most in this world enjoy a carefree afternoon. I had such a smile on my face that my cheeks hurt. This was what life should be, the joy of a proud mother watching her baby grow up.

Basking in splendor, I thought to myself, *My baby was born ten years ago, and how time flew by. It seemed like just yesterday, I was holding her in my arms, kissing her sweet baby cheeks, and smelling that wonderful baby smell.*

She didn't stay in my arms long, my precocious girl. She skipped crawling and started to walk quite early. I could see that she was ahead of other kids her age, always searching for a new experience. Her marvel at the world always kept me in awe; such sweet innocence, such an adventurous soul. My little wanderer ... I was lucky that she had long copper curls that I could always spot in a crowd because she got away from me sometimes. Before I could say her name, she would be off ahead of me to her next conquest. She was my life; all that I had was centered on her and in keeping her safe. Safe from the pain that the world offered in heaping doses, sometimes.

On the day she was born, my life changed both for the better and for the worst. I never knew I could love someone so much; that someone could capture my heart and hold it so strongly. When she was born, other things changed; he changed. I thought that her father, Mike, would be just as enamored with her as I was; she was amazing for her age.

Her father was the smart one. The *A* student with nothing but promise ahead of him; he could be anything he wanted. He didn't study and always had the top grades in school. I had to work real hard to get the *C*s that I managed. I really wasn't a school person, much to my mother's dismay. I know she was happy when Mike and I started dating. She hoped that his intelligence would get into me through osmosis. "Osmosis," now there's one scientific word that I retained from high school science! Math, science, debates, essays, Mike could do it all. He was a star athlete as well—football, volleyball, and basketball. He was the valedictorian the year we graduated together.

I just barely made it through high school. The robe that I wore on graduation day was large enough to camouflage the bump forming in my belly, something we all tried to keep secret. Nobody wanted my pregnancy to impede Mike's chances of getting into a good college. He was accepted at Harvard, his first choice, influenced significantly by my mother, a Harvard alumnus herself. My mother wrote a glowing reference letter to the admissions board at Harvard, and considering her standing in the legal system, and her contributions to her alma mater, Mike was a shoo-in. Since my mother wasn't blessed with the brilliant daughter that she had hoped for, she lived vicariously through Mike, as proud of him as though he were her son. She promised Mike that if his parents couldn't afford his schooling, she would help.

My mother didn't give it a second thought when I told her I was pregnant—eighteen and pregnant! I spent many sleepless nights wondering how I would tell her, how would she take it and all for nothing. In fact, I think she was secretly happy because she could use this to influence Mike all the more. She could mold him into the lawyer prodigy that she wanted. He would be her son-in-law, the father of her grandchild. She told me the day I graduated she was thankful that I was beautiful, and able to attract a bright guy that would become something.

Mike came from a moderate home, with both parents working grunt jobs, as my mother called it, stuck up as she was. Mike's father was a foreman in a factory, being groomed to take over the plant manager position. His mother was a nurse. He never lacked for anything, but what he craved was notoriety. He wanted to be someone important, someone others looked up to. When we were first together, this part of him fascinated me. He wasn't charming per se, but charismatic. He could sway others to his side of any argument. This trait was perfect for becoming a lawyer, and he put it to use as the president of the debate club.

Mike's mother was very warm and caring, a trait that seemed to skip a generation. Mike was not an outwardly emotional or loving person. He was very logical, and his brain seemed to run twice the speed of anyone else's in our graduating class. I felt lucky to be with him, that he chose me, someone who wasn't really smart or talented. Despite the fact that I couldn't elicit much emotion from him, I knew he loved something about me, but what, I never was quite sure.

The one person whose love I could count on was my father, Ron. He was a warm, loving people person who enjoyed every day of his work as a high school teacher. He worked for the same high school year after year, teaching freshman and sophomore sciences, although I'm sure my mother would have preferred him to be a house husband. His enthusiasm for science was evident in every class he taught, in every lesson prepared, and in every experiment demonstrated. He loved high school kids, and they loved him. He was the type of teacher and person who believed that everyone deserved respect. Students, teachers, janitors, and everyone else were all equals in his eyes. Each person's opinion mattered, and each person's rights mattered. The kids really responded to this. Other teachers would yell, give detentions, and send kids to the office. They never earned the respect of students the way he did.

Kids would do their homework, they would look forward to his class, and when possible, he would let them contribute to the class plan. One year, he held a class competition on who could make the best potato cannon. The class created a target that was a huge caricature of the principal painted in water soluble paint, of course, on the back wall of the school. It was quite a spectacle.

Ron was also the senior football coach. The team worked hard for him, and he was known to influence many of the not-so-studious athletes to keep up their grades. Many students made college football teams, and for this, the high school treasured my father and created an award in his honor, the Ron Lewis Award, for the player demonstrating the most heart during a season. I still went every year to the school to help commemorate him and all that he gave to that school.

My parents met in their last year of college, and Ron was more than willing to follow Meryl wherever she needed to go to start her law career. She was well into her career when they finally married, and I believe that she did it to please her parents. Although a feminist with her career, she was still a traditionalist as far as family was concerned.

My mother became pregnant in the first few months of marriage. For her, the whole thing couldn't be over soon enough. I knew this because she often reminded me of the burden I was to her career once the pregnancy became obvious. It put a dent in her image, excluding her from the old boys club that she tried hard to be part of.

I believe that my mother stayed with my father for my sake. She could never understand me, but she did see the strong bond that my father and I had. She worked so much that it was more convenient to have my father around than to have to look for a babysitter. To her, my father was like a pet dog—very loyal and loving and obeyed his master. My father was in awe of my mother's strength, her intelligence, and mostly her confidence.

I don't think my father had a bad life. He was too jovial to let Meryl bring him down, and his love for his work made every day rewarding. He had an easy smile and a warmth that could take my worst days and turn them completely around. When I was down, I would imagine my father's easy smile and his loving embrace, and for a moment, I could be happy. It was always a bittersweet moment though, because it would flitter away, replaced with the memory of the worst day of my life.

It was a Thursday. I waited at school to be picked up by my father, like every other day. He had told me he might be late because the championship football game was that afternoon. He anticipated a win and knew that there would be some celebrating on the sidelines before they got back on the bus to return to the school. This was his best team ever. They had gone undefeated in the last half of the season. College scouts were looking at several of the players. My father was the happiest I had ever seen him. I sat on the curb, bouncing a small ball when Mr. Garrison, the principal of the primary school I attended, walked by.

"Ivy, Ronnie is going to be very happy today, I just heard the news on the radio. The Mustangs won the championships by twenty-one points."

A smile took over my entire face as I could picture my father being hoisted up by his players and paraded around the field or maybe dripping wet with Gatorade that his players poured all over him. My daydream was cut short by Mr. Garrison yelling from his car window as he pulled away from the curb, "He should be along soon, say hello for me . . . and tell him congratulations too."

"I sure will, Principal Garrison. Have a good night," I said as I waved my hand until his car disappeared out of the school parking lot.

Vice Principal Smith was still in the school. She always stayed late. Another twenty minutes went by, but I didn't think anything of it. I knew my dad would be a bit late, especially since his team won. Another fifteen minutes had gone by when I heard the door behind me swing open in a loud thud as it hit the wall. I turned back to see the horrified face of Vice Principal Smith. There were tears streaming down her cheeks, and I wondered what could be wrong. I was sitting on the curb near her parked car, so I stood up and got out of the way quickly, thinking she was running to her car. *Something serious must have happened*, I thought, by the way she was sobbing. My heart swelled for her very obvious pain, and as she got closer, I asked, "Are you OK? What's wrong?"

She stopped just in front of me, silent, looking at me with tears pouring out of her eyes, her breathing was labored and her eyes . . . her eyes had this deep sorrow in them. She tried to speak, but it seemed like she had marbles in her mouth. We stood looking at each other for what seemed like forever, then she lunged out and grabbed me in her arms sobbing my name.

"What," I questioned. "What's going on?" She grabbed me by the hand and ran me back into the school, practically dragging me along the walkway. She could still only get out huge sobs. When we got to the principal's office, she motioned for me to sit in a chair beside another kid, Joey Lafferty, who was there because he was in trouble. She entered her office and closed the door, while Joey looked at me with a "ha-ha" expression, thinking I was in trouble too.

I could hear Vice Principal Smith in her office, behind her closed door, on the phone with someone. She had managed to pull herself together for this conversation. I heard her say, "Yes . . . no . . . ah, hum." Then, a long pause. "I'm so sorry." Another long pause and finally, "Please take all the time you need, all the time she needs." She hung up the phone, and I heard her sigh and gasp, the kind you do when you have been crying for a long time. I heard her chair slide back and the sound of her heels on the floor.

With a bit more composure than before, she requested that I come into her office. Joey snickered with a snide smile as we were both thinking that I did something wrong. I searched my day and my week to see if there was something that I did that could lead to a detention. I wondered who could have made up some story to get me in trouble. Nothing was coming to me. As I entered the office, Vice Principal Smith motioned again to a chair, avoiding my eyes. She walked out and closed the door.

After about ten minutes of me thinking up the worst scenarios in my head, wondering what my punishment would be, I heard a car door outside. Then my heart started to race. My dad had arrived, and Vice Principal Smith was going to tell him what I did, and I didn't know what I did. How could I come up with a good story to cover something I didn't know? I heard the sound of high heels coming into the principal's office again, but I heard two pairs of high heels. *Phew*, I thought. It was Joey's mother, not my father. Then the office door opened.

I kept my eyes down, suddenly feeling guilty for something I did, even though I didn't know why. I heard a voice say my name, but it wasn't Vice Principal Smith; it was my mother.

"Mom?" *Why was my mother here?* I wondered. She never came to pick me up. Her face looked calm, almost warm. For her, this was not a usual look. It made me feel uneasy, like she was hiding something. Again, I asked, "Mom?" And I stuttered as a feeling of dread washed over me. "Wh-what are you doing here? You should be at work. Where's Dad?" Still looking at me with an eerie calmness, she swallowed hard, so hard that I could see a golf ball in her throat.

"Ivy . . . ," she said, and took a deep breath, "Ivy, there has been an accident." My young brain couldn't comprehend what she was getting at. I just stared at her blankly. She crouched down beside the chair and took my hand. She looked into my eyes in a way that I had never seen before. I could see pain. The pain that she was not showing on her face was there in her eyes. She couldn't hide it.

Although I knew there was something seriously wrong, my mind couldn't come to the conclusion that I was going to be affected by it so I asked naïvely, "Where's Dad? Wasn't he supposed to pick me up today?"

She squeezed my hand tighter and clarified, "Your father has been in an accident. We need to go to the hospital right now." The words entered my ears, but my brain refused to process them for a moment. I shook my head as though trying to get the words out of my ears, but it didn't work. I looked up at my mom and questioned very faintly, "Accident?" I think my mouth hung open as tears welled in my eyes, and I shrieked, *"Accident?"* She looked at me apologetically and did something she rarely did. She scooped me up into her arms and held me tight. She didn't say anything; she just held me.

She carried me to the car, and I reasoned things out in my mind; surely the hospital could fix him. "He's at the hospital, Mom. They can fix him, right?" I said with a very hopeful voice. "I had an accident before. I fell off my bike, and they put a cast on my broken arm, and I was good as new. He can get a cast, right . . . and he'll be fine!"

She looked at me this time, bewildered. She didn't know herself how he was and didn't know how to tell me that. "Let's not think the worst," she said. "Let's listen to some music, and we'll be at the hospital in no time." She switched on the radio and held my hand while we drove. I was able to hum along with the music. It was a familiar song, and briefly, my mind was clear. Another song came on, and this one I really liked. I concentrated on the words, so that I wouldn't think of anything else.

When the song ended, a news reporter came on and announced, "A tragic accident on Route 3 may have claimed as many as ten lives when a school bus collided with—" My mom quickly let go of my hand and shut off the radio midsentence. I looked over at her, and it suddenly became clear: the school bus on the news was the school bus that my dad was on with the football team.

This time, I was the one who had the golf ball in my throat to swallow. I looked at her and she looked at me, and all I could say was "Mom?" And she nodded with tears welling in her eyes. We pulled in to the hospital emergency parking lot and ran into the hospital, up to the first desk we saw, and my mother requested with as much calm as she could, "My husband, Ronald Lewis, was brought here. Please let me see him."

The person at the desk responded, "Please have a seat over there," pointing to a room with a bunch of people in it. "I'll find out what I can and have someone inform you as soon as possible."

We entered the room, and there were several adults there. Many were hugging and crying, some were sitting with blank stares on their faces, others were pacing back and forth. A very pretty young woman walked over to my mother and asked, "Are you Mrs. Lewis?"

"Ms. Howard, but yes, my husband is Ron Lewis."

A few of the people standing close to us stopped their hugging and talking and crying for a moment to look at her, and then they looked at me and their faces changed. They looked even sadder than they had been before.

The pretty girl said, "Ron, um, Mr. Lewis taught me biology and chemistry. He's a really good teacher." She tried to smile, but was obviously uneasy. "My boyfriend, Randy," she continued, trying to hold her composure, "is the quarterback." And she gasped as tears started to stream down her face.

My mom reached out to her but couldn't come up with any words. My young brain still didn't have a clue on what was really happening here in this room. One by one, different families were called out to speak with doctors. Some walked away screaming and crying; some walked away relieved, but looking guiltily at the other families, the ones who were crying. So many people hugged each other. So many people said, "I'm so sorry for your loss." My mother held my hand tightly as we sat and watched the spectacle before us, her face blank. She had no words for me.

A doctor came to the door, and I heard him call, "Mrs. Lewis?" A common mistake, everyone always referred to my mother as Mrs. Lewis.

Like always, my mother corrected the doctor, saying, "Ms. Howard. I'm Ronald Lewis's wife," as she got up from her seat. She still held my hand tight and walked over to the doctor, pulling me with her.

The doctor crouched down, his face level with mine he asked, "What's your name?"

"Ivy, Ivy Lewis," I answered, looking over his face for a sign of good news. "Ivy, can you please go over there to the desk and see the nurse in the pink flowered uniform? She'll get you a popsicle while I speak with your mother."

I looked in the direction he was pointing; and I saw a woman, who looked about the same age as my parents, waving hello to me with a popsicle in her hand. I reluctantly let go of my mother's hand and walked toward the woman in the pink flowered uniform. I stopped partway there and looked back at my mother. Her eyes met mine. She forced a smile and waved her hand in a "Go on" motion. I put my head down and continued to walk to the lady. She greeted me with a smile and led me to a room with some toys, books, and a television playing a movie that I had already seen at least five times. There were other kids in the room. Some were coughing, some were sniffling, and some had tubes in their arms; but they all seemed happy enough to be playing.

I watched the movie for a bit, and then I browsed the books they had. Most of the books were too young for me. I found a princess puzzle book and amused myself with the puzzles. After quite some time, my mom came to get me. Her eyes were red and puffy, her face was sad, but she really tried to smile for me.

We walked to each other, and she picked me up again, the way she did at school earlier, and she just held me. Before I could say anything, she walked with me out of the room. She held me and walked toward the exit. I stiffened up in her arms and cried, "Wait, I want to see Dad. Where's Dad?" I was struggling to get out of her grasp, so she put me down.

She looked at me through eyes that had no more tears to cry and said, "Baby, Dad's not OK. They couldn't fix him."

"Take me to Dad. I want to see Dad," I demanded again as though her words were in another language.

She knelt beside me and held both my arms tightly and explained, "Ivy, we have to go home now. Your dad is . . . not going to be able to come home." And she started sobbing again as she looked at my horrified face, her words taking hold of me completely, and then I knew what she was saying.

"Is Dad dead?" I whimpered, hoping that I drew the wrong conclusion from her words. She scooped me up with ease, a strength that she pulled out of her grief, her grief for me and my loss. Holding me tight to her, she nodded her head; no words were necessary. I knew the answer. This was the worst day of my life . . .

The sound of barking dogs pulled me back to my favorite spot at the dog park, and I thought of my dad's face. I thought of his easy smile and felt a smile light my own face. I had his smile, my mom always said. My peaceful moment was interrupted by a faint awareness that someone was calling my name; it seemed like far in the distance. I looked back, and as I searched for the source of the mystery voice, I started to feel like I couldn't breathe, like I was having a panic attack or something. I kept gasping. My body was getting warmer, and the voice was getting louder and louder. I was trying to take off my sweater. I'm too hot; I can't breathe. Then my head was spinning. The trees at the park were whirling around me. I slammed my eyes shut to stop the spinning.

The voice kept saying, "Ivy, it's OK. Breathe. Slow down. Open your eyes, Ivy." Again, I was aware of my body heat. I was hot, still hot, too hot! I was clutching at my clothes, trying to get them off. I needed to cool down. The voice was louder but peaceful, and I could feel a hand on my forehead.

"Ivy, wake up. Open your eyes." The voice seemed vaguely familiar and soothing.

The hand on my forehead reminded me of my father, of how he used to tuck me in at night, and stay with me when I was afraid of the dark. He would stroke my forehead until I was asleep. He kept the monsters away; he kept me safe. I felt safe now, for a moment, with the voice. My eyes started to flutter. They felt less heavy, but I was leaving now, leaving Ana and Sam, leaving the park.

"I want to go back to them. I don't want to leave." I could hear my own voice in my ears, pleading to go back, but the dimness started to come through. I could see a faint light. I became more aware of my shaking body. My hands were clutching at something, something that might be sheets. My body was on fire. My eyes opened slowly, and I could still hear my own voice—although more faint now—saying, "Ana, Ana . . ."

Gasping again, my eyes shot open, and I could see two faces over me, two kind-looking faces but not familiar. The panicked feeling was back again, and I tried with all my strength to say something, but my throat felt like it was glued shut. Gagging and gasping, I reached out for them, trying to get out the words, "Who are you? Where am I? Where is Ana?"

My mouth just wouldn't work. One of them took my hand and started to stroke my forehead again, and both of them said something together. It sounded like singing in harmony. "Ivy, everything is all right."

The woman explained, "You are OK. Ana is OK. We have spoken with her. Please, take some deep breaths, follow me. Now focus, breathe in and hold it. One, two, three . . . breathe out and hold it, one, two, three. Again, in, one, two, three . . . and out, one, two, three . . ."

This voice kept me focused, mesmerized really. I followed the instructions and concentrated on my breathing. In, one, two, three . . . out, one, two, three, and in, one, two, three . . . out, one, two, three. As I focused on the breathing, I could feel my body relaxing, and I heard the voice, "Good, Ivy, that's it. Just think of breathing. Everything else is OK."

Still concentrating on breathing slowly, looking from one to the other repeatedly, I tried my questions again. "Wh-where am I?"

"You're in our house," the woman replied. "You had an accident, and we have been taking care of you."

"An accident, what accident?" I inquired, concerned. "I don't remember anything . . ."

"You were mugged, attacked in Central Park," the man said. *Mugged*, I thought as my heart and breathing started to race again. I quickly searched my memories, but there was nothing, a blank.

"Breathe more slowly, Ivy. There is no danger now. We found you there hurt, and we brought you here to help you," he continued. "What's the last thing you remember?"

My mind was a complete blank, and I'm sure I looked confused because the woman put her hand on my arm in a soft motherly way, saying, "You're in Manhattan. Do you remember coming to New York?" My eyes shut, and I tried to concentrate. *New York?* I thought.

"Your driver's license says you are from Boston," the man added.

"Do you remember why you came to New York?" the woman questioned. I thought to myself, *A vacation? Yes, a vacation.* I came to New York to see the sights. I never had the chance to visit New York for any length of time, and get to really enjoy it. It had always been a draw for me since my high school trip to a Broadway show. I knew that I had to come back and spend some time visiting the city.

"*Ana?*" I forced out suddenly. "Please tell me Ana is OK."

"We have spoken with your daughter. She's fine. She's in London," the man reassured me. "Do you remember that?"

I slowly nodded to acknowledge that I did remember now that Ana was away in London. She was going to start school there soon. I felt relieved that I knew Ana was OK and said, "Oh yes, I remember now. School . . . she's going to school there." Thank God she wasn't with me when this happened! I couldn't bear it if she was hurt.

"What did you tell her?" I implored with a feeling of panic. "I don't want her to worry."

"We told her that you were hurt, but that you were recovering," the woman explained.

"We urged her to stay in London and told her that you would contact her once you were up to talking," the man added.

"How did you know about Ana?" I asked.

The woman answered, "We found a photo in your wallet, someone with the same beautiful copper curls as you, and we found a phone number on a piece of paper with Ana written on it. We tried the number, and Ana filled us in on the rest."

"Do you remember anything else?" the man probed.

I lay silent for a few minutes, thinking, and the pieces started to come together. After seeing Ana off on the plane to London, I impulsively decided to look for a seat sale to New York. I was on my own now. My daughter was away at college in London. This was my time, and New York had always been on the top of my to-do list. I remembered the plane and my hotel room. I had a list of places to see, and I didn't have any set schedule. I remembered some sights that I visited, the usual places: the Statue of Liberty, the Empire State Building, the Metropolitan Museum of Art, Central Park . . .

My memory ended in Central Park. I tried to focus on what I did in the park but drew a blank.

"Why can't I remember?" I was tightening my fists and pounding them onto the bed. My breathing was getting erratic, and the rush of heat started surging through my body again. "This is frustrating!" I hollered. "I want to know what happened. What happened to me?"

The heat was getting very intense, and I was no longer able to think straight. *I'm so hot . . . I'm too hot,* I thought. *Make it stop.* My two visitors were fading, and my head was spinning. I gasped for air. I felt like a weight was on my chest. A curtain of black fell over me. I heard faintly in the distance, "This will put her out for a few hours."

"Rest, Ivy, we'll take care of you." The voice fluttered like a butterfly in a breeze, and I felt peaceful again.

My eyes followed a beautiful butterfly, and as I stepped out from behind a row of sculpted hedges to see where it was going, I found myself in a park. *What an absolutely beautiful day,* I thought to myself as the warmth from the sun gently touched my skin. It was a day of perfection. Just enough sun, just enough breeze; the smell of the midsummer blooms. It was evening, my favorite time of day in the summer. The sting had gone out of the sun, the rays like a comfortable blanket. A few cotton ball clouds floated above me, and I was surrounded by a multitude of plants in Shakespeare Garden. My feet were tired from all the walking I had done. I sat for a while, closed my eyes, and reviewed the day in my mind.

I had started with a carriage ride then made my way to the Conservatory Garden. I was a budding photographer, now that I was going to have a lot of time to myself. With Ana away at school, I needed a hobby to fend off the empty nest feelings that kept creeping up on me. I was registered to take a class in September, a Photoshop class, that would keep me busy. The camera that I bought for this trip was foolproof. It had all the gadgets I needed to take the most incredible photos.

I spent a few hours taking photos of the flowers in the conservatory. It was easy to get caught up in the beauty, the aroma. The Phlox and Rose of Sharon were breathtaking, but still nothing in comparison with the majesty of the roses. I always loved roses. Every Mother's Day, my father and I would buy my mother a new type of rose for our front garden. Together, Dad and I would plant them and tend to them all season long. My favorites were the yellow roses. After my father died, I tried to keep the garden as lovely as he did, but eventually, the motivation slipped away.

Pulling my mind back to the present, I took a few last photos of the roses and decided to head for the Ramble. When in the Ramble, it was like being miles away from any city. There the sounds took center stage. The rustling leaves in the light breeze, the trickling streams, the singing birds . . . I couldn't help but think of the movie *August Rush* and how amazing it would be to make music like this.

I captured birds with my camera, birds that I had never seen before. Blue, red, and yellow . . . species that I thought were only found in tropical forests. I was amazed by it all. I could have spent the day just in this one place and be satisfied with my journey. I finished my tour of the Ramble on Bow Bridge, circled the lake, and visited Belvedere Castle, another picturesque venue that gave me many more magnificent photos for my collection. I finally ended my visit in Shakespeare Garden, thoroughly satisfied with my day at the park.

Feeling decidedly hungry, I made my way to a restaurant named the Boathouse for dinner. I sat with a lovely couple from Tennessee. We enjoyed the ending daylight together on the outside bar and grill. We told stories of our lives and our homes over cocktails, and as they started becoming romantic with one another, I said goodbye. We exchanged e-mail addresses and vowed to look each other up on Facebook.

Feeling very light despite my full belly, I headed back to East Drive with a skip in my step. Admittedly, I didn't drink much, so the few drinks that I had definitely made me tipsy. I started humming a tune from *Cats*, the Broadway show I had seen in high school.

> *... Memory*
> *All alone in the moonlight*
> *I can smile at the old days*
> *I was beautiful then*
> *I remember the time I knew what happiness was*
> *Let the memory live again ...*

My mind was on my day; it was getting dark, and I was tired. I walked toward Bethesda Terrace to see it in the twilight and then down the Mall a distance. My hotel was on Park Avenue and Sixty-first. I cut through a trail that I thought led back to East Drive, according to my map. As I was looking at the map, trying to figure out if I was going the right way, I suddenly saw a flash of light and felt heat in my head. The only noise that registered was my camera crashing down on the ground then nothing. I became aware of a voice and some footsteps. The voice cut in and out of my hearing.

"You go after them, and I'll stay here," ordered a soothing female voice. I tried to open my eyes. Everything seemed to flash like a strobe light was on.

The female voice was talking to someone, and then I heard a petrified scream. The strobe light still flashing in my head, I could barely make anything out. My eyes and my head were not right. I felt awfully cold and heavy; I couldn't feel my body anymore. The female voice spoke again, but I couldn't see her.

"My head!" I hollered as I bolted straight up from my pillow. I had a sudden sensation of extreme pain and flashes of light, heat ... was all of this a dream? I shot out of bed, holding my head in my hands.

The woman was with me in an instant with her usual calming voice reciting her mantra, "Breathe in. One, two, three, and out, one, two, three ... Ivy, try to stay calm. Take it easy."

Now, the man joined in with "Get back into bed. You need your rest." I was pacing and holding my head. The flashes were fading away, but the confusion remained.

"I heard your voice. I recognized your voice in my dream," I told the woman, looking at her wide eyed. "You were there too, weren't you?" I snapped, directing my eyes to the man. "Why did you do this?"

She came near me, and I moved out of the way fast, faster than I had ever moved before. They both looked at me with sympathetic eyes.

Again, she said, "Calm down, Ivy. You can't waste your energy with such excitement."

"Screw you," I yelled. "I want answers. I want out of here."

I began to feel weak; my legs were giving away from under me. The man caught me and asserted, "You won't get any answers if you leave here." He paused then added, "You won't survive if you leave here."

"What do you mean I won't survive? I'm fine now. I want out . . . NOW!" I screamed as I struggled in his grasp.

"Ivy, we won't let you leave, not until you're feeling better and we can talk rationally. You have a lot to learn," the woman explained calmly.

"What the hell are you talking about?" I sneered back at her.

I was absolutely powerless in the man's grasp and had no more energy to fight. He put me back in the bed as the woman clarified, "We must help you. We're sorry for the forceful tactics, but you are leaving us with no choice. Please don't make this hard on yourself, Ivy." She approached me. "Your struggle is completely unnecessary," she whispered as she put her hand on my arm, stroking it lightly. "If you calm yourself, I'll give you the answers you are looking for."

"You don't have to fear us," the man assured me as he eased his grip. "We have not hurt you. We saved you." My head was filling with flashes of my day in Central Park, the sounds, the sights, the pain . . . it ripped through my head again.

"Ow . . . the pain, it's splitting my head open. Why do I have it? What's wrong with me?" I pleaded.

"Please take some deep breaths, focus on your breathing," the woman commanded as she looked straight into my eyes. Her eyes made me listen; they made me want to do what she asked. She put her hand under my chin to help keep my eyes locked on hers, and together we breathed slowly until I began to regain my composure.

The pain was subsiding; my irrational thoughts and anger were dissipating with every breath.

"Will you please lie back now so that I can tell you your story?" she questioned.

Without answering, I let go of all my resistance, relaxed, and lay back on my pillow, drawing the covers over me. I did in fact feel quite worn-out from this episode, and the bed felt good. I closed my eyes for a moment to refocus my thoughts and told them, "OK, I'm ready."

"My name is Tavia," the woman declared, and until now, I had never really focused on her face, only on her voice which was so soothing and caring that it captured me. Her eyes were a smooth and warm light brown, like a latte, very comforting. Her skin was pale but had undertones of olive. Her hair was dark, long, and straight, very silky looking. She was probably in her mid to late thirties, in good physical condition, and not a gray hair in sight. I would call her beautiful, but not in an obvious way. She's more subtle, more genuine than the drop-dead gorgeous type. My mind wandered, wondering where she was from. She had a slight accent, but I couldn't make it out.

"This is Anton," she said. The man nodded and smiled as warmly as he could. He was a much more gruff character. He was squat, with a square head and body, with no neck in between. He was very solid looking with a short military-type haircut. It was difficult to tell his age because his skin looked leathery, like someone who spent a lot of time out in the elements. His name was no big surprise; I would have guessed him as Russian or Romanian by his accent and his stoic demeanor. His eyes were blue, pale blue with a dark blue ring around his irises. They really stood out against his pale tough skin because they were delicate looking.

Tavia held my hand, took a deep breath, sighed, and started the story. "We found you in the park. You were being attacked by two men." My heart began to beat faster, and my breathing was speeding up too. I could feel tears welling in my eyes. I pulled up my knees and wrapped my arms around them. I needed to make myself small, to protect myself from what was out there. Tavia gave me that look again; the one that said *calm down*. So I tried.

As I looked into her eyes, I remembered the breathing, and I focused on it to calm myself down. Rocking back and forth, I closed my eyes and counted to myself. In, one, two, three . . . out, one, two, three . . . in, one, two, three . . . out, one, two, three. When I opened my eyes, I could see Tavia smiling at me. She approved of my self-control. Her approval was important to me, but I didn't know why.

"Can I go on?" she requested.

"Yes," I responded. "I think I have it under control."

"You were injured, seriously injured," she continued. "They had beaten your head with something." As she told me this, I felt the sharp pain in my head, and the flashes of light started again. I had a sensation of something warm running down my face. I reached up to my head to feel where the pain came from, to feel what was running down my face. As I touched my head, my anxiety started to peak again. I suddenly realized there was nothing on my head. No bump, no scar, no blood running down my face, no hair.

"What the hell?" I cried in a panic. "My hair . . . where's my hair?"

Tavia set her eyes on me again, luring me into her calmness, and she reassured me, "It will grow back. It was necessary."

"But there's no scar. I don't understand," I said, confused. "I keep feeling pain when I think about it, but my head is perfectly normal . . . well, other than being bald. How long have I been here for it to heal completely?" I asked, with a swirl of random images filling my head.

"Let's take things slow," she reassured in her comforting way. "One part of the story at a time. You will know it all soon."

"You were bleeding very profusely. It couldn't be stopped," Tavia remarked with an apologetic look on her face. This look confused me. Why was she apologetic? She saved me. I looked at her, very puzzled, but didn't say anything. She paused at my expression, took a deep breath, and then continued. "We didn't have much time to make a decision, so we just had to take action," she described, still looking guilty.

"What happened to the men that attacked me?" I probed.

She looked over at Anton and then back at me and said, "They ran off when they heard us."

"What did you do with me?" I began with my machine-gun questioning. "It must have taken a long time for an ambulance to get there. What did you do to help me? Why am I not in a hospital now?"

"There was no ambulance. There was no time for that. You wouldn't be here now if we didn't intervene," she advised.

"OK, one of you must be a doctor then?" I inquired, obviously confused.

Tavia paused with a look on her face that indicated she was searching for words. "No, we are not doctors," she clarified. "But we do have a cure for the condition you were in. You were going to die. You were almost dead when we found you."

My stomach dropped the way it can on a roller coaster going down the steepest rise. Die, dead, without them I wouldn't be here. Tavia noticed that I was off in my own thoughts and waited for me to be ready before she continued.

"It's always better if there's time to consider all the implications," she indicated. "But that wasn't possible in your situation. I had to do it. There was something about you that made me want to do it. You're special, I could feel it. So I had to change you."

She paused a minute, just looking at me, trying to read my face or gauge my reaction. My head was clouded with a fog, but in the fog, I could see images that were stored in my brain, images that didn't seem real but I think were real.

Looking at me with a combination of guilt and apprehension, she stated, "You are different now, forever."

Shaking my head to clear the fog, I said to her, "You're kind of freaking me out here! What exactly are you trying to say? I'm here. I seem healthy enough. My head is healed, not even a scar. This is a good thing."

"Your head is healed. You are healthy enough," Tavia agreed, "and you will get much healthier and more robust than you ever were, but at a price."

"What price?" I questioned. "I have health insurance. I'm covered no matter the cost." She looked at me then looked up, like she was gathering her thoughts again, and continued in a very calm voice, "You don't need insurance when you're immortal."

My mind rolled the word *immortal* around for a moment, and I said, half laughing, "OK, now I'm getting the picture. You guys are nuts. I must be in a nut house, and you two are just a couple of patients like me." I started to get out of bed, saying, "I'm going to look for a nurse or a doctor. I have to get outta here because this is way too 'out there' for me. I'm not interested in any cult . . . but thanks for the story. It was definitely interesting. You must have some superhero delusion or something."

Instantly, Anton's hands were holding me down as Tavia said, "Ivy, I know that this seems unbelievable to you, but it is the truth."

"Get your hands off me. Don't touch me!" I shouted, trying to rip his hands off my shoulders. It was a rather futile effort because his hands were like boulders holding me down. As I struggled, I watched Tavia get up from the bed, walk over to the medical supplies, and grab some scissors. With Anton still holding me down, she stood right at the foot of my bed and started stabbing herself in the stomach repeatedly with the scissors. My eyes popped open, I think they could have popped right out of my head and gone rolling off the bed. I opened my mouth to scream, but nothing came out. My throat was clamped shut, like in those dreams when you're running away from some bad guy and you try to scream but nothing comes out.

Finally, I got the words, "Oh my god, oh my god," out before the curtain fell over my mind again and everything went black.

CHAPTER THREE
Life or Death

I slowly opened my eyes, hoping it was all just another dream. I was prone to crazy dreams lately. They were both hovering over me. Tavia was smiling. My head flashed back to the sight of her stabbing herself, and I gasped. I looked at her stomach, and there they were, as plain as day on her shirt—many spots of blood, small holes; it wasn't a dream! The heat was coming back; my whole body was burning up. I couldn't breathe. I kept staring at the bloody holes in her shirt, and all I could get out between gasps of breath was "But . . . but . . . why?"

Why did she do that to herself? Why was she standing here smiling? Are they going to hurt me? Who are they? Who am I? I'm not me . . . I don't feel like me anymore. Twirling around in my head like a tornado were all these questions, I couldn't get them out of my mouth. She took my face in her hands and looked into my eyes, and the gasping slowly dissipated.

"We are not going to hurt you. What I did to myself didn't hurt me. I did it to show you . . . show you what your mind can't comprehend without proof from the senses," she explained without blinking and with complete calm. She put her finger over my lips and said, "Shhh, relax now . . . see, I'm not hurt," as she lifted her shirt to show me the wounds. They were there but were almost healed. How could this be possible?

It is like she plucked the question right out of my mind and answered it. "You can't hurt the immortal with such trivial wounds. It's like a paper cut to the average mortal. As unbelievable as it is, this is what . . . who you are now, Ivy." This time, I believed her. I don't know if it was the blood on her shirt, the tone of her voice, or her eyes that indicated she was not lying. I felt the goodness in her, and I just knew it must be true.

I lifted my hands up in front of my face to examine them. They looked the same as before, maybe a little pale and a little dry. I checked out my arms, felt my legs, and I came to the same conclusion.

Tavia again seemed to know what I was thinking. She handed me a mirror and turned on the light above my bed. I lifted the mirror to my face, and I was both horrified and amazed at the same time. I touched my skin; it was cracked and peeling like I had a bad sunburn. The old skin was peeling away to expose the new healthy skin underneath. My eyes darted back and forth; from the mirror, to Tavia, and back again.

"Don't worry. You're shedding your mortal skin. Your new immortal skin is under it, and once you'll see it, you will not have that horrified look anymore."

It was the first time I had seen either of them with the light on. Although they did look pale, their skin also looked radiant. Tavia's skin was smooth looking and beautiful; Anton's skin, although more weathered than Tavia's, was also appealing. I looked again at myself and stared into my own eyes, eyes that were the same but vastly different. I had green eyes with yellow flecks that always drew attention, especially when framed by my copper curls, but now . . . my eyes were like a lush green field of grass with golden flowers. Bright, quick, brilliant, exquisite! I was in awe. These eyes that I have looked at every day looked back at me, and I couldn't recognize them.

They were indeed beautiful, but there was also something entirely new behind them. I wasn't sure if what I saw behind them was good or bad . . . yet. I slowly turned the mirror up to my head, where my lovely curls used to be. I rubbed my bald head and looked at Tavia inquisitively.

"It will grow back soon," she said. "The hair and skin are always the last to transform. It will take another month or so."

Still teetering on the edge of sanity, trying to absorb, believe, and understand what I was and who I was. I started to formulate many questions, so many questions that they started to burst out of me.

"What exactly does immortal mean? What's life going to be like? Can I even call it life? Does my body work the way it used to?

Do I need to eat because I feel kind of hungry? How old are you guys? Are there others like us?"

"One question at a time, we have forever to answer them all," Tavia declared as she winked at me. "Immortality is wonderful when you choose for it to be. Just like mortal life, you can view it positively or negatively. The transition is challenging. It can be exhilarating as you discover your new body and your new abilities, but you still have all the emotions that you possessed before and you will mourn the loss of your mortal self. You will grieve, hurt, question, cry, and hopefully, you will eventually accept and thrive in your new life. We do call it life, eternal life. Most of us find happiness in our immortality, but some do suffer. Some never accept it and live very unfulfilling existences. I truly hope that you find peace and contentment in this life."

She stopped talking and looked at me to see what my reaction was. I didn't know what to say and just looked at her.

"When I found you in the park," she continued. "I sensed a soul that needed to be given strength, a genuinely good soul that longed to do good for others. This life gives you the strength, talents, and abilities to do some good. Many great discoveries, works of art, and humanitarian acts have been achieved by our kind. There can be a lot of good in this life and a lot of satisfaction."

Anton cut in, "Don't paint only the rosy picture, Tavia, there can also be a lot of evil in immortal life as with mortal life. Many of our kind have also been the source of unspeakable acts of cruelty and destruction. The strength and other superior qualities can also be used to hurt instead of help. We always have to be on guard for the malevolence that exists among some of the immortals," Anton cautioned.

"Yes, it is true. Just like mortals, there are the good and the bad. And throughout time," Tavia interjected, "there have been periods where the bad did surpass the good, but our immortal population has evolved and become more and more civilized . . . developed rules and codes of conduct."

I sat for a minute, looking straight ahead at nothing in particular, pondering. *How could she stab herself and be perfectly fine?*

"Our bodies, although similar to mortals in the way we look, are very different on the inside. Most of the mortal parts do not function anymore. Our genetics are reprogrammed, and when we are damaged in some way, our cells regenerate very fast to repair the damage," Tavia explained.

Looking again at my hands and my arms for any sign that I was different or maybe the same, I asked, "How does it happen?"

Tavia was now pacing the room as she explained, "Think of it like an infection, a virus that can get into your cells and take over your DNA. The infection is transmitted through the saliva of the immortal to the blood of a mortal. Of course, our saliva is different than mortal saliva. The virus is concentrated in it. When the virus gets into a mortal, it starts to change the cells. The change is a gradual process that starts from the inside out. It takes two to three months for a full transformation.

I thought about what Tavia explained, and many questions still spun in my head. "How will I know that the transformation is complete?" I inquired.

"Feel your throat. Anton, show her," she directed Anton to pick up the mirror for me. I felt a scar on my throat as Anton held the mirror so I could take a look. The scar looked like a bite mark—visible, but barely.

"I had to bite you to transfer the virus," Tavia said. "It had to be in a large blood vessel because you didn't have much time, regretfully." Touching my scar, I had a sudden flashback of a stabbing feeling in my throat, a burning sensation, and then nothing.

"Bite?" I probed. "Are you a vampire?"

"That's one of the names we have been given over the centuries," she said, rolling her eyes. "There are many other names. We prefer immortal, but yes, biting is the way we transmit the virus. It is also the way we eat. You obviously know the fictional stories about vampires. Some of the fiction is rooted in truth, but much of the fiction is just that," Tavia described. "Now, back to your question. We'll know when your transformation is complete when you have no more scar on your throat." I was still holding my hand to my throat and staring off into space when Tavia finished speaking.

"I'm not going to burn up in sunlight, am I?" I blurted flippantly.

They both laughed, indicating that the answer was obvious!

"A new immortal is very vulnerable to destruction," she cautioned more seriously.

"But I thought that being immortal meant that you can't die?" I inquired.

"An immortal can die, if they don't get enough blood, or if they get seriously injured during transformation and in the first few years of immortal life," she cautioned. "Fire is always a danger. There's too much cell damage when burned significantly that even immortal cells can't regenerate fast enough to prevent death." She paused to look at my worried expression and continued, "A new immortal does not possess full strength and speed and does not have the experience to know their limits. A newborn should be with an experienced immortal for at least a decade."

My mind was overwhelmed by everything. I was taking it all in like it was just a story, not reality.

Tavia sensed my state of mind and said, "That's enough information for now. There is much more to learn, but in time. You are looking rather pale." She walked over and touched my cheek. "Your skin is only tepid. You need blood. Anton?" she said, looking over at him; and he disappeared, returning with an IV bag of blood.

I felt queasy at the sight of the blood, but I also felt intensely ravenous. I was salivating and disgusted with myself for it. "Vampires have to drink blood to live, is that part true?" I asked, hoping the answer was no.

"That part is true," she replied gently, knowing that I wanted a different answer. "Your body is unable to process food any longer. Your digestive system is no longer active in the same way as before. Your cells still need the two basic ingredients of life, like mortals, oxygen and sugar. You still breathe for oxygen, but you can only get the sugar and other nutrients directly from blood." She was looking at me for signs of hysteria. "Blood doesn't get made by your body now, but your body can go a lot longer without replenishing it as compared with a mortal and food," she clarified optimistically.

Anton hung the blood, and as it flowed, I started to feel warmer, better.

"When will I have to drink blood? I don't think I can do that," I expressed with concern.

"You can feed with an IV for a while longer," Tavia advised, placating me, "and we won't worry about the rest for now, OK?"

She looked at me with her calming eyes and I felt the apprehension melt away. I lay back in the bed, allowing the sensations created by the blood to take hold of me. I tried not to look at it, because every time I did, I was foaming at the mouth, and this was definitely disturbing me. I was repulsed by it but deeply desired it at the same time. Tavia stayed with me as Anton left. She curled up on the bed with me like a mother, making me feel cared for. It took two bags of blood to make my color perk up. I felt more energetic, more alive, and also, my head was clearer.

"Now that your strength is up, come and meet some people," Tavia requested.

"What about the way I look?" I questioned.

"Don't worry, they've all been through it," she said while taking my hand and leading me out of the room for the first time.

We toured their house, which was a twelve-room, five-floor brownstone, built in the mid to late nineteenth century. My room was on the third floor, along with the master bedroom. My room was painted light blue with white trim, white crown molding, and had a beautiful ceiling centerpiece. All the bedding accented the light blue walls as did the dainty eyelet curtains. It was simple, light, and fresh.

The master bedroom was breathtaking! The centerpiece of the room was a luxurious Egyptian canopy bed with exquisite carvings, including Corinthian caps and acanthus accents. The cascading gold veil bed curtains shimmered with the setting sun entering the windows. The antique furnishings adorning the room paled in comparison! I asked Tavia if I could lie in the bed, which she obliged, and I felt like royalty enveloped in the lush blankets and pillows. A fireplace, with the firebox converted to a planter, displayed an array of colorful and exotic flowers and foliage that livened up the dark burgundy, gold, and black walnut tones of the room.

The top floor was the living space for two other immortals whom I was about to meet. There were two very manly bedrooms and a shared living room area that sported all the top-of-the-line entertainment equipment. There was an outdoor patio on this level, overlooking the back garden. The overall ambiance was definitely a bachelor pad.

We descended to the parlor level, and I noticed that even the stairwell and hallways were decadent. The hallways were lined with dark, rich crown moldings and wainscot. The steps and the intricately carved balustrade seamlessly flowed from the hallways that led to them. On the landing of the parlor level, my eyes were drawn to the double arch built over the last step of the staircase, from the final handrail post, stretching over the hallway to the entrance of the front parlor. Bordered by dentil molding and a stained-glass sash, the open double doors exhibited a magnificent fireplace that bore the same styling as the doorway.

The floors, as with the rest of the house, were an original parquet design, and the parlor level ceiling rose to probably fourteen feet. The ceiling was lined with a cornice of dark dentil molding enclosing an ornate, sculptured centerpiece. Light straw yellow walls gave warmth to the room, which was primarily used to display a collection of photos and other interesting artifacts. Containing minimal furniture—only an antique settee, a chair, and a coffee table—the room was like a gallery of sorts.

The main feature for the room was photos, tons of photos—on the wall, on the mantel, and even in a panel room divider, taking up each rectangular slot. The photos were old, sepia toned, black and white. There were several old cameras on display and other pieces like statues made of stone, ivory, and onyx. I recognized some Greek gods among the pieces as well as gargoyles and other mythical creatures.

The front and back parlors were separated by a medium-sized dining room with archway entrances. The dentil molding—white instead of brown—along with the white wainscot, bordered the windowless room. A large rustic table and chair set was placed prominently in the center of the room, blending perfectly with the ecru-colored walls. The cornerstone for the room was a display of wine glasses and goblets in two elegant buffets. There was everything from ancient-looking pewter and silver goblets to the finest-looking crystal, each piece with a story, no doubt, that I would ask about eventually. This room appeared to be used often, but not for dining, of course.

The back parlor was converted into a library with lavish red mahogany shelving from floor to ceiling, throughout. Bookshelves lined the archway entrance, filled the walls, and surrounded the windows. To retrieve books on the top shelves, there were sturdy gliding ladders. Two wingback chairs with a matching settee were arranged near the windows, to allow for natural light while reading.

They were also made of carved mahogany and upholstered with floral tapestry, rich green and burgundy on beige. The books looked old, very old. I picked out the oldest-looking book I saw, and it was in some script I didn't recognize.

After spending some time in the library, we moved on to the garden level, which had two guest bedrooms and a huge living room. It was apparent that it had been substantially converted from its original design, now fashioned with a log cabin and chalet appeal. Tavia explained that they had no need for a large eat-in kitchen, as would be found in the traditional layout of the garden level. Instead, there was just a small kitchen for mortal guests, although they were rare. The main purpose of this level was family and fun. The large rec room provided several amenities for family entertainment: a pool table, a huge television with home theater system, a stereo system that would rival most dance clubs, an immense fireplace, and much more. I had the feeling that the bachelor pad touch had made its way from the top floor down to this recreation haven. There was a sunroom at the back leading out to a spectacular garden and terrace.

Finally, we reached the basement level. I felt like there was some top-secret operation going on. This level was an extreme contrast to the others I had seen. The entire space was filled with technology. It was like being in the control room of a TV station. I could see different parts of the city on monitors. There were reports coming in on computer speakers, on printers, and police scanners; you name it, it was all here.

Operating all this technology were two men, young men. They were facing away from me, monitoring the equipment, wearing headphones, typing, speaking with each other, or maybe speaking with someone else through their headsets, I couldn't tell. They didn't appear to hear us coming in. One had golden short hair; the other had longer hair and wore a baseball cap turned backward. We watched them briefly, working together as though they were ballroom dancers. Both knew instinctively what the other was doing, synchronously completing the other's task.

"These are the boys," Tavia said proudly, looking at me and smiling. They both turned around to look at me, and it was like having double vision. They looked exactly the same. They had slightly different clothing styles, and one had longer hair, but their faces were identical. They had beautiful faces, young vibrant skin, and violet-blue eyes like iris petals or Elizabeth Taylor's eyes. I'm not sure if they noticed, but I think my mouth was hanging open. Then I remembered how horrible I looked and turned my eyes down to the floor.

"Hello, Ivy," the one with the shorter hair began. "I'm Justus, and this is Magnus." He gestured to the one with the baseball cap. "As you have probably already figured out, we're twins."

"The boys are obviously our tech gurus," Tavia pointed out.

I gathered from all the technology that they were involved in some kind of surveillance, but of what and why, I didn't know. I looked at her inquisitively.

"We run a watch over the dangerous parts of the city," Justus declared excitedly.

"Looking for bad guys," Magnus added.

"Are you part of the police?" I speculated.

"No, definitely not. We're better than the police!" Magnus boasted. "We take care of what they can't." He went on. "They're bound by laws, mortal laws that don't impede us at all."

"The reality is," Justus elaborated, "we do work with the police, but not for the police. When they have cases that need our particular brand of justice, we collaborate."

"If you want to know who really cleans up the city," Magnus interjected with an air of superiority, "it's us!"

Justus looked at Magnus and rolled his eyes. I could tell already that they definitely had different personalities, despite their identical appearance. "Can you take over?" he asked Magnus. "I'm going to explain more about our work."

Magnus winked at me, turned back to the computer screens, and put his headset on.

I had taken in so much already that day. My brain was desensitized to the unbelievable and I was completely open to anything. I wouldn't be shocked if I found out I was going to grow a second head!

Justus motioned to the chair beside him, inviting me to join him and Magnus. I felt shy, like a thirteen-year-old with a crush. They were certainly lovely to look at, and as I approached them, I had to shake off the lustful thoughts of being the center of a twin sandwich.

"Do you know much about what we do here?" Justus inquired while looking over toward Tavia then back to me.

"No, nothing more than what you both have told me so far," I said gazing into his eyes. It was difficult to concentrate around such attractive men. Justus didn't seem to notice, or at least make me aware that he noticed my staring. He looked again to Tavia, like he wanted approval or permission to tell me more, which she granted with a nod.

"Ivy, there's a lot to learn and a lot of time to learn it," she commented. "If you feel overwhelmed at any time, just let Justus know that it's enough."

I acknowledged her with a timid smile and a somewhat feeble "OK," and watched her as she silently left the room.

Justus took a deep breath and said, "It's been a while since we've had someone new. I'm not sure where to start."

Magnus, just off the phone, interrupted with "Just give it to her straight, no sugar coating." It was obvious that Justus was the softy of the two.

"OK." Justus began scratching his head. "This is the gist of what we do," he continued somewhat tentatively. "As you likely know, this city has no shortage of crime! On average, there are two murders per day and at least four sexual assaults, not to mention other types of assaults." He paused to make sure I was following. "We hack into surveillance cameras around the city and look for criminals in action."

"The police let you do this?" I questioned.

"Let us or not, we do it anyway!" Magnus spoke up.

Justus explained, "We assisted the NYPD in setting up their first closed-circuit surveillance system back in the seventies and the expansion of the system in the eighties and nineties. We know their system, inside and out!"

He paused briefly to acknowledge my understanding. I nodded to show I was following.

"Our only concern is for violent crime," Justus continued. "Especially organized crime, murder, and rape."

"That's who we choose to exterminate," Magnus added passionately.

I contemplated on what he meant by exterminate. It must have been written on my face by my expression because he looked at me and clarified, "We make sure that they won't be repeat offenders."

"D-do you mean you kill them?" I stammered.

"Most definitely," Magnus asserted very concisely with a satisfied grin. I had to take a few deep breaths to keep my head from spinning. It was difficult to control these moments of anxiety, but I was learning.

"Yes, we kill them, not just for the fun of it," Justus insisted.

"Speak for yourself!" Magnus remarked zestfully.

"As I was saying," Justus cut in, giving Magnus a harsh look, "it's not just for the fun of it . . . for most of us. We do need to eat, and by now you know what we need to survive, right?"

"Yes, I do know," I muttered meekly.

"We decided as a group, a long time ago," Justus explained, "that if we must kill, then we might as well make it worthwhile—a public service of sorts. We get what we need and clean up the city in the process. Not really a bad deal!"

He sounded incredibly convincing that it made sense to me, yet how could it make sense? We're talking about murder, killing, death. How could I just accept this as a day's work? How could they accept it as a day's work? My mind was swimming again. My eyes must have glazed over because Justus had to put his face right in front of mine to pull me out of my vortex of thoughts.

"Are you OK?" he asked. "Is this too much for you right now?" I regained my bearings and looked at him without saying anything. "Let's talk about our team, our family, for a while," Justus suggested while reaching out to touch my shoulder gently.

Just then, Magnus made a call and dispatched someone out to a part of the city that I didn't know. I didn't want to look at the monitors because this was not a movie. If someone was killed on these screens, it was reality TV.

Justus took my hand and led me away from the surveillance room so we could talk uninterrupted.

"If it makes you feel any better, we don't always kill," he said reassuringly. "Sometimes all that's needed to prevent worse crimes is a little nudge in the right direction!"

This was good news to me, but killing was part of the reality that I now had to live . . . had to accept. We sat on the overstuffed beige couch in the rec room, and Justus looked at me in silence for a moment. I was calmed by him, by his demeanor, as he began to tell me about his family.

"Tavia is our elder, our surrogate mother," Justus began. "She is the oldest in immortal years, and Anton is her partner, as you know, and is the second eldest of our team. There is no leader, per se, but Tavia is the closest to a leader that we have. We all respect her wisdom and look to her for guidance. She is very objective, compassionate, and thoughtful. Some of us are children in comparison, and you, my dear, are an infant. No offense, of course!" he teased while winking at me.

"She is very motherly," I affirmed, thinking of how Tavia made me feel.

"Ethan and Helene are together. They're roughly the same immortal age. Ethan was changed during the American Revolutionary War in 1781. I met him during the American Civil War where we were Underground Railroad operators, smuggling slaves out of Ohio into Canada.

"The youngest, until you came along, was Yasmine. She is a toddler in immortal years and is still learning to use and control her strength and other gifts. You'll understand what I mean when you meet her!" Justus noted.

"The last member is Jairam, but people call him Jay. He is our organized crime expert. Jay owns a nightclub and uses his love of that world to infiltrate the underground crime scene. Lately, Yasmine has been working with him because of her special talents that are useful to his cause," Justus finished.

"Wow," I exclaimed, "sounds like an interesting group." That's about all I could get out because my mind was too full. I didn't want to know more because I couldn't fathom myself as part of this band of killers. Justus seemed so nice, Tavia so motherly, yet they killed people, probably every day. How could I ever be part of that?

Just then, Magnus bolted out of the computer room and shot past us, saying, "Going to a crime scene with Yasmine."

Justus sprang up and returned to the surveillance equipment. I followed reluctantly, but I was unsure that I wanted to see or even know what was going on. Possessed by curiosity, like someone rubber-necking an accident on the highway, I watched as Magnus arrived at a vacant lot to find two young punks beating up an old man. Magnus began to beat the punks down as a woman arrived and tended to the old man. He was sputtering blood and died right there, in front of my eyes. The woman closed the old man's eyes then joined Magnus in taking out vengeance on the young criminals. They were like savages. I couldn't watch anymore and turned away.

"You're looking a little peaked," Justus pointed out.

I indeed felt nauseated and faint. Maybe from the spectacle I witnessed or maybe from my physical condition.

"Let me take you back to your bed for a rest," Justus suggested as he scooped me up and carried me to my room. He placed me on the bed gently and covered me with my blankets. Looking down into my eyes, he said, "Only time will help what you are feeling now, time and rest. So get some rest. We all went through what you are experiencing, and we understand."

He looked into me, not just at me. And right then, I felt connected to him and instantly felt lighter. He stroked my forehead as I drifted off to sleep.

I'm not sure how long I rested. My slumber was disturbed by horrible images and flashes of violence, and I woke up screaming, excruciatingly warm. I felt pain coursing up and down my legs and in my head, a pain that I had never felt in my mortal life. Childbirth was a one on this scale of pain, and I was at an eight. Tavia rushed in and tried to console me and calm me.

"This pain is necessary," Tavia confirmed. "It is the last vestige of your mortal life. You need it to remember what you have been, and then you can appreciate what you will become."

Tavia stayed with me for what must have been days as the pain continued. I was nearing the end of the transformation, and I wasn't sure if I could bear it. My body shifted from unbearably hot to icy cold. I had uncontrollable tremors and a raging headache. The feeling of imminent death recurred with every cycle.

Finally, one afternoon, I woke from an undisturbed lengthy sleep, and it was over. It felt glorious! I felt fantastic.

The only sound I made was a groan when I stretched my body; and, instantly, Tavia was there, in front of me.

"I feel greeeat!" I declared.

"Oh, you look tremendously healthy!" Tavia noted as she approached. "But you definitely need a shower!"

I showered, and despite feeling pretty good, I still looked like *Nosferatu* with my semi-bald head and molting skin! I tried to fix myself up a bit, but it was futile. I thought of the Dracula movies I had watched, picturing the alluring vampire that was irresistible to their prey. Right now, people would run screaming from me!

"Damn, I look like hell," I cried from the bathroom.

"You don't look that bad," Tavia replied. "Come here, I'll put a scarf around your head and maybe a bit of makeup?"

Tavia gave me a makeover that tamed the beast a little and then requested that I join her in the library.

"I want to call my daughter first," I told Tavia. "I want to make sure she is not worried about me." I lied. The truth was that I was worried about her. I was worried about losing her, never being able to see her again.

I reached Ana, and we talked for quite some time. We were both reassured by one another that everything was OK. I could sense relief in her voice that I was on the mend. She was thoroughly enjoying her experience in the UK, and she had already met someone special. *Someone I may never meet*, I thought. I told her that I was going to stay in New York for a while, and we ended the conversation with a promise to talk every week, which eased my apprehension slightly.

Ana didn't seem to get any sense of just how different I was, how different my life was going to be. I reflected on our conversation and tried to shrug off my negative thoughts and feelings. After a while, I was ready to join Tavia in the library.

CHAPTER FOUR
Creatures of the Night

As I walked out of my room, I stood still in the hall and looked around because I heard voices, like someone was close to me. The voices belonged to Tavia and two other people, and it sounded like they were in her bedroom. I checked but they weren't in there. I followed the voices downstairs to the parlor level, back to the library, and there I saw Tavia sitting with a man and woman I didn't know.

They stopped their conversation to greet me.

"I could hear you from upstairs, as clear as if you were standing beside me," I said with the inquisitive nature of a child.

"You'll get used to it soon enough," the unknown woman explained. "You'll learn to tune out whatever you don't want to hear and focus in on what you do want to hear."

"That's really cool!" I blurted, listening to them and to a conversation going on somewhere outside at the same time.

"Your hearing will eventually be close to the abilities of an owl's," Tavia described. "You're already tuning out a lot. Otherwise, you'd go crazy with all the sounds around you. It is an automatic response to the excessive noise that's always around," she added.

"You can also sense the presence of others by the energy they emit," declared the woman. "You'll sense them long before you can see them. You can already do this too, but it will develop even stronger over the next few months. Mortals and other animals emit infrared radiation; we do also, but in a different spectrum. You'll be able to sense and decipher when warm-blooded animals, like mortals, or when cold-blooded animals, like immortals, are near. You'll feel it on your skin and in other parts of your body. Thus far, you're probably not tuned into it, but we'll teach you how."

"It's really quite fascinating," the man stated. "I had the theory explained to me by none other than the great Einstein himself. An intriguing man indeed! This world would have been better off if only he had wanted eternal life," he alleged, looking disappointed.

"Ethan, you offered, and he declined," the woman said. "We don't force anyone into immortality . . . well, except for under extreme circumstances," she continued, looking at me.

He sighed, looked at me, and introduced himself. "I'm Ethan, and this beauty," he said, extending his hand to the woman, "is Helene, my goddess."

"Oh come on now, how you exaggerate." Helene laughed, taking his hand.

Ethan was an average-looking man. He had average height, average weight, medium brown hair—everything was average except his eyes. He had piercing, light gray eyes outlined by dark lashes that made them look like the eyes of a Siberian husky. Helene was of medium stature and was athletic looking, with ash brown hair cut in a simple bob. Her eyes were yellow-green, like the eyes of a cat. Her essence was feline, and to look at her for any length of time gave the illusion of a cat lying still, watching its prey—just waiting for the right moment to pounce. She was not frightening or threatening but definitely exhibited an intensity that was intimidating. Together, they seemed like a mismatch, the feline and the canine together in harmony, in love.

Tavia said, "Come, sit with us," as she motioned to the seat beside her. "You suffered for days going through the transformation. You will tire easily."

"Horrible, isn't it?" Helene acknowledged.

"It was pure hell," I replied.

"You are lucky to have been sedated for much of the early weeks," added Ethan. "That's when the changes are really uncomfortable, when your organs are changing."

"Tavia told me it's a virus?" I probed.

"Yes, a virus," he began. "A retrovirus to be exact that takes over the DNA of mortal cells, killing many of the internal systems, transforming the body into an immortal, capable of survival through ingestion of blood.

"The various pains you felt were because of the viral process changing your cells and tissues. Your old body technically died giving birth to this new body. Once your hair starts to grow back, the inside will be almost finished transforming."

I reached up and felt my head under the scarf I was wearing, and I could feel the very thin soft hair like that of a newborn, in wisps here and there.

"I feel strong today," I declared, "and more aware of my body. It's tingling and feels like I have pent-up energy that wants to burst out of me."

"That's good, Ivy," commented Helene. "It means you're nearing the end of transformation, but don't let the sensation of endless energy fool you! Your body has been through an extremely draining process, and your energy will plummet, sometimes without warning!"

Just then, Anton stomped up the stairs, muttering to himself. I tried to decipher his words, but they were in another language.

"What's wrong with you, Anton?" Tavia asked, concerned.

"Another rape victim last night," he voiced, exasperated.

"Do you know anything else about it?" Ethan queried.

"Not yet," Anton replied despondently. "Only that they're connected by location and MO."

I looked at Tavia in response to this exchange, and she suggested, "Ivy, you should join us in a few hours when we all meet. We'll be discussing the development of a serial rapist case and what we can do to assist the police. You can learn more about what we do to help our city. For now though, are you hungry?"

Still repulsed by this part of my life, I looked down at the ground and nodded yes. In fact, I was ravenous, and the thought of blood made me salivate.

As we got up to leave the library, Helene warned, "Soon, you won't be able to feed from a tube, you know," looking from me to Tavia.

I sensed that Helene disapproved of the care that Tavia had been giving me.

"There's no big rush to wean her off yet," Tavia declared, taking me by the hand. "We'll cross that bridge when we get there."

Once we were in my room setting up the intravenous line, I asked Tavia, "What does Helene mean?"

"Your system is not fully transformed yet, but is getting close," she confirmed. "Once your hair has fully grown back and your scar is healed, that will indicate you're in the final stage."

"Will there be any more pain?" I probed anxiously. The thought of it made my stomach turn and my heart race.

She sat on my bed and took my hand. "There may still be some discomfort," she answered sympathetically. "But not like what you just experienced. Once in that final stage, you will need live blood to complete the process. For now, you get enough benefit from the blood injected into you, but that will end. With each passing day, you are getting less and less able to use the injected blood because your system is different.

"Believe me, once you allow yourself to drink blood, you will see a huge difference in energy and strength. You won't need to feed as often either," she added. "Although I know you don't want to imagine this yet, the first time you take blood that is fresh from a beating heart, you will see the difference that it makes to your body, and there will be no turning back."

Tavia hooked up my IV, and as the blood entered my system, I was rejuvenated. I thought to myself, *Maybe I could take a little sip*, while my mind was more open to something new. I looked at Tavia and asked, "Can I try a little?" She left and came back with a little shot glass of blood. I looked at it, smelled it like I would wine, and although it did appeal to me, I couldn't bring myself to lift the glass to my lips.

Tavia looked at me with a caring smile and advised, "Don't worry; you don't have to drink it yet. Eventually, your body will take over, and you will have urges that you can't deny. Then you will drink!"

I lay back on the bed, taking in my lifeblood, and drifted to sleep. This time, I had a pleasant dream of Ana, thankfully, and I woke with a smile on my face.

I had agreed to join Tavia and the others in a discussion about a serial rapist and tried to mentally prepare myself. *How does one get prepared for such a thing?* I wondered as I tried to make myself presentable despite my current condition.

Serial rapist, killers, immortals, and drinking blood, this was my new world. My lightheartedness quickly vanished, replaced by a gloomy feeling. *Would I ever be able to live in that world?* I asked myself.

As I started down the first set of stairs, I stopped to listen to the voices I heard. I wanted to practice my newfound hearing skill. Often in my mortal life, I thought it would be so cool to be able to eavesdrop on conversations, to be a "fly on the wall". I closed my eyes and tried to concentrate on the voices. At first, I was distracted by the noise from outside, from the neighbor's house, and from down the street. I pictured Tavia's face and concentrated on her, and I could then single out her voice from all the other noise. I could hear her clearly as though she was right beside me. I then visualized Justus in my mind and was able to hear him loud and clear, unaffected by the other voices and noises.

I heard the front door open, and the image of Helene popped into my head as I heard, "Sorry for being late!"

This was a really awesome feature of being immortal! Proud of myself for honing this new ability, I continued down the stairs, practicing my superlistening skills.

As I reached the bottom of the stairs, before anyone could see me, I heard Justus say, "Hello, Ivy." As I entered the dining room, they all turned to look at me. I gave Justus an inquisitive look, and he described, "It is not just by sound that we can identify other people from a distance. We can also catch their scent." I lifted up my arm and sniffed myself humorously.

Justus laughed and teased, "Scent doesn't imply stink. Your scent is rather enticing." If I were still mortal, I would have blushed at such a statement, but it didn't affect me that way now. Maybe I didn't have enough blood in my system to blush.

"Justus uses his sense of smell as his primary means of identifying someone," Ethan clarified as Justus took a deep breath through his nose. "Each of us is slightly different that way. Some of us are better at sorting out sound, others with scent, and a few are best with sensing the energy of others," Ethan finished.

I paused momentarily to ponder what Ethan just explained and questioned, "Who else knew I was coming?"

"We all did," they answered together.

"It's practically impossible to sneak up on an immortal! It is one of our key survival features," Ethan added.

"Survival features?" I questioned.

"We are immortal, but not indestructible," Ethan replied.

I surveyed the room to see who was there and noticed that Magnus had not surfaced from the basement yet. Sitting around the large rustic dining room table was the most alluring set of people that I had ever seen. They weren't all exceptionally gorgeous—but there was something extraordinary about them. Beside Helene was a stunningly beautiful black woman. She stood up swiftly, walked toward me, and greeted me with a firm handshake, saying, "Hello, Ivy, I'm Yasmine." I shook her hand and smiled. She was intimidating because of her beauty, her stature, and her demeanor.

She was about 5′11″ or taller, with legs that took up two-thirds of her body. She enhanced her already amazing physical attributes with elegant but revealing clothing. She would give any supermodel an inferiority complex! Her facial features were flawless, her skin was chocolate brown, and she had wild hair. Her eyes were fierce, black, and shiny like hematite.

The way she moved had an animalistic quality. I remembered seeing her with Magnus on the surveillance equipment when the old man died. The ferocity with which she killed seemed to match her general style. *If I met her in a dark alley, I would be afraid*, I thought as she smiled and her eyes softened.

"Pleased to meet you, Yasmine," I said, feeling a little more at ease.

Tavia invited me to sit beside her. "We'll get Jay on the phone and get started," she suggested.

Justus dialed, and a calming, melodic voice replied at the other end. "Hello, all, let's get this party started," he said. I could hear music and voices in the background. His voice pierced through all the background noise, and my body shuddered.

"Jay, you dog, wazzup?" Justus prodded playfully.

"I'm talking to you to find out wazzup. I'm here in my little world, isolated from the bad street of New York," Jay answered.

I could feel my breathing speed up and my heart pounding like it was going to burst out of my chest. I looked around to see if anyone noticed. I thought I was having some symptoms from the transformation again. Nobody was paying any particular attention to me, so I just let it pass and tried to focus.

"Who's on the line?" Jay inquired, and Tavia answered with all our names. "Ivy," he said. His voice provoked a chill down my spine.

"We'll have to officially meet soon, but until then, welcome to the family."

Trying to find my voice, I stammered and managed to get out, "N-nice to meet you." Tavia gave me a weird questioning look, and without drawing any attention to me, mouthed the question, "Are you OK?" I nodded and sat there wondering what was going on with my body, fearful that I was going to feel ill again.

"Ladies," Magnus cut in as he entered the dining room.

"Magnus!" Yasmine cried, jumping up to hug him.

As Magnus swung Yasmine around in an embrace, Helene interrupted with "We don't have all night here . . . can we get to it?"

"Helene, as always, a pleasure!" Magnus directed at her while winking at Ethan. "Let's get down to business!"

"Magnus, you decided to come up from the dungeon. To what do we owe this pleasure?" said the enticing voice on the phone.

"This case is getting under my skin," Magnus retorted. "I want to make sure we're all on the same page."

"Well then, what information do we have so far?" Tavia inquired.

"There's some good news this time," Magnus began. "The latest victim saw the attacker's face and was able to give enough detail for a rudimentary composite. We're waiting for O'Shea to get it to us."

I looked at Magnus, puzzled, of course; and Tavia put her hand on mine saying, "We'll explain it all to you after. For now, just take in as much as you can."

"Captain O'Shea is just starting to piece together a serial case file," Justus began. "We know that they're looking for a white male, about thirty, likely with an athletic build, and attractive. They have no solid leads other than this new composite and expect that the attacks will continue and likely escalate."

"Could that information be any more vague?" Anton stated.

Everyone paused at his comment, contemplating the challenge of the case.

"Anyone else have any other sources we can go to?" Tavia probed, looking around the table at everyone.

"Hey, Mag, didn't you date a hotshot reporter from the newspaper a few months back?" Yasmine scoffed mischievously.

"Yep," he answered. "But I doubt I'm on Ms. Flaherty's good side right now. I don't like to keep things long term with mortals, you know. She didn't take it well!"

Helene groaned at this exchange, throwing a dirty look at Magnus.

"I don't think O'Shea is holding anything back from us," Justus interjected. "He really wants our help."

"Wait, quiet, everyone," Magnus cut in. "Something's coming in on the scanner . . . it's a 911 call from the East Side, some kind of disturbance in an apartment building."

Everyone listened to the police dispatch blurting from the scanner in the basement. I could hear it loud and clear too!

"Only 11:00 p.m. and we have to get to work already? Who's up for this one?" Anton asked.

"Yasmine and Magnus," Justus advised.

"OK, Mag," Yasmine blared enthusiastically, "let's move. I'm hungry!"

"Happy hunting," Justus offered.

"Who's on police patrol tonight?" yelled Magnus as he was already out the door.

"Dunn and Johnson," Justus replied.

"Jay, we'll have to call you back," Justus said as he hung up the phone and hurried to the basement.

"Car 62, assault in progress at 279 East Fourth, apartment 408, a neighbor called it in. Are you in the area?" said a voice over the police frequency.

"We're on it, Dunn, out," replied a firm female voice from the police cruiser.

Officer Mel Dunn and Edwin Johnson of the Ninth precinct, patrolling in East Village, eagerly switched on their lights and siren. Arriving at the scene, the two uniformed officers parked their patrol vehicle in front of 279 East Fourth and rushed into the building.

Johnson, a very large, black, thirty-something, ex-college football player, rang the superintendent's unit. "Come on, come on, let us in!" he muttered under his breath.

"Hello? How can I help you?" answered an uninterested voice, through a crackling intercom.

"This is the police, let us in," demanded Johnson. "There's a disturbance in 408."

"OK, you'll have to show me your badges. Hold them up to the camera please," requested the voice indifferently. The officers held their badges in the direction of the surveillance camera. Buzzing the officers in, the lanky, indolent superintendent opened his unit door and questioned in a monotone voice, "There's a disturbance? I haven't heard any report of a disturbance."

"Who's in apartment 408?" probed Officer Mel Dunn, a 5'8" stern-looking female officer.

Standing with his hand to his temple, appearing to be deep in thought, the superintendent sluggishly informed the officers, "That unit is supposed to be occupied by Melvin Schwartz, but I haven't seen him around for a few months. He probably has sublet it to someone. They're supposed to let us know if they sublet."

"Thanks, sir," Dunn said. "Please go back to your unit and be on standby for other officers."

Somewhat disappointed to be missing the action, the superintendent griped, "Won't you need me to open the door up there?"

"Don't worry about it," Johnson exclaimed fervently while patting his holstered gun.

The two officers raced up the stairs, and upon reaching the landing of the fourth floor, they stopped at the hallway entrance. Dunn quickly looked through the rectangular window on the door and pulled back. Silently, she motioned to her partner to go in while she covered.

The fourth floor hallway was clear. Johnson proceeded quickly to unit 408, with Dunn covering the rear. The door to 408 was slightly open, and there was no sound coming from the unit.

Johnson took position to the far side of the unit door as Dunn approached silently, listening for noise. She knocked on the door saying, "Police, we're coming in!" as she pushed the door open with her foot, gun drawn. Then she quickly pulled back out of the doorway, shielding herself from possible gunfire. Johnson peeked into the unit, motioning that Dunn follow him. Johnson entered slowly, gun forward, with Dunn following him. They quickly scanned the visible part of the unit, finding nothing.

Johnson whispered, "Whatever happened here is over."

Dunn yelled, "Anyone in here?" while they both continued searching the unit. Feeling more at ease, they split up, checking all rooms and closets.

"Johnson, come here," Dunn called out from a back room as she reached a female victim lying motionless on a bed. The victim's skin was ashen with visible redness around her throat. Dunn assessed for a pulse and reported, "She's unconscious but has a weak pulse. Looks like she's been choked!"

"Raped?" speculated Johnson as he signaled headquarters to give an update.

"Don't know for sure, but it looks like it," answered Dunn.

Johnson looked over the room, noting an open window leading to a fire escape. He reported to dispatch describing the scene, "White female, approximately thirty, unconscious, labored breathing, red marks on her neck, possible sexual assault. Perpetrator has fled, probably through the bedroom window to the fire escape. Send out units to the surrounding area."

Officer Dunn, while tending to the victim, said, "I hear an ambulance. Go after the perp. I'll stay."

Johnson stood out on the fire escape, looked around, but didn't see anything suspicious. Hearing squad cars on the way, he descended the fire escape into the alley. A patrol car pulled up as Johnson was returning to the front of the building. Officers Smale and Martinez acknowledged Johnson, who gave them a brief summary of the situation.

Smale, a heavyset male officer, looked like he had consumed his fair share of donuts. His stomach overflowed in his too-snug pants, but his demeanor suggested he could take on any hoodlum who deserved a good beating. Johnson and Smale took off together in the direction they estimated the perpetrator had fled. Martinez, a middle-aged, medium-build, intense-looking Latino, began to secure the scene.

Searching near Third and Avenue C, Johnson stopped, followed by Smale.

"Shhh, Smale," Johnson whispered, "Listen, I hear something . . . from over there."

Pointing toward an alley, Johnson motioned for Smale to follow him. Hearing the sound of footsteps running off, they hurried toward the alley with their weapons drawn. Smale called for any squad car in the vicinity to close off the other end. As they entered, they noticed a body on the ground.

"Hey, you, can you hear me? Can you get up?" probed Johnson. There was no sound or movement from the body on the ground. Cautiously, the two officers approached the body. Johnson scanned the scene, while Smale kicked the victim's foot, trying to rouse a response.

"Johnson, check the pulse, I'm going to call it in," Smale directed.

"No pulse, Smale, request a bus," Johnson alerted. "There's a gash on his neck and a pool of blood," he continued. "I don't think there is anything we can do here."

"I'm calling for more backup," Smale advised as he joined Johnson. "We need to check the neighborhood for whoever did this. Maybe it's the same perp?" The sound of an ambulance siren could be heard in the distance. Smale walked to the end of the alley to flag down the ambulance.

"Put on my coat," Magnus told Yasmine as they walked leisurely on Park Street. "You got some blood on your shirt."

"Oops . . . my bad! I can never seem to eat without making a mess." She laughed.

"You'll get the hang of it with practice. Look at me, not a drop spilled," Magnus replied flippantly.

"I hope that woman survives," said Yasmine more seriously.

"We're almost home. I'll check with the hospitals when we get back," Magnus advised. "I should be able to find out something."

Arriving back at the house, Magnus and Yasmine joined us in the dining room.

"Hey, that was fast!" said Anton.

"Yes, swift justice," replied Yasmine as she took off Magnus's coat.

"Nothing like fast food!" Magnus added frivolously.

"I see you had success," voiced Tavia, pointing at Yasmine's bloodstained shirt.

"She's still an infant," Magnus wisecracked as he slapped Yasmine's butt. "We should have her wear a bib."

"Bite me!" Yasmine taunted Magnus, and with lightning speed, Magnus had Yasmine pinned in his arms with her neck exposed.

"Gladly!" he said as he ran his tongue up her long neck. Everyone laughed, but I was unsure what reaction to have to this display. We were talking about death. I knew what they just did; they just killed someone. They both looked refreshed, their skin more radiant, their eyes more brilliant, a bounce in their step.

Tavia reached for my hand under the table. Her touch brought me out of my spiral of disturbing thoughts, and I noticed that everyone was looking at me. For a couple of seconds, the room was silent. I think everyone just remembered that I was new to this.

Yasmine broke the silence by asking, "Does anyone have a shirt to lend me? I never come prepared."

"Come with me," Tavia said, and the two of them left the room.

"Tell us, what happened, Mag?" Anton probed.

"It was an easy one," Magnus began while looking at me tentatively. "Yasmine lured and captured him as easily as offering candy to a child. She has real talent." He continued with a play by play of the incident, and as he went on, I began to feel queasy.

"Ivy, you're looking a little peaked. Do you need some time away from this conversation?" Helene asked me.

"N-no," I stuttered. "I can handle it."

While we waited for Tavia and Yasmine, the conversation was changed to something more pleasant for my sake. Magnus joined Justus in the basement so that he could inquire about the status of the female assault victim.

The precinct captain Fergus O'Shea arrived at the murder scene, glanced briefly at the victim, then walked away to make a call. He was a lean but strong man in his late fifties, about 6′1″, with sparse hair and a weathered face. He worked his way through the ranks of the New York police department honestly without connections, proving himself as the best precinct captain the department had seen in years. He earned respect from his officers and colleagues by walking the talk and working the streets.

Addressing Smale, O'Shea ordered, "Call the medical examiner's office and ask for Drake. Let him know it is a 10-33."

"What's a 10-33, boss?" Smale questioned.

"Nothing that you need to know right now, Smale," advised O'Shea.

Smale radioed the ME's office and repeated O'Shea's request. There were no questions asked, so he just accepted it reluctantly and walked back to Johnson, who was questioning potential witnesses from the small crowd that had formed at the scene.

Smale assisted Johnson with securing the scene and taking statements. There was no clear information about the victim or what happened to him.

Dr. Percy Drake from the medical examiner's office arrived and approached the paramedics. After a quick assessment, he pronounced the exsanguinated victim dead. Smale and Johnson gave Drake a synopsis of the situation and emphasized that Captain O'Shea said to proceed with a 10-33.

"That's all I need from you boys," Drake advised, "you can get back to policing."

Walking back to O'Shea for further direction, Smale asked Johnson, "Hey, do you know someone named Justus?"

"Why?" asked Johnson.

"The boss was talking to someone on the phone, and I think he called him Justus . . . and what's a 10-33?" Smale continued questioning.

"Smale," Johnson replied, exasperated. "Just do what the captain asks and don't question his orders. You're new at the Ninth. There's a lot to learn in good time."

Captain O'Shea approached them and said, "Give me your notes on this one. I'm going to take over the investigation."

Smale hesitated, looking confused.

Johnson slapped Smale on the back and announced, "Less paperwork for us. Thanks, boss. What about Dunn, do we need to get her notes too?"

"No, I'm just heading to that scene now," O'Shea advised. "I'll get her story and notes, if I need to."

After the scene was cleared, Johnson and Smale met Dunn in a nearby small neighborhood coffee shop. The three exchanged opinions about the incidents they had just worked while coming down from the adrenaline rush.

"That was weird. Why would the boss take over the investigation?" Smale asked.

"Don't worry, Smale," Dunn replied, "You'll get used to it in time. He takes over some cases as he sees fit, and it is not up to us to question it. He and Drake have worked together for a long time, and they take care of some cases together. That's all you need to know."

"Don't sweat it. Just be happy that we have less paperwork for the night!" added Johnson.

"What unit did you transfer from, Smale?" Dunn questioned.

"I was at Claremont Park," he answered.

"Things are done differently at the Ninth. Just follow the boss's orders. Don't ask questions," Johnson cautioned. "You'll be given what you need to know, trust me! I've been at the Ninth for ten years, and I wouldn't want to work anywhere else."

"O'Shea is the best captain I've worked for," insisted Dunn. "He always has your back and doesn't just sit on his ass all day shuffling papers."

"Your partner, César, has been at the Ninth longer than me. He'll steer you in the right direction," explained Johnson.

The officers finished up exchanging some banter about sports as officer César Martinez arrived. They talked shop for another while, threw down a healthy tip, and made their way to the door. As they walked away from each other, Johnson asked, "Hey, Smale, what's your first name?"

"John," he answered.

Justus and Magnus returned to the dining room as Tavia and Yasmine did.

"Good, we're all here," said Helene. "Let's get Jay back on the phone now. There's work to do."

My thoughts were scattered as the phone rang, and Jay's voice pulled me back to reality.

"That was fast," he commented.

"Yes, but we had to arrange for some cleanup," Magnus admitted. "The cops were there too quickly for us to deal with discrete disposal."

"Did it look like another one from this serial rapist?" Jay queried.

"No," Magnus stated, "this was definitely a different MO."

"O'Shea is at the scene, so we still don't have any details to share about the assault from last night," Justus declared.

"Jay, give us an update from your projects," Anton requested.

"Nothing much has changed over the past month," Jay explained. "The Bloods and the Kings are still lying low since the cocaine busts last month. There's talk of a big weapons deal, probably organized by MS-13, but I'm not a hundred percent sure yet. My girls say that a Colombian kingpin will be passing through in a few weeks and may swing by my place. I'll need a few of you around if that happens. There's a new guy who has been sniffing around, but I think he's undercover DEA. I'll keep my eye on him to see what comes up. "What about this rapist?"

"As of the last college area attack, it's officially considered the work of one perpetrator, and he's being dubbed as the College Rapist," Justus explained.

"I haven't heard or seen anything about this in my circle, but I'll ask around and see if anyone has any information. What's his MO and victimology?" Jay requested.

"The victims have been in their late teens, early twenties, and out clubbing in the college area," Justus began. "He attacks them from behind, and they never see him. He gags them and binds their hands behind their backs. When he's done, he knocks them unconscious, hitting their heads against the ground."

"Have any of the victims been at my club before being attacked?" Jay inquired.

"Not as far as we know, but we didn't speak with the victims directly," Justus answered. "Our information is secondhand from O'Shea."

"All right, if that wraps things up, I'm going to get to work," Jay said. "I'm expecting a busy night! Later, guys!" he added while hanging up the phone.

During the entire conversation, I was taken hostage by my body's reactions. My heart was pounding; I was breathless and had tremors. My mouth was dry, and I couldn't concentrate or sit still. I assumed that my reaction was related to the transformation, so I tried to shake it off. Tavia could tell that something was wrong but I didn't really know what it was. Maybe I was overwhelmed by what I heard, by what I could envision in my mind? She suggested that I go and get some rest. The last part of the transformation was imminent, and I was going to need energy and more blood to get through it.

I flopped on my bed, mentally exhausted but physically riled up. I was distressed by everything I had just experienced. Serial rapist, police connections, drug lords, killing! I curled up in a little ball on my side and closed my eyes. With images swirling in my head, I eventually fell asleep.

I woke several times, restless, frightened from nightmares. I felt like a child again, wishing for my father to be there, to reassure me that it was all just a dream . . . that none of it was real!

CHAPTER FIVE
The Making of Justus and Magnus

I woke up and noticed that Tavia had started an IV for me. The rest must have done me some good because I didn't feel as overcome and edgy as I remembered. I wasn't sure how long I had been resting. I took my IV bag with me and went to the basement, looking for Justus.

"Hey, sleeping beauty," Justus said as I entered the surveillance room. I sat beside him, and he brushed back the wisps of hair from my face. "How are you feeling?" he asked affectionately.

Hair? I thought as I touched my head. I wasn't bald! I had baby-soft hair just barely covering my head.

"You look beautiful," Justus remarked as he noticed my expression of astonishment.

"How long was I sleeping?" I asked.

"Several days," he told me.

I felt my face and looked at my hands and arms. There was barely any molting skin left. Somewhat elated but also troubled, I reached for my neck and ran my fingers over my scar. I could still feel it there, rough to the touch but definitely shrinking.

"It is only a matter of days now," Justus asserted, watching me assess my scar. "Then it will be done."

I didn't know how to feel. I was happy that there would be no more pain; that I would look normal and feel good, but there was a price, a price I didn't think I would be able to pay!

Justus looked at the IV bag that I had carried along with me. It was almost empty. "I'll go and get you some in a glass," he offered as he got up from the surveillance equipment. "You're going to have to get used to drinking it, sooner than later."

I shuddered as I thought of drinking a glass of blood. It somehow just didn't have the appeal of a nice, tall glass of milk or water. This was going to be a huge step for me.

While Justus was away, I looked at Magnus, studied him, and noticed his very staid appearance as he worked, watching the cameras that were broadcasting footage from some of the worst parts of the city.

"What?" Magnus grunted. It made me jolt upright, and I looked at him more intensely but said nothing. "I can feel you looking at me," he observed. "Peering into me . . . you won't get answers that way. Ask your questions."

"What does it feel like to have a person's life end in your hands?" I wondered with a childlike innocence. "How can you handle the guilt?"

"I feel no guilt," he asserted and paused. "There was a time that I did, when I was young and torn between anger, compassion, and need. When the only warm bodies for miles were people that I knew, people who didn't deserve to die. When I had to leave everyone I loved for fear that I would one night not be able to control my hunger," he said all this with an emotionless voice, a voice that had long since surrendered to what must be.

"As a mortal," he continued, "did you eat steak, chicken, or pork?" He stopped his surveillance and turned his chair to study me. I nodded my head, and he continued. "Did you feel sorry for the cow that was slaughtered, or for the pig whose throat was slit so that you could enjoy your dinner?" he prodded. "Did you have one thought for the chicken and its life as you sat down to a fabulous roast chicken dinner?"

"No," I admitted. "But I once went to an Asian market and marked a fish for death. It was a luscious-looking rainbow trout. I pointed it out in the tank. The sales clerk took the fish out of the tank and clubbed it in the head right there in front of me. I was completely appalled. My appetite was ruined."

"You twentieth century people," Magnus exclaimed while shaking his head in disbelief and disapproval, "never having felt true starving hunger, never having to kill your food with your bare hands. That's why there's a lot of waste. The mortality has been taken out of everyday life. If you eat what you kill, you take life more seriously . . . take death more seriously. Unless you enjoy killing, which some do," he asserted with a grin, "you kill out of necessity and you will keep it at a minimum to be able to live with yourself."

Magnus had never spent this much time talking with me, so I listened without question, without batting an eye. I didn't think he would have any emotions tied up in killing, but it seemed that he did.

"I learned my respect for life from the Navajo Indians," he described. "I spent several years with them, learning all they had to teach me. Learning about real spirituality and Mother Earth, not the man-made spirituality of Western culture used to control and manipulate." As Magnus was finishing his sentence, Justus slid into the room with the grace of a dancer, with him, the lifeblood that I was to drink.

Magnus shuddered as he said, "Nasty . . . I like my blood warm and alive. I don't know how you can choke down that cold, stale syrup."

"Thanks for making it sound appetizing, Mag. That's just what I need," I replied as I brought my hand to my mouth for fear of retching.

He turned his chair back around to avoid watching me swallow the dark red, pungent blood that was to sustain me for a few more hours.

"What were you talking about?" asked Justus. "I thought I heard one of the four forbidden topics."

"We were just starting to touch on religion," I answered as I plugged my nose about to take a sip of the blood. "Please keep talking to me, distract me so that I won't think about what I am drinking," I pleaded.

Before I could change my mind, I took one big gulp and swallowed as hastily as I could. It was cool, thick, and mildly sweet. I could compare it with drinking cold coffee. You expect it to be warm, but when you get it in your mouth, it isn't. You're not sure if you should spit it out, or if in fact it doesn't taste that bad after all. Still, I shuddered, retched mildly, and asked, "What are the other three?"

Justus looked at me inquisitively as I took another big gulp, then he looked away to hide his disgust.

"Other three?" the two questioned in unison.

"The other three forbidden topics?" I affirmed.

"Oh . . . ," They both laughed together.

Justus rhymed off, "Politics, money, and sex . . . don't discuss those unless you are willing to argue and probably be insulted or put down by someone else's views."

Magnus cut in, "Wars have been waged on these topics . . . over the years, I've had men and women alike try to kill me over them."

"Magnus, if you would stop taking money from bikers in pool halls, young beautiful women from the arms of crooked politicians, and wine from priests, then nobody would want to kill you," Justus teased.

"But then, what fun would life be?" Magnus replied with a smirk.

"Any other lessons of great value I should know about?" I queried as I took my last big mouthful.

"Don't ever ask a fat woman when the baby is due . . . that doesn't go over well either," Magnus warned shrewdly.

I almost spewed out the blood all over both of them as we all laughed together. This was now starting to feel like home. These guys were like my family. I hugged Justus and winked at Magnus and said, "Thanks!"

I had managed to drink almost all of the blood, and to my surprise, it was not revolting. Justus sat beside me and pulled the IV out of my arm and affirmed, "You won't need this anymore. You can drink dead, cold blood for a little while and work your way up to small live animals or preferably humans."

"Really?" I questioned, thinking about cute bunny rabbits and kittens. "I couldn't kill a cute little animal!"

"There must be some animal that you hate or that creeps you out?" he suggested.

"Well, probably skunks and raccoons . . . rats, all the ones that skulk in the night," I declared.

"They're perfect to start with because our usual prey also skulk in the night, so you should be able to transition just fine," Justus said.

"Seriously though," I wondered. "How much time do I have before I'll need to kill a mortal to survive?"

"Just to survive?" Justus repeated. "You could exist off the blood of animals, but you wouldn't thrive. You would survive the way a street person survives on the scraps from a dumpster, but you wouldn't have the strength or vitality needed for long-term survival. I remember when I tried to live off of small animals," he continued, looking off into the distance. "That lasted about a month before I was so ravenous that I couldn't take it anymore."

"My first human kill was a stranger passing through town," Justus recalled. "I was famished, I just couldn't help myself. He had a wound, not a serious one, but one that produced a scent that I couldn't resist. I still wasn't completely transformed. I looked hideous, and I was hiding in the outskirts of town, eating the blood of jackrabbits and gophers. I followed the scent, and with barely any regard to remaining inconspicuous, I took him like a ravenous wildcat, in an alley behind the general store. Some men heard my victim's scream, so I had to retreat out of town and hide. I had torn the man's throat apart. The town thought that a cougar had killed him and initiated a wildcat watch.

I had no mentor, so I had to learn everything on my own, learn to curb my desire for blood."

I couldn't picture this crazed behavior of Justus; his demeanor was too nurturing. I also could never picture him looking hideous!

"When were you changed?" I asked Justus.

"I'll tell you my story, if you promise to reserve judgment and remember who I am now, not who I was then," Justus announced, looking very serious.

"I promise I will not judge you for who you were," I assured.

"Mag and I were born in 1831 to James and Abigail Evans. We were the last of eight children. Our mother almost bled to death when we were born. She was damaged by the birth and was unable to have any more children. Our family lived in Kirtland, Ohio, but soon moved to Caldwell County, Missouri, a vibrant, growing Mormon community.

"Our parents had been following Mormon leaders for years wanting to be in Zion, the gathering place of the Mormons. Our parents and family were very devout, and our childhood consisted of constant preparations for the second coming of Christ. Our father was a mild-mannered man, and our mother a very loving and giving woman. We were the only two boys among six sisters, needless to say that we didn't lack for mothering.

"Neither of us remembers Missouri much, but we do remember when we had to leave everything behind and move again when we were about ten. The Mormons were driven out of Missouri, and some of our relatives were killed by militia in a nearby town. We ended up in Nauvoo, Illinois, where two of our sisters, Maisy and Priscilla, died of cholera. After a few years there, we had to move again, when we were about fifteen.

"The Mormons were driven out of the state and headed west along the Mormon Trail to Utah. In this migration, we lost my oldest sister, Lucille, and her newborn son, Thomas. They both died in childbirth. I think the migration was too difficult on my sister, and she just ran out of energy. Her husband and now young widower, William Earl Harris, had become a close friend of ours. The death of his wife, our sister, really soured him on non-Mormons. His family too had been moving with the church leaders and had suffered losses due to illness, persecution, and migration. Anger was seeping out of him, and he was growing violent in his thoughts.

"We arrived at Salt Lake Valley in Deseret, now Utah, in the summer of 1847. In a couple of short years, one of our own, a Mormon, was designated as the governor of the territory, and we finally felt that we had a home. Magnus, William, and I joined the Nauvoo Legion, the Mormon militia. Our governor called upon all strong, young, and healthy men to keep our great territory and religion safe.

"William still blamed the death of Lucille on anti-Mormon hatred and was growing more bitter as time went on. He quickly rose to the rank of captain in the Legion, and Magnus and I were part of his infantry. By fighting, William felt he was avenging the death of Lucille and Thomas. He volunteered our company for all the missions we could take. We fought in raids during the Walkara War in 1853 and 1854 against the Ute Indians, and in other small battles and skirmishes leading up to the Utah War in 1857.

"When you live on nothing but hatred day in and day out, hate starts to become your core belief. We felt that our families and our beliefs had suffered the injustice of wrongful judgment by ignorant people for too long. Our war now became a mission of killing as many who opposed us as we possibly could.

"During the Utah War, there was great paranoia that the entire United States was against us and was bent on obliterating all Mormons and the religion. By this time, we were killing out of self-righteousness in a guise of entitlement, as though God had told us to do it. We found ourselves in southern Deseret by the end of the summer in 1857. Some travelers on their way to California from Arkansas had the misfortune of meeting us and the rest of our troupe along the Spanish trail. We were then thinking with mob rule mentality and didn't wait for any official order to attack. We just attacked the group of migrants and killed most of them.

"I was fatally injured in this attack and was left to die along with the many innocent non-Mormons. I remember Magnus and William mourning over what they thought was my corpse. I wasn't dead, but I was so near death that they couldn't tell the difference. I remember the swirling thoughts in my head. I could see my mother's face and Lucille and our little house back in Nauvoo.

"Lucille spoke to me in my dreamlike state. She told me that it was God's will to have taken her and little Thomas, and that nobody was to blame. She said that I was to live in shame, if I lived. If I died, my soul would not ascend to heaven because of the brutal murders that I had taken part in. She was saddened and would feel forever guilty and tarnished that such brutal deeds were done in her honor. She told me that she loved me despite my actions because I was her blood, her little brother.

"As she was fading away from me, I felt an immense pressure in my chest and a burning sensation that couldn't be given words. I thought that this was my descent to hell. I felt that I was moving, and then all went black. I awoke sometime later to find myself in a small hut. Somewhere beyond the hut, I could hear voices and chanting. I could smell food cooking on an open fire. It was like I was hearing and smelling for the first time. It was all extremely defined and clear. As I made my way to the door of the hut, a native man appeared in the doorway.

"I had learned some native language in my travels and was able to just barely understand him with a combination of simple words and hand gestures. He brought me liquid to drink, and it was only sometime after I left him that I realized it was blood in which he had put some sort of herbs. My transformation was swift and uncomfortable, and it was when I saw my wounds heal completely that I knew something unnatural was happening to me.

"My native caretaker never let me leave the hut and never let anyone see me. I never had any cravings for food, the food that I used to eat. I just waited every day for him to bring me my cups of elixir to drink. One night, he brought me out of the hut when everyone else was sleeping and took me a great distance on his horse. We dismounted the horse, and he motioned for me to follow him and to watch him. He ran insanely fast and caught a jackrabbit, ripped its head off, and drank the blood. I was mortified and petrified by this spectacle. He then tapped my shoulder and motioned to me that I should do it. I wasn't able to bring myself to do this. It seemed very barbaric.

"He eventually gave up, went back to his horse, and motioned that he was leaving. I followed and was waiting for him to help me mount the horse when he put a knife to my throat instead. He motioned for me to go away, and with the few words we could exchange, he advised me not to come back to his village. He looked at me with chilling eyes. I knew he was serious. He turned away from me, and like a bolt of lightning, he was gone.

"It took me a few nights to be able to bring myself to hunt small prey, but once I did, I couldn't stop thirsting for blood. For a few weeks, I continued to drink from animals as I made my way back toward Deseret. I already told you about my first mortal kill, and after that, there was no turning back to small animals!"

"How did you feel about killing back then?" I inquired.

"Well, I knew I had to do it. Killing was definitely not a foreign concept to me, so I didn't have any particular hang-ups about it. I could still hear what Lucille had said to me in my death dreams. She felt guilty and tarnished by the actions that Magnus, William, and I had taken to avenge her death. I have never been able to forget this, and she guides me to do the right thing even still.

"My quest back to Deseret led me to Salt Lake City where I hoped to find my family. The town was in conflict, but this time it was more serious than ever before. I couldn't find my family and was preparing to continue north in search of them when one night, as I loitered around Commercial Street, waiting for the right time to hunt, I heard a scream that chilled my spine. I went in search of the cause and found myself in a brothel where I came upon some men who were raping and torturing a working girl. I felt sorry for the woman, although I didn't approve of her lifestyle.

"Without regard to hiding my true nature, I took great pleasure in killing the men swiftly, so that I could get them all. I didn't want any of them to escape and cause unnecessary problems for me.

The local sheriff came to the door because of the screams, but the Madame took care of him. This was my first exposure to using my gift as a death sentence. The women were scared, but I assured them that I had no desire to either use their flesh or hurt them. For some reason, they believed me easily, and they trusted that they were safe with me.

"The women told me that a few months earlier, two of their girls had been very brutally beaten, and one would never fully recover from it. They had me stay on with them as their guard, and with a bit of time together, we came up with a plan that gave all of us what we wanted. Keeping in mind that I couldn't kill every man that came through the door, I reserved my death sentences for those who showed a tendency toward violence with the girls or in the community. They would use their talents to lure specific targets to the brothel, men that I had handpicked for execution. Law in those days did run somewhat on a Wild West mentality; therefore, I took it into my own hands when warranted.

"One woman, Elizabeth, whose looks reminded me of my sister Maisy, became very special to me. Magnus and I were closest with Maisy as children. She had the same blonde hair and blue eyes, very delicate and angelic.

"Elizabeth was barely a woman. She had been orphaned a few years earlier at the age of fifteen. Her survival depended on her living at the brothel. Madame Young, the house owner, took Elizabeth in, sparing her from a life of begging on the street and starving to death.

"The arrangement that I had with Madame Young was mutually beneficial, and I stayed with them for several months. It didn't take long for me to fall in love with Elizabeth. She called me her white knight, and she was my princess. If I had known then that I could change someone, I would have changed Elizabeth. She asked to be like me so she could be strong too. At that point, I had no idea that I was immortal, just that I was really strong and hearty.

"A few years passed, and I began to feel that the differences between Elizabeth and I would, in the end, make either or both of us unhappy eventually. I knew that I couldn't have a normal life, the kind that Elizabeth wanted.

"I suspected that I couldn't have children since none were conceived between us. I was discovering other aspects of immortality, such as my worsening sensitivity to the sun as time went on. I wasn't sure what I was, and I feared that in time, I may change in some way that would make me a danger to Elizabeth. It broke my heart, but once I helped her secure a respectable job where she could support herself, I left."

"Did you ever find out what happened to Elizabeth?" I questioned.

"We did exchange letters a few times, and I know that eventually she did meet someone, got married, and had children. I always hoped that she would be happy," Justus said longingly, lost in a feeling. After a moment, he continued his story.

"I really wanted to see what had become of Magnus and William," he began. "I started to search for them. As I passed through various towns, I fed my hunger with the blood of criminals, vagrants, and the occasional crooked politician.

"I finally tracked down Magnus, William, and the rest of my family in Rock Springs, Wyoming. All the men were working in a coal mine. I kept myself scarce during the day because I didn't want anyone to recognize me or know that I was there. William was courting a woman and seemed to be less angry than he had been. He really was a good man.

"My parents and sisters were fine, and one of my sisters was married, and I was an uncle again. She had a sweet daughter, blonde and curly, named Sarah. As much as I wanted to be part of their lives, I knew that it would be too complicated to reveal myself to them. I wasn't even fully aware of what I was and what I was capable of. I noticed that my hunger was not as strong as it had been, and I could go longer between the need to feed. I was much more aware of what my body was capable of.

"For a few weeks, I just watched, followed my family, and paid particular attention to Magnus. I sensed that he wasn't happy with his life. I sensed he was lonely. A few nights I stayed in his room, watching him, wondering if I should tell him what had happened to me. I really missed him. We had been inseparable since we were born.

I looked over to Magnus. He remained with his back turned to us, but I could sense his smile.

"One evening, at dusk, I followed Magnus on a walk. He went to the cemetery, and there he sat by a grave, talking to it. My new body allowed me to move very quickly and with quiet agility, I moved to a spot close to Magnus without making a sound. I stayed behind a tree, and with my immortal vision, I could see that the grave was mine. My family gave me a proper burial, despite not having my body to bury.

"I could hear Magnus clearly, of course, because of my improved hearing. He was talking to me, telling me that his life wasn't the same. He couldn't feel peace for me or for himself," Justus said as he looked at Magnus, playfully egging him on.

"OK, stop making me look like a pansy in your story!" Magnus commanded with a smirk, looking at Justus sternly.

"But you were a big pansy, and you still are, Mag. Face it, I got the manly genes for the two of us . . . ," Justus teased while catching Magnus in a headlock. The two of them started play fighting, and I took the opportunity to drink some more blood, which I was actually somewhat fond of.

"Don't keep me in suspense, what happened at the cemetery?" I probed, looking from one to the other.

Magnus was the first one to speak up, saying, "Justus just suddenly appeared beside me, and I reached for a knife, ready to kill him. I had very well-developed fighting instincts from being in the Legion for years."

Justus cut in, badgering Magnus, "You turned as pale as me that night, looking at me stunned, mouth agape. I thought I was going to have to pick you up off the ground."

"Then what?" I urged, preventing another mano-a-mano duel.

Magnus continued his story, "Well, I reached out to touch Justus, because I thought I was seeing a ghost. But to my surprise, he was real. Justus reached out to me as well, without saying a word. We stood there for a couple of minutes just looking at each other, then, we hugged for a long while," Magnus finished.

"Ahhh!" I said, watching them looking at each other.

Justus began again, "I apologized for staying away so long and letting Magnus go on thinking I was dead. "Then Magnus asked me if I had gone to see anyone else in the family yet. He was excited that I was alive, and he wanted everyone to know. He kicked the headstone and told me that he had a feeling all along that I wasn't really dead, and that's why he couldn't put me to rest.

"That's when I had to explain to him that I wasn't the same. I had him touch my skin, which was cold because I hadn't fed in a long while. I told him the entire story of what I had been through since that day when I died on the battlefield. I told him about Elizabeth and how I was beginning to discover what this new life meant for me. I explained that I didn't really know who or what I was and if he, or anyone else, could be safe around me.

"I described how I had to survive on blood, that I couldn't eat real food anymore. I knew I had to minimize my time in the sun because it affected my skin and my eyes. I told him that I didn't think I was alive, that maybe I was a ghost of sorts. I showed him some of my improved abilities too, like how fast I was, how far I could see and hear, and how strong I was. We talked all night out in the cemetery, and finally, as dawn was breaking, I went back to the room I had discretely rented and Magnus went home. We agreed to meet again for the next few nights in the cemetery.

"After a week of spending time together, I decided to say goodbye to Magnus because I felt I couldn't live freely there and I needed to find a way to live some sort of satisfying life. Magnus wouldn't hear of it. He didn't want me to leave, or if I was going to leave, he wanted to come with me. I told him that I didn't know if I was dangerous to him or not, that I really had no idea what I was capable of, if I got too hungry or angry.

"Magnus suggested that if the native man changed me into whatever I was, there must be others out there too. Maybe we could find others, and they could tell me more about what I was now," Justus finished.

"Either way, I wasn't afraid of Justus," Magnus said. "And I was interested in knowing more. I found a journalist from the local newspaper who did some research for us. Justus and I met most nights to come up with a plan. The journalist told us that Louisiana was the place that had the most reports of night creatures, so we decided that we would head there in search of information. The journey was long. We had to steal money to pay our way to Louisiana. One night, I asked Justus if I could watch him hunt," Magnus explained.

"I wasn't sure what I thought of that," Justus stated. "But I reluctantly agreed. I had already made clear that I didn't kill randomly and that I only killed when I really needed to.

"That night, we stalked a few taverns in a town that we were passing through, hoping to find someone with the killer instinct. Instead, we found one of my favorite prey, the rapist. I killed with such prowess that it was over in no time. Magnus touched my skin to see how warm it was when I was freshly fed.

"From that point on, Magnus helped me select my victims. We eventually arrived in Louisiana and settled in the heart of New Orleans, where we had heard the most rumors about night creatures. We had been collecting money and valuables from my victims and resorted to stealing as the need arose. We found a small place to rent, and we spent our time following leads about the existence of night creatures. One warm humid night, we found what we were looking for or, should I say that they found us.

"It was a night when I needed to hunt. I was blanched and voracious from a long stretch without blood. The French Quarter, as always, was alive. Magnus was helping me choose my prey from the vast selection of crooks, criminals, killers, and rapists that were available aplenty.

"I tracked my meal into an alley, putrid with garbage and vermin, and as I was about to indulge, I heard a pleasing voice say, 'Are you going to share?' I whipped my head from side to side, looking for the one who said it, but I couldn't see anyone. I heard a pleasant giggle, and suddenly, beside me was a meek-looking, light-skinned, light-haired beauty, looking both ravishing and ravenous.

"My victim, already stunned from the grasp I had on him, and from the quarts of cheap beer he had drunk, just looked from me to the lady with his mouth hanging open. 'By all means,' I told her, 'please help yourself. There's plenty more!' Before I had finished my offering, she had swiftly enjoyed her first kill of the night.

"From behind me, I heard Magnus say, 'Justus, can you help me out here?' He was in the grasp of a sleek, dark-haired temptress dressed in a white flowing gown. With his head pinned back, throat exposed, she was looking at me to see what I would do. With ease, I was instantly beside them, standing pressed against the woman, looking directly in her eyes.

"'He's with me, ma'am,' I warned, 'Please let go of him.'

"She chuckled and said to the other woman, 'They're both so delicious. I could just eat them up.'

"She gently kissed Magnus's neck and then let him go. We all just looked at each other for a few minutes, prancing around in a strange kind of group dance, with no one knowing what the other was going to do. Finally, I said, 'Ladies, I'm Justus, and this is Magnus.'

"'Why is he not immortal?' the dark-haired one probed, pointing at Magnus. 'Immortal?' I questioned. 'Is that what I am?'

"The light-haired one was instantly beside me, touching my face, 'Yes, darling one, from the temperature of your skin, I can tell you are immortal. Didn't your maker tell you?' she queried.

"'My maker didn't speak my language, and he didn't seem to want to keep me around, so no, he didn't tell me anything.'

"Now both women were around me, fondling my hair, stroking my face, touching me.

"'You poor dear, how long ago were you changed?' they chimed in unison.

"'A few years,' I replied. 'We came here to find others like me who could tell me what I am and what will become of me.'

"'What you are is immortal. Virtually indestructible. Strong, fast, resilient, a hunter.' The blonde continued as she circled me then Magnus. 'You are smarter than mortals, you have heightened instincts and senses, and you are beautiful,' she said and kissed me.

"It had been a while since I kissed a woman, and I found myself eagerly indulging in the moment. This kiss was different than the kiss of a mortal; it was more potent and raw. It was as though she became part of me for the time that we were gripped together in this kiss.

"'Wow,' I stated as she pulled away from me. She giggled again and walked over to Magnus.

"'Why are you keeping him as a weak, fragile mortal?' she asked me.

"'He smells scrumptious. How have you been able to resist?' said the dark-haired one.

"They were both circling Magnus, and you know that I am better with the ladies, so I did the talking for him.

"'He is my brother, as you can plainly see, and I don't want him to be like me because I don't know what I am, what I am capable of. I don't want him to become a killer.'

"'But I want to be like you, like all of you,' Magnus declared anxiously, looking from one of us to the other, like a child hoping to be picked for the team.

"The women were both fondling his hair and face, 'Delightful,' announced the dark-haired one. 'Magnus, not yet, wait until we know more,' I pleaded, but I could see by the look on his face that he was quite keen on changing. The women stepped away from him, kept a safe distance, and introduced themselves.

"'I'm Savannah,' said the light-haired one. 'And this is Haven,' she continued while pointing at the dark-haired one. 'We live with Victor, our maker. Would you like to come and stay with us for a while?' Savannah asked.

"'What about Magnus, will he be safe?' I questioned.

"'We have been immortal for a long time. We are very good at controlling our appetite,' Savannah replied, then she added, 'If we have to.' She winked at Magnus, which made him beam like a teenager about to get laid for the first time.

"We followed them to their plantation home, a two-story, colonial mansion with slave quarters, lush trees, flowering vines, and plants everywhere. The fragrance was breathtaking. In the starlit night sky, I felt the gentle breeze and was content for the first time since I had become an immortal. I finally had some hope that I would know who I was.

"Victor was a tall, slender, dark-haired gentleman. Very refined, well spoken, and well dressed. He had the air of affluence and grandeur about him with every movement and spoken word. He invited us in with enthusiasm and made us feel welcome and comfortable. The house was majestic on the inside with the best of furnishings and trimmings. There were housemaids and butlers available to tend to our every whim.

"Never had Magnus or I lived in such splendor. It wasn't at all difficult to take. The girls took us out to buy clothing from the best tailors in town. We had our hair coiffed in the latest style. The best foods were brought in for Magnus, and they indulged nightly in parties and blood feasts. I still kept myself on a strict diet, only feeding when I really needed to, and I would go out hunting for my usual low-life prey.

"'Why do you deny yourself so?' Haven asked me one night. I described the experience with my sister and that it was just part of my moral code to kill only when absolutely necessary and to kill only those that the world could do without anyway.

"'What a lovely thought,' Victor said. 'Maybe I will give up random killing for lent one of these years.' They all chuckled. We lived in acceptance of our differences, and Mag and I thoroughly enjoyed that way of life that we had never known.

"The evenings were full of people, pleasure, music, and sex. It was an orgy for the senses. Although Victor and the girls were bonded by a maker relationship, they shared each other freely with physical indulgence. Poor Magnus was worn out and had to spend days at a time in bed to catch up his energy reserves."

I looked at Magnus who was now lost in not-so-wholesome nostalgic thoughts. He had a silly grin on his face as he reminisced—I'm sure—about his sultry companions.

"The house would be full of willing mortals and immortals alike," Justus continued. "It was a veritable pleasure palace. They had their killing system worked out as to not attract any attention, but to provide for them almost every night.

"One evening, a new immortal who was invited to the house almost killed Magnus. The girls, who were quite fond of Magnus—he was sort of like a pet—fought off this newborn, but Haven was scathed somewhat in the skirmish. It was the first time that I had seen a fight between immortals, and I was amazed and frightened. It was like watching wild animals fighting for dominance.

"It didn't take long for Magnus to really press me to change him. The girls were really pushing for it, and the incident put fear into us. Magnus could see only the positive side of immortality, which I guess is still one of his charms! He really wanted my approval, but I couldn't give it. Maybe it was the seeds of religious belief planted in me from my childhood, maybe it was my overly developed sense of morality, but I couldn't be the one to change him. We were both given the knowledge we needed to understand the full consequences of immortality, and we were also schooled about the culture of various immortal populations around the world.

"Periodically, we would have visits from other immortals that came from places in the world that we had never even heard of at that time. After consulting Victor, who was the elder of the house and immortal for a few centuries, Magnus was convinced he wanted to change. The girls were all too happy to be the ones to change him."

Justus paused as we both looked over at Magnus, who was still sporting his devious grin as he was obviously remembering his change.

"Tell me about it, Magnus," I requested.

"My change," Magnus began with a little chuckle, "guaranteed, was a more sensual process than either of yours. It takes several days to initiate the change process and then several weeks to go through the change, as you are well aware. You have to be infected daily for several days. You were close to death and unconscious through the initiation part and for a few weeks of the change. I wasn't. The girls tempered the unpleasantness of the initiation and change process with as much physical pleasure as I could endure. It really was quite invigorating for my body to go through the extremes of pleasure and pain simultaneously. As far as changes go, I would recommend it." He was still grinning from ear to ear and turned back to his work.

"Wait a minute, I want to hear more," I said.

"What do you want to know?" Magnus demanded.

"After your change, did you live like Justus or like Victor, Savannah, and Haven?" I probed.

"I lived like my makers and loved it at the time. It was strange because my mortal life was strongly bonded to Justus, especially because we are twins. There is also a strong bond with your maker, and I had two makers. I felt torn between the girls and Justus.

"Eventually, all the frivolous indulgence became something that Justus couldn't live with anymore, so he decided to leave. This was a difficult decision for both of us because he had to decide to leave, and I had to decide whether or not to go with him. These women were my makers, and very alluring too. Leaving them wasn't something I could bear early on in my immortal life.

"Justus left, and I stayed. We were apart for many years. Justus got involved in the Civil War. He joined the North side because he wanted to help free slaves. There were slaves working the plantation, but I really didn't consider them slaves. They were more like employees. They were free to go, if they wanted to, but they all stayed because they were well treated by Victor.

"Justus met Ethan while at war. They are the ones who together started the culture that we live by today. They worked the Underground Railroad out of Ohio and Pennsylvania into Canada. I stayed with Savannah and Haven until they decided to leave the United States to go to Europe with Victor. I didn't want to leave my homeland, and I was missing the west, so I returned west and made it as far as New Mexico.

"There I joined a Navajo tribe, and that's when I started to change my thoughts and ways. I learned a lot from the Navajo. Their prime belief is that they must do everything they can to live in harmony with Mother Earth, Father Sky, and the many other elements such as man, animals, plants, and insects."

"How long were you guys apart?" I asked, surprised that they separated.

Justus took over the story now and explained, "After the Civil War, Ethan and I lived in the northeast United States, cleaning the streets in our own way. We became involved in the First World War where we traveled to Britain. When the war was over, we ended up in Chicago, mob central.

"We met up with Magnus in the late 1920s, in Chicago, during the Prohibition uproar. We coincidentally ran into each other while staking out Al Capone and his people. Magnus had befriended an immortal Irishman named Keiran O'Riley, who was very motivated to take down the Capone mob. He had lost some countrymen to Capone back in New York City before Capone moved to Chicago. The twenties gave us a lot of social upheaval to feed upon. The four of us—Ethan, Magnus, Keiran, and I—formalized our culture of living off those who deserved to die."

He stopped talking, and I waited to see if he would continue with more. This story was extremely interesting. I wanted to know more. Justus smiled, pushed my hair back from my face, and kissed my forehead.

"You look tired," he remarked. "You should rest some more."

"But I want to know more about you and Magnus!" I cried, like a child wanting one more story before bed.

"In time," the two of them said in unison.

Justus shooed me away, and I walked slowly up the two flights of stairs to the library where I immersed myself in historical books. There was a radio on in another room, and a news report caught my attention:

"Another attack by the rapist dubbed as the College Rapist occurred in East Village last night. The city is on high alert, and the Mayor insists that the police are working the case intensely. If they're working it, why isn't there anything more than a rudimentary sketch of some blond guy who could be anyone? Phone lines are open, tell me what you think of all this?

"We have John on the line. John, what do you have to say?"

"I live in East Village, not too far from one of the university residence halls, and I don't think students are taking this seriously. I'm a blond guy, I could be the guy in the sketch, and girls are still hooking up with me, no questions asked. Maybe this one will make them more cautious."

"You look like the guy in the composite, huh. Maybe we should haul you into the police station, John! We now have Debra on the line . . . Debra, what do you think . . . are women more cautious?"

"John has a point. When students are drunk, all caution goes out the window. I know that I'm taking more precautions. I thought someone was following me the other night when I was coming home from work, so I went into a coffee shop and called one of my male friends to come and meet me there and walk me home."

"You're definitely using your head, Debra, but don't we deserve to live in a city where we don't need escorts home? Shouldn't women be able to walk freely? Where are the cops when we need them? Abe, what's your beef?"

"Well . . . I'm a cop, and I don't think that beating down the boys in blue is going to help solve anything. People need to be vigilant, always. This is New York after all. You chose to live here, you chose to take some risk, and you have to assume some responsibility for maintaining your own safety. My advice to women is to be very watchful when out, don't be alone, take a cab instead of walking, use campus security escorts. Make sure to study the composite, as generic as it is, and if you think you see someone who resembles it, steer clear and call your local precinct or 911 to report it."

"Thanks, Abe, good advice and good point . . . this is New York with all its crazies roaming the streets. Back after this . . ."

CHAPTER SIX
Love at First Sight

It had been a few weeks since my first human kill, and my thirst for blood had grown to a serious addiction. I thought about blood all day and all night. I dreamt about blood when I rested, I could smell and taste it when I closed my eyes, and I thought about it constantly.

Someone always had to be with me to make sure that I didn't go on a killing rampage. Tavia and Helene wouldn't hunt with me anymore because I was a liability to their long-term projects. They had been working with Jay, trying to eliminate the leader of a drug ring for three months, and I completely ruined it. They left me alone for just a couple of minutes one night, and I killed the only source of information that they had. They were supposed to question him before killing him because he was just a small distributor in a much larger operation.

Another big blunder was when I was hunting with Anton and Magnus one night. Justus had been working on a child pornography ring, posing as a buyer. He set up a meeting with the key distributor, but we needed to find out who the producer was. Again, I couldn't help myself. Somewhat driven by the fact that it was child pornography and by my extreme thirst, I killed the distributor when Magnus and Anton let down their guard for a moment.

I was supposed to be learning about self-control!

Afterward, I always felt guilty. I couldn't seem to kick that feeling. I was seeing flashes of my victims' lives when I killed them, and this disturbed me. None of my victims ever had decent lives. They were able to communicate their pain to me through their thoughts, but I still didn't understand why, or how, this was happening to me. What was the purpose? All it did was haunt me.

Most of them had very disturbing lives—lives full of neglect and violence. They chose to hurt others out of anger and self-hatred. They felt like they were alone in the world, unable to trust because of their experiences. Their realities were fending for themselves and taking no shit from anyone. I felt sorry for them and wished that I could find a way to help them. I wished I could turn back the clock and meet them before they had turned to violence, somehow change the course of their lives. But of course, that was not possible; and the crimes they committed caused real pain, suffering, and death to others.

Killing humans made me a "normal" immortal. Everything was new to me again. Taking blood from humans created new sensations in me, increased my strength and speed, brought more changes in my body, and gave me intensely acute senses. I had to learn how to use them with efficiency. I was starting to accept my fate and felt somewhat content with my new life. I was learning to accept the good with the bad.

Yasmine was my guardian for the evening, and I had never been to her place, so that was our plan, a girls' night in. Maybe we would watch movies or just sit and talk. It was late afternoon when we met at the entrance to Tompkins Square Park at Avenue A and East Seventh Street. We walked through the park, and Yasmine knew everyone there; it seemed. There was a strange mix of people, business people and street people, sitting on the benches, some interacting with each other.

We meandered through the park, stopping to talk with many people. An old homeless man entertained us with stories of riots and upheaval that had taken place in Tompkins Square in the past. Yasmine slipped a little money to the homeless people, and they all knew her by name. She lived in Christodora House across the park, and as dusk fell, we arrived there. Her building was seventeen stories and very plain-looking from the outside. It had an "institution" feel to it with its evenly spaced small windows, each of which was divided into six panes; it reminded me of a building made of Lego. The only hint of decorative detail was the odd carvings of mythical creatures at the top of the massive entrance and the first floor windows.

"What an interesting building," I commented as we entered the lobby.

"This building has history," Yasmine stated. "That's why I like it! It was built in 1928 to serve as a settlement house for poor families, mostly immigrants. There's an old guy in the building who lived here as a kid in the forties. He said he met his wife at one of the dances they ran here on Saturday nights. Apparently, George and Ira Gershwin gave their first public performance here."

"I never would have pictured you into nostalgia," I remarked. She looked at me, not sure how to take my comment.

"I live in the moment, but I do appreciate history," she said.

As we arrived in her unit, I was in awe. It was colored like the African savannah. She had wicker, wood-carved and weaved furniture, clay pots, and sculptures. Egyptian and Moroccan rugs hung on the walls and were strewn on the floors. It was really very unique. She had dark wood moldings, dried wispy grasses in vases, and beautiful orange and purple flowers adorning the window sills. Her place was exactly what I would have expected from her.

"This place is really you, wild and free, beautiful and chaotic," I observed, hoping she wouldn't take chaotic as a bad thing.

"Thanks," she said. "It reminds me of my roots. I am originally from Africa."

"From where in Africa?" I probed, hoping she would tell me more about herself.

"Rwanda," she responded abruptly.

I got the feeling that she didn't really want to share much more than that. I didn't say anything else, giving her the freedom to share or not.

"Tompkins Square has been my home for a long time," Yasmine continued after a brief pause. "I lived in the park for a while, homeless, like the people we visited today. It was the park people who showed me how to survive in the city."

As I was pondering what Yasmine had told me about herself, she went to her phone and checked her messages. A smile lit her face as she listened.

"I know what we're doing tonight," she said as she hung up the phone. "We're going to Gotham Citi."

"What's Gotham Citi?" I asked.

"It's Jay's club," she answered. "You've never been there?"

"No, it seems that the others are not big nightclub goers," I pointed out. "I'm not a club person either, but a change of pace would do me good."

"I'll make sure that you have a great time, and I'm sure that Jay will give you the VIP treatment as well," she declared excitedly.

We had a few hours to kill before going out, so I decided to look through Yasmine's library for something to read. She was not an avid television watcher, but she had an extensive collection of history novels. I usually read suspense and supernatural novels, some Stephen King and Dean Koontz, but today, it looked like history. Her collection included several U.S. history novels. She had some colonial choices like *Great Johnson* by Edison Marshall, *Into the Valley* by Rosanne Bittner, and several James A. Michener books. I settled on a novel called *Cryptonomicon* by Neal Stephenson.

The story started in the past, in 1942, with a captain in the U.S. Navy, who was also a math genius. His mission was to keep the Nazis ignorant of the fact that the U.S. Navy had cracked their secret code. Then the story moved to the present where his grandson uncovered a Nazi submarine that brought to light a conspiracy related to his grandfather's navy detachment and the Nazi code called Arethusa.

It seemed interesting enough, and I immersed myself in the book for an hour or so and finished it. It seemed that another enhanced skill as an immortal was reading speed! I was absorbed in the story and hadn't noticed what Yasmine was up to. I called out to her, and she answered from her bedroom.

"Finished your book?" she asked.

"Yes," I hollered back.

"You don't have to yell . . . immortal hearing, remember!" she said.

"Oh, yeah . . . sorry," I replied.

"Come in here. I'll help you get ready for tonight," she requested.

I was generally a very conservative person in all aspects of my life, never drawing too much attention to myself, keeping a low profile. I always dressed conservatively and wore my hair in a business style, usually tied back in some way.

I entered Yasmine's room, reluctantly, because I already had visions about what she had in store for me. As immortals, we attract attention. There is a certain aura about us that makes mortals notice us and become attracted to us. We're not all drop-dead gorgeous like Yasmine; but still, to mortals, we were enticing. Yasmine loved the attention; therefore, she accentuated her already stunning qualities with fashion that turned heads. When money is no object, owning a one-of-a-kind Versace and Prada nightclub outfit is par for the course. In her immense walk-in closet were wall-to-wall strapless, low-back, low-front minidresses, skirts, and tops—all labels, all colors, all styles, all short and revealing, some exceptionally short. She had every shoe and every boot that you could find on Fifth Avenue.

I could picture any of them on her, but none of them on me. She walked around me, sizing me up, thinking, not saying anything. She went into her closet and came out with a black, lace-up back, corset top with a short crinoline skirt.

I must have had a look on my face that communicated "No way! Absolutely no way!" because she said to me, "Shut up! You're wearing it." She gave it to me and ordered, "Go put it on . . . NOW!"

I followed her command and put the outfit on. It was unlike me, but then again, I was unlike me these days. A new life can mean a completely new me. She tied the corset laces for me and fixed me in it in such a way that my cleavage was busting out of the top. I'm not a large-breasted woman, but in this dress, anyone could look like they had quite a rack. Yasmine then did my hair in a wild, curly style, letting it hang down my back and over my shoulders, partially covering one side of my face. My curls were vibrant copper and looked like fire. She did my makeup to accent my opulent green eyes and to enhance my Kewpie doll lips.

Next, she pulled out knee-high black lace-up boots and to accessorize, a black velvet choker with a crystal pendant in the shape of a teardrop. Then she put me on display in front of a full-length mirror to admire her work. A masterpiece, indeed! I saw myself, but it wasn't me. I could picture the person looking back at me on a runway, modeling the latest fashions. I turned around to see all of me and still couldn't believe it was me.

"Look at you rocking a Lolita minidress and Sergio Rossi boots," Yasmine stated.

"Sergio who?" I wondered.

"The people that I attract from Jay's club are the Fendi, Prada, and Versace crowd, so to fit in, one must know fashion. The high-end drug suppliers gravitate toward the rich, and it's my job to lure them in. You look amazing, you know."

"I know," I said. "Thanks for the makeover. I never would have done myself up like this, but I like it. I really like it. If my daughter would see me like this, she would never believe that it's me. I barely believe that it's me."

"Should we take a picture and send it to her?" Yasmine teased.

"No way. She'll think I have gone out of my mind and would want to come to see me," I explained. Then it hit me, *I won't be able to see my daughter ever again,* and the elation melted away.

"What's wrong?" Yasmine asked.

"My daughter, I won't be able to see her again," I agonized with a lump growing in my throat and tears welling in my eyes.

"You will be able to see her, for a few more years, but eventually, you will need to fake your death and leave behind your mortal family," Yasmine confirmed. "Some of us decide not to see our families again because it's harder to say goodbye each time. You don't have to make that decision now, try to perk up. Let's go have some fun," she said with a warm voice and smile.

"You're right. I have denied myself fun for a long time!" I grumbled.

Yasmine, as always, was a vision. She chose a black sequin-covered halter dress with a plunging neckline, revealing her perfectly sculpted braless cleavage. *She must never have had children*, I thought to myself. Her breasts looked too perfect for someone who breast-fed a baby or two. I then looked down at my own cleavage and realized that my breasts no longer looked like I had breast-fed a child either.

Yasmine wore ankle-length patent boots with heels so high that she looked garishly tall. She wore a collection of thin silver-band bracelets on both arms and a set of silver hoops on her neck that made me think of the Long Neck Hill Tribe in Thailand. Her hair in a wild Afro was perfect to top off her style. She could make anything work. Yasmine had been scouted by several modeling agencies, but she didn't bother with that. Living in the spotlight would bring complications to all of us immortals.

She looked extravagant and seemingly happy, but when I would catch her eyes and hold them, I could see a soul damaged by something far worse than I had ever known. Immortality can restore and enhance many physical attributes, but the inner damage can't be repaired. It seemed that only time could dilute the poison of psychological and emotional damage, and not enough time had passed for Yasmine.

"Let's go," she said. "It's a wonderful night for a walk."

"In these boots?" I questioned.

"You're immortal. You won't feel any pain from them, and you will be as agile as a cat, believe me," she assured.

I remembered in the past when I had to take off my heels after a few hours of wearing them. I walked back and forth in her apartment and said, "You're right. These boots feel no different from wearing sneakers. This is great. Maybe I can be more fashion conscious if it is going to be pain-free!" I exclaimed.

"I'll make a diva out of you yet," Yasmine declared while laughing.

We walked for at least an hour, talking small talk, people watching, and just looking around. New York was still very new to me, so Yasmine gave me the tourist treatment, showing me different landmarks as we went along. I was very aware of the looks we were getting and the attention that we attracted without provoking it. Yasmine seemed oblivious to it. I assume that she had become desensitized to the attention, but it made me uncomfortable.

As we came around a block, I heard music and saw sky lights coming from a church tower. There was a huge line up outside the church, with taxis and limos pulling up nonstop. As we walked toward it, I asked, "Is this it?"

"Yes, this is Gotham Citi. Amazing, isn't it?"

The outside still looked very much like a church. It was a small church, the kind that you would usually see in the country. It was made of light-colored brick and seemed very old. It had a beautiful circular decorated window in the center of the front face, up high above the doorway. The bell tower looked like a castle turret, and out of its windows poured sky lights of various colors. Although it had an overall rather plain architecture, the structure had many subtle decorative features like brick offset to create the impression of frames around the smaller arching windows. It was impressive to look at, and who would have thought of a nightclub in a church?

A long lineup had formed in a maze created by dark heavy-chain guard rails hung on solid wrought iron posts out front of the entrance. We walked up to the front of the line, and immediately, the doorman recognized Yasmine. He was likely a football player or boxer moonlighting, because he was enormous.

Yasmine hugged him and kissed him on the cheek, and he inquired, "Who is your striking companion?"

"Ivy," I answered, extending my hand for a handshake. He took the back of my hand to his lips, instead of a handshake, and introduced himself as Bruno.

"I'll take a handshake this time because we're just meeting, but next time, I expect at least a hug," he teased. "You need to pay for special treatment somehow," Bruno continued while winking at me. He led us to the door, and as he let us in, he said, "I'll let Jay know you're here."

"Thanks, sweetheart," Yasmine replied as we disappeared through the massive double-door entrance.

Just inside the doors was the vestibule where those who had to pay cover charge or check a coat would line up again. The music was loud here so I could only imagine what it was like inside. We were greeted by another huge guy wearing a headset. This bouncer was much less friendly, but it was understandable since he was dealing with the mayhem inside the club. After our brief introductions, he motioned for us to follow him.

As we entered the main inner doors, my gaze was immediately pulled upward, where an exquisite light show was dancing on the vaulted ceiling. Massive pillars that merged into ornate arches gave the room an air of majesty. Every accent in the hall seemed to point upward—vertical lines everywhere, pointed arches, long vertical painted windows. It was breathtaking. The decor was definitely modern but done in a way to preserve the neo-Gothic overall atmosphere. I found myself standing still, looking around lost in the beauty, and then I realized that I was lost in the crowd. Yasmine had gone ahead of me, and now I was alone.

The music filled every part of the hall. It felt like it was rising to the ceiling then floating back down. I could feel the music in my body, like my atoms were reverberating with each sound.

Everyone around me was moving in a frenzied wave. The crowd, as though joined together by invisible threads, moved together like marionettes being controlled by some invisible force. Usually, I would feel uncomfortable being surrounded by people, having complete strangers touch up against me, but here, I felt like part of the whole, like a vital piece of some intricate machine.

I'm not even sure what music was playing, but it didn't matter; it swept me up like everyone else and made me a slave to it. I was no longer in control of my movement; the energy field around us all kept us in time with every beat. It didn't matter that the person beside me was young enough to be my daughter, or that the person behind me was a punk with earrings and tattoos everywhere. We just all danced.

I'm not sure how much time passed, but eventually, Yasmine came and found me. "Hey, there you are," she said as she took my hand. "I lost you! I forgot that you're a New York nightclub virgin. It kind of sucks you in, doesn't it?"

"This place is amazing," I yelled over the music.

"Immortal hearing," she reminded me. "If you want to catch the attention of one of these delicate mortals," she indicated while grinding her body up against a very delicious-looking man, "you don't have to yell either. They'll all notice you anyway. It's part of being immortal."

Now that I wasn't as caught up in the architecture and the music, I did notice how every head turned as we walked by. I also realized how incredibly powerful the smell of mortal blood was, closed up in this room of heaving bodies. It was a good thing that I had fed the night before because, otherwise, I might have been uncontrollable.

We maneuvered through the crowd that parted like the Red Sea, down the center of the church. I had walked down the aisle of a church many years ago, contemplating my life. In this walk, I was absorbing life. I was becoming energized by the intense mortal contact. I wondered if this was the same for every immortal. Some of the people were more potently attractive than others, and their scent was hypnotizing.

I began to concentrate on the scent; I felt my body reacting to it, preparing for a feast. My thoughts became focused only on the scent, my other senses heightened and sharpened. I felt the hunger coursing through me. I closed my eyes and drew in a deep breath to track the most enticing prey, and just as I had him in my sights, Yasmine saw what was happening to me; that I was approaching the point of no return. To avoid a public spectacle that would surely ruin the evening, she grabbed my arm, hard, and dragged me through the crowd. She was strong, much stronger than me, and prevailed against my attempts to break her hold on me. We ended up in the staff bathroom, and luckily, it was empty.

Once away from the crowd, my rational processes regained control; and I pleaded, exasperated, "Is there some sort of patch or gum for this craving? I'm not sure I can cope. One minute I was doing OK, and then suddenly, my hunger took over."

"I didn't really think of how the exposure would affect you . . . Sorry," she said. "Can you handle it?" she verified, looking into my eyes for the truth from the predator within.

"I think I'm OK now," I insisted as the burning sensation of hunger was starting to wane throughout my body. We stayed in the bathroom for a while, letting my urge to kill subside.

"It is a lot at once for you, so we'll take it more slowly," Yasmine said. "The upper balcony is for Jay's VIPs. We'll go there for a while because most of the VIPs are other immortals."

We made our way to the balcony, avoiding the crowds as much as possible. I was now much more in control of my cravings but had to concentrate and remember the counting technique that Tavia taught me when I first became immortal.

"Focus . . . breathe in, one, two, three . . . breathe out, one, two, three. Breathe in one, two, three . . . and out one, two, three." I could hear Tavia's voice in my head repeating this to me.

"Are you good?" Yasmine confirmed.

"Yes," I replied, "I'm OK."

Entering the balcony, I could tell that there were other immortals there. The energy was different, the auras were potent, and I was feeling on edge. Yasmine, almost abandoning me for the fun of mingling with her peers, realized that again I was experiencing some discomfort.

"It's obvious that I have never trained an immortal before!" she declared sympathetically. "What you're feeling now is normal." When you are around other immortals, those not in your clan, your body prepares to fight. You'll become a good judge of character with exposure to new immortals. You'll develop a sense to read them, their intentions. Don't worry. You're safe here!" Yasmine expressed as she led me by the hand.

The balcony spanned the width of the building and was large enough to house the original church organ, a long bar, and some quaint seating nooks arranged for lounging and conversation. It was definitely exclusive, and 90 percent of the people there were immortals—beautiful immortals—chic, wonderfully dressed and cosmopolitan. I felt a little out of my league!

I was introduced to people as we went from table to table, meeting other immortals that my family associated with. We walked over to the balcony's edge. The wrought iron rails were fashioned like vines and allowed for an unobstructed view of the lower floor that was truly spectacular. The synchronized movement of the crowd could be seen in action from the height of the balcony. It was like tall grass with wind blowing through it, a wave of movement one way then another. It was as though I could see the energy field connecting everyone. I closed my eyes, and the music was inside me again.

At the altar, DJ Dread, his associate the Reaper, and Phantasma, the dancers, entertained with performances that blended various dance styles and martial arts to an amazing light show. I was absorbed in a performance when I heard Yasmine calling me.

"Ivy, this is Blaze and Dietrich," she announced. "They're in town for a few months."

Blaze was somewhat taller than average height and had olive skin that appeared blanched by hunger. He had droopy green eyes, but not like mine; his were a gray green and hazy. His hair was dark and messy, like someone had run their fingers through it for hours. He was a pretty boy but sporting a five o'clock shadow that made him slightly manlier, like a college boy trying to look like a man. It was difficult to tell how old he was when he was changed. I would guess that he was in his mid to late twenties.

"Bella, Ivy," he said with a Mediterranean accent as he took my hand and kissed it.

Dietrich was blond, very blond, with very pale skin. His eyes unbelievably pale and creamy blue were almost white. His contrast to Yasmine resembled chess pieces. He had a model-like face, a square jaw, and lovely lips; and his blond hair was short, with long sweeping bangs. He didn't live a long mortal life because I would say that he was barely twenty.

"Hello, Ivy," he said with some Northern European accent.

Both were dressed in casual high-end outfits, looking ready for the runway.

The four of us made small talk for a while. Both Blaze and Dietrich told us about their lives, mortal and immortal. It was especially interesting for me, because they were the first new immortals that I had spent any time with. They were as charming as they were beautiful—well traveled, well learned, and could spin wonderful tales. Yasmine was engrossed in the conversation, but I became distracted by a sensation of being watched.

I was already used to being looked at, admired by mortals, but this was different. My eyes searched for the source of my sensation and found them—eyes that locked on mine the instant that they connected. Despite the expanse separating us and the myriad of people in our path, we drifted together like we were powerless against an unknown force.

He was a stranger that I already knew. I instantly understood why his voice alone would take my breath away. Everything else in the room faded to the background, and I felt hypnotized and light. I couldn't feel my feet on the floor as they swept me to him. We drifted into each other, our bodies and lips melding into one. Everything else was nonexistent; we were alone among a crowd. All of my senses were drawn into us—no music, no words, just passion like I have never felt in my mortal life.

I kissed him with the same uncontrolled eagerness as when I made my first kill. Base animal behavior took over my entire being. The most perfect kiss, I'm not sure how long it lasted; it made me weak, but he held me close.

When our kiss ended, my eyes still closed, a warm sensation enveloped my body. He kept his hold on me, both physically and emotionally.

"What took you so long?" he whispered in my ear, creating a shiver down my spine. "I've been waiting."

"You know me?" I asked.

"You know me, don't you?" he whispered.

"Yes," I answered. "I feel like I have known you forever."

"Likewise," he affirmed. "Ivy, I've been waiting for you since I first heard your voice."

When he said my name, a wave of weakness passed through me again. My eyes still closed for fear that when I opened them, the feeling would pass . . . the moment would pass never to be felt again.

Our embrace ended, and he gently put his hands on my face. I opened my eyes and looked deeply into his. His face was so close to mine. I could feel his energy. No words were spoken, but silent vows were exchanged and two souls merged in an instant. We kissed again, this kiss as amazing and perfect as the first. I knew that he was the one.

As a mortal, I never had such a sense of assurance about anyone or anything. Having lost my father quite young, I was damaged, unable to connect fully with anyone. I feared the pain of loss. The pain I felt when my father left so suddenly created a huge hole in my heart and in my life.

In this moment, I was absolutely sure that I could trust this man entirely, that he would value me as himself since we were now part of the same whole. Was this sensation possible for mortals, or was this something else reserved only for immortals?

We stood together in an embrace, dancing slowly along with Enya's "Only Time." The sound of that song carried perfectly by the church acoustics was like nothing I had heard before.

Who can say where the road goes
Where the day flows, only time
And who can say if your love grows
As your heart chose, only time

Who can say why your heart sighs
As your love flies, only time
And who can say why your heart cries
When your love lies, only time

Who can say when the roads meet
That love might be in your heart
And who can say when the day sleeps

If the night keeps all your heart
Night keeps all your heart

Who can say if your love grows
As your heart chose
Only time
And who can say where the road goes
Where the day flows, only time

Who knows? Only time

This was our first dance, shared with everyone but felt by us alone, in our little world. We had nothing but time.

We came back to reality when we noticed Yasmine standing beside us with a strange look on her face.

"I see you've met Jay," she remarked in a tone that was both a question and a statement in one.

Jay and I looked at each other with silly grins and didn't say anything. I now had the opportunity to take a good look at him to see just who I had been kissing. With wide eyes, I scanned him from head to toe. He was close to six feet tall, with tan-colored skin, hazel eyes, a little more brown than green. His hair was dark brown, full of body, and his skin was smooth. His lips were full, and when he smiled, his teeth were so white they almost sparkled. His body was lean, and I could see that he was strong from the outline of his muscles beneath his casual black T-shirt.

"Invite your friends over. We'll grab a table," Jay told Yasmine, looking over at Blaze and Dietrich, snapping me out of my lustful, scrutinizing gaze. He led us to a secluded table, and we all took a seat. He edged his chair over to mine and sat with his hand on my thigh. Yasmine sat between the two handsome men both focused on her, competing for her attention. Little did they know that there was no competition required! She would gladly entertain both of them.

"This is a great club," Dietrich commented. "The atmosphere is quite unique. I've been in many clubs around the world, and this one has a certain *je ne sais quoi*. How long have you owned it?"

"About ten years," Jay explained. "It's been through a few transitions to make it what it is now. I'm happy with it, and now, it almost runs itself so I can enjoy it."

"Not that you are pressed for time," Blaze added.

"True," Jay said, smiling casually.

"How long have the two of you been together?" Blaze asked, looking from Jay to me.

Jay and I looked at each other at the same time as Yasmine giggled.

"We just met," Jay stated as he ran his fingers lightly along my exposed thigh, making my stomach swim with butterflies. I had never had this reaction before and hoped that it would never end. Both men looked at us with disbelief. I guess while we were locked in our own world, we were making a spectacle of ourselves.

Yasmine cut in, questioning Blaze and Dietrich, "What brought you to Gotham Citi tonight?"

"Are you kidding?" Blaze responded fervently. "This place is known by immortals everywhere. It's the place to go if you are in New York."

"Does it measure up to your expectations?" I inquired.

"Absolutely!" Blaze answered, and Dietrich concurred with a nod of his head.

"Do I detect a Mediterranean accent?" Jay asked Blaze.

"Yes, I'm from southern Italy. Blaze, of course, is not my birth name. My name is Benito Fuoco."

"Fuoco . . . fire. I see where Blaze comes from," Jay said.

"Parla l'Italiano?" Blaze asked Jay.

"Si, una delle mie tante lingue," Jay replied.

"Impressionante," Blaze added.

I looked at Jay, surprised.

"I speak many languages," Jay acknowledged. "I've been around a long time and lived in a lot of places."

Jay looked at Dietrich and said, "Wo kommst du her?"

"Norddeutschland," Dietrich answered.

"Your name gave you away. By your looks, I would have guessed Sweden," Jay observed.

"How about the rest of us?" Yasmine requested.

"Ah, yes, sorry. Dietrich is from northern Germany," Jay explained. "When we have guests from abroad, I like to make them feel at home. How best to do that but to speak their language," he added.

"We newborns are not as sophisticated as you old men," Yasmine teased.

"Old men?" Jay said, raising one eyebrow.

"Our friend Dietrich is pushing one fifty, and Blaze is more your age, Jay," Yasmine continued.

I spoke up because my curiosity was now peaked. "How old are you, Jay?" I prodded.

"I'm thirty-seven," he stated with a grin.

"Really," I said and turned my gaze to Blaze. "How old are you, Blaze?" I repeated.

Immediately, Jay whispered to Blaze, "Don't burn me . . . no pun intended. I just met her. She might get turned off if she knows my real age."

"From the way she is looking at you, I don't think that is a concern," Yasmine commented. She leaned over to me and whispered in my ear, "He's three hundredish," not that whispering is effective for immortals.

"Is that all?" I said. "That's nothing compared with Tavia and Anton! You're practically a kid."

Just then, the lighting changed, and DJ Dread spoke. "We have a treat tonight. Some of my very special friends are here and will grace us with one of their shows. Please put 'em together for the SuicideGirls!" And the crowd went crazy.

I had no idea what or who were the SuicideGirls.

Jay said, "We should watch this. They're friends of mine, and they'll want some feedback on this new performance."

We got up and walked over to the balcony railing. I had no idea what to expect. The lights went out, and one small spotlight lit up center stage. A woman dressed in an outfit that reminded me of Little Miss Muffet sat quietly on a stool. The place went completely silent.

They put on a risqué burlesque rendition of *The Brothers Grimm* story "The Wolf and the Seven Little Kids."

I looked over at Yasmine, somewhat shocked. I hadn't seen this kind of show before.

"From the look on your face, I guess you've never seen them," Yasmine observed.

"Never heard of them . . . what are the SuicideGirls?" I inquired.

"They're a community that celebrates alternative beauty and culture," Yasmine described. "They have a Website with worldwide members and a large number of followers. Their image is non-mainstream, wild hair color, piercings, tattoos, and general shock and awe."

Jay added, "They've been performing their burlesque shows here for a few years. In my opinion, they're the next big thing since the Club Kids of the late eighties, early nineties."

"I'm the daughter of a conservative judge . . . can't say that I've ever heard about them or even had an inkling that a group like this would exist!" I said. "I guess I'm pretty green as far as alternative culture goes."

The performers were adorned with tattoos and piercings all over their bodies and with wild hair, true to their image.

"Are all their tattoos real?" I asked.

"Absolutely!" Yasmine asserted as she lifted her skirt to reveal a tattoo of a Celtic cross that she had on her upper thigh. "This is as inked as I'll get!"

"Why a Celtic cross?" I probed.

"Its meaning is ambiguous, but one of the interpretations is eternity," she answered. "Eternity defines me now."

We went back to our table, and in a short time, some of the SuicideGirls joined us. We had interesting conversations, and I understood a bit more about why their movement was growing. They promoted acceptance with nonmainstream, challenging the norms and expectation of society, especially for women. It was empowering.

Blaze and Dietrich flirted with the Girls incessantly as we continued to talk; and eventually, despite the strong allure of immortal charm, they moved on to visit other guests.

Blaze remarked, "Sitting with them made me thirsty. Where can a guy get a drink?"

"Not in or around the club," Jay cautioned.

"Let me take you out for a drink, gentlemen," Yasmine offered. "I hope you don't mind our standards."

"What do you mean by your standards?" Dietrich questioned.

"We only hunt criminals," Yasmine explained.

"Blood is blood," Blaze noted. "Let's get out of here!"

The three of them left together, Yasmine arm in arm with both of them. Jay and I sat quietly for a couple of minutes.

"We sat here for a couple of hours and didn't drink anything, kept the same glasses in front of us most of the night," I said to Jay. "Don't the mortals notice and wonder?"

Jay answered, "I suppose some might, but generally, they're concentrating on their own lives, what they're going to drink, who's checking them out, who they're going to pick up. The only ones who may notice are the bartenders and servers. That's why I have my immortal guests come up here. The few people who work up here know about me, about us, about immortals."

I was surprised and asked, "I thought we couldn't tell any mortals about us."

"I have a few people here that I trust with that knowledge, just like Magnus and Justus have a few cops that they trust with it," he commented. "Besides, those who do know, I'm sure, are afraid enough that they wouldn't say anything. I made sure to let them know how easy it is for me to kill a mortal."

He looked at me with a smile, kissed me gently, and said, "I'll be right back. I have to help close up."

When he left, I moved to his seat. I could still smell his scent that lingered there, and it comforted me. From where I sat, I could see him at the bar, working with his employees to get the night's business wrapped up. I just stared. He mesmerized me.

As I looked at him, he looked at me, smiled, and winked. The white of his teeth and eyes gleamed in contrast with his dark features. Again, the butterflies and a sensation of weakness rushed through me. I couldn't stop the feeling, even if I wanted to, but I definitely didn't want to stop it. When he left the balcony and blew me a kiss, my mind wandered. I replayed the evening in my mind, lingering on the sensation of our first kiss. I closed my eyes to fully relive that moment again. The kiss went right through my body again. Then, as his scent became stronger, I felt my hair gently lift off my neck and the sensation of light kisses on my neck.

He whispered, "Let's get out of here," which sent a shiver down my spine right to my toes. He took me by the hand and led me out.

It seemed that despite his age and experience, he had a difficult time controlling his urges. Before we reached the door to leave the building, he pushed me up against the wall and kissed me so urgently that I lost my breath and became weak again. I didn't want it to stop, our hands exploring each other.

Jay then got a hold of himself and said, "Sorry." I couldn't speak but thought to myself, *Sorry . . . sorry for what? I would have you right here, right now, if that's what you wanted.* He took me by the hand again, and in silence, we walked to his car.

It was a red 1967 Mustang. I knew this because he and Blaze discussed cars at one point in the evening. It was a sexy car, although I knew nothing about cars to really be a judge. He opened the door for me. Mike, my ex-husband, had never done this for me, even when I was in labor for our daughter Ana. How nice it was to feel important and cherished. He got in and just sat there for a moment.

Jay looked at me, which triggered an uncontrollable reaction in me. Before I knew what was going on, I was on top of him, fingers in his hair, kissing him with a wildness that was impossible to tame. He had his hand on my back, pulling me close to him. He took hold of my wrists and pushed them up against the ceiling of the car, not letting me kiss him or touch him.

"Wait!" he ordered. "You're making this impossible. I don't have much control left in me. Be good . . . get back in your seat and keep your hands and your lips to yourself."

Like a scolded child, I listened and got back in my seat and put on the seat belt as an extra precaution, not against an accident, but to keep me off him. Not that a seat belt could really do that. I could rip the bolt from the car frame if I really wanted to. But with the belt on, I would have some restraint, hopefully.

He put on the radio as a distraction. The perfect song came on, "Whenever You're Near Me" by *Ace of Base*, and I started to sing along with it.

Whenever you're near me
I give you everything I have
Someone to believe in
When things are good and when they're bad
You know how to please me
Ooh, like nobody can
Someone to believe in
Be my love and be my friend

When every race is run and the day is closing in
I feel the need to hold you
Let the night begin
Come softly to me
Show me why

Whenever you're near me
I give you everything I have
Someone to believe in
When things are good and when they're bad
You know how to please me
Ooh, like nobody can
Someone to believe in
Be my love and be my friend

I cannot wait to feel
The beating of your heart
The days are long
They're just keeping us apart
Come softly to me
Show me why

Whenever you're near me
I give you everything I have
Someone to believe in
When things are good and when they're bad
You know how to please me
Oooh, like nobody can
Someone to believe in
Be my love and be my friend

Whenever you're near me
Love is the reason
We can feel this way inside
Oh, oh
Turning the world around and making us wild
Love is the music

Beating in our hearts tonight
Oh, oh, lighting the way
To take us deeper inside

Whenever you're, whenever you're near me
I give you everything I have
Someone to believe in
When things are good and when they're bad
You know how to please me
Oooh, like nobody can
Someone to believe in
Be my love and be my friend

I looked over at him, conveying the message without words that this song said what I wanted to say. Even though we just met, I knew it was perfect. He took my hand, and we drove the rest of the way in silence. Luckily, he lived very close to the club. We made it back to his place in no time.

My seat belt was off in a flash, and he was out of the car in an instant. It was like he was running away from me. In a blink, he was at the parking level elevator. I was there right behind him. The door opened, and we both stepped in. He stood on one side of the elevator and me on the other. No sooner had the doors closed than we met in the middle mauling each other. The elevator stopped at the main level, and we pulled away from each other. A few people got in. The ride up to the thirty-seventh floor seemed like an eternity.

When we stepped out of the elevator, he took my hand and led me down the hall, completely in control. 3711 was his unit number. He fumbled with his keys, and I thought to myself, *Just break the door down. You can fix it later*. Finally the door was opened. As he shut it, I backed away out of his reach, this time being the coy one. He turned to me, and we just looked at each other for a long while. With every moment that we just stood there, my breathing became more and more labored. He walked to me slowly, took my long hair in one hand, and put the other hand on the small of my back. Gently pulling my hair, forcing my head back, he kissed my neck. His lips were perfect, full, soft. His kisses were just right, light and tantalizing. His touch and grip were firm but gentle. I was completely taken. He owned me in that moment.

Jay then picked me up and carried me off to his bedroom. He laid me on the bed then stepped back to look at me. He took off his shirt, revealing a well-sculpted, smooth upper body, like that of an Olympic swimmer. I wanted to touch his skin. He approached the bed and took off my boots, running his hands on the exposed skin of my legs. He climbed on top of me but kept his body from touching me. He peered into my eyes. I touched his naked arms and chest, while he closed his eyes, being drawn into my touch. It was like torture, having him so near me but not touching me.

He took my arms, held them above my head, and pressed them into the bed. He kissed my eyes to make me close them then whispered in my ear to keep my eyes closed. He lightly kissed my neck and ran his tongue up to my earlobe. His breath in my ear made me shiver. I tried to move my arms so that I could touch him, but he held them tighter and whispered, "No touching, not yet. You're too eager. Promise to keep your arms above your head?"

I obliged and replied, "Yes, I promise," which was going to be difficult for me. I had not been intimate with a man in a very long time, and I really wanted to feel his body and touch him.

He slid off me. I still had my eyes closed because he commanded me to, and I kept my arms up as requested. He put his hands on my waist and eased off my skirt. His hand running over my hips made me gasp. He kissed my stomach and my waist, my hips driving me out of my mind with lust. He climbed back on top of me, slowly running his fingers up my arms that were still stretched out above my head. Although my eyes weren't open, I knew that he was looking at me, into me. I could feel that his lips were just above mine. I could feel his breath, getting more rapid as he held his lips just out of reach.

"You're beautiful," he said, his lips just brushing against mine.

"I want you so badly," I whispered.

"I know," he said with his lips so close I could almost feel them. "I love you," he told me, and that was it. The anticipation was too much for me. I thought I was going to pass out, but he kissed me, bringing me back to him. I touched him and felt his skin on mine, and it was heavenly. I was lost in the moment when suddenly I felt a sensation that was both thrilling and alarming at the same time. Jay bit me and for a brief moment was drinking from me. It gave me a strange sensation that was erotic in a different way from kissing. I guess I must have had a shocked look on my face because he moved away from me, and I reached for the small puncture wounds on my neck. It wasn't bleeding but had a warm tingly sensation.

He didn't say anything but reached for me, leading me to sit up then to kneel on the bed beside him. He kissed me again, holding me tight to him, which gave me a sense of reassurance. He pulled away from me briefly and whispered, "Try it." I kissed his neck, his scent intensifying as we became more and more intimate. It seemed like a normal transition from kissing to feeling his blood enter me. It was enthralling, a mix of the regular physical sensations of lust with the intensity of satisfying bloodlust.

The next several hours were a frenzy of lips, tongues, hands, bodies, and blood together in lust, passion, and love. It was not like anything I had ever experienced in my mortal life. We were tireless; and each sensation, each part of my body touched, kissed, and bitten, brought me to the edge of sanity. We gasped, screamed, and writhed uncontrollably. If being immortal meant an eternity of this, I was all for it.

Eventually, we needed some rest, and by this time, the sun was up. I had no idea how much time had passed. My body felt pleasantly exhausted with the after feelings of intense muscular exertion. I was surprised that my new supernatural body could be brought to this extent of fatigue.

We lay together in silence for quite some time. Jay spoke first and said, "I'm exhausted . . . and hungry. I have never in my three hundred years pushed myself to this level of physical exertion." He looked at me smiling.

"This is a good thing?" I confirmed only half questioning because I knew the answer already. He didn't answer in words. Instead, he kissed me lovingly.

"I'm going to have to hunt tonight," he said. "Come with me."

"I should check in with Tavia," I mentioned. "It feels like she is my mother, and I must get her blessing to be with you."

"Yeah, that's normal," Jay assured. "She is your maker. That's how it should feel. There should be a special bond between you."

I got up out of bed, looked at myself in a mirror, and noticed that my body had several puncture wounds all over. I looked back at him, and he said, "Me too!" as he pulled back the sheets, showing me what I had done to him.

"They'll be gone in a few hours," he assured me.

I threw on a robe of his and walked through his place. He lived in a high-rise condo with a very open concept. It was a corner unit, and both outside walls had floor-to-ceiling windows, allowing the sunlight in, creating a warm glow in the room. The furnishings were very sparse and simple. The style was black and white, boxy, a very modern look. My favorite piece was a lounge chair that was placed by one of the large windows. I lay back in it and let the rays of the sun fall upon me as I took in the view of the amazing Manhattan skyline. It was a wonderful feeling. I could have the heat of the sun on me without the burn and skin rashes that I would get outside. It was the next best thing to sunbathing in full outdoor sun.

It was early afternoon; I was filled with the warmth of love but famished for blood. Jay came to me and announced, "Your bath awaits."

In the bathroom, there was an immense spa tub already bubbling with warm water. The tub was also black, rectangular, and set in the center of a large white room. The minimalist concept continued in this room. There was a rectangular black box mounted on the wall. As I walked over to it, I saw that it was a sink with a motion sensor faucet. There were rectangular mirrors on the wall, and the floor was speckled black-and-white tile. There was a large shower stall, and the floor was heated, everywhere I walked.

We both climbed into the tub and relaxed. Conversation came easily. Jay told me about his club. He said that he opened it in a church for the controversy. In his many years, he experienced firsthand the results of clashing religion and religious beliefs. He studied and practiced a few of the most common world faiths only to be left unfulfilled. He decided to create a place of gathering for those who embraced hedonism, and a church seemed appropriate.

"Why the name Gotham Citi?" I queried.

He thought for a moment and answered, "Most people think it's because of *Batman*, but really, it's because New York was referred to as Gotham City early in the nineteenth century by the writer Washington Irving. He published a magazine of sorts entitled *Salmagundi* in which he made fun of New York's culture and politics. He supposedly based the name on his view of the people from Gotham, Nottinghamshire, in England—simpletons. I don't see the people who come to my Gotham as simple but as people who challenge the mainstream.

"When Gotham Citi first opened, there were protests increasing the exposure in the media, but eventually, the hype died down. Now, the club is what I want it to be. The majority of the people are regulars interspersed with a few newcomers. That's how I like it. You know it's also a haven for significant drug trade, right?"

I nodded to indicate that I knew this. Drug trade is what Jay fed off of, literally. He didn't start into the club life to create a breeding ground for drug dealers, but it ended up being a fringe benefit.

Jay continued, "I feel alive in the club. The music, the energy, and the people make me feel alive. After being immortal for so many years, I long to have the mortal feeling of life again. The club is how I get this feeling—as close to being alive as I can remember." He was very solemn as he talked about the desire to feel alive. A deep yearning for something he could never have. I could see the aching in his eyes, in his being, when he spoke of it.

"Tell me about the people we are going to hunt tonight," I requested both to distract him from his melancholy and because it helped me to hear of the crimes committed by our prey. I still had unresolved feelings about killing, and knowing how much they deserved death eased my conscience a little bit.

"There's an Asian drug gang that's been fairly active lately," Jay explained. "They've killed rival gang members, which doesn't bother me, but they've also killed the family of a traitor in their organization, including his children. I never should have let it get to that," he finished, looking away from me.

"You can't anticipate everything that these thugs will do," I told Jay, but that didn't help him feel any better.

"With all my experience, I should have trusted my own instincts, but I didn't," he said disparagingly.

I knew that there would be no placating him on this, and I also knew that he didn't want to be absolved.

After a few minutes, alone with his thoughts, he asked me, "Are you able to handle a kill by yourself?"

"Yes, my problem is that I tend to get overzealous with my kills," I admitted. "You may find it difficult to control me when I'm in the zone. I get very agitated because when I kill them, I can see what they've done, and what I see enrages me."

"What do you mean by you see what they've done?" he probed.

"Well, when I'm feeding from them," I started, "until their last heartbeat, I can see in my mind their thoughts. It's like watching a high-speed video or slideshow!"

"Wow," Jay said. "I've heard of this phenomenon but never met anyone who experienced it. You have a very special and unusual gift," he finished.

"It doesn't feel special to me!" I exclaimed with vexation. "Without fail, so far, they all know why they're being executed. They all review their bad deeds in their dying moments, and they also have flashes of evil that was done to them in their lives. I get very torn because they've all had bad life experiences that I have to relive with them.

"Evil begets evil!" Jay remarked.

"A few of them communicated thankfulness with their thoughts. Grateful to have their lives ended, their pain ended," I added.

"From what I know," Jay expressed, "this ability comes from a deep connection with others, with their humanity, their souls. It causes a great dilemma for immortals that choose to kill innocents. For you, killing only those that deserve it hopefully makes it less agonizing?"

"My disdain for the acts they committed is strong enough, but I have to admit that I wish the evil could have been stopped in their lives. Would they have become evil, if they had experienced a better life?" I speculated.

"A question that has no answer," he replied.

"Do you know what most of them see in their last moments?" I asked. "Their mother, and if not their mother, then they see someone else in their lives that showed them love. At that moment, I feel their peace."

"Wow, that's both a burden and a blessing," Jay said as he pulled me close to hold me.

For a long while, he held me in the warm bubbling water. Both of our preoccupied minds and souls needed a distraction from the depths they had reached. Blood lust was still strong in both of us, and our physical lust awoke, rising to the same intensity as the bloodlust. We made love again, a welcomed diversion from our thoughts, our thirst, and our inner torment.

Evening fell, and it was time for Jay to get to the club. For me, there was first a stop at home, or that place that had become home. I needed to talk to Tavia about what had transpired in the past twenty-four hours.

When I arrived, everyone was there, deep in discussion. I slipped into the dining room and took my seat between Tavia and Yasmine.

The conversation stopped briefly for everyone to acknowledge me. Yasmine winked at me because she knew where and with whom I spent the night. She gave me this questioning look like a high school girl, in class, looking for the scoop.

I looked away, and Justus was looking at me weird too, so I looked away from him. I decided to focus on Anton who was talking about a new development in the College Rapist case.

I had been listening from up the block, and I was already fairly up to speed with the conversation.

"Do you know what we are talking about?" Anton asked, looking at me inquisitively.

"Yes," I acknowledged. "Last night, there was an assault, and the victim felt someone was watching. The College Rapist might have an accomplice!"

"This changes everything," Helene said.

"Yeah . . . we'll have to change our methods, and so will the cops," continued Justus.

"Speaking of the cops," Ethan interrupted, "what have they got to say about all of this?"

"We'll know soon," Justus noted. "O'Shea will be calling us any minute.

"How are we changing our strategy with this new information?" Tavia questioned, looking around the table.

"Let's see what O'Shea has before we go off on a tangent," Anton advised.

Just then, the call came in.

"Captain O'Shea," Justus announced, "you have our attention." We all stopped our conversations and listened intently.

"We have some new developments," O'Shea began, "that I'm sure you heard about already . . . damn media."

Justus responded with "We heard, but what else is there to know?"

O'Shea clarified, "She's a nineteen-year-old, lives on campus, and was coming back from a house party. He grabbed her close to her dorm building. The rest of the MO was the same, except she felt like someone else was there."

"There how?" Justus probed.

"She said like they were being watched," O'Shea described, "like it was a performance for someone."

"A house party," Ethan commented, thinking out loud, "this is a deviation from the usual MO, why?"

"We have yet to question her thoroughly. She's in the hospital, and Dunn is on her way over there to get more information," O'Shea stated.

"Any evidence left behind? Can she identify him?" Justus questioned.

"We should be so lucky," O'Shea mumbled feeling denigrated. "We have a task force meeting tomorrow to review all of it. Justus and Magnus, I assume you will be there?"

"Wouldn't miss it," Magnus replied eagerly.

As O'Shea left the conversation, everyone sat in silence, pondering the new developments.

"Someone watching?" Justus spoke up.

"Could this have been the work of a pair all along?" Magnus added. "Could we all have missed something this big?"

Ethan, pensive, asserted, "No, I don't think so. I think this is new, but who would join him and why?"

"How do two sexual deviants find each other, generally?" Helene pondered.

"Well," Ethan started, "there are fetish clubs, swingers clubs, strip clubs, online . . . I wouldn't think it's that difficult to find someone willing to try something a little off side."

"This is still just speculation," Justus suggested, "until we get more details from the victim. I'm intrigued at why a house party and not a bar this time. Was the perpetrator at the house party? And if so, then he's probably a student at the university."

"The victim might have lied about where she was because she is underage?" Helene proposed.

"That too will only come out when Dunn questions her," Magnus cut in. "I think we're spinning our wheels here. We'll get the information we need at tomorrow's task force meeting, for tonight, let's keep the streets clean as best we can!"

We all dispersed, and Yasmine followed me to my room, determined to find out about my night.

"What happened last night?" Yasmine urged.

"What about you?" I returned.

"Blaze, Dietrich, and I hunted, and then I went back to their hotel with them. I'm spent today!" she confessed with a wink as she fell back on my bed.

"Is sex with immortals always amazing?" I sighed.

"Like with mortals, they all differ in technique and experience, but yes, it is always better," Yasmine replied contented. "Because our senses are heightened, we can feel everything much more intensely. Since our bodies are stronger and more vital, we can push ourselves to limits that a mortal body would never be able to reach."

We lay on my bed like two teenagers recounting our first time.

"Blaze and Dietrich were insatiable," Yasmine detailed. "The older immortals are always better," she declared and rolled over on my bed, looking at the ceiling, running the night through her mind.

Beaming with satisfaction, she continued, "Hunting together was our foreplay. The chase and the taunting were like a sensual dance. They were cunning and merciless with their kills. They did enjoy the element of hunting criminals and said that it made the meal more like a delicacy.

"The sex was like sugar and spice. Dietrich was the sugar, and Blaze was the spice. I've had threesomes before, but this one was definitely one to remember! It was a very pleasing game of twister . . . half the time I didn't know who was where doing what," she finished.

Yasmine oozed with confidence and was so comfortable with herself, with lust and with sexuality that nothing seemed to faze her. I doubted that there was anything she hadn't tried. This is one of the ways that she and Magnus were kindred spirits, both adventurous in all aspects of life.

We both lay silent, briefly, then Yasmine spoke, "I'm definitely going to see them again. What about you?" she asked again.

Feeling a little awkward and shy, I covered my face. I thought I would blush just thinking about my night. I wasn't used to having girl friends to talk to. In my mortal life, I spent most of my time alone with my daughter. I certainly never had stories like the one I had now to tell.

Yasmine was peering at me . . . into me, and said, "I would ask Jay, but he is not the kiss-and-tell type. I've always wondered what he would be like." She winked at me again. It made me feel more awkward knowing that Jay and Yasmine were close, but from her comment, I could surmise that they had never been intimate.

"Common, spill it," she ordered with a manner that forced compliance.

"OK, first, I don't even know what happened to me at the bar," I explained, lying on my back, staring at the white ceiling.

"One minute I was just looking around, and then the next, I was making out with some stranger, but he wasn't a stranger," I asserted. "It was like time stood still . . . everything around us disappeared, and the only thing I could see, hear, touch, and feel was him." I covered my face again out of habit, not having the same confidence and openness as Yasmine.

"I remember that our eyes locked on to each other's, and then the rest was a blur until I felt the most incredible kiss I had ever shared in my life," I continued.

"We were mauling each other as though nobody else was around . . . me, the reserved, shy, timid, loner, grabbing some guy's ass in the middle of a crowd? I don't know what came over me!" I exclaimed.

Running it all through my mind, I lay silent, still looking at the ceiling.

Rolling over, I looked at Yasmine and wondered, "Is it the immortal thing that made me so weird?"

Pausing briefly to look me over, Yasmine said, "No, I don't think that it is the immortal thing that made you behave the way you did."

I lay there staring at Yasmine, both of us in silence.

"I think I'm in love with him," I said feebly, like I was forced to against my will.

"I know you are," she said.

"This sort of thing doesn't happen to me," I said.

"I don't fall in love with a stranger I don't go home with strangers. I don't let my emotions take over my reason!" I admitted bewildered.

Rolling over on my back, I lay in silence with the vision of Jay in my head and the sound of his whisper in my ear. Butterflies filled my stomach again, and a wave of weakness flowed over my entire body. It was a good thing that I was lying down because I may have withered to the floor, otherwise.

I closed my eyes and ran over in my mind the sensual details of my night with Jay, in his apartment, in his bed. My heart fluttered, and I sighed with delight.

"Tell me more about it?" Yasmine probed.

I rolled over to look at Yasmine and described, "It was incredible." A smile took over my lips, my entire face.

"Jay and I were instantaneously joined by some force that I can't explain. I can still feel him now," I acknowledged as I touched myself to feel grounded in the here and now. "It is so cliché, but it was love at first sight for me. I never felt this as a mortal. That's why I think it is an effect of being immortal. The feelings are so much stronger than they have ever been for me. When he touched me, I felt weak and faint. When he spoke to me, I shivered and felt like I had electricity running through my entire body. Thinking about him now makes me feel the same," I admitted.

"I swear that my body doesn't even belong to me. It has been taken hostage by something, someone," I said, feeling overwhelmed.

"There's only one thing that can explain what's happening to you," Yasmine suggested. "It's love, bonding, and yes, it is stronger than mortal love and comes only once, when you have met your mate, your eternal mate."

"You know, like Tavia and Anton, Helene and Ethan," Yasmine added. "They're weird with each other all the time. I asked them once how they knew that they had met the right one. Both described the same thing . . . that when you meet that person you know, you know it with every molecule in your body. Even if you don't understand it, you can't stop it. Imagine Ethan not being able to explain some rational or physiological reason for why he was uncontrollably drawn to Helene?" Yasmine stated with a laugh.

"Do you hope to find someone special?" I asked her intently.

"No, I think that I'm not sending eternal mate vibes out for anyone to pick up on at this point," she claimed.

"I wouldn't have thought that I was sending out vibes of that sort either," I responded.

"You're definitely mate material," Yasmine said. "I, on the other hand, have too many wild oats to sow, although they tell me when it happens, you have no control over it. Until then, I'm going to have as much fun as possible!" Yasmine declared with assertiveness.

I lifted my shirt to show Yasmine the very faint bite marks that were still on my skin from making love. She showed me hers.

"I was like a savage in bed," I told her, "from what I can remember. I was somewhat in a trance and completely at the mercy of my hormones or whatever it is that controls me now."

"What's next?" Yasmine demanded.

"He wants me to live with him . . . I have to speak with Tavia about it," I replied tentatively.

"Tavia understands the depth of mate connection, so I doubt there will be any issue with the decision you make," Yasmine asserted. "I'm assuming that your decision is to live with him, right?"

"The last time I had this decision to make, I was pregnant and eighteen! Then I did it out of necessity. This time, I would like to say that I am making a rational, conscious choice, but I would be lying," I admitted.

"Of course, I'm going to live with him. I couldn't picture anything else. But it isn't a rational, conscious decision though . . . It is 100 percent irrational, subconscious, and based on something I don't understand at all. With all of that said, I know it is the best decision I have ever made.

"Has Jay been with many other immortals? Or mortals?" I inquired hesitantly.

"Not since I've known him, but that's not that long," Yasmine acknowledged. "He concentrates on the club and on making drug trade connections. He feeds the least of all of us . . . but that will change, if you're going to be using up as much of his energy!" she teased.

If I could blush, I would have because I knew that I intended to use up as much of his energy as I could!

We sat in my room for at least another hour talking about love, sex, and lust, giggling like a couple of teenagers. Yasmine still wouldn't give up much about her past, always evasive when I tried to slip in a question.

Our school girl chat ended when there was a knock at the door. It was Tavia.

"Look at the two of you," Tavia said. "Rosy cheeks, giddy, acting like sixteen-year-olds ready to sneak out to see your secret boyfriends."

"I'm guessing my boyfriend isn't secret?" I said bashfully, looking at Tavia for a reaction.

"No, there's no secret. You can't really keep secrets from immortals . . . unless you don't talk at all," Tavia replied. "Not that any of us were eavesdropping, but it was hard to resist the temptation to find out a little about where you were last night."

"We never have to guess what Yasmine has been up to. She always shares so eagerly!" Tavia declared with a sly look at Yasmine.

"You old married couples live vicariously through me . . . you know it!" Yasmine jibed.

"And when you and Magnus decide to take advantage of your 'friends with benefits' relationship, we have no choice but to hear it and hear about it," Tavia said while rolling her eyes.

"You're just jealous that you don't have as much fun as I do," Yasmine teased with a wink as she got up to walk away.

I knew they were joking with each other, but I could see in Yasmine's eyes that really she was the jealous one. Despite her portrayal of being free and easy, she longed for a connection with someone so deep that it was ingrained and everlasting.

Yasmine left the room, leaving Tavia and I alone, and closed the door. Not that this would matter . . . Anyone who wanted to hear our conversation could. Tavia looked at me silently for a while, like a mother looking at a daughter. She reached for my hair and pushed it back from my face. We took each other's hand, and she said, "I know I don't have to ask you if you are sure, because I know that you are. I remember the feeling. I remember like it was yesterday when I met Anton," she said with a smile.

We continued to hold hands, and I recalled my wedding day with Mike. My mother, unaffectionate, helped me to fasten my dress over my pregnant belly. All she told me was "Mike is smart and has a great future in law. You couldn't do any better."

Drawing me back to the present, Tavia noted, "It's quite incredible that you have found your mate this quickly in your immortal life. Most of us have to travel the globe and through decades or centuries to find the one. I am infinitely happy for you and Jay. He has waited very long for someone. I thought he had given up hope."

Smiling, a smile that seemed permanently painted on my face, I hugged Tavia and said, "Thanks."

"You'll always have a home here," Tavia whispered to me while she held me in a motherly embrace.

Once we let go of each other, we both knew that it was definite. All I had to do was tell the others and pack the few things that I had. She left me alone, and I lay on my bed. My exhausted body needed rest. I drifted and had visions of Jay, feeling the glow and tingle of happiness throughout my entire body.

After a brief catnap, I woke feeling wonderful. I showered, packed my things, and psyched myself up to say goodbye to my family. Tentatively, I made my way down to the garden level where Tavia and Anton were lounging. Tavia smiled, and Anton winked; I knew nothing more had to be said to either of them. I continued on to face my biggest challenge since speaking with Tavia. I silently descended the basement stairs and snuck up on Justus and Magnus, which, of course, is impossible. As I reached Justus, I put my arms around him and begged, "Forgive me?" And I kissed his cheek.

He sat motionless for a moment and replied, "Just when I had a sister again."

"You still have a sister. You'll always have a sister," I affirmed.

Of course, he wasn't really trying to make me feel bad. He was just playing with me. Justus stood up, picked me up, giving me the strongest hug I had ever had, then put me down gently on my feet. He held my face in his hands and looked into my eyes for a moment then kissed my forehead and said, "I am truly happy for you, and Jay is a great guy."

Magnus turned to look at me and grumbled, "Get out of here!" And he smiled.

I left the house for the last time as a resident and would only come back as guest.

CHAPTER SEVEN

Partners in Crime

Justus and Magnus arrived at the precinct for a task force meeting and were greeted by Captain O'Shea. Sitting in the cold white meeting room was an assortment of blues and suits, waiting for a briefing from Dunn, Johnson, and O'Shea, the task force leaders.

There was a collection of photos on a large portable whiteboard with details about time, location, and particulars for each College Rapist attack. There were seven photos, seven lives that would never be the same again, each victim young, with hope in their eyes, happy smiles, and brilliant faces with promise of great futures ahead. For each photo, there was a matching file displayed on the table in front of the whiteboard. Each file detailed the moment where life changed forever for each victim, photos showing their injuries, their pain, and notes outlining their horrifying ordeal.

For some in the room, this was business as usual; for others, it was a first. The task force brought together the expertise of many, including seasoned investigators, beat cops, and an FBI profiler specialized in team sexual assaults. Everyone had a part to play in the plan to find and apprehend the College Rapist.

"We're all here, so let's get this started," Johnson began. "As you all know, this latest incident introduces a possible change in MO. The College Rapist, which we'll refer to from here on out as CR, has possibly engaged a partner in his activity."

"The latest victim, although not a hundred percent sure, described a feeling that someone was watching," Dunn explained. "She said that as she was in a semiconscious state, after having her head pounded against the ground, she believed she heard another voice. This alleged person did not participate in the attack, at least while the victim was conscious."

"She heard another voice?" reiterated one of the task force members. "It could have been the first responders she heard, with blurry timelines."

"Yes," acknowledged Dunn, "but we have to take the victims 'feeling of being watched' into consideration along with the voice and investigate the possibility to the fullest. She couldn't describe anything in particular about the voice, unfortunately, but did say that throughout the assault, she felt like CR was performing for someone. She didn't see him, because like other attacks, she was blitzed from behind and bound, but there was a sensation of putting on a show."

"Let's review the first six CR attacks to make sure everyone is up to speed," insisted O'Shea.

He skipped over the first photo, and while pointing at the second photo on the board of an attractive young woman with light brown, long straight hair, a beaming smile displaying perfect teeth, O'Shea outlined the first attack of the series that was investigated.

Flipping open the file, he began. "This offense occurred on June 25. The victim, a twenty-two-year-old student, was out in the college district at two clubs that night. She was assaulted in the Third Avenue Station. Her alcohol level was point one six, so she had only a sketchy recollection of the incident and what preceded it.

"The victim and her friend were on the subway together. Both remembered noticing a blond guy on the train, in the same car. He stood out because he was attractive. The victim's friend thought she had seen him in one of the bars that night. The victim left the train at Third Avenue, and her friend continued on to First Avenue.

"The man followed the victim off the train, and the notes indicate that she felt relieved that she wasn't alone in the station. She didn't fear him," O'Shea described and paused to collect his thoughts.

"He is attractive, frequents the same bars as his victims, and doesn't raise any suspicions or concerns in them," Justus paraphrased while writing down some point form notes.

"That's part of the current profile," acknowledged O'Shea, then he continued with the account of the subway victim's story. "The subway platform was deserted, besides the two of them, the victim described. Her instincts and reaction time were compromised from the alcohol, and she didn't suspect him of being a threat. The victim doesn't remember much of the assault. The witness who found her and the EMS responders relayed the details of the scene. She was unconscious when discovered, lying in vomit with a large contusion on her forehead. Her hands were bound with a tie wrap, and there was a sock on the ground close to her face. The attacker must have knocked her unconscious by driving her head into the floor.

"At the time, the MO had no connection to any other case that we were working. We canvassed the bars, but the only description we had was that he was an attractive white male with blond hair. Unfortunately, we didn't have any success in finding leads. There was no DNA evidence from the attacker, so it was also a dead end," O'Shea concluded and pulled the gory photos from the file, displaying them so all could see the scene and the victims' injuries.

Everyone sat in silence, repulsed by the photos, pondering this initial data, making connections in their minds to other evidence that came up since that first, or thought to be first, assault by the serial rapist.

"Has she been interviewed again since the initial evidence was gathered?" Magnus inquired, breaking the dead silence.

Through the sound of shuffling papers, O'Shea said, "Let me see . . . no, she hasn't been contacted again . . . not yet anyway."

O'Shea, slightly uncomfortable, cleared his throat, pointed to the third photo—a dark-haired beauty with sparkling black eyes—and began to describe the next attack in the series. "About a month after the subway attack, on July 21, a twenty-three-year-old student walking through Washington Square Park was assaulted. She was pushed down from behind, bound like the previous one, but managed to dislodge the gag and scream. The attacker fled before the victim was raped. An officer patrolling near the park responded to the screaming. The notes indicate that she felt like she was being followed, but despite being hypervigilant, she still fell prey to the perpetrator. This victim was only mildly inebriated and had a better recollection of the event but had still not seen the attacker.

"When questioned about the men she met during that evening, she did remember a couple of attractive blonds who had bought her drinks. Neither of them gave her an uncomfortable feeling or said anything that would make her suspicious. There was no evidence left at the scene to assist in identifying the attacker. The officer didn't catch the perpetrator despite an extensive chase. This confirms the assumption that the perpetrator is athletic, and the officer indicated that he must know the city well to have evaded capture during the chase.

"Two nights later, July 23, a nineteen-year-old student was assaulted with the same MO in an alley in Noho," O'Shea continued while pointing at the fourth photo of a sweet-looking childlike young woman with blue innocent eyes. "Distracted by her cell phone, she was easily grabbed from behind and pulled into an alley. She was bound, gagged, and raped, same as the other two preceding attacks. She had an extensive head wound indicating that her attacker used substantial force to subdue her. She said that it happened so fast, she had no time to react. The attacker threatened her into silence and submission and at the end told her, 'You made this easy, easy like you,'" O'Shea stated.

"Did the perp say anything to the Washington Square Park victim?" Justus asked.

Flipping through the file, O'Shea answered, "Yes, he said, 'Shut up, bitch, I'll kill you if you don't shut up!'"

"When questioned about the men she spoke with that night," O'Shea continued, "the Noho alley victim recalled an attractive blond. She provided a very rudimentary description of a white man with short blond hair, average height, attractive, and clean-shaven. She couldn't provide enough detail to create a composite.

"With that incident, we determined that there may be a link among the three cases because the MO and victimology were similar," O'Shea advised as he displayed a photo from the file of a broken girl, eyes no longer innocent.

"The key MO details consist of a blitz from behind, the use of plastic tie wraps to bind the wrists, use of a gag, uttering verbal threats, and ensuring escape by rendering the victim unconscious with a blow to the head.

"Victimology indicates that his preferred targets are white women in their late teens or early twenties, who frequent clubs in the college area, and who are vulnerable due to inebriation.

"We finally got a break in the case when a twenty-five-year-old law student was assaulted just behind her apartment building and managed to fight back. This occurred on Fifth near First,"

O'Shea detailed as he pointed at photo number 5, that of a spunky-looking blonde, with a cute crooked smile and smart eyes. "This was on September 30. He beat her quite severely, leaving her with considerable facial wounds." He paused to show the ghastly photos of the facial damage sustained by the victim; and, as the room reacted with various sounds of disgust, he continued with the account of her attack. "She wasn't raped because the perpetrator gave up on the assault. She did see him clearly and was able to give a good enough description for the first composite."

While showing the composite, O'Shea provided the description, "CR is a white male in his late twenties or early thirties with short light hair; cold, narrow eyes; clean-shaven; strong-angled jaw; approximately six feet tall with an athletic build. He dresses in high-end casual wear and presents as a very confident person.

"The victim remembered the perp from Zax Club. She said he approached her, and was very charming. He didn't come on to her like other men at the bar did that night. He told her he had been watching her all night, watching her turn down one guy after another. They spoke for a while; he asked her about what she studied in school and other small talk. He never requested her number or tried to pick her up. She had no idea he had followed her home, where he blitzed her from behind as she walked through the small parking lot behind her building. Despite her struggle with him, there was no DNA recovered.

"After the composite came out, a victim came forward identifying CR as her attacker," O'Shea said as he pointed to the photo of the first victim in the series on the whiteboard. "She was assaulted several months earlier but never reported it," he explained while observing the faces in the room, repugnant, as they looked at this victim. She looked so young—long brown hair, beautiful features, but still the face of a child.

"This seventeen-year-old high school student," he declared with great disdain, "was assaulted in her own backyard in East Village. She admitted to being out clubbing in the college bars with her older cousin, a student at NYU, using fake ID. She got home after curfew and was going to sneak into her house through a back entrance. The attacker assaulted her in the backyard, and as with the other victims, he grabbed her from behind. Her face was down during the assault, and she didn't see him. The attacker used threats and verbal assaults to force her compliance and at the end whispered in her ear, 'If you're going to come out to play with men, be a woman, a whore.'

"This girl was a virgin before her attack. Ashamed and scared of what her parents would say, she snuck back into the house and made up a story about her bruised forehead. She was able to get out of the binding that he used on her wrist because it was a shoelace, not a tie wrap like the others. He obviously determined that a shoelace wasn't adequate or was too cumbersome, so he changed it in subsequent assaults. The victim did remember talking to someone that looked like the composite drawing at one of the bars that night, but because of inebriation, she couldn't remember much more."

Everyone in the room became more and more agitated as each assault was detailed. The first victim's story put everyone over the edge with disdain, disgust, and rage, which was apparent on the faces staring back at O'Shea—furrowed brows, tight lips, clenched jaws and fists.

The room was thick with revulsion. O'Shea, with only one more solo assault to detail, began. "The sixth victim," he said, pointing at the photo of a creamy-white-skinned, dark blonde-haired, blue-eyed country-girl type, "a twenty-one-year-old, was attacked in the stairwell of her Gramercy apartment. The attacker must have followed her home on the bus, but she didn't remember seeing him. As with the others, her face was down, so she wasn't able to identify or describe him. There was no DNA evidence recoverable from the scene. She did remember talking to someone similar to the composite at Fascination, the last bar she frequented that night. He used verbal assaults to subdue her and also said, 'A tease needs to be taught a lesson' before pounding her head on the concrete."

There wasn't one person in the room who didn't imagine themselves with the College Rapist in their trigger sights, knowing what they would do.

The FBI profiler, a staid-looking Asian woman in her fifties, wearing a very conservative gray skirt suit, took over the conversation. "I'm Agent Chan," she began with a mild Asian accent. "I have a few details to add to the profile already detailed by Captain O'Shea."

"The MO involves a planned attack, which we surmised from the fact that he was prepared with the tie wraps used to bind the victims' wrists, the use of a gag, and he took precautions not to be identified, nor leave any DNA at the scene.

"He is an organized offender who will display many of the following characteristics," she outlined as she turned on a projector displaying a computer screen with the following points:

- Generally concerned with appearance so will take good care of himself and will be well groomed and well dressed
- Will most likely be highly intelligent and very streetwise
- Will probably have completed high school and may have some college
- Was possibly known as a troublemaker in school
- Will likely work in jobs that project a macho image or an authority figure
- Can be sociable and outgoing when it suits his agenda and he is a master manipulator
- Will be a pathological liar with a chameleon personality
- Probably lives far enough away from the crime scene in a middle-class area, in an exemplary home environment
- May have past arrests for violence and sex offenses
- Will often collect trophies such as personal items from his victims
- Will follow news media related to his offenses and may communicate with the police, taunting them with his perceived superiority

"We have not ascertained if he fits the profile of a power rapist or anger rapist. Some of the behaviors tend toward power, but other behaviors tend toward anger.

"The power-assertive rapist," she continued while advancing her slide, "will generally use a con or surprise attack and display fantasy behavior, such as

- Demeaning and humiliating his victim
- Using excessive profanity
- Giving very explicit commands about the sex acts that he wants performed

- Threatening the victim into submission
- Tearing the victim's clothing

"He will be concerned for his pleasure only," she continued as she paced the room, advancing her slides with a remote, presenting the information that she knew all too well. "He won't kiss or engage in any other foreplay. He may sexually punish or abuse the victim and inflict painful stimuli like pinching or biting. The assaults may be prolonged where the victim is raped repeatedly.

"He will choose a location that is convenient and safe. He will apply moderate to excessive force that will increase as the victim resists or with any sexual dysfunction that he experiences during the offense.

"The MO will indicate that the victim is selected for characteristics that feed his fantasy. The choice will be influenced by availability, accessibility, vulnerability, and location. The victim may be held captive while being assaulted, and a weapon may be involved.

"The power-assertive rapist asserts his identity through his power over the victim. He doesn't want to hurt her but wants to dominate and possess her. He'll generally use only the force necessary to accomplish the assault.

"The anger rapist, on the other hand, is much more violent and may be motivated by retaliation or may just be sadistic. He will generally use a blitz attack and display fantasy behavior including blaming the victim for past wrongs in his life.

"The MO will indicate that the attack is unplanned. The victim might be known to the offender or might symbolize a person that he knows. The offenses are random and will happen when the offender is angry. Excessive force is applied throughout the assault. There will likely be use of a weapon of opportunity found at the scene. The attack is usually short, and anger is evident from the crime scene.

"The anger excitation rapist, unlike the simple anger rapist, enjoys the hunt and will be able to manipulate his victim into trust. He will use a con to lure his victim. The fantasy behavior includes demanding to be called a name such as Master, or Sir, so that the victim is subservient. He wants to inflict pain and may make the victim verbalize how much something hurts and make them beg for more. He'll call the victim by demeaning names and command her to call herself these names also.

"This type of offender will have built his fantasies partially through viewing pornography and will likely own an extensive collection of violence-based pornography. He is sexually stimulated by the victim's response to physical and emotional pain. He will likely practice bondage and other sexual experimentation with willing partners. He may have rehearsed the rape through fantasy role play with a sexual partner. His victim may be tortured with devices. This offender type is the most likely to record the assault.

"The vicious level of force used and the brutality inflicted against specific areas of the victim's body sets him apart from the other offender types. The intensity of brutality will increase with his anger, which in turn increases with the level of sexual arousal.

"The MO will indicate an attack planned in great detail. This offender may have an occupation where he is an authority figure, assisting him in accessing victims and in eliciting their trust. The attack will be very methodical playing out his fantasy. He is skilled at identifying victims who are vulnerable, nonaggressive, and who have low self-esteem. He'll have a rape kit, containing weapons, bindings, and sexual apparatus. The assault can last a long time, possibly days. The levels of aggression will likely increase with each of his attacks and may escalate to murder.

"The anger excitation rapist is the most complex. He is motivated strongly by his fantasies, and the goal is total victim fear and submission. He has learned to eroticize physical aggression and becomes aroused through the victim's suffering. This offender type will become more confident and efficient over time. He is a narcissist who believes he is superior to all others. He can maintain complete control over his motives and actions, unlike the anger retaliation rapist. He preserves his identity with great skill and will kill to protect it.

"A final point about the anger excitation rapist is that he exhibits all of the behavioral indicators of a psychopath.

"The majority of the evidence that we have, based on the scenes and victims' statements, indicates a higher level of physical force than necessary was used in the CR attacks. You can also surmise this from the victim and crime scene photos. It is more likely that he is an anger-based offender. His assaults are planned and organized, and he does have a rape kit of sorts with bindings and a gag. Although he does show characteristics of both types of anger-based rapists, I believe that he is a budding anger excitation rapist. I expect his violence will escalate as he gains more and more experience.

"I also believe that CR is a psychopath. His interpersonal traits will probably include guile, superficial charm, arrogance, pathological lying, and mastery of manipulation. He'll lack remorse and feelings of guilt. When it suits his purpose, he'll interact with others but may demonstrate a shallow affect, a lack of empathy, and be unable to control his anger. He may seek stimulation in the form of risky behavior and impulsivity and will not conform to social norms or rules. His past will reveal childhood behavior problems, juvenile delinquency, and past criminal offenses." Agent Chan paused as she turned off the projector.

"Motive is unclear at this point. If he is a psychopath, motive is most difficult to ascertain because it is mostly internal, driven by fantasy. There will be few to no external indicators of motive. This will complicate our investigation and make it much more difficult to predict behavior and progression of offenses. It is obvious from the offenses that anger, humiliation, and degradation are integral, but these may be motive or may be fantasy or both.

"Another interesting point is that CR is very skilled at evading the NYPD CCTV surveillance system and also leaves no physical evidence behind. He has obviously done some research and understands the basics of crime scene analysis. He is likely an avid reader of criminology and forensic science works and may be a student in either of these departments at the university," the profiler finished, waiting for any reaction from the group.

"So what you're saying is that we have a smart psychopath driven by some internal fantasy that obviously involves anger and demeaning women," a task force member began. "The force he uses will probably increase, and he may potentially escalate to murder. We really have no leads and not much to predict future assaults. This isn't giving me much hope at this point."

Captain O'Shea interjected, "That's why we have this task force, and no perpetrator is infallible. He'll eventually give us something. We have to examine and reexamine everything. We can't afford people to become unfocused." He looked around the room, catching the eyes of the team members, and waited for comments. Nobody had anything else to say. O'Shea looked at Agent Chan.

"Turning now to the team assault," the FBI profiler stated as she pointed to the seventh victim's photo on the whiteboard, a pale-skinned, gray-eyed girl with long light brown hair and glasses, "we have to investigate two different offenders now: one solo offender who perpetrated the first six attacks and one team that has perpetrated the most recent seventh attack," she reported as she turned the projector on again.

"We can presume that CR is the leader from his profile, and the partner is a voyeur for now. Based on research of team offenders, we know that teams are generally led by one person with a strong fantasy. This person is very persuasive and able to inspire the other or others to serve his fantasy. There could be more than two people in a team, but more often than not, it is two offenders. The dominant one will maintain psychological and sometimes physical control over the partner and control over devising the offenses.

"The primary catalyst for the dominant partner comes from a need to have power and control over others. The crime must be both a participation and a spectator endeavor. Sometimes the dominant one will derive as much or more pleasure and power from having the partner perpetrate the crime while he watches. The weaker partner will probably be coerced or forced initially into taking part in the criminal activity but then may develop a lust for and psychological need for voluntary participation. The pathology of the relationship operates in a way that each partner finds a sense of power through the assaults, somewhat like a child bullied in school seeks power by in turn bullying their younger sibling at home.

"The additional level of control can fuel the dominant partner, having several possible outcomes:

1. Shortened cooling-off periods between offenses
2. Escalation to more violent activity
3. A change in MO and/or victimology
4. A change from organized to disorganized behavior."

Agent Chan announced as she outlined each point on the projector screen with her laser pointer, and then paused to scrutinize the team for understanding.

"As a team, everything can change. Two minds engaged in the activity can create a completely new set of behaviors, a new profile altogether. One thing on our side is that the greater number of offenders involved, the greater the possibility of mistakes being made and of evidence being left at the crime scene.

"A final possibility to consider is that this latest attack is not CR," she proposed with a demeanor that suggested it was very unlikely.

Brewing in the room was a determined atmosphere, with each person analyzing the facts laid out. Led by Johnson and Dunn, the group continued to brainstorm a plan that included increased surveillance, looking more closely at the blond men, a.k.a. the blond parade, who voluntarily came to the precinct for questioning, and re-interviewing all victims, hoping to get details that would help flesh out a more specific profile. They needed to determine whether there was a connection between victims that was not obvious. Were they all members of some group? Did they go to the same gym? Did they attend the same church?

All students currently enrolled in criminology and forensic sciences would be interviewed, and attempts would be made to track down alumni as well. Any related patterns of offenses in other jurisdictions would be investigated for connection to the College Rapist case.

As the meeting was ending, O'Shea was called out briefly. As he reentered the room, there was a look on his face that was difficult to read. On one hand, it indicated some hope, but on the other hand, it indicated dismay. He motioned to everyone to pay attention, and he announced, "A new assault victim has just come forward. She is a twenty-one-year-old student who was assaulted last spring on campus but never reported it. When she heard of this latest assault on campus, she was compelled to report her attack. By the brief details I was just provided, she was likely the first victim in this spree. There are only a few details that we could get over the phone. She didn't come back to school this year, so we're waiting for her to come in from South Dakota. We'll be interviewing her tomorrow."

The meeting wrapped up, and everyone felt a renewed sense of purpose and drive with the investigation. Justus and Magnus stayed behind to speak with Agent Chan.

"Hello, Agent Chan," Justus said as he extended his hand to hers. "I'm Justus Evans, and this is my brother, Magnus."

"A pleasure," she replied while shaking hands with them. "Please call me Mai-Lee. I'm already aware of who you both are. Fergus told me about you," she acknowledged while nodding at Captain O'Shea.

They exchanged some small talk briefly, then Justus asked, "With the little information that we have so far, who do you think they are, CR and his accomplice?"

Agent Chan stood pensively and answered, "Well, if I had to put an initial guess on it, I would suppose that CR is a senior forensics or criminology student, a teacher's assistant, or may even be a postgraduate student. The accomplice is probably a freshman or sophomore in the same program. They may be roommates. The older student may be a resident assistant in the younger student's residence hall or may be the younger student's TA."

"It does seem like he has a lot of forensic knowledge," Magnus pointed out. "On what basis are you making your initial prediction?"

"On the skill, planning, and knowledge required to ensure no evidence was left behind for one, and because of the college bar and college student connection," she asserted. "I'm having all senior-level students in those programs assessed for past violent acts, for violence in their upbringing, and for general psycho-sociopathology."

Justus and Magnus nodded in agreement of her plan to background check the senior students.

"Boys," Captain O'Shea cut in while looking at his wristwatch, "Agent Chan and I have to take off now for a press conference. Sorry to have to cut this off."

"No problem," Justus asserted, looking at Captain O'Shea; then looking toward Agent Chan, "This has been a great pleasure meeting you, Agent Chan . . . Mai-Lee," he corrected himself. "We have read many of your works and value your expansive knowledge and experience."

She smiled and gestured to shake hands with them again as Captain O'Shea said, "See you tomorrow for this new victim's interview."

"Of course," they both answered in unison.

At the police station, the next afternoon, Justus and Magnus were led to an interrogation viewing room where they joined Captain O'Shea. They were preparing to watch an interview with the sexual assault victim who was likely the College Rapist's first. She had just come forward to report her attack.

"One of our best will be conducting the interview," O'Shea declared. "She's an expert with rape victims and with cognitive interview techniques. The victim is Jamie Myers, attacked last spring, on April 16."

O'Shea left Justus and Magnus in the observation room and joined Dunn, absorbed in the case file, in the interview room. Officer Dunn was dressed in a conservative navy blue suit with her dark hair pulled back into a knot. She was plain but pretty, not delicate, and she exuded self-confidence, creating an attractive allure.

The interview room was cramped and uninviting, with a dim light, a one-tone paint job, furnished with a table and chairs that looked like they came from a liquidation store at best. An officer led in a languid-looking young woman with dirty blonde hair, somewhat unkempt in appearance, wearing a baggy sweatshirt and jeans. Her glance shifted back and forth from O'Shea to Dunn.

"Please have a seat, Ms. Myers," O'Shea offered to the victim.

Reluctantly, she sat at the small table across from Dunn.

"This is Officer Dunn . . . Melanie Dunn," O'Shea finished as he sat down.

Officer Dunn extended her hand, introducing herself, "You can call me Mel."

"I'm Jamie," the victim replied as she looked back and forth from each officer then down at the table.

Dunn started the discussion. "I understand that you were assaulted last spring, correct?"

The victim kept looking down and responded, "Yes."

"I'm going to talk to you today about the assault," Dunn continued. "I know that it will be uncomfortable and difficult for you. I have spoken with many rape victims, and I hope that once you have been able to talk about the event, you will feel a certain amount of relief. You will be contributing to finding this perpetrator with all the details that you can remember and tell us."

Jamie looked at Mel, maybe evaluating her sincerity, and gave a slight smile and nod, indicating a readiness to begin.

"When exactly did your attack happen?" Dunn began.

"It was April 16," the victim informed her.

"You never reported it, correct?" confirmed Dunn.

"No . . . I didn't want anyone to know." The victim continued looking down at the table.

Officer Dunn paused briefly to give the victim time to continue speaking. The victim sat silent and then turned her gaze to Officer Dunn.

"I wish that I had said something because maybe it would have helped me get over it faster," she acknowledged in a monotonous, listless voice.

Dunn continued to look at the victim in silence. Jamie slowly turned her hands over, exposing her scarred wrists from an attempted suicide. Dunn extended her hand in a gesture of support, making sure not to touch Jamie's hand unless she initiated contact.

Jamie reached for Mel's hand and broke down in tears.

After several minutes, Jamie stated, "When a schoolmate from last year sent me an e-mail telling me about the campus rape and the composite, I had a total breakdown. Everything from that night flashed back to me. I was drunk and had no worries, with first year of school almost done. I was going home to my family and boyfriend for the summer." She continued to sob.

"Take your time," Dunn advised, while holding Jamie's hand. "Do you want some water?" Dunn suggested as she motioned to O'Shea to get some water.

"Yes, please," Jamie replied through her sobs, looking at O'Shea through tear-filled eyes.

The officers gave Jamie some time to compose herself.

"Is it normal to feel this way?" Jamie asked feebly.

Dunn took a deep breath and affirmed, "Yes, everything you are feeling is completely normal. No two people react the same way. No two people feel the same, but having a strong reaction to what happened to you is very normal. Many sexual assault victims have physical and emotional symptoms for a while after the assault, but getting help from a professional can really help you to process the experience and learn to go on with your life. Do you have someone to help you back home?"

"Yes, I do now, since doing this," Jamie admitted as she displayed her wrists again.

Dunn sat silently, waiting for the victim to give an indication that she was ready to continue. Jamie stared at her wrists for a few moments, took a deep sighing breath, closed her eyes briefly, then opened them, fixing her gaze on Officer Dunn.

"Do you feel ready to talk about what happened that night?" Dunn asked tentatively.

Jamie looked at Captain O'Shea then back at Officer Dunn and answered, "I don't know."

Captain O'Shea left the room, taking the cue that Jamie would probably be more comfortable without a man in the room.

Both Officer Dunn and Jamie looked at each other for a moment, and Dunn asked, "Where were you the night of your assault, Jamie?"

Jamie closed her eyes again, took a deep breath, and began, "I was out at the Animal House with some friends. We were celebrating my dorm mate Tara's birthday. We made a big deal out of it so that guys would buy us drinks. I had to work in the morning, so I left early. It wasn't a long walk to my dorm. I had done it many times before. Most of my friends didn't have to work because their parents paid for everything. I had to work to be able to stay in school."

Jamie's lip began to quiver as she paused to recall her walk home from the club. Officer Dunn reached out to touch Jamie, who recoiled away from her.

They were silent while Jamie composed herself.

"I walked home the same way I always did from the club. I was thinking about my boyfriend, back home, probably humming some song that I heard that night. Then the next thing I remember is being on the ground, facedown with pressure on my back. I felt like I didn't have any air in my lungs."

Jamie started to tremble and cry. Dunn passed her a box of tissues, offered her more water, and waited.

"Where were you when you were pushed down?" Dunn inquired.

"I was walking between two of the buildings at my dorm hall," Jamie answered.

"Picture yourself walking there that night. Is there anything that you notice?" Dunn questioned, trying to prompt Jamie's memory.

"No, I had no reason to feel uncomfortable or cautious, which was obviously a mistake, I should have been more aware," Jamie admitted while displaying obvious frustration on her face and clenching her fists.

"Your assault was not your fault, Jamie," Officer Dunn acknowledged in a calm reassuring manner.

"I wish I could believe that," Jamie retorted tersely.

Dunn waited for signs that Jamie was ready to go on. Once her breathing regained a slower pace and she unclenched her fists, Dunn assured, "You're doing well with this, and I know it's very difficult. Are you ready to continue?"

Jamie nodded her head indicating yes.

"You felt pressure on your back and couldn't breathe, then what happened?" Dunn began again.

"Something was put in my mouth, like a sock or something like that, and I couldn't move my hands. They were tied somehow behind my back. I was trying to scream . . . I was crying. Then he raped me." She sobbed.

Dunn walked over to Jamie and put her hand on Jamie's shoulder, and this time, she accepted the supportive gesture and cried for a long while.

They took a break, and Dunn entered the observation room, where O'Shea, Justus, and Magnus had been observing the interview.

"Good work, Dunn," O'Shea expressed. "You seem to be building good rapport with her."

"Thanks, Captain," she replied.

"Dunn, you remember Justus and Magnus Evans?" O'Shea asked.

Extending her hand, she acknowledged, "Yes, from the College Rapist task force, right? You are consultants on this case?"

Nodding, Justus shook her hand, as did Magnus.

"Dunn, here are some specifics to probe," O'Shea suggested.

"Did the perpetrator seem nervous or hesitant?

How much force was used both in the attack and at the end of the attack?

She didn't have a rape kit done. Did he leave any DNA?

Did she resist, and if so, did this increase his force used?

Did he have a weapon?"

Dunn noted O'Shea's questions and looked at Justus and Magnus.

"We also want to know if the attacker said anything, and when he said it," Magnus requested.

Justus added, "We would like to find out if she thinks that someone else was there, watching."

"Show her the composite again and try to get her to recall exactly what interaction she had with the perp when she was at the club," O'Shea advised.

Dunn reentered the room with a chocolate bar for Jamie that they shared while exchanging small talk. Then Dunn informed her, changing the tone, "I have a few more questions for you. Are you ready to continue?"

"Yes," Jamie affirmed, "I'm OK."

"Was the attacker hesitant at all?" Dunn began.

"No, not that I remember, but it all happened so fast," Jamie advised.

"Did you resist at all?" Dunn continued.

Jamie's bottom lip began to quiver again as she answered with an agitated voice, "I couldn't breathe. It was too fast. Should I have resisted? Would he have stopped if I tried?"

Dunn reached out to Jamie, touching her shoulder and calmly explained, "There's no 'should have' when it comes to your situation, there's no blame, and there's no right answer. You followed your instincts in the moment, and you are alive. That's what's most important. We're asking these questions to get an idea of the type of attacker we are dealing with. In no way are we trying to suggest how you should have reacted or what you should have done."

Giving Jamie some time to process, Dunn kept her hand on Jamie's shoulder and waited for a sign that she was ready to go on.

Jamie took a deep breath and recalled, "The pressure on my back took my breath away, then my mouth was stuffed with some kind of cloth, making it even more difficult to breathe. I couldn't say anything. I was crying. I may have tried kicking my legs, but then his weight was on my legs."

"It sounds like he was quite forceful. Did he hit you?" Dunn probed.

"He grabbed my hair hard and hit my head on the ground, then I only remember waking up, and he was gone," she described.

"Did he bite you or inflict any other pain, besides the pain of forced intercourse?" Dunn questioned.

"Not that I recall, but the whole ordeal was painful," Jamie insisted.

Dunn paused briefly, reviewing her notes. Jamie closed her eyes and took several deep breaths. When Jamie opened her eyes, Dunn looked directly in them to assess if she was ready for more. Her eyes were showing more determination, which Dunn took as a sign to continue. "Was there any semen?"

Jamie answered hesitantly. "No, I don't think so, but I obviously showered, I almost scrubbed my skin off. I was completely disgusted. I also went to health services the next day and got a morning after pill. When I got back to South Dakota, I had an AIDS test, and thankfully, it was negative."

"OK," Dunn continued, "did the attacker say anything to you?"

Jamie was quiet, looking down at the table for a moment, and then she blurted, "He yelled at me and threatened to hurt me."

"When did he yell and threaten?" Dunn asked.

"When the pressure was on my back, he told me to shut up or he would kill me," she answered. "He called me a bitch and a slut."

"Did he threaten with a weapon or say that he had a weapon?" Dunn probed.

"No," Jamie responded, "not that I can remember."

"Do you remember him saying anything else, Jamie?" Dunn prompted.

She closed her eyes and quoted, "If you're not selling, don't advertise."

"When did he say this to you?" Dunn verified.

"He said it just before he smashed my head into the ground, and that is the last thing I can remember until I was walking around, and someone came to help me" Jamie recollected with relative composure.

"Did you get any feeling at all that someone witnessed what happened to you?" Dunn probed.

"No!" Jamie exclaimed, shocked. "I know that New Yorkers are cold, but I can't picture someone from the campus just letting this happen to me."

Dunn asked, "Who helped you?"

"It was a couple, but that is all that I remember," Jamie replied. "They walked me back to my dorm, and from there, one of my floor mates took care of me."

"I want to go back to the couple," Dunn directed. "What did they look like?"

"I don't remember too clearly because my head was dizzy and sore," Jamie explained.

"I'm going to try to help you remember things that are locked in your mind. Please close your eyes and focus back to that night, just after the attack. You're dizzy, your head is sore, and you are stumbling. Can you picture your surroundings?"

Jamie nodded, indicating yes, with her eyes still closed.

"What do you see?" inquired Dunn

"I'm seeing double," Jamie began, "a light in the distance. The lamppost at my dorm hall is going in and out of focus."

"Is there anyone around?" Dunn probed.

"There are two people," Jamie began. "Their voices sound muffled. One is definitely a woman, and the other a man. The woman has a light-colored coat or sweater on."

"What about her skin?" Dunn questioned.

"She has light skin and hair," Jamie remembered. "The guy is darker, like Indian or Arab. He took his coat off and put it over my shoulders. My hands were still tied . . . I remember that they tried to get the thing off, but it wouldn't come off. I remember saying, 'I'm OK. Just get me back to my room,' over and over again."

Jamie was getting agitated, so Dunn took over the conversation briefly. "Keep your eyes closed but take several deep breaths." She coached Jamie through her breathing, and they paused until her breathing slowed.

"Do you remember the names of the people that helped you?" Dunn began again.

Now feeling calmed, Jamie responded, "No, I don't think I asked, and I don't think they offered their names. When we got to the front of the dorm, they left, but he told me to keep his jacket."

"Where is the jacket now?" Dunn interjected.

"It was thrown out, the next day, along with all the other clothes I was wearing that night," Jamie confirmed.

"When you got back to your dorm, what happened?" Dunn continued.

Through tears and sobs, with her eyes still closed, the victim recalled. "Only one person was up. Most were still out at the club, and any others that stayed behind were in bed already. I tried to get in without anyone seeing me, but I couldn't because I broke down at my door. I couldn't get into my room with my hands still tied," Jamie described.

"Who helped you?" Dunn inquired.

"Pamela Stanton," Jamie stated, and she opened her eyes. "She wanted me to report it, but I made her promise not to tell anyone."

"Is she still at school?" Dunn questioned.

"Yes, she's the one that sent me the e-mail," Jamie advised.

Dunn wrote down the name and asked, "Write down her number here please," as she passed Jamie the sheet of paper. "OK, let me summarize," Dunn suggested. "A couple helped you, a white woman with light-colored hair and a darker, possibly Indian or Arab, man. When you say Indian, do you mean native or do you mean Indian from India?" Dunn verified.

"I mean Indian from India," Jamie responded.

"What about age for this couple?" Dunn continued to question.

"Just normal student age, like in their twenties," Jamie answered.

"What do you remember about the coat the man gave you?" Dunn asked.

Jamie closed her eyes and replied, "It was dark, nothing special."

"Did it have anything on it, like a crest or insignia?" Dunn queried.

"No, not that I remember. Pamela took it off me and cut off what was binding my hands, then she must have put it in a garbage bag where the rest of my clothes went," she explained.

"What were your hands bound with?" Dunn inquired.

Jamie closed her eyes and thought briefly then responded, "A shoelace. It was knotted really tight. It had to be cut off because Pam couldn't undo the knot."

"OK," Dunn paused, "I'm going to show you the composite, and I want you to tell me what you remember about this man."

As Dunn displayed the composite on the table, Jamie covered her eyes and began to shake and sob again.

Officer Dunn turned over the composite and moved over to the same side of the table as Jamie, putting her arms around her.

"This is very traumatic for you, I know," affirmed Dunn. "Can you continue? Every detail you can remember helps us find him."

It took several minutes for her sobs to subside, then Dunn presented the composite again.

"Let's try this again. Look at this composite, and now, I want you to go back to the bar in your mind with this picture in your thoughts," Dunn requested.

Jamie, still shaken, reached for the composite with a trembling hand and drew it closer to her. She studied it, and a look of apprehension washed across her face.

Officer Dunn touched Jamie's trembling hand and said, "Close your eyes and put yourself back at the bar that night."

Jamie reluctantly complied.

"Tell me what you see," asked Dunn as she maintained contact with Jamie's hand.

"It was packed," Jamie began. "Lots of people were out blowing off steam because the semester was at the breaking point. There was only a week until exams, and most people had assignments galore. We were drinking shots for Tara's birthday. There were lots of guys buying drinks for us."

"Think about the guys that were around, those buying drinks. Where was the one that looks like the composite?" Dunn probed.

"He wasn't right around us. The guys that were around us were just regular college guys. The composite guy was older, better dressed, looked like a guy that had a good job," Jamie disclosed, remarkably composed. "I talked to him when I went up to the bar, but I don't remember what we talked about. One of my friends pulled me away to dance because one of her favorite songs came on."

"Did you talk to him again?" Dunn asked.

"No, I never paid attention to him after that, and I wasn't at the bar much longer," Jamie finished.

"Were there any other guys that stuck out in your mind for any reason?" Dunn questioned.

"No, nothing unusual. One guy called me a bitch because he bought me a drink, and I blew him off. But he was a regular at the club and harmless," Jamie claimed.

"What makes you think he was harmless?" Dunn probed.

"Well . . . he was always at that bar and most often had to be dragged out of there by his friends, long after last call, falling down drunk," Jamie described. "He was already so drunk when he was with us that he could barely stand."

"What did this guy look like?" Dunn requested.

"He's a dark-haired white guy, stocky, six feet tall," Jamie answered. "His name is Todd, but I don't know his last name."

"Is there anything else that you think I should know about? Is there anything else that may help the case?" Dunn queried.

"No, not right now, but if I think of anything else, I'll let you know," Jamie finished with a long cleansing breath.

Dunn, taking Jamie's hand again, said, "You did a great job with this. I'll be back. While I'm gone, can you please write down the names and any contact information you have for the people you were out with at the bar the night of your assault? If you know the names of any of Todd's friends, please write them down as well."

Dunn passed Jamie a paper and pen and then returned to the viewing room to speak with O'Shea, Justus, and Magnus. They were deep in conversation as she entered.

"Good interview," Justus congratulated with enthusiasm, giving Dunn a pat on the shoulder.

"Is there anything else you need from this victim?" Dunn inquired.

"Don't advertise if you're not selling," Magnus pondered. "Sounds to me like she was dressed or behaved in a way to attract sexual attention but rejected advances. I'd like to know more about that."

"Is there any background on what she was wearing?" Justus asked.

"No," Dunn responded.

"Let's ask her if there are photos from that night. It was a birthday celebration, someone probably took pictures," Justus suggested. "We can ask her friends about her behavior. Also, we want to know if he took anything from her."

Looking tentative, Dunn returned to the interview room where Jamie sat, hands on her temples, massaging away a tension headache.

"I just have a couple more questions for you," Dunn assured, trying to show that the end was in sight. "Are there any photos from that night?"

Jamie, pensive, answered, "Yes, a few people took pictures. I can get them."

"OK, that will be helpful," Dunn said.

"Why do you want pictures?" Jamie asked.

"You never know who is in the background. All bits of evidence can be useful," Dunn added. "You said that you threw away the clothes that you were wearing the night of your assault. Can you describe them to me?" Dunn requested.

"Well," Jamie started, searching her memory, "I would usually wear skirts out, so I probably had one of my minis on." She paused briefly. "It was black, and I had a red V-neck sweater and some black boots."

Dunn paused to see if Jamie would add any more details to her description, and after a few seconds, she reviewed, "You said there were a lot of guys hanging around your table. Did any make advances on you?"

"Sure," Jamie admitted. "That's how the game is played. You flirt. They buy you drinks."

"You're certain that the blond man from the composite didn't approach you or anyone at your table?" Dunn verified.

Jamie answered, "I wasn't at the table all night, but he didn't come around that I can recall."

"Did the attacker take anything from you?" Dunn asked.

"I'm not sure," Jamie said. "I think I wore a necklace that night, and when I got home to South Dakota, I was missing it. I'm not sure if he took it or if it was thrown out with my clothes."

"Can you describe it?" Dunn requested.

Jamie detailed, "It was a cross pendant on a thin black lace, nothing really special. I just bought it from a street vendor."

Dunn looked sympathetically at Jamie and expressed with warmth, "You have been very helpful and brave to face this. We have no more questions right now; you're free to go. Your parents are down the hall to the left. Thanks for your assistance. Here's my card. You can send the photos to this e-mail address."

Jamie took the card, stood up, and made her way to the door. Before leaving, she looked back and said, "This was really hard, but I do feel a bit better. Can you please tell me when you catch him?"

"Yes, I'll make sure that you know when he is caught. Take care and keep seeing your therapist. After going through this today, you may need some extra support," Dunn suggested. "Talk to your therapist about a procedure called EMDR. It stands for Eye Movement Desensitization and Reprocessing. Some victims find this to be very helpful in dealing with traumatic events."

Jamie left the room. O'Shea, Justus, and Magnus entered.

O'Shea stated, "Sounds pretty clear that this is our guy. I'd like to track down that couple that helped her and the roommate. What was her name?"

"Pamela Stanton," Dunn advised.

"Let's track down these people as well," O'Shea said, holding the list of the victim's friends. "We have the seventeen-year-old victim coming in later today, and tomorrow we're bringing in the subway victim and her friend again."

"Is Dunn interviewing all the victims?" Magnus asked.

"Yes, we want to keep consistency and dig at the same details," O'Shea answered.

"One of us will be here for both interviews," Justus told Dunn and O'Shea.

After several days of interviews, Justus and Magnus were ready to share the information with all of us. We met at the house, Jay with me instead of on the phone. The seating arrangement shifted now with Tavia to one side of me and Jay to the other. This made our relationship seem official, like bringing home my boyfriend to meet my parents for the first time.

We exchanged some small talk until Justus was ready to begin with a brief synopsis of the eight assaults.

"The first victim came forward after the recent campus attack," he began. "She was attacked on campus as well, mid-April, last school year, but didn't report it at the time. She did recognize the composite as someone she met at a campus club the night of her attack. We reviewed some photos taken from that night, and she recognized the man from the composite in one. She remembered his clothing, but of course, as luck would have it, we could only see the back of him, leading us no further ahead with his identification.

"The second victim came forward after the composite was released. She was attacked in her own backyard after being out for a night of clubbing with her cousin, an NYU student. She remembered meeting someone who looked like the composite. This occurred at the end of May.

"The next victim was the subway attack in June. She was unable to give much information but did remember an attractive blond male from the subway, exiting at her station.

"The fourth victim escaped the full extent of the attack in Washington Square Park. An officer pursued the perpetrator but didn't catch him. The victim did not see the attacker.

"The fifth attack in Noho was only two days after the thwarted park assault, both mid-July.

"There was a break of almost two months then an attack late in September. The sixth victim fought her attacker, suffering a severe beating, but was not raped. She had a fairly clear recollection of his appearance and was able to provide enough information for a composite, which was released to the media.

"The seventh victim was attacked in the stairwell of her Gramercy apartment in October.

"The eighth victim was in November, on campus, and she felt that someone was watching the attack, opening up the possibility that there is an accomplice," Justus concluded.

Magnus added, "So far, the MO has been a blitz attack from behind with substantial force, binding the victim's hands, using a gag, and knocking the victim unconscious with a blow to the head after the rape. He threatens the victims and says intimidating and degrading one-liners at the end of the attack, his signature it seems. His level of violence has escalated over time, and although he appears to be very organized, he has encountered two victims that he couldn't subdue, forcing him to abandon the rape. All the victims are between seventeen and twenty-five, attractive, and frequent the college district clubs. He left no DNA. There was a break of almost two months in the pattern of attacks, and we can only speculate why."

Anton surmised, "Maybe it was because of the botched attack in the park, he was rattled by it?"

"Maybe, he met his accomplice in that time?" Ethan speculated. "Or maybe something completely unrelated happened. Maybe he attacked in another part of the city. Serial offenders are successful sometimes because law enforcement doesn't connect the crimes. I assume O'Shea has looked at potentially similar assaults in other parts of the city?"

"Yes," Justus confirmed, "they are looking at patterns nationally to see if there are any similar sprees over the past few years.

"What is MO?" I asked. "I watch cop shows, but it's never explained because all the cops on the show know what it is!"

Everyone chuckled, and Helene responded, "MO means modus operandi, and it's what the perpetrator does to commit the attack. It is the necessary steps he takes to make sure the attack is successful. It's learned and dynamic based on what the attacker encounters from offense to offense. He may try something in one attack and find that it almost got him caught or almost caused him to be identified, so he'll think about it and try something different the next time. The MO becomes refined with time, and then once it is perfected, it is repeated fairly ritualistically."

Helene looked at me to ensure understanding and then added, "For the College Rapist, he seems to feel it necessary to bind his victim's hands and attack from behind to successfully accomplish the attack. This could indicate many possible characteristics such as he may not want to use a weapon, for whatever reason. He doesn't want to be seen, which makes a lot of sense. He doesn't want the victim able to use her hands to fight so that there is no potential for her to scratch him and get DNA under her nails. It opens up the door to a lot of speculation that could help lead the investigation into various directions."

Justus expanded on Helene's answer with "A signature is what the perpetrator has to do because of some psychological need. It is not necessary to the attack, but he does it anyway and will always do it. For instance, Magnus mentioned that the College Rapist says a degrading one-liner to his victim just before he knocks her unconscious. He doesn't need to do this because he has already committed the rape successfully, but it gives him some sort of satisfaction to do it. If he does it every time, then it is a signature. To make things tricky, the fact that the College Rapist binds the victim's hands could just be part of the MO and totally functional in accomplishing the rape, as Helene described, but it could also be a signature based on fantasy and psychological satisfaction. If he is a strong guy and intimidating enough, he may be able to accomplish the rape without binding the hands but does it for the psychological thrill that he gets from it. If an aspect of the crime seems to be a bit overdone, beyond the point of functional, then it is probably a signature."

Ethan concluded with "Ultimately, the MO and signature allow us to make educated guesses about the perpetrators character, what type of attacker he is, about when the next attack will take place, where it may take place, if the attacks may escalate to more violent behavior, and to connect various crimes together."

"What's with the one-liners?" Anton interjected.

"Well, to one victim, he said, 'If you're going to come out to play with men, be a woman, a whore,'" Magnus recounted. "To another one, he said, 'You made this easy, easy like you.' And to another, he said, 'If you're not selling, don't advertise.' He had something of that nature to say to each of them, except for the two who fought back, making him give up on the attack."

"He feels women are whores and teases," Justus surmised.

Helene offered, "It could indicate that he is retaliating against behavior that he perceives to be demeaning to him in some way, something that happened out in the bars where he met the women."

"He may be punishing his victims for something real or imagined," Magnus reasoned.

"Ethan, you will need to pull it all together to see what can be connected and if there's anything else that's been missed," Justus said as he handed Ethan a pile of papers from the task force meetings.

"What about the team angle?" Anton queried.

"There isn't much to say about it yet," Justus advised. "It's still speculation so other than generic team assault assumptions, there's nothing. This guy is evasive. All we can do is assist with surveillance, take it up a few notches, and hope that we get him before he escalates. He has dodged the NYPD public CCTV system quite skillfully, so we'll try to hijack more commercial cameras in his target area and hope to get something," Justus summarized with trepidation in his voice.

December, my favorite month, had already come and gone without any new concerns related to the College Rapist.

I thought that without my daughter, the holidays wouldn't be worth celebrating. She stayed in Britain, which was somewhat of a relief because I wouldn't have been able to see her, if she had come back to the States. My mother retired and was in the Bahamas with no expected date of return. Jay had given up on celebrating any holidays a long time ago, but I convinced him to humor me. We put up a tree, a magnificent tree. We bought each other gifts that we exchanged on Christmas Eve, sitting by the fireplace, watching the diamonds falling from the sky. We went up to the roof of our building and caught snowflakes on our tongues. It felt invigorating to be out in the cool breeze.

We spent New Year's Eve at Madison Square Garden, something I had always wanted to do, and then in the wee hours of the morning, we went skating in Central Park. We were alone in the crisp winter air, the clean smell of fresh fallen snow. It was magical, and my love for Jay grew stronger every minute.

As December became January, there was less criminal activity; winter did tend to have less violent crimes compared with the rest of the year. We enjoyed the brief hiatus, but it also meant less feeding, which for me was difficult. The others needed to feed less because of their immortal ages, and they were not suffering from the cravings that I still lived with. I smoked briefly in high school, but quitting was a breeze compared with this.

I spent hours with my new family, trying to stay distracted from my hunger, learning about history, about being immortal, and about their lives. They were a set of living encyclopedias. I learned firsthand about the past, and I found out how much of the history we learned in school was wrong or at least twisted to give mortals the illusion of being civilized and good.

I spent many of my nights at Gotham Citi with Jay. I was settling into night life without difficulty since I was always more productive at night anyway. I had never been a regular of the bar scene, but I was enjoying the liveliness and energy. I had dabbled in accounting in my mortal life, so I took on the project of bookkeeping for the club. When we weren't there, Jay left the club to be managed by Eirinn, whom he had known since he bought Gotham. Jay had purchased the club from her father, and she had worked there since her teen years. To Jay, Eirinn was like a daughter, especially since both her parents were killed in a car accident when she was eighteen. She knew our secret, and he trusted her wholeheartedly.

Eirinn was a lighthearted twenty-seven-year-old who looked younger than her years, with a soul that was much older. She was a natural beauty, with light brown hair, freckled skin, and razor-sharp gray eyes, slight of build but with a natural leadership that commanded respect from everyone. Her demeanor, although strong, was subtle, and she kept the club running smoothly. I once saw her jump over the bar, between two guys ready to tear each other apart, and diffuse the situation in seconds. Jay didn't like these tactics, but he knew that spark in her couldn't be put out. The club was her life; she said that it was how she kept her parents alive.

Jay was onto a new developing project that he and Yasmine were collaborating on. They were closing in on a major connection to the Los Zetas cartel, a criminal organization from Mexico, major players in the international drug trade. Also known for assassinations, extortion, kidnapping, and other organized criminal activities, the Drug Enforcement Administration considered Los Zetas as the most violent drug cartel in Mexico. The cartel was founded by a group of former Mexican Army Special Forces deserters, expanded with Guatemalan Special Forces and corrupt police officers. Jay had wanted to get to the Mexican leaders for a long time.

He had some DEA partners who fed him drug trade intelligence. Yasmine was posing as a girlfriend to Carlos Vargas González, the cousin of one of the original Los Zetas. Carlos was the New York connection, the leading distributor throughout the eastern states. A major cocaine shipment was destined for the United States in a few months, and one of the cartel leaders was personally ensuring its safe arrival to New York.

Gotham Citi was one of the first stops on the Zetas leader's itinerary allowing him to personally examine the club and meet Jay. Gotham was the cartel's proposed regular meeting place, and Jay was their facilitator in New York. Gotham was known in the drug trade as a major underground connection.

Jay worked in tandem with the DEA and O'Shea, eliminating several major distributors over the years. His DEA connections ensured that the reputation of Gotham Citi as a haven to trafficking held strong.

In mid-January, there was a break in the College Rapist case, confirming that he did indeed have a partner . . . a woman. We all waited patiently at the house for O'Shea to call with details. Of course, the media was already all over it. The would-be victim was almost abducted, but the attempt was thwarted by her vigilance and by a nearby plain-clothed officer.

The phone rang, and we all sat in anticipation of the details, hopeful that this would help us find and eliminate the College Rapist once and for all.

"We're listening," Justus told O'Shea.

"As you and the rest of the city already know, he's back!" O'Shea declared halfheartedly. In these situations, there is both a sense of hope and doom all mixed together. "The victim said a woman that she befriended at a bar lured her to a car, saying she would give her a ride home. As they approached the car, she noticed something moving in the backseat, and she had a gut feeling that something wasn't right. She abruptly declined, and as she started to walk away, the back door opened. A man attempted to grab her but she screamed loudly enough to attract attention. The two perpetrators pushed her down, got in the car, and left the scene. Moments later, an undercover officer was there, but neither the victim nor the officer got a plate number."

"What about descriptions?" Magnus requested.

"Both perps are blond, attractive, and the car was a dark sedan," O'Shea added. "The description of the male seemed in line with CR, but there never was a car before. As always with a change in MO, there is a possibility that it's not CR, but my instincts say it is," he asserted. "We feel that the existence of an accomplice is now confirmed! The victim is giving a description to a composite artist as we speak."

"Where are we with this now?" Magnus asked.

"The task force is meeting in an hour," O'Shea replied. "See you there."

Justus and Magnus left for the meeting, and the rest of us stayed on alert, as usual, while Anton ran the surveillance equipment for the night.

At the task force meeting, Dunn, eager to begin, spoke up. "Back to business . . . we now have some fairly solid evidence that CR has a female accomplice."

"We have two ways to look at this," Agent Chan, the FBI profiler began. "We either have a coerced, fearful woman who has been emotionally and possibly physically abused by the dominant male, or we have a willing partner who is likely a psycho-sociopath, or suffers from borderline personality disorder, or an addiction.

"If she has been coerced, a psychopathic male will generally follow a pattern in breaking her. Starting with charm and seduction, he'll be the perfect mate until he senses the appropriate time to start the emotional control.

"Remember that the psychopath is charismatic and very alluring when he wants to be. He lacks empathy but knows how to read emotion in others. He understands emotions at an intellectual level, although he doesn't feel them. Once the emotional timing is right, he'll start the rest of the process required to control and manipulate his partner. It will likely start with reshaping their sexual norms, guiding them toward his fantasies. Then like other abusive relationships, he'll use degradation and instill social isolation. Finally, to ensure obedience, punishment, both psychological and physical, will be used.

"He will then look to play out his fantasies on others, luring his partner into it. Once she is involved, he'll convince her that she is guilty of the crime they committed and hold this over her to force compliance and silence.

"This type of woman is psychologically damaged but will probably protect her abuser when push comes to shove. Sometimes though, the female partner will come forward, if the physical abuse becomes too intense. Once she is apprehended, she'll likely talk freely about the crime or crimes committed."

Agent Chan paused briefly, looked around the room for signs of understanding, and waited for questions or comments.

"If she is a coerced partner," Johnson noted, "CR has probably been with her for a while. He could be married to her."

"Many psychopaths are married," Agent Chan claimed. "Remember, not all psychopaths are criminals. Some lead normal lives, but they generally know they are different from others."

"We could check with hospitals and clinics for blonde women in the twenty to forty age range with repeated physical abuse," Dunn suggested.

"Yes," O'Shea replied, "but still quite the needle in a haystack, I would imagine. What's the other scenario, Agent Chan?"

"The female psycho-sociopath has not been studied substantially," Agent Chan acknowledged, "but some research shows that the difference between men and women psycho-sociopaths is the expression of deceitful, manipulative, and exploitive traits. Women may be more likely to express these personality traits through behaviors that are associated with other mental illnesses such as borderline personality disorder and are therefore more difficult to identify.

"Where men generally portray a very confident, charismatic, arrogant persona, the woman may be extremely fearful of abandonment and appear to be needy. She may have very noticeable extremes in mood and behavior and may be very impulsive. She may also be just as callous as the male psychopath victimizing others and running elaborate cons to get what she wants.

"There is a possibility that she'll have an increased testosterone level, which can lead to hypersexuality, engaging in impersonal sexual relationships. She may also have a more muscular build and other male developmental traits," Agent Chan concluded.

"We're looking for a horny tomboy with severe PMS?" one of the task force members teased, trying to lighten the atmosphere. His comment elicited a few lackluster chuckles, but beyond that, everyone was very serious and had no sense of humor under the circumstances.

"Thank you for this informative summary, Agent Chan," O'Shea said. "As for the changes in MO, we now have to consider abduction and all the complications this will introduce into the investigation.

Not to mention the huge potential for escalation in violence toward a victim."

"We have to get this out through all media channels with appropriate facts and precautions," Johnson affirmed. "I'll get this done ASAP."

"Dunn, alert all college area clubs and bars with the updated information, and we'll do another campus campaign as well," O'Shea ordered. "I'll ask the techs if there were any camera images of the vehicle, although I doubt it. He has evaded cameras so far."

Once the meeting wrapped up, O'Shea, Johnson, and Dunn met separately with Justus and Magnus.

"We'll have Ethan get to work with this new information," Justus assured O'Shea. "We'll check our cameras for signs of the vehicle, but there aren't too many commercial cameras in that area."

"I fear that the next time we meet, we'll be dealing with a much more detrimental outcome," O'Shea concluded with apprehension.

CHAPTER EIGHT
"Who's on First?"

The hype surrounding the attempted abduction faded as no new developments came from the January incident. There were now two composites of attractive blonds, strong media coverage, a safety campaign at the colleges, but no suspects in custody. With the public attention, the perps likely were no longer blond and smart enough to lie low for a while.

We fed our needs with other criminal activity. Jay, Yasmine, and I kept working the Los Zetas connection. Jay and Yasmine were getting ever more deeply entrenched with the organization, but Jay didn't want me to be involved. My only role was to join Jay during dinners and to act as the doting girlfriend as we entertained the Zetas guests who came to scrutinize us and Gotham Citi.

It took six weeks for the College Rapist to rear his ugly head again, and this time, it was the worst. We were all called to the house for an update on the latest developments.

"There's been a significant change in the College Rapist case," Justus reported to open the meeting. "The cops believe that he's escalated to murder. A thirty-two-year-old stripper was found dead in a vacant apartment in Noho," Justus declared as he showed us a photo of a dark-haired, light-skinned, heavily made-up woman. "It looks like the College Rapist because the victim's hands were bound behind her with a tie wrap, and she was gagged in the same way as his other victims. She was strangled to death with a scarf left tied around her neck in a bow. It happened at least three days ago. She was just discovered today by the unit owner."

"A stripper," Helene said, "that's not the College Rapist."

"May not be," Magnus interjected, "but we're better off to consider it."

Tavia asked, "Was there any sign of an accomplice?"

"No," Justus advised, "but no sign that there wasn't an accomplice either. With such a significant change in MO, something has changed."

"What strip club was she from?" Jay inquired.

"The Scratching Post in Hell's Kitchen," Justus answered.

"I know it. I'll talk to the owner. He'll be straight with me," Jay offered.

"Let's brainstorm some ideas," Anton proposed as he took a fresh piece of paper and pen ready to scribe ideas.

Ethan threw out the first thought. "What would cause this change in MO?"

"Repeating the same MO gives the perpetrator a comfort zone to operate within," Helene noted. "Going outside of his comfort zone takes a greater risk. Why would he increase the risk level?"

"One option is a natural escalation caused by nothing other than the need to get a better thrill," Justus suggested.

"Could be, but I would suspect that he would have evolved to adding risk to rape, not going full out to murder," Magnus postulated. "Maybe he would have escalated to abduction with captivity, prolonging the attacks or something like that."

"The attempted abduction in January is in line with what you're saying, Magnus," claimed Anton. "Maybe there is another victim or victims out there that haven't been linked to this case."

"All possible," maintained Ethan. "Let's rein it in to what we do know right now. There's a murder with some facets of the College Rapist MO, there's a significant change in victimology, and there may or may not be an accomplice for this offense. Let's assume that something triggered a change, a significant change that wasn't just natural escalation," Ethan summarized.

"Let's bring it back to the beginning," Justus proposed. "We have to answer all the questions again.

Why this victim?
Why this day and time?
Why this location?
Why this behavior?"

"With the sexual assaults, we had these questions somewhat answered, but now, with murder, the questions all have to be repeated," Ethan proposed.

"If we are considering this murder victim as one of the College Rapist's, then 'why this victim' is an enigma," observed Helene. "Why change from young school girl types to a skanky stripper?" she queried.

"Not all strippers are skanky," Magnus interjected, winking at Ethan.

Ethan just shook his head, waiting for the rebuttal.

"I presume you're speaking of the ones you've dated?" Helene retorted with disdain, giving Magnus an equally contemptuous look.

Magnus snickered and clarified, "There's an age difference. The murder victim was thirtyish compared with the late-teen, twentyish rape victims, and, to rephrase Helene's description, this victim appeared to have a few more miles on her odometer compared with the young innocent types that were raped."

I was thinking out loud and offered, "Jealousy!"

Everyone stopped and looked at me.

"Jealousy," Justus pondered, looking at me inquisitively.

"Maybe his accomplice felt threatened by the young, pretty school girl types," I reasoned. "I probably would, if it were me."

"Simple human nature," Ethan speculated. "That's a real distinct possibility. Any other thoughts?"

"Maybe it was unplanned, and she was a victim of opportunity?" added Anton.

"Equally as plausible," replied Ethan while nodding his head.

"Yes, but if unplanned, why would he be walking around with tie wraps handy?" Justus speculated.

"Maybe he intended to rape someone but got sidetracked and ended up at the strip club," Helene surmised.

"Maybe his tie wraps are like his VISA card, and he doesn't leave home without them," Magnus mused with a chuckle.

"A Boy Scout . . . always prepared," threw in Anton with a smirk.

"OK, OK, you two," urged Ethan, "I'm feeling safe to assume that he did have the intention of rape, especially if we look at timeline. So far, there has been an assault roughly every six weeks since last spring. It has been almost two months from the attempted abduction and almost four months since the last assault on the books for this perp."

"Then he must have really been 'jonesing' for a fix," Magnus interpolated. "Maybe he was just a little overzealous, and the murder was accidental?"

"A pretty bow tied around the victim's neck doesn't scream accidental to me," insisted Justus.

"There was never a scarf before. If he was into erotic asphyxiation, you think there would have been some sign of it before now?" Helene pondered out loud.

"The bow has a woman's touch," I offered, convinced that the change was related to the female partner.

Magnus pointed out, "Men are generally the erotic strangulation practitioners, and usually, it's a solo activity."

"More men are found dead because of autoerotic strangulation, but that's just because women are smarter, not because they don't do it," Helene retorted to Magnus's comment.

"Point taken," Ethan intervened and added, "If there is a couple, they may engage in erotic strangulation and decided to add it to the rape repertoire."

"Tying a bow with the strangulation device . . . that's callous," Tavia insisted.

"Let's keep with this train of thought," Ethan suggested. "What kind of woman are we dealing with?"

"The obvious answer is that she is a sociopath or psychopath," Magnus concluded.

"Sure, that goes without saying," Anton remarked.

"What's the difference between the two?" I asked.

Of course, Ethan was the one to answer this question. "They are similar in many ways, but the psychopath integrates with society better than the sociopath. The psychopath usually appears normal where the sociopath sticks out as being different. Both lack empathy and remorse, and are characterized by shallow emotions, egocentricity, and deceptiveness. They'll do whatever they want, regardless of laws and social norms, to obtain the thrill they seek."

Justus added, "She would likely have had an abusive childhood, experiencing repeated sexual abuse."

"She likely had issues with the law, and/or she may have been in foster care," Helene surmised.

"These are all the usual traits, gender neutral," Ethan claimed. "There have been studies that indicate that hormone ratios, with increased testosterone, are found in psychopaths."

Helene responded with "Those studies are not conclusive and can't be relied upon."

"The study of psychopathy is young, but we all know psychopaths have been around for a long time," affirmed Justus.

"Remember the Lonely Hearts Killers?" Magnus recollected. "Our only mistake with them was not anticipating their extradition to New York."

"What about Bundy?" pointed out Justus. "We could have saved Florida an electric bill, if only they would have told us about his prison break faster!"

Anton broke in by declaring, "There's a reason that Jack the Ripper was never caught," winking at Tavia, the two of them looking like cats who had just swallowed canaries.

Of course, everyone else knew each other's stories, but they took pride in their noteworthy cases and enjoyed divulging them to newcomers!

"You killed Jack the Ripper?" I stammered with surprise, and they only smiled.

Ethan gave them their moment of glory and continued with the discussion of psychopaths. "The most accepted theories about psychopathy blend genetics and environment," Ethan stated. "It's known that genetics, brain chemistry, brain damage, and history of mental illness are all factors in the development of antisocial personality disorder. Psychopathy falls under the antisocial personality disorder umbrella, as does sociopathy. It has also been proven that children who grow up in violent homes don't develop the social skills that they need to function as normal adults. A strong factor in the development of antisocial behavior is a person's lack of connection with others. They escape their childhood trauma by creating elaborate fantasies, and this carries on into their adult life."

Taking a breath, Ethan continued with "The question then is which one is the cart, which one is the horse? Do the physical factors like brain chemistry changes cause the social issues or do the social issues trigger the changes in physical factors?"

"I think they are so intricately intertwined that there is no way to ever predict if someone will be a sociopath or psychopath," Justus added.

"OK, sure," said Helene, "Nothing is definite, but studies have shown that women psychopaths tend to fall in four categories: the caretaker or angel of death, the profit killer, the revenge killer, and the team killer."

"The woman we are looking for, based on our assumptions, would be a team killer, but there could be some revenge thrown in as well," explained Magnus.

Justus summed up with "The team killer usually kills with a male partner but generally is not the one to initiate the killing. The killing usually involves some sexual assault, and generally, there will be a weapon involved."

"What about the revenge killer?" I asked.

"A revenge killer won't necessarily be a sociopath or psychopath," explained Ethan. "Generally, women who kill for revenge will do it once in a crime of passion. If a serial killer does so out of revenge, it often involves jealousy, or the victims represent someone or a group that the killer finds offensive in some way. For instance, if as a girl the killer was repeatedly molested by her own father, out of revenge, she may target men who look like her father or who act like her father."

"Have you heard of Aileen Wuornos?" Helene asked me. I shook my head, indicating no.

"She was a prostitute that murdered johns because she claimed they were going to rape her," Helene explained. "She had a brutal upbringing involving rape and prostitution at a young age. She definitely was not sane, but she may not have been a psychopath, just an extremely damaged person," Helene suggested grimly.

"Do you mean the woman from the movie *Monster*?" I inquired.

"Yes," she answered.

Justus pulled us back on track with "We have hypothesized some characteristics of the potential partner, and we surmise that the change in MO may be related to the partner. I for one don't think that the murder was an accident. I think two very devious people have found each other and are exploring the depth of their sadomasochism."

"I second that motion," offered Magnus.

"I think the woman is the catalyst for the escalated behavior," added Helene.

"We need to explore the MO a little more," suggested Ethan. "The victim was taken to a location where a more prolonged rape could take place. There were no indicators of excessive anger. She wasn't beaten severely. She wasn't stabbed repeatedly. The room was not in disarray. There were no signs that the victim resisted."

"She probably started off as a willing participant," Justus speculated. "The lack of signs of anger means that either she was completely compliant and therefore didn't cause any anger response in the perp, or that anger was not a motive. We know that CR's attacks demonstrated anger as an element, so this confuses things."

Helene noted, "The fact that he has changed victimology also clouds the idea of motive because as we have already discussed, there is a vast difference between the 'school girl' and the 'slutty stripper.' It seemed that a key piece of the fantasy was the school girl, especially the school girl who acted like a tease."

"The hunting ground changes significantly as well, with a change in victimology," Magnus added.

Everyone sat silently pondering. Ethan broke the silence and proposed, "Let's move on to question number 2. Why this day and time?"

"I think we have covered this one with the analysis of timeline," Justus said. "The College Rapist was overdue for an attack. We'll need the ME to ascertain the time of death, but based on the victim's occupation, the time of day probably matches CR's usual pattern."

"Any other thoughts on that?" Ethan asked.

Everyone nodded, communicating that there was nothing to add.

Ethan continued with question number 3, "Why this location?"

"This is more intriguing!" Helene stated. "Why move from the college district clubs to a strip club in Hell's Kitchen?"

"I think it was the partner's choice," I offered. "Is there anything special about this club?"

"Nothing out of the ordinary for a strip club," Jay commented. "It is not a gentlemen's club. It's lower on the totem pole but not the bottom of the barrel either."

"Maybe there's a tie to Hell's Kitchen?" Magnus suggested. "Can anyone think of any connection?"

Everyone sat silent, searching their minds for any significance, but nobody could come up with anything.

"No significance for the Scratching Post or Hell's Kitchen, but what about a strip club in general?" Helene requested, looking at Magnus, of course.

"If they were looking to pick up someone to have a threesome, a strip club could offer that opportunity," Magnus suggested, "but picking up a hooker would be easier."

"True," agreed Justus. "Maybe they wanted a little entertainment first?"

"A more significant question is why the empty apartment?" Tavia probed. "How did they know it was empty, and how did they get in?"

"When selecting a location for an assault, a rapist would consider isolation, easy entry and exit, chances of being seen, interrupted, or caught," Ethan said, thinking out loud.

"A vacant apartment covers these key points as long as the victim is willing to go into the apartment with them," remarked Magnus. "Once inside, they could do whatever they wanted."

"Maybe the victim was really drunk or drugged, easy to persuade into the apartment," Helene pondered.

Justus looked back on his notes from the conversation with O'Shea and said, "I'll have to get her tox screen results. I don't have anything written down about drugs in her system."

"I get the feeling that this guy wants the fear in his victims, that he wouldn't want them roofied on GHB or E," Magnus proposed.

"The binding and gagging of the victims makes me agree with you," Justus added. "He wants them to feel helpless, terrified, and controlled."

"So they must use some ruse to get the victim into the apartment," Helene suggested. "Like a party!"

"That makes sense. I would be more likely to go to a party with a couple than to go with some guy I just met," I admitted. "It would seem safer. I wouldn't suspect the woman of being a rapist."

"That's what makes this pair all the more dangerous," Ethan cut in. "Women in general would think the same as you."

"How would they get into the apartment?" Anton speculated.

"Let's examine the possibilities," Ethan suggested. "They picked the lock or broke in some other way. They had a key, or it was left open."

"They have their victim with them," Justus began, "under a ruse of some sort, and they start to pick the lock or have to sneak in a back window to get in? This would put the victim on alert that something wasn't right and would lead to problems. I think this is the least likely scenario."

"I agree," reasoned Helene. "Maybe they broke in earlier in the day and left it open?"

Magnus, looking focused, suggested, "That's a possibility but could still be risky. Someone else could get into the apartment and ruin their plan."

"This apartment was ideally located where there wouldn't be too much traffic or people hanging around. It wasn't chosen haphazardly!" Helene assured. "One of them knew about this apartment and had access to it."

"We need to check past tenants," noted Justus.

"We need to check if keys are changed between tenants," Ethan added, "and we need to do a background on the landlord and maybe past owners too."

"O'Shea must be doing this, so I'll see how far they've gotten with it," Justus said.

"Now, the most fascinating of the questions . . . why this behavior?" Ethan queried with a mixture of enthusiasm and apprehension. "We're looking at two heads engaged in the same incident, one we already know something about and the other we don't know anything about."

"The male has been raping for almost a year that we know of, but very likely, this is not the only criminal behavior this perp has been involved with," Justus surmised. "Sex crimes don't just happen. They need a buildup, and if we looked at this guy's past, we would likely find break-ins, robbery, date rape, or some other crime."

"From the behavior demonstrated by this perp, I would peg him as an anger rapist more than a power rapist. As a murderer, since there were no significant signs of overkill, I would say he is a power seeker," offered Magnus.

"What does all this mean?" I asked.

Ethan began with, "A power rapist needs to assert his manhood or dominance. He probably has low self-esteem but overcomes this by acting confident. People wouldn't see him as a person with low self-esteem. They would see him as confident to the point of being arrogant. He would use a con or blitz attack and would likely verbally threaten and degrade the victim. This type of rapist doesn't intend to kill his victim, he just wants to intimidate and control her.

"The anger rapist is more dangerous. His motivation is rage, often against women in general. He is much more violent than the power assertive rapist. He may not intend to kill, but in the fit of rage, he might kill, especially if the victim tries to resist. This rapist is most likely to degrade his victim in some way. He is usually the macho type, married, but has affairs."

"The first one sounds a bit like my ex-husband," I disclosed, remembering the times that Mike forced me to have sex with him. I hadn't revealed much about my past so far because I was always much more interested in hearing about everyone else's history.

"Sounds like you have some experience with deviant behavior?" Justus commented, looking at me with compassion.

I had uttered this, thinking out loud, and really didn't intend to draw attention to myself and my past. Feeling a little uncomfortable with everyone now looking at me, I said, "It took me a while, but I finally did the right thing and had him put away."

"Imagine what you could do to him now . . . ," Magnus hinted, winking at me, changing the mood of the conversation.

"I've definitely thought about it!" I conceded enthusiastically. "What is a power-seeking murderer?" I questioned, changing the focus back to our task.

Magnus took over the technical discussion, describing the details of a power-seeking killer.

"Similar to the power rapist," he described, "this attacker often has underlying feelings of inadequacy because of some childhood emotional trauma. The ultimate power is over life and death, and this killer revels in holding this power over the victim, terrorizing, and ultimately killing. The first murder fuels his fire, so, if I'm correct with my assumptions, there should be more murdered women with the same MO showing up soon."

"Where did this information come from and how accurate is it?" I queried.

"There's been lots of research on serial rapists and killers, but nothing is absolute," Helene advised. "There's still a lot of controversy and no consensus on how reliable profiling is when tracking a deviant. They're called deviants for a reason . . . they deviate from the norm and usually continue to deviate from what we anticipate or expect."

"As a group," Ethan explained, "we have a lot of experience with deviants, but each new one gives us a challenge. There isn't one that is the same, but over the years, we have certainly seen firsthand the patterns that emerge among serial rapists and killers."

I amazed myself that now I was able to handle such conversations, and was even intrigued by the criminal element. It was in my blood after all, with a criminal attorney and judge for a mother.

Jay, Justus, and Magnus left for the Scratching Post to question the owner and some witnesses. Tavia, Helene, Anton, and I continued to discuss the case; and they taught me more about crime analysis.

Johnson and Dunn were already deep into the interrogation process at The Scratching Post when the guys arrived. The establishment was like a three-ring circus—but, in this case, the rings were elaborate stage setups where the dancers performed. What the owner invested in stage design he took from the décor for the rest of the club. There were cheap tables, cheap chairs, plain walls, but in the dim light at performance time, none of that mattered. There was a huge bar with every type of bottle you could possibly imagine.

Greeted by Johnson, they were directed into a room off the main club area. Gathered in the room were several dancers, servers, a bartender, and the club owner. Dunn was interviewing the bartender who had been working the night that Tandy Masterson, the murdered dancer, was killed.

Jay broke away from the group and walked over to greet the owner, who was sitting alone at a small table, reading the newspaper.

"Niko," Jay said while extending a hand to the establishment owner.

"Jay!" Niko replied ignoring Jay's outstretched hand, giving him a bear hug. "How's business at Gotham?" he asked with a thick Greek accent.

"Good, how's business here, other than this recent tragedy?" Jay inquired.

"You know how it is in this business. I'm always losing girls to the competition and now this . . . ," Niko expressed bitterly.

As Jay continued his discussion with the club owner, Justus and Magnus were escorted to meet some of the dancers that remained to be questioned.

"Hello, Miss?" requested Justus, speaking with a tall blonde double-D, scantily clad dancer.

"Missy," she answered, extending her hand.

"OK, Missy, pleasure," Justus said while shaking her hand. "I have some questions about Tandy. Please sit with me," he continued while showing Missy to a table.

"Missy, were you working the night that Tandy disappeared?" he asked.

"Yes, Tandy and I worked together most of the time," she confirmed.

"What do you remember from that night?" Justus probed.

"Everything seemed normal to me. She was working the room, like usual. She always made a lot of money with table dances. We took a smoke break around midnight. I was working a bachelor party. She told me she had some rich old Wall Street type hooked."

"Did she say anything else about the Wall Street guy . . . what he looked like?" Justus questioned.

"No, nothing," Missy responded. "Around two, I looked for her and noticed she was sitting at a table with a blond couple."

"Tell me more about the blond couple," Justus prompted.

"I didn't pay a lot of attention," she admitted. "They were both good looking, midtwenties to midthirties . . . hard to tell."

"Close your eyes," Justus requested. "Remember the atmosphere of the bar from that night. Can you see it?"

"Yes," Tandy replied, eyes closed tight.

"Tell me about it," Justus probed.

"It was a busy night. People were spending a lot of cash. A bachelor party was rare for this time of the year. I was going to ask

Tandy to join me so she could make some extra money. Bachelor parties love to see two women perform together."

"Look around. What else do you see?" Justus asked.

"I see Jim, the bartender. He winked at me and gave a nod toward the bachelor party . . . he makes more tips, the more we keep the parties entertained. The crowd was usual for a busy night, some businessmen, some college boys, some skanks."

"What song was on?" Justus inquired.

"What song was on, I can't remember every detail," Missy declared incredulously, opening her eyes.

"Trust your own mind. It is in there. We just have to dig it out," Justus confirmed. "Close your eyes and let's try again."

Missy closed her eyes, and Justus directed, "Look at Jim again . . . can you see him?"

"Yes, I see him," Missy stated.

"What is Jim wearing?" Justus asked.

"His usual black dress shirt, but he had something pinned to his collar, something pink, maybe a breast cancer pin?" she noted.

"OK, who do you see at the bar?" Justus queried.

"Lots of people. I see them all but don't see any one in particular," she answered.

"What song was playing?" Justus asked again.

Missy paused but kept her eyes closed. "'Back in Black.' Yes, that was playing. All the routines were done, so requests for table dances were the only ones playing."

"Is there anyone near you, anyone standing out from the crowd?" Justus inquired.

"There's a voice from behind me . . . a skank wants to pay for a table dance, flashing his money," Missy responded. "I told him I was already booked for the night."

"Good," Justus said. "Now look over to Tandy. What do you see?"

"She's OK. She's talking to the woman. She's smiling, acting friendly," Missy recalled.

"Is she trying to sell a table dance?" Justus inquired about her behavior.

"It doesn't look like it. She is just socializing. When she's trying to sell, she doesn't sit down. You can't display the merchandise if you're sitting down," Missy continued.

"Describe the woman that Tandy is talking with," Justus requested.

"She's sitting down, so I can't see much," Missy explained. "She's blonde, quite blonde. I'm sure it is a dye job. She is pretty, but not soft. From the little bit I see, she appears to be in good shape and probably in her twenties."

"Do you think you could describe her to a sketch artist?" Justus verified.

"Sure, I could try," she confirmed.

"What else is going on at that table?" Justus requested.

"The guy is watching the girls talk. He isn't really participating in the conversation," Missy described.

"Describe this guy," Justus asked.

"He's blond too, but darker, more natural. He is definitely attractive. I can see more of him than the woman. He is dressed in a casual shirt, probably some light pastel color and light-colored khakis. He is probably thirtyish, well groomed, and fit. I remember he looked at me, like he sensed someone looking at him. His eyes were cold and piercing. I had to look away."

"Sounds like you could give a good description of him to a sketch artist," Justus observed, hoping that this would lead them closer to the College Rapist.

"Yes, I definitely can. I especially remember the eyes," Missy acknowledged.

"What happened next?" Justus asked.

"When I looked away from the blond man, one of the bachelor party guys was standing beside me, and he told me to come back to their table, so I did. That was the last time that I saw Tandy," Missy replied sadly as she opened her eyes.

"Is Tandy her real name?" Justus questioned.

"Yes, it is. Mine is Melissa . . . Melissa Baines," she answered.

"Melissa, was Tandy drinking that night?" Justus tried to ascertain. "Or was she taking any other drugs?"

"Niko is very strict about that, no alcohol, no drugs," Melissa informed him. "We let guys buy us drinks, but we take only a sip and then leave it. They're usually too drunk to notice that we're not drinking. Niko says we are here to make money, not to party. Tandy may have done some drugs recreationally but not when working. I didn't see any signs that she was an addict or a drunk."

"Wearing your dance costumes, I'm guessing you or Niko would have noticed track marks," Justus speculated.

"For sure, Niko makes a point of checking us out every now and then," she advised, showing her arms to Justus.

"What about prostitution?" Justus asked point-blank.

Melissa was taken back a bit by his blunt tone and explained, "It's not part of the job description," and paused briefly, "but what people do outside of work is none of Niko's business."

"Did Tandy have a side business?" Justus questioned, looking Melissa in the eyes.

"Not that I was aware of," she acknowledged, looking straight back at him.

"What was Tandy like, you know, her personality, her character?" Justus probed.

"She was quiet enough. She worked here a lot longer than me. I only started a year ago. She was here for at least three years. You would have to check with Niko. I didn't see her outside the club, but I know she was taking classes at a community college," Melissa explained. "She was a really good dancer. I think she took lessons when she was young because she had really good technique."

"Is there anything else you can tell me about Tandy that could be helpful?" Justus requested.

"No, I wish I could help more, but that's all I know," she answered with a distraught look.

"Your help with the composites of that couple will be very valuable," Justus assured while gently touching her arm to console her. "Thank you for your time," he added as he signaled to a sketch artist.

Once Justus had Missy set up with the sketch artist, he met up with Magnus and Jay.

"What did you get?" Justus asked Magnus.

"Jade, over there," Magnus indicated, looking toward a raven-haired Asian woman, "has only worked here for a few months and didn't have a lot to say about Tandy or the night in question . . . but she did invite me back for a VIP package some night." He finished with a sly smile.

"You're such a dog," Justus scoffed and turned his gaze to Jay. "What did Niko have to say?"

Jay glanced at his notes. "Tandy worked here for almost three years, one of his longest standing dancers. She was straightforward, did her work, was clean, quiet, and didn't mix personal life with work life. She helped choreograph routines for new dancers and was a headliner. She drew a regular following and recently started doing a doubles routine with the one that you were talking with Justus."

"Was Niko around the night that Tandy disappeared?" Justus verified.

"Yes," Jay confirmed, "but not in the club. He was in the office. He couldn't say who was here and who wasn't, other than by payroll records. There is a security tape that we can look at, but it mainly covers the bar area to watch over cash transactions."

"My girl saw Tandy socializing with a couple and can give a decent description," Justus informed them. "She is with the sketch artist right now."

Johnson and Dunn joined Justus, Magnus, and Jay.

"What's next?" Justus asked Dunn.

"We'll get the composites out and alert the college bars and the strip joints," Dunn advised.

"There are too many clubs to stakeout," Johnson added. "We need to concentrate on finding out if there's a connection to the Scratching Post."

"We need to find out if there was any strangulation or threat of strangulation with any of the previous CR rapes," Magnus interjected.

"We need to look into any rapes or murders involving strangulation in general," Justus suggested.

"We can get Vice to work their prostitution connections to round up any johns with strangulation habits," proposed Johnson.

"Ethan will reevaluate the likely zones to patrol based on the history and the change in MO," Justus reported, "but it is going to be an educated guess at best."

"We'll stay on this one full time," Magnus added.

"I'll get the word out to the clubs," Jay advised.

They interviewed a few remaining dancers and servers and wrapped things up. Jay still had a busy night ahead at the club.

He came home just before dawn and joined me on the couch, laying his head in my lap. He was warm and looked satiated. I knew he had fed and probably even overindulged. He looked up at me, his eyes soft and adoring, saying nothing but saying everything. I kissed him and went back to reading my book, leaving him to his thoughts.

After a while, Jay got up and went to his computer. I could hear him typing frantically. I followed him into the office, rubbed his shoulders and neck, and ran my fingers through his hair as he sat facing his computer screen. I quietly left the office and made my way to our bed, hearing his footsteps just behind me.

Jay had excess physical and mental energy to expend. I enjoyed being with him most at those times. He focused all that excess energy in pleasing me. He could read my every move, sound, and thought it seemed. It was like time was standing still, but the reality was that hours passed.

As we both collapsed, physically drained, me lying with my head on Jay's shoulder, I traced the outline of a tattoo on his chest with my finger. I could hear his heart beating, and his scent was intoxicating. I never felt more content and could have stayed there, like that, for hours, maybe days.

"What is this tattoo?" I asked as I traced its circle shape.

"It is a Tomoe, a Buddhist symbol," Jay answered.

"What does it mean?" I asked.

Jay responded after a few seconds of thought, "It means circular energy, and the three flames represent the earth, the heavens, and humankind. The Tomoe embodies a never-ending source of energy from the interaction of the three forces."

He took my hand and put my finger to the diamond-shaped tattoo he had on his arm and described, "This one is the endless knot. It represents the intertwining of wisdom and compassion."

His third tattoo, which intrigued me the most, was on his back, between his shoulder blades. It was a swastika with four dots. I couldn't picture Jay promoting Nazi or Neo-Nazi beliefs, ever. "What about the tattoo on your back?" I questioned.

"That one is the oldest one. I've had it for centuries. It's a swastika, as I'm sure you know. The word *swastika* comes from the Buddhist Sanskrit word *svastika*, which means lucky object . . . lucky charm," Jay finished.

"You are my lucky charm," I said, locking my eyes on his.

With all the warmth his eyes possessed, he looked deeply into me and confessed, "You are my lucky charm . . . you have charmed me, and my life will never be the same. The empty feeling that I have lived with forever has been replaced by a peaceful glow like embers." He kissed me tenderly.

Our beautiful moment was cut short when Jay's phone vibrated with a text requesting us to come to the house.

We arrived to find everyone already there, waiting for us.

"About time," Justus grumbled, winking at me.

Of course, we already knew that they were talking about us before we arrived because we could hear it all.

"Here is the latest," Justus began. "The rental unit where Tandy Masterson was found is managed by a property management firm, and there is no apparent connection to the victim, to any blond couple, to anyone at The Scratching Post."

Magnus added, "It seems random, but I really doubt it."

"It isn't random," Ethan cut in. "We just don't have the connection yet. We'll have to keep working it, digging deeper. Something is there . . . I know it," he finished with frustration.

We sat silent briefly, and then Justus resumed with his report. "Johnson reported that their canvass of known prostitutes revealed one who had a couple matching the description almost kill her a few weeks ago."

"OK," Ethan declared, "that gives the escalation a more subtle progression. It didn't make sense that murder would just suddenly be the perp's next step."

"What was the story?" Helene asked.

Magnus read the prostitute's statement from a printed sheet:

> They picked me up at Twenty-eighth and Lex, and we went to a hotel in Soho. They told me that they were married, and that this was the first time they wanted to try a threesome. We talked about price and safety, and when all the business was taken care of, we drank for a while.
>
> The woman then took out a tie wrap and gave it to her husband and said that she wanted me to pretend to be a rape victim.

Her husband tied my arms behind my back, and then she brought over a cloth from the bathroom and went to put it in my mouth. I've done kink before, so this was no big deal, but before I let her gag me, I told them that this increased the price. The woman agreed and shoved the cloth in my mouth.

The guy then forced me down on the bed on my front and started to rape me from behind. The woman gave him a scarf, a pink sheer scarf, and I didn't know what he was going to do with it. He put it around my neck and started choking me with it as he raped me more. I was trying to scream but couldn't. I tried fighting against him. I couldn't make him stop, and just before I passed out, I heard the woman say, "Pull tighter," and then all went black.

When I woke up, they were gone, and there was no money. I didn't report it because I didn't want any cops on my case.

"The woman is the aggressor with strangulation," Helene remarked. "She must have some hatred issues toward women."

"If we looked into her past, she was probably abused or mistreated by a woman."

"Or women," Helene interjected. "Young women, girls, can be very cruel."

"They didn't kill the hooker," Magnus pondered. "Was the intention to kill her and they chickened out, or was the thrill just in the choking act?"

"This raises the question again about the death of the dancer. Could it have been accidental from an overzealous role play?" Justus queried.

"Tying a ribbon around the victim's neck tells me that it wasn't an accident. It was designed and enjoyable to them," Tavia pointed out, thinking out loud.

"Unfortunately, we won't know for sure until there is another victim, dead or alive," Ethan cautioned with a miserable look on his face.

"The cops have some undercovers from Vice working the various sex trade districts, and the composites have been circulated to the strip clubs," summarized Justus. "Here are the updated drawings of both suspects, as given by the prostitute."

We studied the drawings. The male I had seen already from the rape victim composite, but this drawing gave more detail. They had a very similar look, like they could be siblings. It's never easy to tell if a woman's hair color is natural or not, but both were described as blond. Both had attractive faces but with cold blue eyes.

Now that murder was imminent, we decided to join the surveillance effort at the bars and clubs. The strength of our immortal senses could help pick up clues that police officers couldn't. We were all now weekend bar hoppers since the College Rapist's pattern was to attack on Friday or Saturday nights.

"OK, ladies," Magnus reveled with a glint in his eyes, "you hit the college bars. Guys, we hit the strip clubs."

"What a horrible assignment to be on!" Ethan quipped as he threw an innocent look at Helene.

This was going to be an interesting night of surveillance!

Jay went to Gotham Citi. Yasmine was still playing girlfriend to Carlos, the Los Zetas New York distributor, and would meet up with Jay at the club. Justus and Magnus split up so they wouldn't attract attention. Either one on his own could attract enough attention in a crowd, but the two of them would definitely not go unnoticed. The idea behind tonight was to be under the radar, not to draw attention.

Ethan and Magnus went to Chelsea, while Justus and Anton went to Alphabet City. Dunn joined Tavia, Helene, and I as we headed out to the college bars. I was teamed with Tavia for the night, and Helene was partnered with Dunn. The rest of the police force was out on overtime, patrolling the college bars, some notable strip clubs, and the busy prostitution areas.

We were assigned a specific radius to cover, so Tavia and I started with the first club we encountered, named Hammer Time. We stood out in the crowd not only because of our usual aura but also because of our age. Hammer Time lived up to its name because it was basically a beer swilling bar, with the cheapest pitchers of beer in the area. There was no dance floor, just long wooden tables that looked somewhat like picnic tables made out of logs. The bar was immense, and there were televisions showing sports of all types. There was a boxing match on the main screen that seemed to be keeping most of the boys in the club entertained. The music and atmosphere was in the genre of *Spirit of the West's* "Home for a Rest."

Almost immediately, a pack of young boys surrounded us, asking to buy us drinks; I don't think many cougars made their way into Hammer Time! Needless to say, this was not the target bar that we expected for the College Rapist and his accomplice. We flirted innocently with the young college boys for a few minutes and then left on our next bar conquest.

The Dusty Rose was up on the next block. It was a more upscale dance club. This one was a complete contrast to Hammer Time. Everything was silver and black—tall tables, tall bar stools, tall glasses, stiletto heels. The black leather barstools seats held by thin silver legs were populated by beautiful people—sleek dresses, suits, trendy glasses, high cheek bones. We were surrounded by people that rivaled ourselves in mystique and attraction. The atmosphere was euro and trance. Flashing lights made people look robotic on the dance floor. Tavia and I quickly determined that this too was not the likely target scene for the College Rapist.

Next was Jam-boree, a live music club with rock, classic rock, modern rock, blues rock, jeans, T-shirts, a casual atmosphere. We stayed long enough to see a great *Hootie and the Blowfish* cover of "Let Her Cry" by a college band. We didn't consider this one a target for our perps either.

Finally, we found the right type of club, with *Britney, Beyonce,* and *Rihanna* blaring at the Back Room, the perfect school girl bar, where the young energetic, pretty girls went and the horny, cocky, hopeful boys followed. This is the type of place our perps would be, if they decided to come back to the college bars to hunt.

Here we could settle in for a while. We watched everyone who came in, everyone on the dance floor. We listened to everyone. We knew all their little secrets, all the lies, all the deceptions, the games that mortals play! Watching and listening made me think of Jay and how happy I was to have an absolute certainty that he loved me, that I was the only person for him.

Tavia noticed me slipping away into my own thoughts and gave me an elbow.

"That infatuation period can be all consuming," she groaned.

"How did you know I was thinking about Jay?" I asked.

"By that silly smile and your eyes. They tell it all!"

We had to concentrate on looking for the couple who could destroy the life of one of these young women, women just like my daughter. It made me think of my Ana being out in one of these bars with these unsavory boys looking to get into her pants. Again, Tavia had to snap me out of my own thoughts. I guess surveillance wasn't my forte.

"I'm hungry," I announced. "It has been a while since I fed, and I'm due."

"We'll troll a few more bars, and then we'll go get something to eat," she suggested. "I know of a sure thing. I've been keeping my eye on a certain pimp."

We did exactly that. We found another couple of bars that fit the profile; we watched and listened for clues, for people who may know our criminal pair, but came up empty.

"Let's go," Tavia said, once last call was over at Zax, the last bar we frequented for the night.

Famished, I followed Tavia through the city at top speed. I could finally keep up with her. I was reaching my full power, and it was exhilarating. I could hurdle things too, like cars and other minor obstacles. As we were on our way to the anticipated kill, I heard a cry for help and stopped dead in my tracks.

I could smell it, bloodshed, not far. As the frenzy built up in me, I could now sense it in time to control it, to focus that energy toward the hunt. As my maker, Tavia was in tune with me. I didn't have to say anything; she followed, letting me lead.

I tracked the scent and the dying breaths to an alley with a putrid stench of garbage and the delicious scent of blood, fresh and guilty. A homeless man lay in a pool of his own blood, starving and in pain from fatal stab wounds, the perpetrator not far. Tavia stayed to take mercy on the victim while I gladly tracked his murderer.

I always found it amusing how these cowardly killers would flaunt their weapons. He looked at me, and I saw in his eyes that he knew it was over for him. I was learning to savor the moment. I took in the aroma, as you would a hot meal or a wonderful wine. Still so intoxicating, I smelled his throat while he was paralyzed in my grasp. Biting in, slowly, drinking, letting the warmth flow over my tongue, tasting it, I allowed his visions to take over my mind.

This man, like many others, had a pitiful life, a painful life. I was learning to accept these visions and letting the life flow out of my prey, giving them mercy from their painful existence. This wretch stabbed the old man in the alley for a bottle of booze; to think that a bottle of booze could be more important than his fellow man. His last thought was the face of his beautiful daughter, when she was five years old, before he went to prison for the first time . . . a sweet smiling girl with flowers in her hair, wearing a yellow Sunday dress.

The last beat of the heart was always invigorating for us, our kind, who need to take lives to have life. It sent a shudder through me every time, a flood of heat, strength and power.

After dropping his corpse into a nearby dumpster, I returned to the alley to find Tavia. She too had the glow of having just fed, alleviating the pain and suffering of a slow death for the old man in the alley.

Forsaking our planned target, Tavia and I made our way home, advising Justus that there was an unintended "mess" to clean up.

At Gemini, an exotic dance club in Chelsea, the twins, Anton and Ethan, met to wind down their evening of dancers and debauchery.

"I hope everyone kept their focus on scanning the crowd for a blond couple?" Ethan snickered.

"I kept my ears on task, but my eyes were distracted occasionally," Magnus countered with his gaze directed toward a tall, dark-haired, Mediterranean seductress.

"You can play later," Justus warned, as he drew Magnus back to the conversation with a force that can only be understood by twins.

"Any credible intel?" Justus put out to the group.

Ethan reported for him and Magnus. "We started at the Toy Box, an interesting club," he announced, looking over at Magnus, watching the smile grow on his face. For his age in centuries, Magnus was about as mature as a thirteen-year-old boy! "For all the times that I have already experienced it, I'm still amazed at how women throw themselves at Magnus!" Ethan exclaimed.

"OK, so besides the free lap dances, was there anything of use from this club?" Justus requested impatiently.

"No, nothing," Ethan continued. "Next we went to Juggs, and this was also a bust, no pun intended, except for the phone numbers that Magnus collected."

"We did get a lead from the bartender at Black Magic," Magnus cut in. "He told us he remembered a blond couple there about a week ago, talking to some of the girls."

"He noted that the woman looked familiar to him, but he couldn't remember from where," Ethan added.

"Interesting," Justus observed, kicking Magnus under the table, luring his focus away from the Mediterranean dancer who was tempting him with some overt flirting.

"We got nothing and lost money paying for table dances," Anton ranted disappointed, describing his night with Justus. "I want to go out with Magnus next time," he whined, winking at Ethan, who chuckled.

"Where did you guys go?" Magnus asked, directing his gaze above Justus's head at the approaching temptress.

"The Game Room, Scarlet Letter, and the G Spot," Anton advised.

"Basically then, for our night of T&A, we have one bartender who remembers a blond couple with a familiar-looking woman," Justus summarized.

"Don't forget the phone numbers I got," Magnus threw at Justus, pushing his luck.

Justus gave Magnus a sideways glance and chose to ignore his brother's attempt to get his goat.

"Where was that club located?" Anton inquired.

"Just close to Hell's Kitchen," Ethan stated. "There is definitely some significance to that. Two clubs reasonably close to each other where a blond couple has been seen talking to dancers. I'll have to crunch this along with some other factors and see what our next target area for surveillance should be."

Justus looked at Magnus, who was completely absorbed in flirting, and conceded. "OK, go get her." No sooner had the words come out of his mouth than Magnus was gone, like a flash.

"Anyone up for a warm one?" Ethan proposed.

"I'm just going home," Justus announced. "The two of you enjoy."

"Let's hunt!" Anton exclaimed eagerly to Ethan, and they too took off like sprinters out of the starting gates.

Justus sat there looking at his brother, already heading for the door with his catch of the night. Although he couldn't stop the brief smile from forming on his lips, Justus deeply felt loneliness that he knew couldn't be fixed by picking up random women. He sat for a while longer, tuning into the conversations going on around him, scanning for any useful information, then went home.

CHAPTER NINE
Obsession

I was set to partner with Dunn for the first time on a bar-hopping intelligence mission. I felt like *Agent 99* in a covert operation.

"How much does Dunn know about us?" I asked Justus.

"She knows it all," he answered.

This was going to be awkward for me. I generally wasn't good just hanging around with new people. What would we talk about? I was always a tagalong in groups, usually stayed on the fringe. I found this weird. Here I was an immortal who should have no worries. After all, what is there to worry about when you're immortal? I realized that although I was virtually physically indestructible, I was still emotionally vulnerable. Immortality didn't change my essence. I still had petty worries, I still felt insecure at times, I still judged myself, and I was still my own worst critic. Despite my great physical strength and abilities, I was still that hurt and tentative young girl who lost her father at a young age; that shameful wife who was abused by her husband.

I met Dunn at the police station, and wow, did she look different. I had the impression that she was very reserved and kind of butch, but she definitely wasn't dressed to give that impression this evening. She had me beat by tenfold as far as sexy school girl looks were concerned; I was going to have to learn from her for next time! She was wearing a sexy tight skirt that was a far cry from business wear, and she was definitely sporting a push up bra. As we were leaving the precinct, some of her colleagues made cat calls and whistles, which she rejected by flipping the bird.

The previous focus for surveillance had been on clubs near those that the College Rapist victims had frequented. Tonight, we were to focus on clubs in a radius just outside that area.

Dunn and I started at ZanziBar, a two-story, darkly lit, quasi-Goth club. We made small talk for a while—the weather, where each of us was from, and so on. We sat silently for a few minutes, and then Dunn asked, "You're the newest one, right?"

"I'm the newest what?" I questioned.

"You know," she whispered, leaning toward me, "immortal."

"Yeah, I guess," I answered, feeling self-conscious.

"How long have you been . . . that?" Dunn probed.

"For several months," I replied.

"What's it like?" Dunn continued.

"Being immortal?" I returned.

"Yah, you know, what does it feel like?" Dunn continued to probe.

"Well, my body doesn't feel much different, but I'm incredibly strong and fast," I explained.

"How strong?" she queried.

"Real strong," I told her. "I'll show you later when we're done with all of this."

We sat in silence again, somewhat uncomfortable, looking around at the people frequenting the bar. I could feel Dunn looking at me, as I tried to tune into various conversations.

"I hear you can read minds," Dunn said, inquisitively.

"Read minds . . . who told you that?" I scoffed, smirking, already guessing who it was.

"Magnus alluded to it," she disclosed.

"He's just messing with you," I told her. "We can hear conversations from a distance, but we can't read minds."

"That's good," Dunn admitted. "If he knew what I was thinking about him when he was around, it would be really awkward!"

"You too?" I agreed, "If Magnus and Justus could have read my mind when I first met them, we'd all have been very embarrassed. Well, at least I would have been!"

"It's hard to stop fantasizing about that man . . . ," Dunn continued with a sigh and a distant look in her eyes.

"Give it up," I warned. "He's nice to look at, but he is a real dog when it comes to women."

"I'll throw him a bone," Dunn taunted, giggling, and we both laughed as the server came to our table.

"What'll you have, ladies?" the tiny energetic barmaid asked.

"A Heineken," Dunn requested.

"I'm the designated driver," I said. "Nothing for now, thanks."

As the server bounced away, Dunn declared, "All right, time to get down to business. Let's work the room."

As we waited for the server to return, I noticed a blond couple dancing. I pointed them out to Dunn. I tuned into their conversation but heard nothing but drunken talk of exams and who in the dorm got the drunkest the night before.

"That's a dead end," I told Dunn, thinking out loud.

"How do you know?" she asked.

"Because I can hear them as clear as I can hear you," I answered enthusiastically, still in awe of my new talents.

"That's cool," she said astonished. "What are those guys over there saying?" she asked playfully.

I looked over to where Dunn was indicating, spying two well-dressed, classically handsome men. I listened briefly and replied, "They're talking about money, stock trades, and the like."

Dunn pointed out another set of men, dressed in T-shirts and jeans, and inquired, "What about them?"

It didn't take long for me to answer. "They're just talking trash!"

"That skill would be incredibly handy for police work. I'm jealous . . . Make me immortal?" she demanded lightheartedly.

"Be careful what you wish for!" I cautioned as the barmaid arrived with Dunn's beer. "It's not all fun and games," I asserted as she paid the woman.

We got up and strolled the club, Dunn using her police-trained observation skills and me using my immortal hearing and eyesight. So far, nothing seemed noteworthy at this club. There were TV screens showing the crowd dancing on the second level, assisting us with our recon mission. As we approached the stairs leading to the second floor, I overheard two girls speaking about the composite of a woman that was hung in the rest room.

"Come on," I ordered Dunn as I grabbed her arm and pulled her through the dense crowd of young college kids, swaying somberly to "Don't Let It Go" by *HIM*. We entered the restroom and approached the two girls that I heard speaking.

"Excuse me," I interrupted, "what did you say about the woman in the composite there?" I requested as I pointed to the drawing on the wall of the suspected College Rapist's accomplice.

The two girls turned to see us simultaneously, as though startled. The one girl had dyed red hair and not a natural red, fire engine red, dressed in fish net stockings, Doc Marten boots and a short black dress. The other, a slender brunet, long hair, wearing torn jeans, thigh-high boots, and a wide-neck black shirt said, "Um, I met that woman . . . why?"

Dunn flashed her badge and ordered, "We need you to come outside."

"O . . . K," she agreed reluctantly, looking over at her friend. "I'll meet you back here after?"

The redhead, looking curiously at me, muttered, "Yeah, whatever," and walked passed Dunn, giving her a disrespectful glare.

We left with the witness to the back alley of the club where we could talk more clearly.

"What's your name?" Dunn asked the girl.

"Allie," she answered sheepishly.

"OK, Allie, you said that you met the woman in the drawing," Dunn questioned, peering at the girl, the way that cops do.

"Yes," Allie responded.

"Tell me about it," Dunn continued.

"What do you want to know?" Allie threw back at Dunn, seeming concerned to give any information.

"Look," Dunn revealed, "I don't care if you are underage, if you were doing drugs, or even hooking the night you met the woman. I just need to know the details . . . all the details."

"Well, it was at the Back Room," she began, "a couple of weeks ago, I think. I was hanging out with a different crowd then." She paused to look at Officer Dunn. "My friends had left, and I was talking to this guy, who turned out to be an assho . . . a jerk . . . and she came up to me after he left me. She seemed nice, and she talked to me about how guys are all jerks and other stuff."

Allie paused and looked at me, scrutinizing.

Dunn demanded, "And then what?" snapping Allie out of her trance.

She looked away from me to Dunn and continued, "We had a couple of drinks together and talked usual girl talk . . . you know, that guy is hot, that chick looks like a bitch. She was like an instant friend. She told me she would give me a ride home, and just as we were getting to the door to leave, my roommate showed up, out of nowhere, and wanted me to stay with her. It took only a second, then when I looked around, my new friend was gone."

"What was this woman's name?" Dunn requested.

"Cassie, she told me," the girl answered.

"Did she ask you your name first?" Dunn queried.

Allie looked up briefly, thinking, and declared, "Yes, I think so."

I looked at Dunn inquisitively.

"Who did most of the talking while you were together?" Dunn probed.

Again, Allie paused to think. "I did. She seemed so easy to talk to that I just talked a lot. It's kind of weird when I think about it now."

"Did she share any personal information with you?" Dunn continued.

"Yes, she talked about the same stuff as me, being single, having just left a bad relationship, taking classes, exams," Allie explained.

"Did you notice her looking around a lot or looking at a specific guy?" Dunn inquired.

"No, I don't think so," Allie explained. "She said that her friends left too."

"Did she say anything about where she lived?" Dunn asked.

"Hmm," Allie uttered as she thought, "I told her where I lived, and she told me that my place was on the way to hers, so she could drop me off."

"How certain are you that the woman you met is the same woman as in the drawing?" Dunn requested.

"I'm pretty sure, like 90 percent," Allie confirmed, assertively.

Dunn studied her face carefully as she answered then verified, "Have you seen her since then?"

"No," Allie responded.

"I want to find her," Dunn indicated. "Is there anything else that you remember about her and your conversation that would give me an idea of where to find her?"

"Nothing that I can remember," she advised. "What has Cassie done?" Allie questioned Dunn.

"Her name is probably not Cassie, and all I can say is to stay away from her and call me if you see her," Dunn warned as she handed Allie her business card. "She knows where you live so take precautions, keep your doors and windows locked, don't open the door to anyone you don't know. We might need to contact you again. What's your full legal name, address, and phone number?" Dunn requested.

As Dunn was taking down the information, I picked up on a conversation I heard from around the block.

"I'll give you a ride home, come on. I live the same way you're headed," a female voice coaxed.

"Well, my friends might come back," replied another female voice tentatively, "but maybe I should leave."

I left the alley and hurried toward the voices, and just as I was getting close to them, I cut in, "Excuse me," and both women turned to look at me. Both had brown hair, one light and one dark. "Do you have the time? I'm supposed to be meeting someone, and I'm late," I explained.

The woman with the darker hair looked at her phone and gave me the time. The lighter-haired woman rushed back into the club before I had a chance to speak with her.

"I'm waiting for my friends too," the dark-haired woman said as she put her phone away and turned to look at her new companion who had just vanished.

"Where did she go?" the young woman asked.

"Did you know her, the one who was here with you?" I requested.

"Just a little. I met her tonight. My friends ditched me, and so did hers, so we talked for a while, and she offered me a ride home."

"I need to find her," I said as I hurried toward the door of the club. "Stay away from her and don't take rides from strangers," I advised as I disappeared through the door.

I maneuvered my way through the crowd with ease and listened for clues but didn't find her. She might have been the College Rapist's accomplice or was I just too suspicious?

I returned to find Dunn finishing up her notes.

"Hey, where did you go?" Dunn asked.

"I heard a conversation that concerned me, and I followed it," I answered.

"Oh yeah, what was it?" Dunn questioned.

"It may have been the College Rapist's accomplice, but I lost her."

Dunn looked at me soberly and asked, "What does your gut say?"

"I think it was her," I confirmed.

"What did she look like? What was she wearing?" Dunn probed as she dialed headquarters.

"I didn't see her for long . . . light brown, straight, medium-length hair, my height, a short dark skirt but not black, ankle boots, a short-waisted dark jacket, a blousy top of some sort," I described as quickly as I could.

Dunn called headquarters to put out an immediate BOLO in the college bar vicinity for the description I gave. She advised that the suspect would likely be with a male, six foot, attractive, and well dressed. "Stop vehicles for DUI checks and bring people in that remotely resemble the suspects," she finished as she hung up the phone.

"Those descriptions don't narrow it down too much, unfortunately," Dunn conceded, "But you never know. We may get lucky. You did great following the lead and your gut."

"If it is her, she changed her appearance," I told Dunn.

"Not unusual," Dunn returned. "The composites have made it necessary, and in fact, we expected it. The guy probably isn't blond anymore either."

"I didn't understand some of your questions for that witness," I told Dunn.

"What do you mean?" she queried.

"Well, it seemed that you were asking about trivial things like who said what first," I described.

"There are a couple of reasons for that," she began. "One was to observe her while she was speaking to get clues for how much truth she was telling. What she does with her eyes, her hands, and her general demeanor tells me a lot. Second was to get a sense of the style of conversation they were having. The woman was using mirroring to try to instill a sense of comfort, to build some trust. It appeared to me that she was building a con to lure our witness into a possible trap."

"Wow, there's a lot for me to learn," I acknowledged. "It's so interesting. I'd like to learn a few of those techniques. It could come in handy!"

Dunn returned to the station to monitor the BOLO, and I went to Gotham Citi. Every time I walked in, the majesty of it never ceased to catch me and make me stand in awe. Tonight there was a tribute to the Cure, and as I walked in, "Just Like Heaven" was starting. I made my way through the dense crowd on the dance floor, right to the center where I was consumed by the music. Soon, a set of familiar hands were circling my waist, and familiar lips kissing my neck, sending shivers through me. As always, time seemed to stand still when we were together. I heard nothing but the music and felt nothing but him as I turned to look at his handsome face.

"How did you know I was here?" I asked.

"I tracked your scent," he whispered in my ear, sending shivers down my spine, again, and the tingles didn't end there.

Jay always knew exactly how to entice me, my sensitive spots, where to touch me, how to hold me, what to say.

Our embrace ended as the band called Jay to the stage. It was time for his customary thank you to the band, the crowd, the staff, and these days, to me, for being part of his life. I watched him on the stage with the feeling of bursting inside because he loved me. It was like being in a perpetual crush. Then he requested my favorite Cure song, "In Between Days" as the encore; we danced, alone among the crowd.

Jay led me to his office where he spared no time in seducing me, even though I was eager to tell him about my night. Every time I tried to tell him about the College Rapist's accomplice, he interrupted me with torrid kisses until I couldn't remember what I wanted to say. Soon, I was the aggressor, pushing him down on to his work chair, using him for my pleasure.

Interrupted by a knock at the door, Jay picked me up and whispered, "I'll deal with you later," kissing my cheek and setting me down gently.

He went off to take care of some work emergency, leaving me roused and disheveled. I straightened myself up and made my way to the balcony to help Jay deal with business.

"Ivy," I heard from across the vast balcony.

There I saw Dietrich and Blaze surrounded, of course, by a harem of beautiful women, mortal women.

"Hello, my lovely," Dietrich said as he took my hand and kissed it.

Blaze, less courteous to the women hanging on him, hugged me and in European tradition kissed both my cheeks.

"I didn't know you were back in town," I commented.

"We love American women," Dietrich answered, winking at the most beautiful member of his adoring entourage. She perked up like a peacock displaying her feathers.

"They smell so sweet," Blaze asserted as he kissed the long exposed neck of the woman by his side.

"Join us, please," Dietrich invited me.

I spent the rest of the evening catching up with Blaze and Dietrich, hearing all about their gallivanting until Jay passed by with a request for me to help with the close.

I said my goodbyes to Dietrich, Blaze, and their entourage.

"Remember," I whispered in Blaze's ear, "no one from the club."

"Worry not," he returned. "We know the rules. There are other means of entertainment with our current company," he proposed then kissed the woman on his right and then the one on his left, winking at me.

I wondered, *Was Jay ever a dog with women, like Dietrich and Blaze?* Although I couldn't picture it, he had lived a long time. Magnus would probably enjoy a few nights out with these hounds, a trio of womanizers out on the prowl!

We closed up the club, and by the time we got home, it was almost dawn. I could finally tell him about my brush with the College Rapist's accomplice.

"I was so close to her," I blurted, exasperated. As I thought about the experience, I felt both invigorated and incensed. "If only I would have followed her more quickly, I might have caught her," I continued, getting more wound up. Second-guessing is the insecure person's best friend!

"You followed your gut," Jay stated, trying to console me, "and you made sure that her intended target was safe. That's the most important thing."

"I guess," I retorted weakly.

"It's a good sign that we're looking in the right area for our perps," he added. "Come here," he urged as he reached for me, "we started something earlier that I need to finish, and I think it will make you feel better!"

Of course, like always, he did make me feel better, much better!

A few weeks after my brush with the potential accomplice, Justus and Magnus were called to a college campus dorm. We were in another College Rapist dry spell, which made all of us uneasy, not knowing what we would find next.

Arriving, they found Dunn and Johnson searching one of the dorm rooms. It was a typical college student dorm room, with clothes strewn all over, books piled everywhere. There was a stench of old food, dirty laundry, stale closed-up air; this room had not been lived in for a little while.

"What's happening here?" asked Justus as he and Magnus put on some nitrile gloves.

"Look at this," Johnson suggested, handing Justus an open diary.

Justus and Magnus read together.

> Tonight we took it further. She made the fantasy perfect. He was so excited by it, when I told him to pull the scarf tighter . . . I watched the life go out of her eyes, and it was amazing. He told me he loved me after, and that meeting me was the best thing that ever happened to him.

They read on for a few pages, and Magnus asked, "What's this?"

"It's the diary of Marilyn Walker, the student that lives here. We suspect she's a Jane Doe found a few days ago in the East River, no ID," Johnson answered. "We matched the Jane Doe with a missing person report by the university. We found the diary hidden under a false bottom of this jewelry case," he continued as he pointed to a pretty wooden jewelry box adorned with two gold painted hearts on the cover surrounding finely detailed pink painted roses.

"It was just by luck that we found it," Dunn interjected. "Johnson knocked over the case while flipping the bed mattress."

"Look at the date of the entry you read. It corresponds to the first suspected CR murder and sounds like it too," Johnson indicated.

"What else do you know about her?" Magnus probed.

"Not much, she was a twenty-two-year-old, third year student," Dunn replied. "We called you guys and O'Shea as soon as we read a few pages of the diary. We had the residence floor leader assemble all the students from this floor in the lounge, and O'Shea is sending some interrogators."

"Read on, I think it is pretty safe to say that the writer was CR's accomplice," Johnson observed as he resumed searching the room for other evidence that would link the missing woman to the Jane Doe and to the College Rapist.

Justus took the diary to a quiet room and started to read, while Magnus stayed with the officers, continuing to search the dorm room of the missing student.

Flipping through the first few pages, Justus realized that this journal had been started several months back. She had some usual college girl journal entries—complaints about classes, her dorm mates, and work. Several pages in, it started to get interesting.

July 29

Last night, I met HIM, the one. All the other guys have been juvenile, unable to understand me at all. HE is different; it was like HE knew me right away. I've needed some excitement in my life. I can't stand the boring pursuits of students, especially the immature girls I live with day in and day out. It was getting to the point where I couldn't take it anymore, but now it's different; everything else is tolerable because of HIM.

The night we met, I saw HIM watching me but not engaging, and this intrigued me. Older, sophisticated, attractive, he was exactly what I was looking for, not one of the boys from campus.

When we met, there was a meeting of souls, an immediate attraction and an unspoken understanding of how WE differ from others. WE drank and flirted with each other, heightening our desire. It was eighties night at the bar, and when the song "Obsession" came on, we both knew immediately that this was our song; and we took over the dance floor with a wild seductive dance.

You are an obsession, I cannot sleep
I am a possession unopened at your feet
There is no balance, no equality
Be still I will not accept defeat

I will have you, yes I will have you
I will find a way and I will have you
Like a butterfly, a wild butterfly
I will collect you and capture you

You are an obsession, you're my obsession
Who do you want me to be to make you sleep with me

I feed you, I drink you by day and by night
I need you, I need you by sun or candlelight
You protest, you want to leave
You say there's no alternative
Your face appears again, I see the beauty there
But I see danger, stranger beware
A circumstance in your naked dreams
Your affection is not what it seems

You are an obsession, you're my obsession
Who do you want me to be to make you sleep with me

My fantasy has turned to madness
All my goodness has turned to badness
My need to possess you has consumed my soul
My life is trembling, I have no control

I will have you, yes I will have you
I will find a way and I will have you
Like a butterfly, a wild butterfly

> *I will collect you and capture you*
> *You are an obsession, you're my obsession*
> *Who do you want me to be to make you sleep with me?*
>
> *We left together after that song, hand in hand. We didn't have to talk. We both knew it was destiny. We walked a short way when he suddenly pulled me forcefully into an alley. He pushed me face forward up against a wall and bound my hands behind my back. Holding me forcefully into the wall, one hand on my bound wrists and the other on my throat with slight pressure, he whispered in my ear, "Does this scare you?" With heaving breath and butterflies in my stomach, I told him, "I love this." My heart was racing, and without saying a word, he forced himself upon me, like I was his victim, and I played the victim well.*
>
> *This was the most amazing sex I had ever experienced, a mix of excitement, fear, lust, and ecstasy . . .*

Justus read on a little bit more, enough to be fairly convinced that the author was the accomplice for the College Rapist and called Ethan to join them in reviewing the new developments.

O'Shea arrived with a couple of interrogators to question the students who lived with Marilyn Walker. A temporary meeting room was set up in a kitchenette on the residence floor to facilitate the investigation. Justus and Magnus took the newly found evidence directly to O'Shea.

Ethan was thumbing through the journal with a shocked expression, as he read an entry that detailed a night the author watched, with enjoyment, as her partner raped someone.

"Intriguing how two demented people can find each other like that?" Ethan stated, looking around at the others in the room. "Definitely blows away the concept of opposites attracting. You know some social studies indicate that despite the popular belief that opposites attract, we are more attracted to those like us, or at least, we'll create more stable, long-term bonds with those like us."

Magnus looked over at Justus, rolling his eyes as Ethan continued. "You know there's also scientific evidence that we seek out and protect those similar to us. The selfish gene theory by Richard Dawkins outlines how it is biologically beneficial to ensure that ours or similar genes are passed on to the next generation, even to the detriment of the organism itself. A parent will take a bullet to save their children. A sibling will donate an organ to a dying brother or sister. Genes look to ensure their own survival and will seek out other organisms containing similar genes and protect them."

O'Shea, with eyes glazed over, looked at Ethan like a student on Monday morning. Ethan took a breath in anticipation of continuing his monologue when Justus cut in, "OK, let's take stock of what we have learned."

"This Marilyn Walker was a student at the university studying psychology and sociology," O'Shea began. "Her dorm mates say she has not been at school or in the dorm for at least two weeks. The university reported her missing a week ago.

"Jane Doe was found in the East River three days ago. A connection was made between the Jane Doe and the missing student because of her hair color and physical description, the approximate date of disappearance, and a tattoo of a butterfly on the lower back."

"During the search of the dorm room," Justus added, "a diary was found with content that leads us to believe that the author is the accomplice to the College Rapist. She appears to be an active participant in the rape and murder of at least four victims, from what I read so far. The diary details are compatible with the rape and murder of Tandy Masterson and details three other rapes committed together, another one of which ended in murder. There was an assault detailed that took place during the Christmas holidays. This is what the diary says:

> *On New Year's Eve, we picked up a street girl named Virginia and brought her to the hotel. She was innocent enough, for a street girl, so that made HIM more interested than if we had picked up a whore. We kept her roofied for a couple of days and made a video.*

The rest goes into detail about the two days and the videos. You can read that yourself," Justus decided.

"This doesn't correspond with any College Rapist victims we have interviewed," O'Shea concluded. "Did they kill her?"

"Not that it says in the diary," Justus pointed out.

"A street girl named Virginia," O'Shea said while rubbing his temples. "We'll get Vice and Missing Persons on it to try and find her."

"Let's connect the dots," Ethan speculated, "assuming that Jane Doe is Marilyn Walker and that Marilyn Walker is the College Rapist's accomplice, we have now opened up a huge lead source."

O'Shea summarized, "We'll have all possible detectives question students, professors, and other university-related leads. We'll track down family, coworkers, and whoever else we think may have even a remote connection to Marilyn Walker."

Everyone sat silent for a moment, each one contemplating the new evidence and its impact on the case.

"The next questions are," Ethan pondered out loud, "why is she dead and what killed her?" He paused briefly, looking around the room at the others. "I'll need details from the medical examiner and forensic scientists to help build my analysis parameters. Once I crunch all that data together, I may be able to narrow down where we need to focus the investigation."

"I'll be asking Drake to take over this investigation for the ME's office," O'Shea asserted. "And you can work directly with him, Ethan. I'll ask Drake to start the Jane Doe investigation from scratch, and you can participate, if you want to," O'Shea suggested.

"Want to?" Ethan exclaimed, practically jumping up and down. "I would be honored to work with Drake!"

Ethan left with O'Shea to the medical examiner's office. Justus and Magnus sat in the kitchenette meeting room silent, assimilating the new evidence and formulating the next steps needed to catch their nemesis.

At the medical examiner's office, Drake sat at his desk, leaning back on the head rest of his chair, catching a nap. His robust belly looked like that of a seasoned beer drinker. His work shirt, at least a size too small, was like a girdle, buttons tortured by the force that held them in the button holes.

"Watch this," O'Shea whispered to Ethan as he walked over to Drake. Leaning over him, O'Shea yelled into Drake's ear, "Wake up, you lazy bastard!"

Drake fell off his chair as he was startled awake, his comb-over flopping to the wrong side of his head and a drop of drool leaking down his chin.

"You son of a bitch," he hollered back at O'Shea, "can't an overworked silly servant get some sleep round here?"

O'Shea extended his hand out to help Drake up, which Drake refused, saying, "I don't need your charity old man," and got himself back up to his feet.

They had served together in the military and worked together for years at the NYPD. They constantly pulled pranks on each other, a very manly way to show the deep bond they shared.

"Ethan Talbot . . . Percy Drake," O'Shea said as he looked from Ethan to Dr. Drake, shaking hands with each other.

"What can I do for yeah?" Drake asked O'Shea, as he smoothed his comb over back in place.

"Jane Doe number 13, you need to review it all over again," O'Shea answered. "We have some evidence that may be linked to her, but that's all I am going to say on it."

O'Shea looked at Ethan while saying, "Don't reveal anything. I want this to be done completely impartial . . . OK?"

"Yes, sir," Ethan advised, looking like a first year forensics student, excited to witness his first autopsy.

"OK, son," Drake said as he led Ethan and O'Shea out to the lab, "have you seen a dead body before?"

"He's with Justus and Magnus," O'Shea informed him.

"Oh, OK, then there shouldn't be any vomiting!" Drake concluded almost disappointed, winking at Ethan.

"I'll try to wretch at least," Ethan quipped, "if it will make you feel better."

"No bother. I'll enjoy not having to clean vomit off my shoes," Drake concluded as he went over to a filing cabinet and took out a large binder marked Jane Doe #13.

"You familiar with autopsy procedure?" Drake asked Ethan.

"Somewhat," he replied as Drake opened the binder to the crime scene photos.

"Pull up a chair. We're going to be here for a while!" Drake recommended, adjusting his glasses.

They worked nonstop for over twenty-four hours to make sure that the autopsy details were available as soon as possible.

Jay and I were resting after a long busy night, when my phone rang. "Hello," I answered.

"Ivy, can you and Jay come over now?" the familiar and soothing voice of Justus asked. "Ethan is here, and he has a lot to tell us."

"OK, we'll be there soon."

Arriving at the house, it was like Thanksgiving minus the turkey and trimmings. Everyone was there, sitting at the dining room table, socializing like a family, minus the arguing and quarrelling.

I truly loved this family, my family. Usually, you can't choose your family, but in this case, they did choose me. I felt fortunate and grateful to be loved and accepted for who I was.

"Hey, lovebirds," Justus greeted us, and I looked over at Jay's amazing smile.

Ethan broke my concentration on Jay as he started to excitedly describe the evidence discovered through his and Dr. Drake's autopsy of Jane Doe #13.

"Although not 100 percent conclusive," Ethan began, "we are fairly certain that Jane Doe number 13 is Marilyn Walker, and that she was strangled to death. Here are the details." He read from a report:

> The nude body of a Caucasian woman was found at water's edge, face up, with a bloated abdomen and macerated skin. From the skin condition and the state of decomposition, it appears that the body was in the water for two to three weeks.

"This coincides with the disappearance of Marilyn Walker," Ethan indicated with great enthusiasm. "Since hair resists putrefaction, samples were taken to compare with samples taken from Marilyn Walker's hair brush at the dorm. Information has been requested from the college regarding her records so that dental comparison can be initiated."

Ethan continued reading:

> The physical description details a 5´7˝ Caucasian female with stocky bone structure and athletic features, weight approximately one hundred and thirty pounds, well-nourished and strongly developed musculature. Medium-length light-colored hair, which had recently been dyed brown, and blue eyes. Age, approximately twenty-five years old.
>
> Facial features: Square shaped with prominent jaw bone structure, high cheek bones, slightly prominent, long forehead, large almond-shaped eyes, and a small symmetrical nose.

"These physical characteristics are compatible with photographs of Marilyn Walker," Ethan explained and continued.

> The most telling characteristic is the butterfly tattoo on the lower back of Jane Doe #13.

"Marilyn Walker's dorm mates indicated that she recently had a butterfly tattoo done on her lower back as a gift to her boyfriend," he continued. "Photographs of the tattoo found on Jane Doe #13 will be shown to Marilyn Walker's dorm mates for comparison."

> There was some trace evidence and postmortem injuries that indicated the body did not originate in the water where it was found.
>
> The body was discovered by passers-by. The identity of the victim was unknown by

witnesses. Background checks on witnesses revealed no cause for suspicion.

The cause of death could not be ascertained because the body was submerged for too long, and putrefaction had begun. It is fairly conclusive that death was by asphyxiation, but the exact cause of asphyxia can only be interpreted by viewing the autopsy findings along with the crime scene evidence.

The body may or may not have been dead upon entering the water. If death occurred in the water, there are several possible causes of death, including drowning. It is difficult to prove drowning with 100 percent accuracy. Some reliable signs of drowning are:

- Weeds, stones, or other objects from the water firmly grasped in the hands
- Fine white or pink froth at the mouth and nose
- Fine froth or mucous plugs in the lungs and air passages
- Water-logged lungs and water in the stomach and intestines
- Diatoms in the tissues
- Signs of hemodilution in cardiac blood and altered blood chemistry

Not all of these signs will be found in every case of drowning. If the victim is incapacitated before submersion, or injured during a fall into water, or experiences vagal inhibition, many of the signs may not be apparent.

In death from strangulation, the general characteristics of asphyxia are present. If the asphyxial features are concentrated in the head and neck, it's strongly indicative of strangulation as the cause of death. Other indications of strangulation include:

- Evidence of compression or constriction of the neck
- Presence of bruising on the outside of the neck
- Hemorrhage in the muscles of the neck, in the tissues around the trachea and larynx, and in the larynx
- Petechial hemorrhage around the eyes, and elsewhere on the head and face, and on the mucous membrane inside the lips

The presence of petechial hemorrhage often indicates death by strangulation, hanging, or smothering. The hemorrhages occur when blood leaks from the ruptured capillaries in the eyes, due to increased pressure on the veins in the head, when the airway is obstructed. If petechial hemorrhages and facial congestion are present, it is a strong indication that asphyxia by strangulation is the cause of death.

Suicide by strangulation involves venous congestion above the ligature and is prominent at the root of the tongue. The angle of the ligature is dependent on the mechanism used for strangulation.

Hanging, whether done with rope or other implement, always leaves an inverted "V" bruise, making it easy to distinguish from ligature strangulation, which leaves a straight-line bruise.

Homicidal strangulation and hanging can be staged to mimic suicide, therefore making certain determination of suicide difficult. Strangulation should be assumed to be homicidal until the contrary is shown. A murderer would generally use more force than necessary, causing injuries to the deeper tissues and structures.

Evidence of struggle is often found unless the victim is blitz attacked without warning or is incapacitated. Loss of consciousness can be so rapid that the assailant is able to single-handedly tie the ligature, subduing a victim without a struggle. If there is a struggle, the victim may have abrasions and contusions.

Ligature marks may be present, may be indistinct or absent. Ligature marks can be produced by applying a ligature after death and are therefore not conclusive of strangulation.

Signs of asphyxia cannot be relied on as evidence of strangulation in cases of putrefaction. If there are signs of mechanical violence applied to the neck, an opinion about strangulation can be given, although not conclusively.

It is strongly indicative, although not conclusive, that the cause of death for Jane Doe #13 was strangulation by soft ligature, and that the body was submerged in the water after death.

The examination of Jane Doe #13 revealed general signs of asphyxiation as would be found in drowning or strangulation. There were no objects grasped in the hands or diatoms in the tissues.

On examination of the head and neck, both external and internal signs of strangulation were identified. The victim showed signs of petechial hemorrhage

```
        and deep tissue damage, including hyoid
        fracture.
           There were no defence wounds. There was
        evidence of ligature marks on the wrists in
        a pattern consistent with both wrists being
        tied together using a thin, hard material.
        There were no other injuries, antemortem,
        indicating possible incapacitation of the
        victim prior to strangulation.
           There were some postmortem soft tissue
        injuries likely obtained during submersion.
           The toxicological screen revealed MDMA
        (Ecstasy) at elevated levels.
           No nail scrapings could be obtained.
           No evidence of foreign hairs on the
        body.
           No rape exam could be performed.
```

Everyone sat silent for a moment contemplating the technical data that had been detailed.

"Sounds to me like a whole lot of nothing," Anton exclaimed.

"From that, I gather that she was drugged, raped, strangled, and dumped," Magnus summarized.

"Yes, that sounds reasonable to assume, but what else can we get from it?" Helene speculated. "Ecstasy says willing participant to me, not rape."

"Maybe," Justus added "but cases have been made for rape using Ecstasy instead of roofies or GHB."

"No defensive wounds and thin ligature around the wrists," Ethan reminded. "Sounds familiar, doesn't it . . . Tandy Masterson?"

"So maybe the College Rapist and his accomplice replay the rapes and murders in their own sex life for a thrill, and it went too far?" I suggested.

"Did the diary indicate that they practiced erotic strangulation?" Helene queried.

"Yes," Justus indicated, "there was some mention of that, but I can't remember the details exactly. I'll have to rescan the journal and find the specific details."

"Let's suppose that they were reliving a fantasy of rape and strangulation and he held the ligature too long, accidentally killing her," Helene theorized, "why didn't he stage it to look like the other vacant apartment murder?"

"Maybe because he didn't take precautions regarding evidence left in or on the body," I surmised.

"What better way to eliminate evidence than a water dump?" Justus added. "That's probably why there was a change in MO. There hasn't been a water dump associated with the College Rapist and murder that we know of, until now."

"That's something we'll have to discuss with O'Shea," Ethan said. "Maybe there have been others, but no connection was made?"

"They were likely at his place or a hotel, so staging at a vacant apartment would be too complicated," Magnus surmised. "The logistics involved would be daunting."

"Also, maybe she was too personal for him to put on display," I proposed.

"True," Helene agreed.

"Let's take another angle," Ethan suggested. "What if he intentionally killed her?"

"The diary did indicate that the bloom was going off the rose," Justus surmised. "She did give him an ultimatum of doing things her way or she was done with it."

"That would definitely give a reason to get rid of her," Anton observed. "She would be a concern to him if left alive. In the words of William Congreve, 'Hell a fury, like a woman scorned.'"

"If he did kill her intentionally, why do it that way?" Helene probed.

"Think about it," Magnus interjected. "She would be completely vulnerable in the midst of what she thought was intimacy and very easy to kill."

"That would be cold, even for a psychopath!" Justus proposed.

"He kills her, dumps her, and then what? Lies low for a while," Helene proposed.

"Let's say it was about three weeks ago that he killed her," Justus surmised. "He'll most likely go back to the bars and the victim type that he likes."

"The question is, will he go back to rape only or will he continue to kill?" Magnus speculated. "From the diary, it seems like his accomplice may have instigated the killing, not him."

"From our experience with other serial rapists and killers over the years, once you get the taste for murder, you stay with murder," Helen reasoned. "Remember Gerald and Charlene Gallego?"

"Who are they?" I asked.

"They're a killer couple from the late seventies," Justus explained. "We were helping with that case, but back then, there was no sophisticated technology to help us. They were caught before we found them, unfortunately. We did get to interview them when they were in custody, and we created a good profile for couples that rape and kill together."

"Interesting," Ethan blurted. "The Gallegos and the Sunset Strip Killers do give credence to the woman being the breaking point. In both cases, the women testified against the men."

"The College Rapist would have been smart to dispose of his accomplice, if she was showing any signs of breaking," Helene considered out loud.

"His mental state may be crumbling," Magnus supposed. "The MO and victimology has already changed. I don't think we can predict anything about him right now."

"All we have are patterns and profiling," Ethan announced. "We have no choice but to extrapolate from this. From past timelines, the College Rapist should be due for another attack any time," he surmised, looking around the table. "With that in mind, I need to review all the data and narrow down the areas where we need to focus our hunt. We need O'Shea to look for more water dumps that may be similar, in case this isn't the first. We need to determine positively if Jane Doe is Marilyn Walker and, if so, do an extensive background check and profile on her."

"We can ask for a facial reconstruction of Jane Doe #13," Magnus said. "This may be faster than waiting for the dental and DNA testing."

"I'm going to review Marilyn Walker's journal again to see if I can get anything new from it," Justus added. "Let's talk to the surviving victims of the duo and the dorm mates to see if we can glean any new information."

Justus and Magnus returned to Marilyn Walker's dorm with a photo of the tattoo from Jane Doe #13. They were able to ascertain that the tattoo in the photograph was likely the same tattoo that Marilyn Walker had on her lower back.

The students also provided some background on Marilyn Walker. Justus reviewed the journal carefully, taking note of details that would help build a solid profile.

At the same time, O'Shea requested official documentation from the university and tracked down Marilyn's history from official sources.

Justus, Magnus, Ethan, and O'Shea met at the precinct.

"Time for show and tell," O'Shea initiated. "Here is the facial reconstruction," he continued as he displayed the photo to them.

The photo revealed a feminine face with strong angular features, almond eyes, and high cheek bones.

"Looks like Marilyn Walker to me," Justus and Magnus echoed in unison.

"I agree," added Ethan.

Over several hours, they shared their evidence, devising a probable background and profile for Marilyn Walker.

> Marilyn Walker was born to sixteen-year-old Jennifer Walker in Bluefield, Virginia; population: 6,000.
>
> Jennifer Walker, a high school dropout, gave birth to Marilyn in 1989 and was kicked out of the family home, abandoned by her parents, left to raise Marilyn on her own. Soon after, a son came along, named Anthony, and then another daughter, Stacey. A single mother of three children, all having different fathers, Jennifer, in her twenties, tired and depressed, was addicted to amphetamines. The only work she could get was waitressing in bars. Her children were left in the care of whoever she could find, when she went to work.
>
> By the time Marilyn was ten years old, she had been molested by two of her

mother's boyfriends. By the time she was twelve, she was performing sexual acts to buy herself name brand clothing. Just after turning thirteen, her mother, Jennifer, committed suicide; and the kids were separated in foster care.

Marilyn, a very bright girl, with an IQ in the ninety-eighth percentile, was placed in the care of a family that encouraged her scholastic achievement. The foster family recounted that Marilyn was driven to the extreme to achieve. Marilyn, a natural athlete, developed a strong aptitude for tennis and displayed a ruthless need to win. She was banned from the sport in her senior year because she assaulted another player after losing a match.

Although it was never proven, Marilyn had been accused of petty theft a few times. She was known to keep to herself and rarely dated boys, although she had sex with many. There were rumors that she was involved with her high school tennis coach. She had one close friend in high school, named Patti, but they did not stay in touch once they went to different colleges. Marilyn earned a scholarship to study psychology.

Patti, the high school friend, described Marilyn as brilliant but odd. The basis of their relationship was their focus on academics, not a typical close friendship. Marilyn rarely disclosed information about her past. Patti said that once in science lab, when they were dissecting a rat, Marilyn said she wondered what it would be like to kill a person.

Marilyn did not maintain contact with her brother and sister once they were separated in foster care. Her brother, Anthony, had not thrived in foster care and was living in a group home for juvenile offenders. He had nothing much to say about his sister other than she protected him and their little sister, Stacey, from their mother's molesting boyfriends.

Stacey, the youngest, was sheltered somewhat from the abuse that Marilyn endured. She looked up to Marilyn because Marilyn had raised Stacey until they were sent to foster care. Stacey was very hurt by the lack of contact with Marilyn but was managing to live a productive life in foster care. Stacey was in high school, achieving reasonable attendance and grades.

Marilyn's dorm mates at the university concurred that Marilyn was brilliant and odd. She rarely studied but maintained above average marks. She held down at least two jobs to be able to buy high-end clothes. Marilyn admitted to a college friend that she had stolen some of the clothes she owned.

Marilyn was image conscious and arrogant, according to her dorm mates. She was known to say inappropriate things to draw attention to herself and would purposely take the opposite side of arguments just for argument's sake. Her mood would fluctuate from one moment to the next, and she didn't maintain long-term romantic relationships.

"All indications are that she was a classic psychopath," Justus asserted. "Highly intelligent, confident, deviant, lack of strong connections to people, shows no remorse, and endured an abusive childhood."

"Did anyone find out if and where she works?" Ethan requested.

Justus, Magnus, and O'Shea, looking at each other, all shrugged their shoulders, indicating they had not.

"How about boyfriends, did we talk to any of them?" Ethan questioned.

"We couldn't get any full names of boyfriends from her dorm mates or from her high school friend," Justus responded. "In fact, her dorm mates said she kept somewhat secretive about her relationships, and that since she started dating this new guy, she wasn't hanging out with them or staying at the dorm much."

"We tracked down the high school tennis coach. He died a few years ago in a car accident," O'Shea added.

"Marilyn's journal indicated that she took part in three rapes and two murders," Justus recalled with a pause. "She never mentioned the name of her partner and only mentioned the name of one victim, the street girl named Virginia."

"That means we have one murder unaccounted for!" Ethan exclaimed.

"Yes," O'Shea affirmed, "the rivers are being dragged as we speak. If there is a victim in a vacant apartment somewhere, we won't know until some unfortunate person discovers the gruesome scene."

CHAPTER TEN
Point of No Return

Yasmine, Jay, and I had to multitask, working two very significant criminal elements in tandem. We were still devoting as much time as possible to the College Rapist case that had cooled off once again; no body found in the rivers and no new evidence. With every cooling-off period, we became more and more frustrated because we had nothing; our hands were tied, just like his victims, helpless and under his control. He was effectively evasive, and all we could do was watch, listen, and hope to find some clue before he struck again.

The three of us had to focus on the upcoming Los Zetas visit. Finally, after sending several of his soldiers to scrutinize Jay and his club, it was time for the big boss to visit and ensure that a key shipment of cocaine was in good hands.

I spent my afternoon with Yasmine, getting ready for our big night as hosts to the cartel. It was to be a "pull-out-all-the-stops" affair: dinner at the best restaurant in Manhattan then VIP treatment at Gotham Citi. Jay, Carlos, and the cartel representatives were meeting all afternoon at the club; Yasmine and I were to join them at a restaurant for dinner.

"You have no idea how I can't wait for this charade to be over," admitted Yasmine. "I just want to get back to my normal life. Playing the doting girlfriend with Carlos is wearing very thin with me."

"It won't be for much longer, right?" I asked.

"We won't know until after tonight. It depends on how much they trust Jay. If I still need to get more information from Carlos, I'll have to continue with the pillow talk tactics."

I still used Yasmine's closet as a boutique for all occasions. Tonight, we both selected upscale cocktail dresses, and I wore my hair up with little wispy curls falling down from the nape of my neck and around my face. Yasmine, as usual, could be dressed in sweats and be the sexiest woman in the room. She wore her hair in the wild style that suited her character.

We received a text message advising us that a car would be arriving to pick us up in ten minutes. Putting the last touches to our makeup, I asked Yasmine, "How can you bring yourself to sleep with him?"

"I guess it is no different than being a hooker," she declared. "I just look at it as a job. I gave up the love and sex connection a long time ago. To me, it is just something I do for fun, exercise, or in this case a job. For a mortal, he isn't bad," she commented frivolously.

To have given up on love seemed sad, yet Yasmine still seemed content with her life, most of the time.

An immense limo picked us up; this was not something I was used to. Even though I grew up in a relatively well-off family, we didn't indulge in this kind of extravagance. My mother worked in public service and was always scrutinized. Yasmine and I made small talk in the limo until our arrival at Jean Jacques, the most exclusive restaurant in Manhattan. When we arrived, we were shown to our table where all the other guests were waiting.

The most senior looking of the Los Zetas, Gustavo Ruiz Caballero, stood up to greet me; and he pulled out my chair, taking my hand, and said, "Buenas noches, bella dama." He repeated the same gesture for Yasmine. I looked at him inquisitively, and he said, "It means good evening, beautiful woman."

There was a round of introductions, and then the Zetas entertained us with stories. If I didn't know that they were ruthless drug smugglers and killers, I wouldn't have guessed it by their enchanting company. Perhaps, they would think the same of me, if they knew that I could be a ruthless killer also! Their wives were all relatively quiet, knowing only rudimentary English.

Yasmine seemed comfortable in her role as one of Carlos's girlfriends. She was well aware that he had girlfriends in all the cities that he frequented for business. This would ultimately be her way out of the relationship, once she was given the OK by Jay to end it. She planned to play the jealous and somewhat crazy lover role hoping that Carlos would break up with her.

I had been out to dinner so few times since becoming immortal that I was out of practice with etiquette. We could eat and drink, if necessary, and this was one of those times. The main caveat with eating was that it could only be small portions. Food stayed in our bodies until the next time we had blood. It was like the equivalent of having intense indigestion. Yasmine and I could get away with eating very little, but it was more difficult for Jay.

We could drink, if we wanted to. Alcohol had no effect on us. We could drink drain cleaner, and it would have no effect on us. We didn't feel thirst for water or other mortal beverages, only for blood.

It was Mexican dining etiquette to leave some food on your plate, so we were able to camouflage our lack of eating more easily. Luckily, we weren't dining with Italians . . . Mangi, Mangi!

We arrived at Gotham when it was in full swing. The balcony was, of course, reserved for us; and we had our own private service. Instead of the usual neo-Gothic candelabras and statues, Jay had decorated with colorful Mexican knickknacks for our guests.

"What a truly spectacular club," Gustavo complimented. "Thank you for honoring us with such splendid décor."

"El gusto es mio," answered Jay as he playfully took a sombrero and put it on his head.

After a couple of hours at the club, playing the devoted girlfriend and hostess, Jay summoned limos to take the Zetas' wives, Yasmine, and I home. He whispered to me that they wanted to talk more business, and the women were not to be part of it. Jay gently kissed my cheek and promised he would make it up to me. I loved having him indebted to me.

I woke from a deep sleep, which was rare, to the feeling of Jay running his fingers through my hair. He said, "Come on; let's go get something to eat. I have the perfect target. I got some great leads from my conversations with the Zetas."

"OK," I responded groggily, a little perplexed, but I really needed some blood. The food I ate at the restaurant wasn't agreeing with me!

In a flash, we were off to the Bronx; some expendable rivals to the Zetas were going to provide us with what we needed. Kills that we did together drew us closer every time. We performed together like two ballroom dancers, swift and efficient. As always, I couldn't escape the visions. I couldn't desensitize myself to them, but I had to learn to accept them as part of the process. It was like taking a big spoonful of cod liver oil with a delicious meal.

"What did you see?" Jay asked.

"The usual stuff," I replied.

"Can you make out faces? Do you see things really clearly?" Jay continued to probe.

"I guess I do," I remarked, "but I haven't paid that much attention to it lately."

"I think we can use your visions to help with this Zetas thing," Jay explained.

I stood there puzzled then thought about the visions I had just seen, faces I saw, and I understood what he meant. I vaguely recognized gang markings on some people in the visions. All of them were already dead, but I could see connections between certain crime groups from the murders that I read through my victims.

"I'll concentrate more on the visions the next time and see if there is anything important in them," I told Jay.

"Let's experiment with it," he commented.

We started to walk home hand in hand. I felt light and warm, the feeling you get when you are waking up in a warm soft bed after a wonderful sleep. My bliss was disturbed by a small gang of young wannabes, thinking they were going to rob us and maybe have their way with me.

Initially, Jay tried to talk them down, but they wouldn't have it. His patience grew thin, so he grabbed the closest one by the throat and lifted him off his feet, choking him. The kid dropped his weapon, writhing in Jay's grasp. The others took off in different directions. Once the kid lost consciousness, Jay put him down and took his weapon.

"Stupid kids," Jay growled. "They're starting younger and younger these days!"

"Their parents are probably working night jobs to support them," I suggested.

"Hopefully," Jay commented, "maybe they'll have a bit of a chance to turn things around, but if their parents are at home passed out from some kind of substance abuse, these kids will probably be one of our meals in a few years!"

We walked in silence for a while, and I thought about what Jay said. Those boys were heading down a road to becoming a warm meal. I wanted to maintain some optimism, but it was difficult.

"I didn't see Eirinn at the club tonight," I said as we walked.

Jay explained, "I didn't want her around because of the Zetas. I want to make sure she doesn't get implicated or wrapped up in anything related to them."

"How did things go with Gustavo and his posse?" I enquired.

Jay answered enthusiastically, "Real good. Everything is set up. We laid out the ground rules for our relationship. He seems convinced that I'm his man, and that Gotham is the right spot for his crew to frequent and discuss business. We did, after all, put out quite a spread for him and his men over the last few months. How could he not love us?"

Jay was very excited about this project; his eyes lit up when he talked about it. This "in" with the Zetas would give him access to unlimited information. It was going to take several months of work for him to get enough intel to start planning a coup of some sort, his ultimate goal that I didn't know anything about yet.

The rest of our walk home was pleasant, and dawn was just setting in as we crawled into our bed. I rested in his arms, allowing the blood to rejuvenate me. Jay's warmth was comforting. As I lay with my head on his chest, I realized that I felt for him the same protective feelings that I had for my daughter. I didn't know that I could feel this for someone other than Ana. I knew right away that I would sacrifice myself to protect him. As I was thinking this, Jay broke the silence.

"I would do anything to protect you," he vowed as he gently pushed under my chin, turning my face toward his. Looking into his eyes, I knew that we shared energy and intuition; we could almost read each other's minds.

Swathed together like twins in the womb, our quiet thoughts could be felt by one another as we drifted into a sleeplike state of complete relaxation.

Several hours later, I awoke to a soft hazy sunlit day, the kind that made you want to lie in the grass and feel the gentle rays caress your skin.

I slipped out of bed, completely rejuvenated. Jay looked delectable lying in bed with the sheets just barely covering his body. *There's nothing better than a little afternoon romp*, I thought to myself, and as I did, I saw the glint of a smile cross Jay's lips. Instantaneously, his arms were around me. He was kissing my neck and whispered, "You're not getting away from me."

Then, of course, the phone rang. We were summoned to the house for an update on the College Rapist case and to see what our tasks for the evening would be.

"Damn!" Jay snarled and kissed me. "Work, work, work . . . that's all we ever do!"

As we were set to leave, Jay received a phone call telling him that Eirinn hadn't shown up to open Gotham Citi.

"That's unusual," Jay asserted. "I can't remember the last time that Eirinn didn't show up for work, and she's always called, if she was going to be late."

"Go deal with the club, and I'll catch up with you at the end of the night," I insisted as I touched his cheek with my hand and leaned in to kiss him gently.

"Good night, sunshine," he said sweetly as his arms circled my waist, pulling me close for a sensuous kiss. I held his embrace long enough to breathe in his scent, imprinting on my senses.

As Jay left, I closed my eyes and could smell him and feel him, as though he was still holding me. A few minutes passed and I left for the house, daydreaming all the way about Jay and some of the special times that we had spent together.

Everyone but Jay and Yasmine met, and we reviewed an action plan that included Johnson, Dunn, and other undercover officers. Previously, our surveillance was to be covert. Now, we women were trying to attract attention, hopefully the attention of the College Rapist. We knew what he was looking for, and we had to provide it to catch him.

Dunn and I were partnered again. I now had the college girl look down pat, wearing a shirt that let my boobs practically fall out and a skirt that showed my every curve splendidly. Dunn always chose a bit more of a rebel, bad girl look, sexy in an I'll-kick-your-ass kind of way. It was so *21 Jump Street!*

We came up empty again, other than the reams of advances and phone numbers that we collected. At the end of the night, Dunn went home for some rest, and I met Jay at Gotham.

Eirinn had not shown up, causing Jay to have a lot of extra work to do.

"Can you go check Eirinn's apartment while I close up?" Jay asked. "It will ease me if I know that she is at least not in trouble there and unable to get to her phone."

I arrived at Eirinn's apartment, looked around, but didn't see anything suspicious. It was spotless. Way more tidy than I kept my place. She had no landline phone, and Jay had been trying her cell phone all night. I checked the shower. It wasn't wet. I looked in the fridge; there were some leftovers and a new carton of milk. Nothing seemed out of the ordinary, but still, my gut felt uneasy. I checked her parking spot, and her car was gone.

Maybe she went to visit some friends out of town and just got caught up in having a good time. She had a couple of nights off, so that made sense. I couldn't remember the last time that she went away somewhere, or took time off for that matter. She probably didn't want to bother Jay because of the Zetas thing, knowing how important it was. I was able to talk my mind into believing this very plausible explanation, but my gut was plagued with something else.

I dialed Jay. "Eirinn isn't here, but nothing seems suspicious. Do you remember her saying anything about going to visit some friends out of town?"

"No," he admitted, "but I have been a little preoccupied. Maybe she did."

I waited silently for Jay to speak again.

"If I don't hear from her by noon tomorrow, I'm going to talk to her neighbors and the friends she has here. Maybe we're just too guarded lately," he concluded.

"Yeah," I answered, "I've been thinking the same thing."

"Meet me at home. I'm just locking up," Jay said, sounding uneasy.

Neither Jay nor I slept at all. Noon the next day rolled around slowly. At 12:01 p.m., Jay called Eirinn's cell phone again; still, he got no answer, so he texted. Two minutes later, he was up and out of bed, getting dressed.

"I'm going to talk to Eirinn's neighbors and friends. Can you stay here in case she calls the house phone, please?"

"Sure," I assured as I walked over to hug him. I knew that he didn't want me to stay home as much as he wanted to be alone. He didn't want to hurt my feelings. I already knew by the tension in his face that he would want to be alone.

I called Justus. "Hey . . . how are things?"

"What's wrong?" he questioned.

"What do you mean?" I asked with a feeble attempt to deceive him.

"Don't bullshit me," he continued, "I can tell by your voice that there's something troubling you . . . so what is it?"

"Eirinn didn't show up for work last night, and she hasn't called Jay or anyone else from the club," I explained.

"OK, when was she last around?" he probed, trying not to sound like a police investigator.

"She worked on Wednesday night, then, she had Thursday and Friday off because of the Zetas visit," I replied.

"Did you talk to everyone from the club? They weren't all working last night," Justus asked.

"I think Jay did ask them all. He's out now talking to her neighbors and friends," I relayed with growing concern in my voice.

"Come over here instead of waiting there alone," Justus suggested.

"OK," I agreed, feeling relieved.

I knew I never had to wait for an invitation to go to the house, but it was nice to be invited. I really needed someone to wait with me. I dressed quickly, tied my hair up on top of my head, and bolted out the door. Because it was daylight, I took a cab. As much as a walk in the sunlight would have been soothing, I didn't wish to break out in a rash from head to toe. My skin became more sensitive to light as each immortal day passed.

I arrived to find everyone in good spirits: Tavia reading; Anton watching NASCAR; Magnus and Yasmine sitting on the couch, legs intertwined, listening to Muddy Waters. Justus heard me coming and was at the door ready to greet me with one of his bone-crushing, soothing hugs. He led me across the floor, dancing to "You Shook Me," and I found myself dancing the blues like a pro. We collapsed together on the couch beside Magnus and Yasmine.

Anton and Tavia joined us; and I told them all about Eirinn, sharing with them that my gut was foreseeing something wrong, very wrong.

"We have to keep you distracted," Yasmine insisted.

"Movie?" Magnus proposed, being the media junkie that he was.

I shook my head, saying, "No."

"Cards?" Yasmine asked.

"Euchre," I replied, perking up. Besides Go Fish, which I used to play with my father, it was the only other card game that I knew.

Tavia and Anton were more than happy to go back to what they were doing before I arrived. The four of us got off the couch to play euchre for a few carefree hours, listening to the blues. Justus and I were just losing our last hand when my phone rang.

"It's Jay," I gasped getting up from the table. I was too nervous to sit still.

"Nobody knows where she is, Ivy!" Jay announced with a chilling voice.

Before I could say anything, he wanted me to pass the phone to Justus.

We could all hear Jay as he spoke. The plan was that Jay would meet Justus at the police station to start a missing person investigation.

The rest of us were to continue our patrol of the bars and strip clubs because we couldn't let the College Rapist work slide.

Dunn and I were spending another frustrating night of trolling the bars and clubs together. Time was going horribly slow. All I could think about was getting back home to Jay. We were in midconversation when my ears caught a vague scream from somewhere close by. My body sprang into action immediately, and I was out the door. I followed the direction that the sound came from, and as I rounded the corner, I spotted two people in the backseat of a dark car in a small parking lot on the other side of the street. I could make out what appeared to be a blond man and could only see the back of him. Someone was struggling with him, and I could hear her scream.

In an instant, I was ripping open the car door, and I had his throat in my grasp, pushing him up against the vehicle.

I was squeezing the life out of him when I heard "What the hell?" coming from the car.

I was peering into his eyes, watching his terror grow as his oxygen level decreased.

I felt hands hitting my back, and a voice saying, "Get your hands off him! You bitch, let go of him!"

Dunn was just arriving, and her voice drew me out of my rage as she said, "OK, let go of him. I'll take over," as she flashed her badge.

I let go of him, and he bent over and vomited on my shoes, gasping and coughing. The woman was still yelling at me. Dunn was holding her back from coming at me. My mind became clearer, and I realized that the guy's pants were down around his ankles. The woman was disheveled, but from her reactions, the realization hit that it was consensual; she was just a screamer.

She continued to berate me and concluded with "Can't people have sex in their own car in peace?"

Dunn interjected at that point with "Actually, no, you can't. It is in a public parking lot, so I could charge you with public display of offensive sexual material, which is a class A misdemeanor."

The woman calmed down and straightened herself out. The man, still sputtering a bit, pulled up his pants.

"Sorry, I thought he was raping you!" I explained.

"I want her charged with assault!" the woman ordered Officer Dunn.

"If I charge her, I charge you too. Your choice," Dunn confirmed.

"Forget it," the man croaked. "What are you, some kind of weightlifting, UFC, Roller Derby Queen?" he directed at me between heaving breaths.

I said nothing but "Sorry!" again.

Dunn sent them on their way with a warning about public indecency and then joined me.

"That was kind of funny," she blurted, "other than the part where you almost killed him! You need to learn how to control that."

"I know. I came on a little strong. The Eirinn thing has me on edge. I saw a dark car and a blond guy, and that was it. I completely snapped," I told her.

"Next time, let me know what you hear or sense before you take off," Dunn requested.

"OK, I will," I promised.

We both looked down at my vomit-soaked shoes and laughed.

"That serves you right!" Dunn scoffed.

As we walked back to the bar, Dunn told me she was specially trained to spot domestic violence, and that an abused woman may protect her abusive partner. She was convinced that those two were just two horny people who couldn't wait to get home.

The rest of the night passed without any excitement. I kept hoping to hear from Jay, but I didn't, and it worried me. We finally met at home close to dawn. I was home first, waiting anxiously for him to arrive. When he walked in, I looked at him, and his eyes started to well with tears. He had held them back all night, but now, they were too heavy.

"She's like my daughter," he declared while I held him in my arms. "I know how you must miss Ana, because there is a hole in me right now missing Eirinn."

His tears and my thoughts set me off too. We stood together quietly crying, holding each other.

Jay was the first to break our embrace. Wiping his eyes, he said, "This isn't going to help find her. I need to do something. I need to ask more questions, look in more places. She was at the club the night of the Zetas visit. I told her not to come, but she did anyway. Marcus, the new bartender, told me she was only there for a short while, and that he saw her leave alone by the back door. What if the Zetas suspect me, think I'm working with cops. They may have taken her to use against me!"

"We need a plan, an outside look at the situation," I reasoned tentatively. "Let's call Ethan and ask him to come over."

Jay agreed, and Ethan arrived with Helene.

"The boys were working with the cops all night," Ethan explained, "going over Eirinn's apartment, friends, looking for any transactions in her name, communicating with PD in the cities where her friends live, checking hospitals."

"We're covering all the bases," Helene affirmed as she touched Jay's shoulder in support.

"O'Shea is checking the Zetas?" Jay requested anxiously.

"Yes," Ethan reassured, "he has communicated with your DEA man, and he'll also check for any possible Zetas involvement. The best thing that we can do right now is to stay focused on the College Rapist and let O'Shea make sure the missing person investigation is a priority. You are too close to Eirinn, and your judgment will be clouded."

"I've plotted the most likely zone that the College Rapist will strike," Ethan revealed as he rolled open a map on the kitchen table. "We need to watch this area closely," he continued as he pointed to an area on the map, bounded by Second and Third avenues and Seventh to Ninth streets. "My mathematical analysis tells me this is the place, if he is, in fact, back to the bars."

Helene added, "The strip clubs need to be monitored too, but Ethan strongly believes that he is back to the college clubs."

"Without his partner, he won't want whores or strippers," I blurted. "He'll want the girls he used to rape. I don't think he got the same thrill from the dirty, easy women."

Helene was following my line of thought. "She was the one who wanted the whores. She didn't want him to lust for the victims. Classic jealousy!"

"Why wouldn't he hit a different part of town, where there's less danger of being caught?" I questioned. "I'm sure he's well aware that the college bars have the composites up, and that the police are focusing there."

"True," Helene acknowledged, "but he needs the college girls for his fantasy. Otherwise, it isn't right for him."

"Also, his psychopathic thought process would lead him to believe that he is smarter than everyone else and can continue to evade getting caught," Jay stated as he was pulled into the conversation. "Look at how long he's gotten away with it so far. This would keep feeding his ego and sense of invincibility."

"OK, we need the others and O'Shea's team to organize a tight surveillance plan for the target area," Ethan concluded as he rolled up his map.

Back at the house, we met with O'Shea, Dunn, and Johnson by teleconference and prepared for the night with great expectations. We thought that this would be it—we would get the College Rapist that night—but our optimism dwindled with each surveillance hour that passed.

Another week went by with no new activity or leads for the College Rapist case and nothing from Eirinn. We all knew in our heads that after a week missing, the likelihood was that she would be dead. In our hearts, though, we held on to hope. Maybe she was a Jane Doe in a hospital with memory loss. Maybe she just went away and didn't want anyone to know where she was. After all, knowing about us immortals and what we do must have been stressful for her. Basically, we had nothing to go on at all.

Jay was pulling it together and running Gotham Citi, but I could see that the week had taken a toll on him. He had been neglecting taking care of himself, so I insisted that we hunt together.

He was incredibly fast and knew the city well. I couldn't keep up, so he had to slow down for me. We raced through every shortcut and alley and in no time, we were on the Upper West Side. We reached an apartment building and quietly scaled it from the outside, stopping at a balcony. We listened to the conversation inside. Two men were discussing a job, which I assumed was murder, since Jay brought me there to feed. One was getting paid for doing a job that the other one had ordered.

"I heard about these guys through the club," Jay whispered. "There's one for each of us!"

I was strongly drawn to the one who committed the murder; and Jay, being a gentleman, let me have first choice. We broke in, surprising them both, and the kills were accomplished easily. As I had become accustomed to, the visions appeared as my victim's life was being drained away. When I saw his last criminal act, I broke free from him, peering into his dying eyes with contempt, asking, "How could you kill an unborn child?" I wanted to cause pain, but he was already too far gone for pain to have the effect I desired. I finished him off, turned to Jay, and barked, "Do you know what they did?"

"Yes, but to me, it usually makes no difference. They all die the same way," Jay answered very matter of fact. "All I know is that I need food, and they deserve to die," he added, "but let's work on your memory of the visions. Tell me what he did."

"This repugnant thug!" I hollered, kicking his corpse across the room, smashing it into a big screen television. "He murdered one of his prostitutes because she got pregnant. A pregnant prostitute doesn't make money. An unborn child didn't deserve to die, and neither did the woman!"

"Did you see it clearly?" Jay questioned as he came over to me and put his hands on my shoulders.

"Sort of," I declared, "but I broke away from him, and then it wasn't clear anymore, thankfully! It's not an image I want stuck in my mind. Some of the images stay with me, like haunting dreams that you wake up with, fearful. You know how those can stay with you all day?"

Jay held me for a while, and then we called Justus, advising him of this situation that needed some cleaning. Being out of our usual area, O'Shea would have to pull some strings to be able to deal with it.

I was getting better at feeding without making a mess; but this time, because I was upset by what I saw in my mind, I spilled on myself. Jay had a jacket that I put on, and we left. As we walked back home, hand in hand, Jay quizzed me some more about my visions. I was seeing how they could potentially be useful; but, for that night, my torment was not being alleviated by that thought.

Jay and I spent the week revisiting all of Eirinn's friends and neighbors, asking every possible question, trying to elicit something that would be useful in finding her; but, as had been our streak of late, we came up with nothing.

Jay had to overcome his reluctance to hire someone at Gotham to replace Eirinn. I tried to convince him that it would help him concentrate on the many things he had on his plate. He finally gave in and hired someone with the thought that it would be temporary, until she was back.

We gathered at the house with Dunn, Johnson, and O'Shea over the phone. Our spirits were down, starting another four nights of surveillance.

"How's Jay holding up?" Dunn asked me.

"Not good," I replied, "but he hides it well. He's training someone new at Gotham, and that's really taking a toll on his emotions. Nobody will love that club the same way that Eirinn did. She loved it as much as Jay, you know, maybe more." I looked down, swallowing a huge lump in my throat, blinking away tears from my eyes.

Everyone was quiet for a moment, perhaps all noticing, as I did, that it was the first time that I had referred to Eirinn using the past tense. Tavia took my hand under the table, which comforted me mildly.

"All right, Ethan," said O'Shea, breaking the awkward silence, "what's our target for the night?"

"With nothing happening last weekend," Ethan began, "there isn't much change in last week's predictions. Maybe we can widen the zone just a smidge, say from Fifth to Tenth streets, and still include the area between Second and Third avenues."

We discussed some tactics for the evening, refining our plan and ruse to lure the College Rapist. Our hope was that he would target one of us; but failing that, with any luck, we would at least pick up some credible information about him.

Mel and I were partnered again. I waited for her at the Escape Lounge, making small talk with a bartender. True to its name, the Escape Lounge made you feel that you were escaping your real life. There were comfy couches set up in L shapes, with coffee tables and soft suspended lights. The servers appeared and disappeared unobtrusively, blending into the background. The lighting was soft, and the music was calming.

I was absorbed in my surroundings when Mel arrived. If she hadn't walked right up to me, I wouldn't have recognized her. She clashed with the environment, surely to be noticed.

"Mel, you surprise me every time we're on duty together!" I said as I observed her outfit for the evening. She was wearing a very short school girl kilt, a low-cut black T-shirt prominently displaying her cleavage, and knee-high Doc Marten boots.

"I did have another life before becoming a cop!" she exclaimed. "It's nice to let down my hair and take some of these old clothes out from the back of my closet."

"I could never have pictured you wearing this outfit . . . ever," I remarked.

"If you'd known me in high school, you may have voted me most likely to end up with a criminal record," Dunn retorted with a laugh. "I had a nose ring," she confessed, showing me the very small hole still in her nose. "My usual attire was ripped jeans and combat boots. I skipped school constantly and hung out with the smokers and tokers! I have my share of tattoos as well," she volunteered while lifting her shirt, displaying a floral vine tattoo that started at her ribcage and contoured her waist, disappearing down her hips, hidden by her skirt. "The others I can't show you out here, or I'll have to arrest myself for indecent exposure!" she said while chuckling."

When she was showing me her tattoo, I noticed that she had a belly button ring. "Why a shamrock?" I inquired. "You're not Irish, are you?" Mel looked at me, confused for a moment, and then clued in that I meant her belly button ring.

"Well," she began, "it's a long story that I'll make short." With a less cheerful expression, Mel explained, "I used to work for another precinct, and I dated O'Shea then. When I got transferred to the Ninth, for obvious reasons, that relationship had to end. He bought me the shamrock because, of course, he's Irish."

There was an awkward silence between us, and as I looked at Mel, I could see that for the moment, her thoughts were elsewhere. I couldn't picture her with O'Shea. He was at least twenty years older than her, but then again, Jay was at least three hundred years older than me, so who was I to judge?

In comparison with Officer Dunn, I looked plain; I was wearing a jean miniskirt and slim-fitting halter top with my hair gathered loosely up on top of my head. I blended much more seamlessly with the scene at the Escape Lounge. An odd couple we were!

Despite our clashing styles, Mel and I were finding out that we complemented each other well in friendship. We had been on several stake outs together and were becoming friends outside of "work." Mel was single and had never been married. She portrayed a very tough character as a cop, a natural leader and a force to be reckoned with. When not on duty, she was just your average woman, going out jogging, picking up groceries, and doing laundry. She didn't live extravagantly, although who could on a cop's salary? She came from a blue-collar family raised in Queens.

One of Dunn's high school friends was raped, and this influenced her to become a cop. Mel was a decent person, trying to earn a living helping the community. Her instincts were good for a mortal. She could read a room well and catch subtleties that others would miss. She noticed a man, white, six foot, brown hair, watching us.

"Check the guy out to my left, light blue casual shirt, brown hair . . . you see the one I mean?" Dunn asked as she signaled with her eyes. "He could be the College Rapist. I assume he has changed his hair color," she speculated.

"Yeah, if I picture him blond, slightly different hair style, I could see it," I agreed.

It was time to put on our show; we needed to bait him. The College Rapist wanted a victim that he believed "deserved" to get raped, someone flaunting her sexuality, someone who was a tease. Our undercovers needed to join the ruse. Dunn went to the bar and stood beside one of them and gave him the signal that the game was on. They flirted, and he bought Dunn and me our drinks, but he didn't join us. He called over his friend, another cop, and they made it obvious that they were scoping us out. When we finished our drinks, another set was sent to our table, courtesy of our undercover friends.

All the while, our suspect talked to a few women, but kept watching Dunn, in particular. There were several students there, those who were from upscale backgrounds, so I could see why this club made it to Ethan's target list. The stuck-up girls from a world of entitlement would certainly pique the interests of our target. He was a handsome man, attracting the attention of the more outgoing ladies in the club. Of course, I could hear what our suspect was saying to the women. He introduced himself as Ryan and engaged in small talk. Nothing up to that point gave me reason for concern. He continued to watch Dunn; and she worked the room, flirting with several men, fairly noticeably. Dunn stumbled by the suspect, making sure to fall into him. He helped her steady herself but didn't engage with her.

When Dunn came back to the table, our undercover friends tried to join us, but Dunn turned them down. I watched our suspect as this went on, and he was definitely intrigued by the situation. We drank our virgin beverages, our target none the wiser, pretending to get more and more intoxicated.

Dunn flirted with another undercover officer, and he bought us drinks. When he put the moves on her, she turned him down, very noticeably. Our target was watching her intently now.

Dunn feigned receiving a call on her cell, and she made it apparent that she was getting up to leave for the night. From her behavior and conversation, anyone around us would have guessed that it was her boyfriend, and that they were having a fight. I stayed at my seat, finishing my drink, as she said goodbye and stumbled toward the back door of the establishment. The suspect watched her then threw some money down on the table and left behind her.

It was only seconds before the undercovers and I were out the back door to find Dunn already cuffing the College Rapist suspect.

"What the hell is this?" the suspect blurted. "I didn't do anything. You can't just arrest me for no reason. I only wanted to make sure you got a cab."

Dunn read him his rights and took him in for questioning. "It was unlikely that he was the perp, but right now, all precautions were being taken, and if that meant that a few innocent suspects were hauled in for questioning, so be it. Until it was definite that the College Rapist was behind bars or dead, we would be hypervigilant and wouldn't stop our search.

CHAPTER ELEVEN
Oh, Sweet Revenge!

At 2:15 a.m., Percy Drake arrived at the scene of a body discovery in the East River, near the Williamsburg Bridge. A couple on the Promenade made the discovery and alerted the authorities. The media, also alerted, was quick to respond. Dr. Drake waded through a horde of press, all asking the same thing; "Is this related to the College Rapist and the other body from the East River?" Drake could only respond with a standoffish, "No comment at this time," although his thoughts were reciting a much more colorful response.

With floodlights ablaze, a crew of police and firefighters were lining the shore, waiting on the NYPD Harbor Unit to complete their task of removing the body from the water and searching for any other evidence they could recover.

O'Shea, at the mercy of the divers, was pacing feverishly just beyond the police line. His frustration could be seen in his posture and gait, and as Drake approached him, it could be read through the deep lines in his face. "What do we have?" Drake asked O'Shea.

"I don't know yet," replied O'Shea. "They're just about finished with the recovery."

They both stood in silence, waiting for the dive captain to come and give them a report. In the background, the crime scene techs were foaming at the mouth, eager to observe, collect, and analyze whatever evidence was unearthed.

"Captain O'Shea?" a voice called from the distance.

"Yeah!" he answered as he walked toward the familiar voice. "Lieutenant Valente, come stai?" he continued.

"Sto bene grazie, Capitano," Valente replied as he embraced O'Shea, "although under these circumstances, a jovial greeting is probably not appropriate."

"You remember Dr. Percy Drake?" O'Shea asked as he gestured toward Drake, following behind.

"Lieutenant Valente," Drake uttered out of breath, extending his hand, "congratulations on your promotion to the harbor unit. You look like you're in shape for it, not like this old fart," he added patting his ample belly, as he paused for a moment to catch his breath. "What do we have?"

"A woman, I think. She is in rough shape," Valente reported.

Drake, leaning over the horrific naked remains, looked over the body and affirmed, "Yep, you're right. It is a she, and she's in rough shape. From the look of her, she's traveled a distance to end up here. This is definitely not where she went into the water. What else have yeah dragged up?" he questioned, looking at Valente.

"Nothing useful so far," he noted.

Justus arrived just after Drake. He took a look at the body and backed away, repulsed by the state of the decayed corpse. "What do you think?" Justus queried O'Shea and Drake simultaneously.

"Hard to say," O'Shea advised. "There isn't much left of her to go on."

"She looks to be the approximate size and same hair color," Drake surmised.

"Sorry to be so rude," Justus said, extending a hand to Lieutenant Valente. "Justus Evans."

"Angelo Valente," the harbor unit lieutenant announced, giving a firm, decisive handshake.

"Justus is a consultant on the College Rapist case," O'Shea told Valente.

"How long has she been in the water?" Justus inquired.

"Can't say conclusively, but a few weeks anyway," Drake responded.

"Yeah, that's what I think too," agreed Valente.

"Anything else in the water to go on?" Justus questioned Valente.

"A few trinkets but nothing that seems relevant," he stated, "but we're not finished yet."

O'Shea, Drake, and Justus all feared the same thing. The body was Eirinn.

Valente wrapped up his end of the investigation, ordering that the body and other objects found in the water be transported to the coroner's office, allowing Drake to start the autopsy and identification process. Back at the morgue, Ethan awaited Drake to assist with the autopsy.

"What an atrocious sight!" Ethan remarked with pity in his voice.

"It is unbelievable what the water and its elements can do to a body." Drake returned as he set up the camera for the initial photographs. "Look at the hands, Ethan, but don't touch them," Drake requested. "Is there anything evident in them? I couldn't tell with the lighting at the recovery site."

Just as Ethan was about to answer, Justus entered the lab unexpectedly.

"Holy Mother of Christ!" Justus hollered as he inhaled the stench of the lab and viewed the mangled, bloated cadaver under the light, on the cold metal table.

"Hell on fire!" Drake exclaimed. "Don't sneak up on an old guy like me, or I'll be on the table."

"Sorry," Ethan apologized. "We would have covered the body had you knocked or given some other indication that you were coming in!"

Justus, having turned away, advised, "Here's some hair and a blood-streaked tissue from Eirinn's apartment," handing the samples to Ethan. "Hopefully, this will eliminate her as this Jane Doe," he stated with muted optimism.

"You know that DNA testing will take several days. What about any identifying characteristic or marks?" Ethan asked Justus.

"I don't know," Justus answered distraught. "Maybe Ivy will know something"

Yasmine had joined me at the Escape Lounge, after Dunn left with the suspect. "Hey, my phone," I said as I looked for it at the bottom of my purse. "It's Justus." I assumed he was calling to give us an update on the suspect brought in for questioning earlier.

Looking hopefully at Yasmine, I answered, "Hey, Justus."

"A body was found in the water tonight . . . East River," he advised.

"Is it her?" I asked then held my breath, waiting for an answer.

"They don't know yet," Justus stated, "but I did get a sample of DNA from her apartment. That will take a few days though. Does she have anything, like a physical characteristic, that could help identify her more quickly?"

"Let me think," I said, closing my eyes to visualize Eirinn. "She has a birth mark on one leg, somewhere on her thigh. I remember her saying how much she hated it."

"I don't think that's going to help. The victim's skin is in rough shape," Justus advised hesitantly.

"Um . . . OK," I said and continued to think. "She never wore heels," I recalled, thinking of a conversation I had with Eirinn. "She shattered an ankle when she was younger and has some screws in it, but I don't know which one."

"OK, that might do it," he concluded, hanging up abruptly.

I looked at Yasmine, stunned, and she demanded, "What are you still doing here? GO!"

I didn't want Jay to know. He didn't need the worry; this victim may not be Eirinn.

I ran faster than I ever had toward the morgue, hurdling every obstacle in my way.

Entering the autopsy lab, Justus asked, "Did you guys do the X-ray yet?"

"Just getting to it. What should we look for?" Ethan answered.

"One of the ankles has some hardware in it," Justus informed them.

As Justus left the lab, the swinging door just closing behind him, Jay appeared.

"Why are you here?" Justus asked Jay, trying to delay him from going into the autopsy room.

"It's on the news," he blurted. "A body was discovered in the East River. What do you know about it?"

"Not much yet," Justus admitted, "but the autopsy has just started."

"Did you see? Do you think it's her?" Jay demanded anxiously.

"Yes, I did see, but I really don't know anything. The body was too decomposed to recognize," Justus revealed despondently.

Jay covered his face with his hands briefly, sighed, and sat down on a bench in the hallway. He got back up abruptly and started for the door of the autopsy room, but Justus confronted him and pleaded, "Don't go in there. You don't need to until we know something for sure."

"I want to see . . . I'll know if it's her," Jay insisted.

"Believe me, you won't, and you don't want to see," Justus replied.

Jay, taking the advice, paced the hallway as patiently as could be expected. As he heard the lab door open, he swiftly faced Ethan.

"Tell me about Eirinn's ankle injury," Ethan asked.

"She broke it badly when she was a teenager," Jay answered. "She was into skateboarding and wiped out doing a three-sixty off a stairway."

"What ankle was it?" Ethan requested.

Jay thought and stated, "Her right ankle. She has a plate in it somewhere."

Ethan reached a hand out to Jay, touching his shoulder, and affirmed, "Dr. Drake believes that the body found is Eirinn."

I arrived at the morgue too late. I turned down the lab corridor just in time to see Jay collapsing to his knees, sobbing. I walked over to him, wondering what I could possibly say. I put my hand on his shoulder, and he covered mine with his tear-soaked hand, looking up at me, so devastated. He stood up, and I took him into my arms where he sobbed uncontrollably. Abruptly, he pulled himself away from me, and I saw a look in his eyes that I had never seen before. It frightened me; it was wild, furious, and dark. Justus reached for him, but Jay evaded his touch and darted out of sight in an instant. We ran to see where he went, but he was gone, too fast for us to find him.

I looked at Ethan and Justus, not knowing what to do. Justus came to me and held me. "He just needs some time," Justus insisted soothingly. We stood in silence for a few minutes, then Justus brushed the hair back from my face and kissed my forehead. "Let's go back to the house and wait."

"No, I want to wait for Jay at our place. I think he'll go back there, and I want to be there for him."

"OK, let me take you there," he offered.

Ethan gave me a hug in silence, and as Justus and I left, he returned to the autopsy room.

I waited for hours to hear from Jay, worried. I had no idea how to help him. I didn't know what to do to keep myself sane. Justus called frequently to check on me. I wept, thinking of Eirinn, and imagined how I would feel if it was my Ana who was dead. Eirinn was like Jay's daughter.

I kept having visions in my head of Eirinn, dead bodies, and murders. I couldn't shake it. I thought of my mother, prosecutor and judge, every day dealing with criminals, viewing endless disturbing evidence of crimes, hearing endless horrible stories. It made me understand her stoicism a little more. How else could someone do such a job? You would have to turn off your emotions to survive thirty plus years of it. Was she always so cold, I wondered, or did the job do it to her?

After pacing, trying to read, and taking a bath, I turned on the television for some distraction. A news report was just beginning, and it caught my attention.

> "The slain body of a local known associate of the Los Zetas was found impaled on a wrought iron fence surrounding his upscale home in Queens, New York. As you can see behind me, police and emergency vehicles are still on the scene, and nobody is commenting.
>
> Carlos Vargas González, real estate and construction entrepreneur, evaded prosecution for drug trafficking allegations on two occasions in the past five years. González, having family ties to the Mexican Los Zetas, is suspected of working one of the most lucrative distribution channels for cocaine, reaching the northern United States.
>
> There are no leads on the murder at this time, but it is expected to spark a renewed battle between the Los Zetas and Mara Salvatrucha, a.k.a. MS-13, known to have an ongoing territorial conflict in the region.
>
> This is Morgan Flaherty reporting from channel 6 news. Back to you, Dan."

Stunned already by the discovery of Eirinn's body and now this news, both good and bad; I didn't know how to feel about it. Good for Yasmine, no more charades, but bad for Jay's investigation of the Los Zetas.

I called Justus, and as usual, nobody could ever scoop him.

"Yeah, we know, the body was discovered maybe an hour ago, pretty gruesome," Justus informed me.

"How's Yasmine?" I inquired.

"OK . . . here talk to her," he said as he passed over the phone.

"What are you feeling?" I asked Yasmine.

"Well, I'm not sure what to feel. I was acting, you know when with him, but I did also see that there was a part of him that wasn't all bad," she explained. "I understand a bit what it must be like for you, when you have your visions. Nobody is all bad."

"Do you need me?" I asked.

"Jay needs you more!" Yasmine confirmed.

Just as she spoke, my call waiting alerted me of another call. It was him. My tension increased instantly, not knowing what to say.

"It's Jay," I told Yasmine, voice shaking and stomach feeling nauseated. I answered his call.

"Sorry if I worried you," Jay spoke softly.

"I didn't know what to think . . . what to do for you," I replied, my voice quaking, hands quivering; then tears started to stream from me uncontrollably.

"Shhh," he whispered, "I'm coming home."

It wasn't long, and I heard the door opening. I wiped the tears from my cheeks and met him in the hallway. Standing a few feet apart, we looked at each other. I could see that he had fed a lot from his skin color, he looked vital, his scent powerful and enticing. I felt weak in his presence, pallid and frail. His eyes penetrated me with a look that was both evil and delightful. I was paralyzed in the moment.

Swiftly, I felt his heat behind me; his hand encircled my waist, pulling me close. Pushing my hair aside, he took in the scent emanating from my neck. I heard nothing but his breath in my ear. Closing my eyes, I gave in to my body completely, a puppet ready to be animated. I felt him pierce my skin, taking the energy from my already languid body, his hands exploring me.

My hunger grew intense as he drained me, weak and delirious; his scent was all that I could sense. As his hand swept over the contours of my face, I eagerly sank my teeth into his wrist, retrieving what was mine. His blood trickled slowly over my tongue, sweet and warm. I licked and sucked playfully at the wound, teasing more blood out of it. No mortal could comprehend the ecstasy of taking blood from a lover. Pulling his wrist away from me, he licked a drop of blood from the corner of my mouth, our tongues sharing it. Kissing with complete abandon, we sank to the floor. His hands were desperate to touch me, his lips and tongue eager to please, his body releasing the pent-up tension he had carried for weeks.

When Jay's energy was all used up, that's when he completely broke down. We sat on the floor in the hallway. He laid his head in my lap as he spoke about his past. He had gone a long time without letting anyone into his heart, and Eirinn was the one that melted it just enough to make it beat again. He had his own children long ago; they disappeared, along with his wife, when he was away in battle. He never knew if they were dead, or if they had been taken. He always wondered if his wife had left him willingly. He hadn't been able to trust anyone completely, he admitted, until he met Eirinn.

I could understand loss, but not the loss of a child. I knew I would eventually have to experience it, but I couldn't even think about it now. Eventually, there was nothing left to talk about but the inevitable—what to do next.

We had to plan a funeral, something that Jay had never discussed with Eirinn. He didn't know what she would want, and this made him feel even worse.

"I think she wouldn't want you to stress over it," I offered with as much compassion as I could. "She was always easygoing. She would want all of us to celebrate her life, not despair from her death," I continued. "What flower was her favorite?" I asked.

"The little white bells," Jay answered, and we began to plan her service centered on lily of the valley.

The next week was difficult. The women planned the memorial service, leaving Jay some time to process everything. The new club manager tended to Gotham, and I helped where I could. I took on the task of telling all of Eirinn's friends and regulars at the bar about the tragedy and the memorial service. We needed the service done quickly so that we would all be available for the weekend. If Ethan's estimate was accurate, the College Rapist would be striking then. No more than now were we fully committed to doing all it took to ensure that HE would not live to hurt another woman.

The day of the service took a toll on Jay. We planned a private party on the balcony at the club, in Eirinn's honor, to celebrate her life. The rest of the club was open for people to come pay their respects and pulled in a huge crowd. People came in hordes to toast Eirinn. Patrons she had served over the years and those who had known her father, former owner of the club.

Eirinn had been the quintessential barstool psychologist. She listened to everyone who had a story to tell, who needed to vent, who needed a sounding board. The DJ booth was open to anyone wanting to propose a toast in her honor. All of her favorite songs were played.

A memorial service is not for the one lost. It is for the family left behind. It shows them just how many people were affected, touched by their loved one. As the evening went on, I could see Jay's sorrow lifting a bit when he heard all the great things that people had to say about Eirinn. We had a large poster-sized photo mounted on the wall behind the bar that would stay there for as long as Jay owned the club. There were lilies of the valley arrangements everywhere in the club, and the sweet fragrance lingered like Eirinn's spirit.

Besides our family, our closest friends were here: Gemma, Lars and Christian, other New York immortals, Blaze and Dietrich, even some I didn't know who had come a distance for Jay's sake.

"Ivy, I want you to meet Loreena and Davis, friends of mine from Europe," Jay announced as he introduced me to a handsome couple, of course. She was adorned in the finest jewelry, even in her golden blonde hair, tied in a knot at the back of her neck; her long sleek figure was like a manikin displaying a very high-end tailored suit. Davis, a classic-looking Englishman, was a constant appendage at her side.

After shaking hands and having a brief conversation with them, Jay ushered me to another set of immortals from his past. Aastha, Raheem, and Danish were very old immortals, I could tell by their demeanor, very much like Tavia and Jay. I could tell that they had a special bond with him. After a few minutes of conversation, the language switched to an Indian dialect, so I gracefully bowed out and returned to sit with Justus and the rest of my family in a comfortable little nook in one corner of the balcony.

Dunn, Johnson, and O'Shea were sitting with us, sharing stories of Eirinn and looking at some photo albums. Brandon, one of the bartenders, saw me and approached, asking to speak with Jay. I advised him that Jay wasn't to be disturbed about business-related issues, but Brandon insisted. Of course, Jay could hear this exchange from across the room and was at our side promptly. Although Jay pulled Brandon aside to talk, we all could hear the conversation.

"There was this guy asking about Eirinn," Brandon began. "He wanted to know how she died and if the police knew anything," Brandon explained. "He creeped me out, staring at her photo above the bar."

"What guy? Where is he?" Jay demanded as he looked over the balcony toward the bar.

"He was right there, in front of Eirinn's photo," Brandon recounted, "but I don't see him now."

"Do you remember seeing him before?" Jay questioned frantically.

Brandon answered, "I can't say for sure, but he was definitely not one of the regulars!"

"What was he wearing?" Jay asked aggressively.

"Nothing special," Brandon replied, intimidated.

"THINK!" Jay yelled, startling him.

"A casual shirt, light colored, I think," Brandon stuttered, "and normal jeans, nothing special."

As Jay called down to security at the doors, he asked Brandon impatiently, "What did he look like?"

"My height," Brandon indicated, "white skin, brown hair, looked like he was growing a goatee and moustache.

Justus showed Brandon the College Rapist composite on his phone and said, "Could it have been this guy?"

As Jay was telling security to stop people from leaving, Brandon confirmed, "Yes, he did look like this guy, I think."

Jay was gone in a flash; and in no time, the music was off, the lights turned on, and Jay announced, "Nobody leaves the premises!

The police will be checking ID at the door. You may be questioned before you are cleared to leave, sorry for the inconvenience."

"You did the right thing coming to tell Jay. You know he isn't usually this rude," I told Brandon. "I hope you understand, with the circumstances."

As Brandon sheepishly turned to walk away, Justus requested, "If you can isolate his glass or beer bottle, put it in a plastic bag without getting more fingerprints on it and keep it secure. Brandon," he continued with a pause, "thanks!" Brandon went back to work a little stunned, searching for anything that the suspect might have touched.

Luckily, we had several members of the police force with us. They began with ID checks and questions as they waited for backup to arrive. Justus and I met Jay and Anton in the club office.

"He was here!" Jay roared as he punched a hole clear through a brick wall. "He was here, and we let him get away!" I was startled by his voice and from the noise of the wall shattering. When I saw his eyes, he had that same look, the one he had at the morgue, just before he disappeared for hours; and it made me uneasy.

Justus went to him and put both hands on Jay's shoulders, looking at him intently, and whispered, "You don't want this to end like it did last week, do you? Pull yourself together. None of us can afford to lose it right now!"

Of course, I could hear, and I didn't know what Justus meant by "you don't want this to end like it did last week," but I chose not to question.

"Let's talk this over and determine the best course of action right now," Justus continued. "Ivy, can you please go find O'Shea and Ethan? We need to talk to them now," he commanded, not taking his eyes off Jay.

I left hoping that the two of them were under control and found both O'Shea and Ethan at the main doors, questioning patrons.

When I told Ethan what was going on, he found Magnus and brought him to the office, and O'Shea followed me.

"Let's take stock of the situation," O'Shea began. "All the exits are covered, if he is still here, we'll get him. Could he exit by any of the windows?"

"No," Jay verified, "they're sealed."

"If he did leave and is on foot, then he couldn't have gotten very far," Ethan suggested. "Magnus, Ivy, get some of the others and go search the surroundings. Justus, go talk to the security staff outside to see what they know and ask if any cabs or limos left the club in the past ten to fifteen minutes."

O'Shea cut in, "I'll contact the cab and limo companies and ask them to put out a description to their drivers in the area. Remember, everyone, there is still a College Rapist victim out there somewhere. We need him to talk," O'Shea cautioned.

"You know we're all in until this guy is DEAD," Magnus dared, looking at O'Shea as though in a showdown, trying to provoke a reaction.

O'Shea, taking the bait, declared conclusively, "We don't want this guy in the system other than the morgue, but we still need to question him about the missing victim mentioned in Marilyn Walker's journal!"

Until now, it had never been said openly that our killing was condoned; it was only implied and presumed. There was definitely no question this time, and it was understood by all of us.

Standing there, imagining what Jay was feeling and thinking, I became engulfed with apprehension. I looked at Jay carefully and caught his attention, making sure that he was OK; that it was OK for me to leave him. His eyes answered me with assurance that he was focused and controlled. Magnus and I assembled all the immortals, and we set out on a search in all directions from the club. Our order was not to kill until we had a name and location of the missing victim.

It would take enormous restraint for any of us to control our desire to kill him.

I ran frantically, looking at everyone; looking in restaurants, bars, lobbies, alleys; listening to conversations so much that my head was spinning. I asked people if they had seen someone matching the description, given by Brandon. I showed the composite to everyone who would stop. I searched for two hours with no luck and was called back to Gotham.

There was a forensic team trying to pick up prints from the bar, but this would be almost futile, considering the number of people who had been here. There was one glass isolated that might have had the suspect's prints.

Everyone met on the balcony to discuss their findings. The heavy load we all carried was visible on our faces and in our languid postures.

Yasmine was told that someone resembling the suspect went into an apartment building on East Twenty-third and Second, but the doorman didn't recall anyone with the suspect's description going in. He also said that no one fitting that description or resembling the composite lived there. Some officers were questioning the tenants of every unit as we were meeting.

Everyone who searched the area around the club couldn't find any sign of him. There was no luck with the cab or limo companies either. The suspect simply vanished. With his practice stalking victims, he did know how to be invisible, how to blend in to the background.

"I didn't want to talk about this tonight, but under the circumstances, I think it is appropriate," Ethan announced.

I immediately had a knot form in my gut, and I could see the discomfort taking over Jay's body as well.

Ethan began in a professional manner, "The autopsy findings revealed that Eirinn was killed about three weeks ago. The time frame can be very difficult to ascertain for a body found in water."

He paused briefly because Jay winced. I reached over to take Jay's hand, which he accepted instinctively. The furrows in his brow were deeper than ever, and I could see tears welling at the corner of his eyes.

Ethan looked at Jay for approval to continue. After a moment, Jay looked at Ethan with conviction and told him to go on.

"She was most likely strangled to death then dumped," Ethan continued, painfully. As he said this, Jay's hand tightened like a vice grip around mine, and a few tears painted his face. I felt like vomiting. I wasn't capable of vomiting, but the sensation was there anyway. I couldn't hold back my tears, as much as I wanted to be strong. Neither could Tavia, and then it was like a chain reaction going through all of us.

Ethan waited until we were all able to contain our tears before he continued. "There were ligature marks on her wrists, consistent with those of Marilyn Walker and other College Rapist victims," he said cautiously, looking over to Jay.

"How could it be HIM? She knew better!" Jay hollered and then covered his face with his hands and sobbed with sadness and frustration.

I put my arms around Jay and held him until I felt his body relax. I looked at him, searching for a sign that he was ready to hear more. I needed to be strong for him, even though I was berating myself for having missed my opportunity to catch Marilyn Walker. Eirinn might still be alive if I had only . . .

I stopped myself from going down that road, and finally Jay's hand tightened around mine, and we spoke silently through our entwined fingers. Once Ethan saw that both of us were able to remain composed, he continued.

"She did one thing that was extremely commendable," Ethan revealed with a lump building in his throat. He paused again to swallow hard and continued, "She got a piece of him. She bit him, and there was tissue lodged in her teeth. We were able to isolate a strong DNA sample and get a profile!"

Jay smiled and cried again, knowing that he had taught her well. She knew about evidence and DNA, and she gave us a gift, her last gift to Jay and the team.

This was the first DNA sample collected from all the assaults and murders. The College Rapist was impeccable so far, but finally, someone outsmarted him.

"There was no match in the system," Ethan continued, "but with this profile, we'll be able to screen any suspects from here forward. We also ran the profile against the rape kits and got a positive for all of the cases that we suspected were his."

"There's no better time than now, while everything is still fresh, to get inside his head," Justus proposed. "He came here tonight seeking something. What was it?"

"Many killers will return to the scene of a crime, or attend the funeral of the victims," Magnus stated.

I could see Jay depersonalizing and thinking as a profiler; the look on his face changed from sorrow to determination.

"When we profiled after the Tandy Masterson case," Ethan recalled, "we determined that the College Rapist wouldn't likely risk any contact with crime scenes because of the state of alert in the city. Could we have been wrong?"

O'Shea replied, "Not necessarily. Maybe he didn't come here to feed his fantasies but because he was concerned about the evidence left behind. It is the first time that we know of, that evidence was left behind. That would rattle an organized killer."

"Serial killers like to involve themselves in the investigation," Helene added. "Maybe he's been hanging around the investigation on the sidelines all along, and nobody ever noticed him?"

"I don't get that sense from him," Ethan declared. Jay, somewhat aggressively, demanded, "What makes you say that? We did categorize him as an organized offender. They often follow the investigation closely and get off on thinking they're better than the cops!"

Ethan responded calmly, "It is partly my gut feeling, Jay, and partly because I don't believe any of us would have missed identifying him on the sidelines or masquerading as a witness."

O'Shea cut in, "I agree with Ethan. I still feel strongly that we nailed the profile, and that he was here tonight because of worry, if he is capable of worry, or just to take stock of the status of the investigation. Because he is organized, I think that he knows when to stay out of sight, and that he is using the information to plan his next attack. We have not and will not release to the press that we have DNA evidence. Ethan, do you think that this changes your prediction for the next attack?"

"If we don't get the press any more hyped up than they are now and make sure there's no leak of information, I think my prediction is still solid," Ethan assured. "I believe that he is well into the cycle, probably full on in the fantasy stage. He can't stop now until the cycle is complete."

"What is the cycle?" I questioned.

Justus explained as simply as possible, "You know how there is always a cooling down period between rapes or murders for the serial offender?"

I nodded, showing that I was following.

"In the cooling down period," he continued, "there is a mental process that goes on, building up to the next attack. The mental process includes distorted thinking, where the offender goes through stages of anger that gets pushed outward on to others. This starts the slide down the slippery slope. Something in the offender's thinking triggers a compulsion that starts as fantasy and then becomes reality through an attack. Once the compulsion is triggered, the offender can't stop the process until release is obtained by committing the assault. Just like a drug addict who won't stop looking for a fix, because it is an addiction to the feelings obtained through the act.

Organized offenders can control their actions to some extent, and the planning is part of the fantasy, but they still are ultimately under the power of the compulsion. After the act is complete, the distorted thinking subsides until the next cycle begins. The length of the cycle is quite variable from offender to offender but is fairly predictable for an individual offender."

"Having a victim found and publicized in the media may actually speed up the process, fueling the fantasy," Ethan added. "Showing up here, seeing the photo, might be like throwing fuel on the fire, or it could have the opposite effect of giving some temporary satisfaction, slowing down the process."

O'Shea, nodding his head, advised, "Just in case, we should be on high alert starting tonight. The night is still young as far as bars and clubs are concerned, so let's all get out there and troll the target area. I'll call in as many plain-clothes officers as I can." He looked at Jay and insisted, "Jay and Ivy, you're both needed here. We'll let you know if anything comes up where we need your assistance."

Jay and I knew that we were excluded from the surveillance that night because we were too emotionally invested for the moment. He had to face that the College Rapist killed Eirinn because all evidence pointed that way. We closed up the club and had our own private memorial for her. I watched Jay as he looked at Eirinn's photo behind the bar and I wished I could read minds, without having to kill for it. I was still at a loss for words.

Four nights came and went with no sign of the College Rapist. All we had was another week of anticipation building toward the next hunt for him. It was like preparing for a competition of some sort. We knew what we had to do but couldn't predict what the outcome would be. Everyone wanted to be the one who would catch the notorious College Rapist. We all had parts to play in an elaborate con, designed to entice and entrap someone whose skill for evasion had proven masterful. If we missed our opportunity, we would have to wait another three to six weeks before we would have it again, and another innocent life would be lost in the process.

Surveillance day arrived, and we met at the house, this time with Johnson, Dunn, and O'Shea around the table with us. The atmosphere was definitely thick with apprehension. We so rarely had mortal guests, that we made an occasion out of it. We took out our best coffee set and served them a rich imported, hand-ground coffee. The aroma was extravagant, perking everyone up ever so slightly.

Everyone hoped that Ethan could provide a narrower target; a specific place to search in the radius we had already been working.

After some small talk, Ethan announced with enthusiasm, "I have tweaked my mathematical model after consulting a friend of mine at MIT, and I have pinpointed our zone to the following clubs: Escape Lounge, Club Diamond, or Lavish."

"How did you get that?" I questioned.

"Elementary, my dear Ivy, elementary," he said with a smile. "I used mathematical algorithms similar to those for predicting weather. Using past patterns and other data, I can predict where the College Rapist is most likely to commit his next offense."

"Does this new tweak include timeframe?" asked Justus.

"Somewhat," Ethan expounded. "Most likely Saturday," he finished with a very satisfied look on his face.

Justus, equally as pleased, jumped up and patted Ethan on the shoulder as he praised, "This is great. Ethan, as always, you are amazing!"

"My darling partner tells me I'm amazing too," Ethan jibed as he winked at Helene.

With this new information from Ethan, there wasn't a single officer who was not engaged in the pursuit of the College Rapist. The NYPD technical unit was at the ready with any available police cameras strategically placed to maximally view the target areas. Anton volunteered to stay home and run our video system commandeering as many private CCTV cameras in the target area as he could. Everything was in place, and collectively, we felt ready.

Dunn and I were at the Escape Lounge again. We had a new crew of undercovers with us this time. Tonight, Dunn and I were more synchronized in our attire, fitting in nicely with the students. Our hopes were high, and we had our act down pat.

"Mel, I love that necklace," I observed, admiring her silver and black antique cross necklace displayed conspicuously on her bare neckline.

"Thanks," she replied. "It's old. It was my grandmother's. Tonight, I wore it for luck."

"It's really busy in here," I commented.

"Yeah," Dunn agreed. "Even though this place is relatively small, we won't be able to stay in one spot."

We worked the establishment for several hours, and it looked like the night was going to be a bust. The crowd was thinning, and we were starting to relax, letting our guard down when one of the undercovers alerted us to a man sitting discretely at the bar, just watching. Eerily, he peered from woman to woman.

Dunn asked the undercover officer, "When did he get here?"

"I was scanning the bar area regularly, and he just seemed to appear. If he was here for a while, he was blending in well."

"He's a pro stalker, moving into position when most of the women are drunk and vulnerable," Dunn remarked.

If this was the College Rapist, he changed his appearance again. He had a very short haircut with a perfectly sculpted thin goatee. I scrutinized his face, and as the realization set in that it was him, my heart began to race. Then our eyes met. The brief message his dark blue eyes communicated was beware, but then as a slight smile formed on his lips, his eyes softened and became inviting. I felt as though we sized each other up as opponents, and I thought to myself, *GAME ON!*

We had to trap him. This was our chance. I immediately began my part in the play, acting inebriated, and I put my arms around the undercover officer to my side, which he took to quite kindly. Dunn also went into action, making a fake phone call, standing right by the suspect.

"You're not here, are you?" she said. "I guess I'll have to get someone else to buy my drinks tonight!"

I continued to flirt with Mr. Undercover, and he bought me a drink, of course. Then I scoffed, "Thanks, doll," and walked away from him, past our suspect, over to Dunn; and I put my arm around her.

"What's wrong?" I asked within earshot of the suspect.

"Screw that bastard," she answered.

"What happens at Escape stays at Escape!" we chorused, giggling.

We took a table in the club that was in a perfect location for us to see the suspect but, even more important, where he could see us. Two drinks arrived at our table, courtesy of my undercover admirer. After a while, he and his friend, another undercover, came to our table; but I shot them down. They walked away with their tails between their legs.

We overtly flirted with another set of our undercover friends, Johnson and Francis. They joined us at our table, buying a few rounds. During this time, Dunn and I observed the suspect covertly, hoping we were feeding his fantasy, painting his perfect victim picture. He was hooked, I could tell, so I got up, and looking straight at him, I walked toward the bar, where he was sitting. As I stood directly in front of him, I stopped and held his gaze for a moment. I had the attention of the room, thanks to my immortal charm. I looked away from him with complete disregard; this would be the final pull to set the hook.

I squeezed between the suspect and another patron, waving some money toward the bartender, when a random guy pushed his way in beside me, crowding the suspect and insisting on paying for my drinks. Of course, I accepted. Even though this man wasn't an undercover, his timing could not have been more impeccable!

I could feel the suspect's eyes searing through me, as I walked back to the table. Dunn was now straddling Johnson, kissing and groping him. Our suspect was locked on our table, watching and loathing! Francis whispered in my ear that it was time for the separation. I engaged in a loud bogus phone call, displaying reluctance to leave the club but finally giving in. I said goodbye to Dunn, who was still in a lustful embrace with her colleague. I declined to give my number to Francis and stumbled my way to the back door of the club.

My intention was to take a route providing the most seclusion, the most apt for an attack. Officers had been alerted to be on the perimeter, ready to catch the College Rapist in the act. With everyone eager and ready, it seemed like a walk in the park!

I meandered away from the club, feigning inebriation, seeming to pay no attention to my surroundings, hiding that my nerves were on edge and then . . . nothing. Nothing happened! *Did we miss our opportunity?* I asked myself. The officers and I congregated to decide what to do next.

"I saw him walk toward the back of the club," Francis confirmed. "I had to stay a distance from him so he wouldn't be alerted or suspicious. I really thought he left the club and followed you, Ivy."

None of the officers had seen him. Johnson went back into the club to question some bystanders. Nobody, including the bartender, noticed the suspect leaving, but there was a tip left on the bar, where the suspect had been sitting. Johnson confiscated the tip, but the likelihood of isolating the suspect's prints from money was almost nil. We alerted the other stakeout groups that our opportunity was a bust; they should continue with their surveillance. Dunn had left the club once Johnson went in pursuit of the suspect. She was sure that this was it. We would have him, the College Rapist. She had to initiate the process at the precinct. It had been made clear that no harm would come to the suspect until he revealed the name and location of the missing victim. Dunn had to ensure that he was not officially booked into the system because there were alternate plans for his sentence.

Francis and another two undercovers scoured the area surrounding the Escape Lounge, with no results. I returned to the bar with Johnson, just in case the suspect would come back, however unlikely.

I scrutinized Johnson, trying to get a read on him. He had a tremendous poker face. In my mortal days, I would be scared of him for sure; if I didn't know that he was a giant teddy bear on the inside.

"Looked like you and Dunn had a 'friends with benefits' thing going on . . . ," I prodded with a grin.

He let out a snicker and retorted, "I'm a great actor!"

His eyes said differently though. I believe they had a deeper connection than partners on the job. Dunn never spoke about Johnson in that way, but as I thought about our conversations, I recalled the warmth in her face when she spoke of Johnson. I can imagine it was difficult to work with someone every day, often in extreme situation, without creating an attachment that goes beyond coworkers.

"Speaking of Dunn," he said, "I'm going to call the precinct to let her know that we didn't get him." Johnson went outside, where he could have a noise-free conversation. When he came back, he had a puzzled look on his face.

"What is it?" I asked.

"Dunn didn't check in at the precinct, and there's no response from her car or cell!" Johnson replied, sounding concerned.

"Is there anywhere else she would go?" I asked.

"No!" he claimed, eyes shifting as he thought, and at that moment, we both had the same ominous suspicion. We looked at each other and simultaneously echoed, "HE HAS DUNN!"

It wasn't me the College Rapist wanted; it was her!

Johnson ran out the door, up the street to the alley where Dunn had parked the unmarked car. It wasn't there. Johnson and I searched the immediate area with no luck and no clues.

Johnson alerted the other officers and the precinct; I alerted my family.

"How could this have happened? How did we miss this?" Johnson uttered under his breath as we jumped into his car. I could tell that he was the kind of guy that didn't want to be reassured or placated.

Then it came to me. "He never went for a redhead before. He had no interest in me. It was her!" I reasoned, astonished, such a seemingly small detail.

Johnson looked at me completely incredulous, and he realized it too. Was this a detail that never occurred to anyone?

All the unmarked squad cars sped back to the precinct like a security blockade for the president. The ominous thought that entered my head was how this convoy resembled a funeral procession.

Johnson and I were the first to arrive at the precinct. One by one, officers entered with looks on their faces that varied from despair to determination. Johnson took his frustrations out on a vending machine that looked like it had already suffered a few beatings. Justus and Magnus arrived and joined the police techs looking through video footage from the street cameras in the vicinity of the Escape Lounge.

Jay arrived, and I was stunned to see him.

"Did you close Gotham early?" I asked surprised.

"Finding Dunn alive is more important to me than Gotham. I left the new guy in charge," he confessed as he came to me and held my hand. Whether it existed this strongly before, I don't know, but there was certainly a strong sense of community building between my family and our partners on the police force.

Tavia, Helene, Ethan, and Yasmine arrived, joining the huddle, ready to do what it took to find Dunn. Tavia gave me a silent hug in support, knowing that Dunn and I were building a friendship that was greater than coworkers on a case together.

The CCTV cameras revealed a brief view of what they believed to be Dunn's unmarked car driving east.

Johnson, enraged, roared, "What are we all doing standing here? We need to be out there looking for her."

O'Shea, with an overpowering voice, took charge of the situation, organizing directed action. "Ethan, your geographical predictions for the target clubs were right on. Can you do it again to figure out where he has taken Dunn?"

"I'll try, but I need a powerful computer system," Ethan suggested.

"Johnson, take Ethan to our tech center," O'Shea ordered. "Francis and Stockton, go to Dunn's house," he continued. "Smale, we need the LUDs for Dunn's phone. Martinez, see if you can track her car. Everyone else, just wait here. We need a structured approach. I don't want people going off in different directions without a plan."

Just then, Drake could be heard coming down the hall, spouting a tirade of choice words. "O'Shea," he bellowed as he approached the gathered crowd, "some eegit buried this report under some crap on my desk!"

O'Shea, distracted, asked, "What is it, Drake? We have a situation!"

Drake, oblivious to who was around, announced while shoving the report into O'Shea's chest, "A DNA report that matches the sample from Eirinn Murphy to one of the blond parade guys."

"WHAT?" O'Shea hollered, eyes bulging from their sockets. "How long ago was this report done?"

Before he could answer, I felt Jay tense up, readying to pounce.

"WHO IS THE BASTARD?" Jay screamed as loud as the horn from a train, and with the momentum of a speeding train, he was moving toward O'Shea and Drake.

It took all four immortal ladies to hold him back. His face had that eerie look, and I needed to get through to him, to tame him. This situation wasn't O'Shea's or Drake's fault, but in his current state, I don't think Jay was seeing it that way. The ladies were holding him by the arms, and I managed to get in front of him and put my hands on his chest, pushing against his forward motion.

"JAY, LOOK AT ME!" I screamed, pleading. "LOOK AT ME!"

I saw the change in his eyes; the Jay that I knew flickered through the haze of his frenzied anger briefly, enough for me to take hold of him, to get through to him.

"ENOUGH!" I yelled, pushing back against him again. "It's not their fault, and flipping your lid won't help things. Either calm down or LEAVE!"

I actually freaked myself out; I had never reacted that way before. I had never spoken to him or anyone that way.

He snapped out of it, I think, because he was completely taken aback with my reaction. In fact, Tavia, Helene, and Yasmine were all looking at me with a variety of expressions. Tavia's eyes were darting back and forth from Jay to me with a look of "what's going to happen next." Yasmine's mouth was hanging open, and Helene directed a "you go girl" gaze my way.

O'Shea motioned for us to get into a meeting room, and he closed the door. We didn't need this scene to continue. Not every cop in the station knew about us, and we all wanted to keep it that way.

"Sorry," Jay offered to both O'Shea and Drake.

"Understandable," commented Drake. "I should have been more sensitive about it. Tact is not my strong suit."

"It's done," O'Shea dismissed. "Let's hear more about this report."

"The guy's name is Dane Free," Drake answered.

"How good is the match?" O'Shea questioned.

"Near perfect!" Drake assured.

"Get his name to the techs. I want to know everything about Dane Free and any other alias he's used . . . Dane Free doesn't sound like a real name to me!" O'Shea noted as he handed the report back to Drake. "Find out who left this on your desk!" O'Shea added harshly.

Jay sat humiliated and remorseful because of his behavior. I walked over to him tentatively, not sure how this first confrontation between us would work out. He looked up at me, his hazel eyes like those of a child begging for forgiveness. No words were needed. I extended my hand toward him, which he took happily. I eased him up, and we walked out of the room hand in hand.

Several patrol cars were sent out to troll the river's edge. This ominous detail meant that they expected Dunn would be another river victim. The officers assigned to Dunn's condo reported that she wasn't there and that there was nothing indicating she had been there in the past few hours. The attempt to locate her by GPS failed. Her abductor must have destroyed the unit or jammed the signal. Everything hinged on Ethan. He needed to find a way to locate her, and fast. While we waited for Ethan, all we could do was go over the details.

"He never went after a redhead before," I stated. "Is that why it was her and not me?"

Helene reported, "We did consider hair color, and since it was all over the map, we discounted it in victimology, but you are right. There were no other redheads . . . maybe it was significant?"

"We can't second-guess ourselves," Tavia insisted. "We did everything possible to try and pin this guy down."

Then Jay reached out to my necklace. I was wearing a heart pendant that he gave me for Christmas.

"Was Dunn wearing a necklace tonight?" Jay asked with a very focused look on his face.

"Yes, I commented on it. It was very beautiful," I answered.

"What did it look like?" Jay urged me to continue.

"It was her grandmother's, a very old cross," I described.

Jay muttered under his breath, "A cross." Then he spoke up, "A cross! Eirinn always wore the cross necklace that her parents gave her, and I have not been able to find it."

"What about the other victims?" Helene probed.

"O'Shea!" Jay called out. "Was there anything noted about necklaces taken from the victims?"

"Not that I can recall, but you'll have to check with Ethan," he responded.

Just then, Ethan entered the room, shouting, "I have it. I think he would have brought her near the dump site of the other murdered victims. I've deduced that to be somewhere between the Manhattan and Brooklyn bridges, possibly at Market Slip or Pike Slip. Concentrate your search around the Lower East projects. Most organized killers won't commit their attack at the same place that they dump the body."

"He probably knows that Dunn's a cop now," surmised O'Shea, thinking out loud. "He may draw this out to make a statement to the police force. This could be good, giving us more time to find Dunn alive," he continued hopefully.

In my mind, I thought this also gives more time for Dunn to suffer. This whole situation seemed like a live chess match. All our plays hinged on Ethan's initial, albeit educated guess. Luckily, Ethan was a chess master.

"OK, you heard it, everyone," O'Shea concluded. "Search the Lower East Side. Think about places where a car can be concealed or could go unnoticed. You all know the description and the plates for Dunn's car. Report at least every fifteen minutes."

Justus stayed at the tech center to use the camera surveillance available in the Lower East, ready to feed us information. Ethan went off with Magnus toward one end of the vast projects. Jay and I took the other end. Tavia, Helene, and Yasmine took the center. The officers, mostly in vehicles, a few on foot patrol, were covering the waterfront in the dump zone to the Williamsburg Bridge and all the major park areas.

Jay and I searched the projects near the Williamsburg Bridge with as much speed and efficiency as we could. Jay had a thought, "The projects are patrolled regularly. I think the College Rapist would know this."

"You think Ethan was wrong?" I asked.

"Not wrong, but I think we should be looking on the outskirts of the projects, not in them. Around here, I know the perfect place," Jay revealed as he took off.

I could barely keep up with him. He was like a cheetah on the hunt. I was lucky if I was at racehorse speed in comparison. He was almost out of my sight, but I could still hear him and track his scent. I wasn't sure where we were heading. I had not been to the Lower East Side too often. Not to be noticed, running with our immortal capabilities, we had to stick to areas with tree cover, through parks and alleyways. Jay was a pro with clandestine maneuvers through the city.

I caught up with Jay because he stopped. Just as I was about to speak to him, he said, "Shhh, listen. Close your eyes. Now, listen, but don't just listen with your ears. Listen with your instinct. You know Dunn better than me. You are connected to her."

I stood in silence, hearing everything but hearing nothing. I couldn't get anything. Frustrated, I blurted, "This isn't working! I don't hear anything. I don't feel anything. We're wasting time."

Jay stood behind me, close, and whispered in my ear, "Close your eyes and breathe deeply." A breeze caught wisps of my hair and blew it over my face.

"What do you feel?" he probed.

"I feel my hair tickling my face. I feel your breath on my neck," I described.

"What do you smell?" he continued.

We were close to the FDR, so I conveyed, "I smell cars. I smell trash and water."

"Keep breathing deeply and focus your thoughts on Mel. Keep a single image of her in your mind," Jay directed.

We stood there for a while—I'm not really sure how long—and our breathing became synchronized. I kept an image of Mel in my mind from earlier in the evening. I could picture her dark hair falling playfully in wisps around her face, framing her rosy cheeks, her steel blue eyes, her thin lips smiling, and her necklace, her lucky necklace. My mind stayed stuck on the necklace. I don't know why, but it was burning in my brain, and then I felt it. I felt a queasy sensation in my gut, like jumping off the highest diving platform or jumping from a quarry cliff.

Jay must have known that I was connected because he asked me very calmly, "Where is she?" I hesitated, and then he pressed, "Focus. You'll feel it." My breathing rate increased, and my brain became consumed with Mel and her necklace. Then I knew, and I opened my eyes.

"GO! I'll follow," Jay insisted.

I had no idea where I was going, but I was led by something inside me. I could best describe it as an intense gut feeling. We ran through a park, under the FDR, and right in front of us was a construction site at the water front. Everything inside me told me she was there, close.

"I can feel her," I said to Jay. "She must be alive. I can feel her."

In the distance, I heard a male voice say, "Wake up, you bitch," and the sound of someone being slapped.

Jay took off again, faster than I could possibly go. In the distance, I heard a loud thud. I could make out a car and see that Jay was standing on the roof of it.

Mel was on the ground, her hands were bound behind her, but her clothes were on, a little disheveled, but still on. The College Rapist was straddled over her, hand raised to give her another slap in the face. He was trying to wake her from unconsciousness.

"What the hell . . . ," he stammered, startled by Jay's overt arrival.

He had not noticed me, so I silently approached. I could see that Mel was breathing, and this gave me an instantaneous sensation of relief. I looked at Jay, and he was calmly furious, peering into the eyes of Eirinn's murderer.

Arrogantly, the College Rapist got up and sassed, "You know, the good thing about having snagged a cop is her gun." And he pointed it at Jay.

"Really?" Jay scoffed with a snicker. "Go for it!"

Jay jumped off the car and started to walk toward him, and the gun went off, a shot toward Jay's head, which he dogged quite easily. Next, the College Rapist shot straight at Jay's midsection, opening a small hole in his shirt.

"Ouch," Jay croaked as he continued to walk slowly toward him, "that really does sting!"

The College Rapist, dumbfounded, held up the gun for another shot, which went off as Jay reached for the gun, a bullet going straight through his hand.

"Really?" Jay protested. "Can we just stop this now?" he said, as he took the gun and threw it into the East River. "It's starting to piss me off!"

The College Rapist turned to run, but I blocked his path, saying, "I don't think so!" And I shoved him back toward Jay.

He stood mere inches away from Eirinn's murderer, whose mouth was agape.

"You're that bar owner," the College Rapist remarked.

"That right!" Jay answered with an eerie grin, and he hoisted the murderer off his feet by the throat.

The only sounds that could be heard were the sound of gasping and waves lapping at the shore line.

Jay had that look, the one that I wished to never see again. "You killed my daughter, a crime punishable by death!" he announced unnervingly.

"We need the girl. We need the girl," Mel managed to say as she wavered with consciousness.

"Oh, yeah, that's right," Jay expressed as he launched the College Rapist several feet away onto his back.

As he landed on the ground, he began to gasp from the spasms in his diaphragm. As he writhed on the ground fighting for breath, Jay searched through the College Rapist's pockets and took out his wallet. Standing patiently over him, waiting for his breath to return, Jay riffled through the wallet and read from his driver's license, "Dane Free. Now, that's an interesting name." He took a photo of Marilyn out of the wallet and said, "And here we have the lovely Marilyn Walker."

I helped Mel to her feet and removed the binding on her wrists. She was badly battered but otherwise OK.

"We read your girlfriend's diary," Jay confessed. "We know that you killed two women with Marilyn, then you killed her. One of the two murder victims was a dancer named Tandy Masterson. Who is the other one?"

"I see," the College Rapist hissed, still on the ground, regaining his cocky tone. "We're negotiating now."

Jay kicked him in the ribs and roared, "Negotiate this!"

Through his groans, the College Rapist demanded, "Hey, cop, arrest me." And he started spitting up blood. "I want my rights, and I want a lawyer," he continued, in obvious pain.

Jay laughed and kicked him in the ribs again, saying, "The name, give me the name now."

Still he refused, and I could see Jay starting to lose control. Jay walked over to the car and searched for something. The College Rapist tried to scramble away; but, of course, that was futile. Jay flipped him over and bound his hands, in the same way that his victims' hands had been bound. He knelt on the College Rapist's back, slipped a scarf around his throat, and started to slowly choke him. Just before he passed out from lack of oxygen, Jay let go of the scarf and insisted again for the name of the missing woman. This scenario was repeated two more times, but the College Rapist wouldn't give up the name. Mel and I didn't want to interfere; we didn't want to take the bone away from the dog.

The smell of blood was overwhelming me; I had to concentrate hard to overcome it. Finally, Jay, frustrated, made a small puncture wound on the killer's wrist; and a slow trickle of blood oozed out. Obviously unsure of what was happening, Dane's eyes bulged out of his head, and he made a whimpering noise.

Jay promised, "Don't worry. It will be over soon, and we'll get some information from you, like it or not!"

The blood smelled enticing. I felt my hunger building as the scent permeated me. Jay lifted Dane's wrist as an offering to me. I knew my part in this scenario. I needed to see and remember every detail possible regarding the murder of the missing woman.

I took his wrist and licked the small trickle of blood, savoring it; the blood of a masterful killer seemed more satisfying and delicious. I bit deeply, drawing out his life and his story. I saw images of a sweet little boy with older sisters doting over him; he held the image of his sisters in his mind for a while. I saw a violent father controlling every move a fearful family made. I saw a sister saying goodbye in the night and felt the deep sorrow of a small boy feeling alone. I saw a mother in a jail cell and felt the confusion of a child. There were foster homes, Chicago and then New York. I endured visions of voyeurism, several date rapes, then the string of rapes perpetrated as the College Rapist. I had to keep track in my mind, five date rapes, twelve stranger rapes, then came Marilyn. She was beautiful, and he did love her in his own way.

I had to see their sadistic sex games, then their first joint rape experience. His feelings for Marilyn were strong. Their first kill, Tandy Masterson, I saw through his eyes that Marilyn wanted the kill. Marilyn knew Tandy and enjoyed the kill. Having that power over life and death was the switch. I felt it in him. I saw the quarrelling, Marilyn's jealousy, and I felt his building rage.

This was the one I really needed to remember. She was young, white with dark hair. He liked her and wanted to keep her longer, but Marilyn was enraged by this. His and Marilyn's anger with each other fuelled an even more sadistic murder than the first. There was no name. I couldn't get a name, but it was in an apartment.

I saw more anger, more fights with Marilyn; I felt him seething. I saw him punch Marilyn many times and then him on the floor in fetal position, repeating over and over, "Why do I do this?" I felt his uncertainty, then I felt his decisiveness, and Marilyn was gone. I felt his rage mixed with regret. Then I saw Eirinn. Tears welled in my eyes and spilled over my cheeks as I had to see her suffering. I wanted to stop, but I had to see it all, see if there were more victims. It was horrifying; I would never tell Jay what I saw.

I saw myself in his visions then Dunn's necklace and the beating that he gave her. Visions of his sisters passed through his mind last, and before he took his last breath, he whispered, "Olivia."

I let his arm drop as I swallowed the last part of his life, and I started to cry.

"Marilyn knew Tandy Masterson," I told Jay through my tears. "She wanted to kill her. She enjoyed killing her."

Jay held me and said nothing. Dunn walked off in the distance toward the river, and it struck me that she had just witnessed something foreign, something bestial. I approached her slowly, silently, wondering what was going through her mind.

"Who is Olivia?" she asked, looking off into the river.

"I don't know," I explained. "Maybe one of his sisters. They are what he thought of last. His sisters called him Wayne, not Dane."

"Did you see anything that would help us find the missing victim?" Dunn questioned, still looking into the distance.

"Yes, I hope so," I described. "I saw a young woman and an apartment." I touched Mel's shoulder, and she flinched. I wanted to comfort her, but it was clear that she didn't want to be touched. I wondered what she thought of me now, after seeing what I did, witnessing what I, what we the immortals, really are.

"I need to call it in," Dunn started to say, and before she could finish, I was already handing her my phone. She took it with a shaking hand, and she looked at me, finally; her eyes told me that her distress was not because of me but because of her attack. For the moment, she needed to be a cop, not a victim.

I gave Officer Dunn her space and returned to Jay, still sitting by the corpse of the College Rapist; his face and demeanor were also difficult for me to read. I chose to say nothing and sat silently by his side.

"Is she OK?" Jay asked of Mel.

"No, but she needs to be a police officer right now," I answered. "She's calling it in."

"What did you see?" Jay inquired, and I knew that he was specifically probing for information on Eirinn.

I didn't answer; instead, I closed my eyes and listened to the noise of the night. Jay understood and put his hand over mine, intertwining his fingers with mine. I could see Mel, in the distance, just standing, staring out into the darkness. We were all physically and emotionally drained from months of pursuit.

I sighed deeply. Jay put a hand to his forehead, massaging the furrows out of his brow, and we both looked at the lifeless body, the now frail and vulnerable body of the College Rapist, Dane Free, or whatever his name really was.

I heard Mel collapsing to the ground, and I rushed to her side. She sat in the sand, elbows to knees, supporting her head in her hands, and began to sob. Just then, behind us, we could hear a vehicle, two vehicles, arriving.

I looked back to see Johnson running toward us. He stopped just shy of us and looked down at Dunn. His six-foot-three, two-hundred-pound silhouette towered over us. Mel looked up at him, and he scooped her up as gentle as he would a baby and carried her to the ambulance that had arrived just behind his unmarked squad car. Now, Officer Dunn could be the victim.

Next to arrive was O'Shea and a "meat wagon." O'Shea hesitated as he walked by the ambulance where Dunn was being treated. His eyes met Johnson's, and he knew that his presence would just complicate things, and walked on.

Jay and I were still sitting on the ground beside our victim, silent, when O'Shea approached. He stopped on the other side of the body, gave it a nudge with his foot, and said, "So this is it. This is what terrorized the East End for months. Very boy-next-door. It's no wonder women didn't fear him."

There was a long moment of silence for us all, then O'Shea asked, "What did you get from him?"

"I can give a description," I began, "of the victim, of the apartment, but he wouldn't give it up. All we have is what's in my head."

Jay spoke up, "It's my fault. I got tired of his games. I forced the hand."

"Quite literally," O'Shea pointed out as he nudged the College Rapist's gashed wrist, from which I took away his life.

Jay gave O'Shea a weak smirk and suggested, "You need to check for any missing persons named Olivia, fitting the description that Ivy will give you."

"Oh yeah?" O'Shea uttered. "Where does this come from?"

"His last word was Olivia," I disclosed. "It could be his sister, though."

"We'll check on that," O'Shea assured. "Ivy, you need to come to the station and give your description to a sketch artist before you forget it.

"We . . . I have a great memory," I advised O'Shea. Immortals have superior memory capabilities, but also my visions were like those vivid dreams that stay with you, sometimes for days.

As Jay and I were leaving the scene, we saw the College Rapist being encased in a body bag, and a sense of relief and elation washed over me. I became aware of how useful my gift could be.

At the precinct, I gave a detailed description of the victim that I saw, the circumstances, and the apartment where the rape and murder of the unknown victim took place.

Ethan went to work using the apartment description I gave, the apartment where Tandy Masterson was found, the want ads for rental apartments, and his mathematical modeling to try and estimate where to search for the missing victim. This endeavor took several days, but he did come up with some target units.

Dane Free's condo was searched, and several women's necklaces were found, all of them bearing a cross pendant. There were more necklaces found than there were victims that we knew about. So many sexual assaults go unreported. The police had put out an appeal for women to come forward, if they had been assaulted by Dane Free, the man known as the College Rapist.

The necklace collection was confiscated, and Jay was called in to identify which one belonged to Eirinn. Once the investigation was finished, O'Shea promised Jay that he could have it.

On Dane Free's computer was a collection of articles about himself, the College Rapist, and his desktop background was the composite that had been published in the newspapers. He had a collection of pornographic photos of Marilyn and other unknown women. The movie that Marilyn had referred to in her journal, with the young drugged street girl, was found along with several others.

The missing persons search revealed that a twenty-year-old Olivia Clark went missing ten weeks prior.

Jay accompanied me to the police station to look at her photo.

"What do you think, Ivy?" O'Shea asked. "Does this look like the woman you saw?"

Her photo was very similar to the sketch. "It does. I'm 90 percent sure it's her," I confirmed with anguish, thinking of this woman . . . this girl's family.

"What's happening with the apartment search?" Jay inquired.

"Nothing yet," O'Shea declared in exasperation. "We need to jump through so many hoops to gain access."

"Have you figured out the connection between Tandy Masterson and Marilyn Walker?" I asked O'Shea.

"Yes," he affirmed. "The owner and manager of the Scratching Post were questioned again, and it was determined that Marilyn Walker had worked there, over a year earlier, as a dancer. No connection was previously made because Marilyn had dark hair when she worked there, and people knew her by her stage name Georgia. She worked with Tandy Masterson, and at that time, they appeared to be friendly, according to the manager of the club."

After a few weeks, a connection was made between Marilyn Walker and the vacant apartment where Tandy Masterson was murdered. The realtor for the unit had a son who returned from school in California and identified Marilyn as a girl he had dated the year before. He described that they used to take keys from his father's office and throw parties in vacant units. He ascertained that Marilyn was devious and had some questionable sexual fantasies such as rape and strangulation. This information helped narrow down the apartment search because there were only two of the realtor's units that had been vacant for over ten weeks.

The remains of Olivia Clark were found in one of the vacant apartments and were positively identified. The unit belonged to a foreign buyer whose move to the United States was delayed.

Despite the advanced state of decomposition, it was determined that her hands were bound, as with the other College Rapist victims, and a scarf was left tied around her neck. Her hyoid bone was fractured, indicating strangulation as the cause of death. There was enough evidence, along with what I was able to provide from my memory, to close that murder off as a College Rapist offense.

A thorough background on Dane Free, who grew up as Wayne Freel, was compiled swiftly. There was a substantial children's services file that assisted in piecing together his childhood. Most of his adult life he spent as Dane Free, he was able to mastermind fake credentials and work as a professional in the financial industry.

His mother and sister were advised of his death and were consulted regarding his background.

Wayne Freel was born to Barbara and Joseph Freel in 1976, in Iowa. He grew up in an extremely abusive household. The father, Joseph Freel, a high school dropout, and mother, Barbara Stratford, met and married young. Joseph Freel was unable to maintain work because of anger and conflict issues, exacerbated by alcoholism.

There were three children: Angela, the eldest; Kim, the middle child; and Wayne, the youngest. By the time Wayne was born, tension in the family was very high. His mother was very distant and only tended to Wayne's very basic needs. Family violence was a regular event in Wayne's early life, but only the females in the family were the direct victims of the violence. Wayne, on the other hand, without any nurturing from his mother, looked to his sisters for love and guidance.

Joseph Freel controlled the family's every move with force, as necessary. The family became used to having an unemployed father and no source of income. They lived in various trailer parks and slums. Angela, the eldest daughter, ran away from home at the age of sixteen. A few months later, Barbara killed Joseph in his sleep, stabbing him to death, and fled with Kim and Wayne, then fourteen and eleven years old, respectively.

After a few weeks on the run, they were caught by state troopers, and Barbara went to prison. She was convicted of manslaughter, instead of murder, thanks to Kim's testimony and to a journal that had been written by Angela, the eldest child, depicting the family violence.

During the trial, there was a search for Angela, and it was determined that she was a Jane Doe found dead in Chicago. She had been living on the streets and was murdered in a drug-related shooting.

Kim and Wayne were sent into foster care in the state of Iowa. The foster home where Wayne grew up maintained a very strict religious environment. Both children, too old to be adopted, aged out of the system.

Wayne was described as a quiet child who kept to himself. He didn't integrate well with the other foster children and was often teased and bullied by the older kids. He suffered the same experience in school. Extremely intelligent, he never reached his potential in high school but did graduate. In his last year of high school, he became obsessed with books on how to get rich quick.

Wayne left Iowa and made his way to Chicago. He started to work for a large financial institution in the mail room, still under the name Wayne Freel. He devised a way to embezzle money through checks and money orders received by the financial institution. His scheme was uncovered, but he managed to flee the state before being arrested. There were still pending charges for fraud against "Wayne Freel" in the state of Illinois.

Wayne moved to New York and changed his name to Dane Free, forging some identification and credentials. He started to work as a stock broker, riding the dot-com wave, getting out just before the crash.

Good looking, charming, influential, and highly intelligent, he had no problem securing other professional jobs and forging other credentials, as needed. Living in lavish condos, his life seemed an amazing turnaround from his troubled youth.

Dane Free never associated with anyone from his past and made up a story of an ideal upbringing when speaking with coworkers and acquaintances. It was revealed by his boss at work that a year earlier, Mr. Free had been demoted in his job because he made a costly error that caused the firm embarrassment as well as financial loss. This demotion was probably the trigger that started his rape and murder spree.

Anyone interviewed from his workplace couldn't believe that Dane Free was the College Rapist, and nobody could believe him capable of murder under such heinous circumstances.

Tracking down past relationships proved more difficult. It was determined that he had only superficial relationships with women and that there had been allegations of date rape and other violence.

After several weeks, the hype of the College Rapist case started to settle, and we could get back to our "normal" lives. Jay and I were lost in our own worlds of guilt and regret. For me, it was because I failed to catch Marilyn Walker when I had the chance, and I also didn't attract the College Rapist as planned. Instead, he went after Dunn. Jay was still tortured by the loss of Eirinn, thinking he should have been able to do something, that maybe he could have prevented it.

We both knew that what we needed was forgiveness, to forgive ourselves. Jay certainly had a much larger hurdle than I did, but in time, we accomplished our goal of letting go. An eternity is a long time to carry guilt or any other negative feeling.

Life didn't stop or even slow down just because we were preoccupied. There was still a very large project that we couldn't let slide, after all the work that Jay and Yasmine had put into it.

The rather ostentatious death of Carlos Vargas González caused an uproar in the drug world. MS-13 was taking the heat for the assassination, and a local war was going on in the underground drug trade of New York.

It took several weeks before Jay admitted to me that he killed Carlos, but I had already deduced it for myself. Giving him the benefit of the doubt, he did suspect at that time that the Zetas might have taken Eirinn. What Jay hadn't bargained for was the upheaval that it caused and the war it began.

EPILOGUE

The War Over Transport Routes Escalates

by Enrique Perez Alonso, *The Mexican National Press*

Eight beheaded bodies were found dumped on a highway leading to the Texas border in what appeared to be the latest massacre in an escalating war between Mexico's dominant drug suppliers.

Authorities discovered the bodies at the entrance to a small town on a highway leading from Monterrey, to the border city of Nuevo Laredo. A white stone arch welcoming visitors was spray-painted with a large black letter *Z*. Some of the bodies bore a Mara Salvatrucha tattoo.

Body dumps have increased in Mexico over the past year as the fearsome Los Zetas gang goes head to head with the powerful Sinaloa Cartel and their allies, the Mara Salvatrucha, a.k.a. MS-13.

"This is the ultimate of all the drug wars," said an expert at Mexico's National University. "Under the president's five-year campaign against organized crime, the Zetas and Sinaloa cartels have become the largest in the country and are battling over transport routes and territory, especially along the border of Texas."

This year, the mutilated bodies of five Sinaloa members were left in a truck near Santiago de Querétaro, which has long been controlled by gangs loyal to Sinaloa. Ten MS-13 men were found hanged in Reynosa, and the dismembered body parts of seven people, including family of the Zetas, were found strewn around Veracruz, considered Zetas territory.

The Mara Salvatrucha, allied with Sinaloa, threw three bodies over a freeway overpass in the city of Monterrey last month. Police also found six other bodies outside of Monclova, likely killed by the same gang, several days later.

The war and violence has bled into other cities in the United States such as Houston, Los Angeles, and New York.

Carlos Vargas González, cousin to one of the original Los Zetas, was slaughtered last week in New York, presumably by Mara Salvatrucha, key rival to the Los Zetas along the U.S. Atlantic coast. It is rumored that the Zetas have started to retaliate in New York, while the Mara Salvatrucha reinforce their presence there.

Edwards Brothers Malloy
Thorofare, NJ USA
August 30, 2013